~ Purchased
with interest income
from the
library's trust fund ~

MAGIC STREET

MAGIC STREET

ORSON SCOTT CARD

BALLANTINE BOOKS

NEW YORK

Copyright © 2005 by Orson Scott Card

Published in the United States by Del Rey Books, an imprint of The Random House Publishing Group, a division of Random House, Inc., New York.

Del Rey is a registered trademark and the Del Rey colophon is a trademark of Random House, Inc.

ISBN 0-345-41689-9

Printed in the United States of America on acid-free paper

www.delreybooks.com

9 8 7 6 5 4 3 2 1

First Edition

Book design by Lisa Sloane

To Aaron and Lauren Johnston
Who show us that magic
can be funny and hopeful—
a light in the darkness,
conjured out of love

CONTENTS

1. Bag Man 3
2. Ura Lee's Window 24
3. Weed 32
4. Coprocephalic 47
5. Baby Mack 53
6. Swimmer 65
7. Neighborhood of Dreams 81
8. Skinny House 94
9. Captive Queen 112
10. Word 129
11. Fairyland 158
12. Motorcycle 174
13. Property Values 190
14. Playing Pool 205
15. Yo Yo 217
16. Preacher Man 233
17. Wish Fulfilment 244
18. Witch 264
19. Council of War 278
20. Wedding 293
21. Fairy Circle 312
22. Breaking Glass 330
23. Slug 348
24. Changeling 378
25. One 387

Acknowledgments 393

MAGIC STREET

BAG MAN

The old man was walking along the side of the Pacific Coast Highway in Santa Monica, gripping a fistful of plastic grocery bags. His salt-and-pepper hair was filthy and hanging in that sagging parody of a Rastafarian hairdo that most homeless men seem to get, white or black. He wore a once-khaki jacket stained with oil and dirt and grass and faded with sunlight. His hands were covered with gardening gloves.

Dr. Byron Williams passed him in his vintage Town Car and then stopped at the light, waiting to turn left to go up the steep road from the PCH to Ocean Avenue. A motorcycle to the left of him gunned its engine. Byron looked at the cyclist, a woman dressed all in black leather, her face completely hidden inside a black plastic helmet. The blank faceplate turned toward him, regarded him for a long moment, then turned to the front again.

Byron shuddered, though he didn't know why. He looked the other way, to the right, across the lanes of fast-moving cars that were speeding up to get on the 10 and head east into Los Angeles. Normally Byron would be among them, heading home to Baldwin Hills from his day of classes and meetings at Pepperdine.

But tonight he had promised Nadine that he'd bring home dinner from I Cugini. That's the kind of thing you had to do when you married a black woman who thought she was Italian. Could have been worse. Could have married a black woman who thought she was a redneck. Then they'd have to vacation in Daytona every year and listen to country music and eat possum and potato-chip-and-mayonnaise sandwiches on white bread.

Or he could be married to a biker like the woman still revving her engine in the other left-turn lane. He could just imagine getting dragged into biker bars, where, as an African-American professor of literature specializing in the romantic poets, he would naturally fit right in. He tried to imagine himself taking on a half-dozen drunken bikers with chains and pipes. Of course, if he were with that biker woman, he wouldn't have to fight them. She looked like she could take them on herself and win—a big, strong woman who wouldn't put up with nonsense from anybody.

That was a lot to know about a woman without seeing her face, but her body, her posture, her choice of costume and bike, and above all that challenging roar from her bike—the message was clear. Don't get in front of me, buddy, cause I'm coming through.

He only gradually realized that he was staring right at the homeless man with the handfuls of grocery bags. The man was stopped at the edge of the roadway, facing him, staring back at him. Now that Byron could see his face, he realized that the man wasn't faking his rasta do—he was entitled to it, being a black man. A filthy, shabby, rheumy-eyed, chin-stubbled, grey-bearded, slack-lipped old bum of a black man. But the hair was authentic.

Authentic. Thinking of the word made Byron cringe. Every year there was at least one student in one of his classes who'd mutter something—or say it boldly—about how the very fact that he was teaching courses in nineteenth-century white men's literature made him less authentic as a black man. Or that being a black man made him less authentic as a teacher of English literature. As if all a black man ought to aspire to teach was African studies or black history or Swahili.

The old man winked at him.

And suddenly Byron's annoyance drained away and he felt a little giddy. What was he brooding about? Students gave crap to their teachers whenever they thought they could get away with it. They learned soon enough that in Byron's classes, the students who cared would become the kind of people who were fit to understand Wordsworth, Shelley, Keats, Coleridge, Grey, and—of course—Lord Byron himself. That's what his good students sometimes called him—Lord Byron. Not to his face, because he always gave them his withering glare until they apologized. But he reveled in the knowledge that they called him that behind his back. And if he ever let anyone see his poetry, perhaps they'd discover that it was a name he deserved.

Lines from one of his own poems came to his mind. And from his mind, straight to his lips:

> Into my chariot, whispered the sun god.
> Here beside me, Love, crossing the sky.
> Leave the dusty road on which you plod:
> Behind these fiery horses come and fly.
> No matter how fast we go, how far, how high,
> I'll never let you fall.
>> All your life
> On earth you've crept and climbed and clawed—
> Now, Mortal Beauty, be my wife,
> And of your dreams of light, I'll grant you all.

The bag man's lips parted into a snaggle-toothed grin, and he stepped out into the traffic, heading straight for Byron's car.

For a moment Byron was sure the man would be killed. But no. The light had changed, and the cars came to a stop as he passed in front of them. In only a few moments, he set his hand to the handle of Byron's passenger door.

It was locked. Byron pushed the button to open it.

"Don't mind if I do," said the bag man. "Mind if I put my bags in your back seat?"

"Be my guest," said Byron.

The old man opened the back door and carefully arranged his bags on the floor and back seat. Byron wondered what was in them. Whatever it was, it couldn't be clean, and the bags probably had fleas or lice or ants or other annoying creatures all over them. Byron always kept this car spotless—the kids knew the rules, and never dared to eat anything inside this car, lest a crumb fall and they get a lecture from their dad. Sorry if that annoyed them, but it was good for children to learn to take care of nice things and treat them with respect.

And yet, even though he knew that letting those bags sit in the back seat would require him to vacuum and wash and shampoo until it was clean again, he didn't mind. Those bags belonged there. As the old man belonged in the front seat beside him.

The motorcycle to his left revved one last time and whined off up the steep road to Santa Monica.

Behind him, cars started honking.

The old man took his time getting into the front seat, and then he just sat there, not closing his door. Nor had he closed the back door, either.

No matter. To a chorus of honks and a few curses shouted out of open car windows, Byron got out and walked around to the other side of the Lincoln. He closed the back door, then reached in and fastened the old man's seat belt before he closed that door, too.

"Oh, you don't need to do that," murmured the old man as Byron fastened the belt.

"Safety first," said Byron. "Nobody dies in my car."

"No matter how fast we go, how far, how high," answered the old man.

Byron grinned. It felt good, to have someone know his poem so well he could quote it back to hm.

By the time he got back to the driver's door, the cars behind him were whipping out into the leftmost turn lane to get around him, honking and screaming and flipping him off as they passed. But they couldn't spoil his good mood. They were jealous, that's all, because the old man had chosen to ride in *his* car and not theirs.

Byron sat down, closed his door, fastened his seat belt, and prepared to wait for the next green light.

"Ain't you gonna go?" asked the old man.

Byron looked up. Incredibly, the left arrow was still green.

"Why not," he said. He pulled forward at a stately pace.

To his surprise, the light at the top of the hill was still green, and the next light, too.

"Hope you don't mind," said Byron. "Got to stop and pick up dinner."

"A man's got to keep his woman happy," said the old man. "Nothing more important in life. Except teaching your kids to be right with God."

That made Byron feel a little pang of guilt. Neither he nor Nadine were much for going to church. When his mother came to visit, they all went to church together, and the kids seemed to enjoy it. But they called it Grandma's church, even though she only attended it when she came to LA.

Byron turned left on Broadway and pulled up in the valet parking lane in front of I Cugini. The valet headed toward his car as Byron got out.

"Just picking up some takeout," he said as he handed the man a five-dollar bill.

"Pay after," said the valet.

"No, don't park the car, I'm just picking up a takeout order."

The man looked at him in bafflement. Apparently he hadn't been here long enough to understand English that wasn't exactly what he expected to hear.

So Byron spoke to him in Spanish. "Hace el favor de no mover mi carro, si? Volveré en dos minutos."

The man grinned and sat down in the driver's seat.

"No," said Byron, "no mueva el auto, por favor!"

The old man leaned over. "Don't worry, son," he said. "He don't want to move the car. He just wants to talk to me."

Of course, thought Byron. This old man must be familiar to all the valets. When you spend hours a day at the curb in Santa Monica, you're going to get to know all the homeless people.

Only when he was waiting at the counter for the girl to process his credit card did it occur to Byron that he spoke Italian and French, and could read Greek, but had never spoken or studied Spanish in his life.

Well, you learn a couple of romance languages, apparently you know them all.

The food was ready to go, and the card went right through on the first try. They didn't even ask him for i.d.

And when he got back outside, there was his car at the curb, and the valet was inside, kissing the old man's hands. By the time Byron got around to the driver's side and opened the back door, the valet was out of the car. Byron put the takeout bags on the floor, stood up, and closed the back door. The valet was already walking away.

"Wait a minute!" called Byron. "Your tip!"

The valet turned and waved his hand. "No problem!" he called in heavily accented English. "Thank you very much sir!"

Byron got in and sat down. "Never heard of a valet turning down a tip," he said.

"He only wanted to talk to me," said the old man. "He worries about his family back in Mexico. His little boy, he been sick. But I told him that boy be fine, and now he's happy."

Byron was happy, too. "Well, friend, where can I take you?"

"You go right on home," said the old man. "Don't want that dinner getting cold."

"Oh, it'll get cold no matter what we do," said Byron. "At six o'clock, doesn't matter if I take Olympic or the 10, traffic just takes time."

"Take the ten," said the old man. "Got a feeling we zip right along."

The old man was right. Even at the junction with the 405, the left lanes were moving faster than the speed limit and they made good time.

Byron thought of lots of things he wanted to say to the man. Lots of questions to ask. How did you know the valet's son was going to be okay? Why did you pick my car to ride in? Where will you go from Baldwin Hills, and why don't you want me to take you there? Did you make it so I could speak Spanish? Did *you* speak Spanish to the valet?

But whenever he was about to speak, he felt such a glow of peace and happiness that he couldn't bring himself to break the mood with the jarring sound of speech.

So the old man was the one who spoke. "You can call me Bag Man," he said. "That's a good name, and it's true. It's good to tell the truth sometimes, don't you think?"

Byron grinned and nodded. "Be good to tell the truth *all* the time."

"Oh, no," said Bag Man. "That just hurts people's feelings. Lying's the way to go, most times. It's kinder. And how often does truth really matter? Once a month? Once a year?"

Byron laughed in delight. "Never thought of it that way."

Bag Man smiled. "I don't mind if you use that in a poem, you go ahead."

"Oh, I'm not a poet," said Byron.

"There you go," said the old man. "Lying. Never show those poems, never admit they even exist, and nobody can say, This is all too old-fashioned, you're not a *real* poet."

Byron felt the hot blood in his face. "I said it first."

Bag Man laughed. "Like I said!" Then he turned serious again. "Want to know how good you is?"

Byron shook his head.

"Every bit as good as you hope," said Bag Man.

Relief washed over Byron and brought tears to his eyes. "But you've never read anything of mine."

"How could I?" said Bag Man. "Can't read."

"You're kidding."

"I may lie, but I never joke."

"Were you lying just now? What you said about my poetry?"

"No, sir."

"What about right *then,* when you said you weren't lying?"

"*That* was a lie, of course," said Bag Man. "But don't let logic spoil things for you."

Byron was aware of a strange feeling in his stomach. Nausea? No, not really. Oh, yes. It was anger. A kind of distant, faraway anger. But he couldn't think why he might be angry. Everything was wonderful. This was a great day. Not a speck of traffic. Not a light against them.

Coming down La Cienega he noticed See's Candies. Still open. But he mustn't stop. Dinner hot in the back seat.

He got out of the car and went inside and got a one-pound box of milk patties, those little disks of chocolate-covered caramel. It took forever for the woman to fill each little crinkled-paper cup. And when he got back to the car, he was really pleased to see how delighted Bag Man was to receive it.

"For me?" he said. "Oh, you just too nice, my man." Bag Man

tore open the paper and put two patties in his mouth at once. "I never get this down in Santa Monica."

"They have a Godiva's in the mall at the bottom of the Promenade," said Byron.

"Godiva's? They too rich for my pockets."

There was something wrong with the logic of that, but Byron couldn't think what it was.

Byron drove through the flat part of Baldwin Hills. Modest homes, some of them a little tatty, some very nicely kept—an ordinary neighborhood. But as they started up Cloverdale, the money started showing up. Byron wasn't rich and neither was Nadine. But together they did well enough to afford this neighborhood. They could have afforded Hancock Park, but that would be like surrendering, to move into a white neighborhood. For a black man in LA, it was Baldwin Hills that said you had made it without selling out.

Au-then-tic.

"This *magic* street," said the old man.

"What?"

"I said, this is *Magic Street*," he repeated. "Can't you feel it? Like standing in a waterfall, it's so thick here."

"I guess that's one of the senses I didn't get when God was handing them out," said Byron.

"Pull up right here," said Bag Man.

They were at number 3968, an elegant white house with a tile roof and a triple garage. It was the last house before the hairpin turn, where no houses stood.

Instead, there was a grassy green valley that stretched about a hundred yards before it ran into the thick woods at the base of the Kenneth Hahn State Recreation Area. Not that anybody did any recreating there. It was kept clear because when it stormed, all the runoff from the whole park was funneled down a concrete drainage system to collect in this valley, forming a lake. And right in the deepest part was a rusted tube sticking straight up out of the ground. Must be two feet across, or so it seemed to Byron, and eight feet high. It was perforated at about shoulder height, so water could drain into it when the lake got deep enough.

That's what it was *for.* But what it looked like was a smokestack sticking straight up from hell. That's what Nadine said when she first saw it. "Wouldn't you know it, up in the park it's all so beautiful, but down here is the anus of the drainage system and where do they put it? Right in the nicest part of the nicest black neighborhood in the city. Just in case we forget our place, I suppose."

"It's better than letting the rainwater run right down the streets and wash everybody out," Byron told her.

That earned him a narrow-eyed glare and a silent mouthing of the word "Tom."

"I wasn't defending the establishment, I was just saying that not everything is racism. The city puts up ugly stuff in white neighborhoods, too."

"If it was a white neighborhood they'd make a playground and that pipe would be brightly painted."

"If it was a playground, then every time it rained the children would drown. They fence it off because it isn't safe."

"You're right, of course," said Nadine. And that meant the argument was over, and Byron had lost.

But he *was* right. The pipe was ugly, but the meadow around it was pretty, and the tangled woods behind it were the closest thing to nature you'd find in the Mexican-manicured gardens of the City of Angels.

Bag Man sat patiently. Finally it dawned on Byron what he was waiting for.

Byron got out of the car and opened the door for the old man. "Why thank you, son," said Bag Man. "It's not often you find a man with real manners these days. Why, I bet you still call your mama 'ma'am,' am I right?"

"Yes sir," said Byron.

The old man leaned on him as he got out. "I leave my blessing with you, son," he said. "I bless you in the blessed name of Jesus. I bless you for the sacred sake of your mama's mama, who never lived to see your face, but she loves you in heaven all the same, son. I hope you know that. She's up there pestering God to watch out for you. How do you think you got tenure so soon?"

"Affirmative action," said Byron, even though it wasn't true. It was what he always said to other professors when they asked him questions like that. It wasn't even a joke anymore, just a habit, because it was so fun to watch the white professors look at him without a clue how they were supposed to answer when a black man said something like that. He could see their brains turning the alternatives over and over: Is he joking? Or does he mean it? Is he a Republican? Or does he think *I'm* a Republican? Is he making fun of me? Or himself? Or liberals? Or affirmative action? What can I say that won't make me look like either a racist or a politically correct brown-noser?

But Bag Man just grinned and shook his head. "Here I tell you about your mama's mama and how she love you, and all you answer me with is a joke. But that's okay all the same. I don't take back no blessing once I give it."

"Thank you for your blessing, sir," said Byron. "And for my grandma's blessing, too."

"Well, ain't you the polite one. Now you just go on home and have dinner with that sweet pregnant wife of yours. I'll be all right here."

So Nadine was pregnant—and hadn't even told him! Wasn't that just like her, to keep a secret like that.

Byron watched Bag Man walk right up to the chain-link fence and open the gate and go on through into the meadow. Then he knew he shouldn't watch anymore. So he closed the passenger door and walked back to the driver's side and got in.

Not two minutes later he was pulling through the electric gate into his driveway and waiting for the garage door to open. Nadine's car was there, and it made Byron happy just to see it.

And then, suddenly, it wore off all at once, and the anger that had seemed so far away just moments ago now erupted. He beat on the steering wheel with his open palms until his hands hurt.

"What did you do to me? What did you do to me?" He said it over and over again as he thought of that man just getting in his car as if he had a right, and the way he made Byron do things and say things. Making him buy See's chocolates for him! Saying Nadine was pregnant and he believed it! Was Bag Man a hypnotist? In the moment when Byron looked away from that motorcycle mama, was that when Bag Man caught his eye and hypnotized him without him even knowing it?

If I see him again I'll run him over even if they put me in jail for it. Nobody ought to have power like that over another living soul.

Word, his ten-year-old son—named for Wordsworth—came through the door from the house and rushed to Byron's car window. The boy didn't look excited, he looked worried.

Byron turned off the engine and opened the door.

"Dad, there's something wrong with Mom. She's really sick."

"All right, I'm on it." Byron headed toward the house. Then he stopped and looked back at Word. "Son, would you get dinner out of the back seat?"

"Sure," said Word. "I'm on it." And without a word of argument, the boy headed right back to get the sacks from I Cugini. That's when Byron realized that whatever was going on with Nadine, Word thought it was serious.

She was in the bedroom and when he knocked on the door, she said, "Go away."

"It's me," said Byron.

"Come in," she said.

He came through the door.

She was lying on her back on the bed, naked, breathing rapidly. Or was she crying? Both. Short sobs.

She wasn't just pregnant. She was as big as she had ever been with any of the children.

"By, what's happening to me?" she said. She sounded frantic, but kept her voice low. "I just started bloating up. An hour ago. I got home from work and I had to get out of my clothes, they were strangling the baby. That's what I kept thinking. Only I'm not pregnant, By."

He sat on the edge of the bed and felt her stomach. The skin was stretched as tight as it ever was at the peak of pregnancy, completely erasing her navel. "You sure feel pregnant," said Byron. And then, without thinking, he blurted: "That son-of-a-bitch."

"Who?" she said. "What are you talking about?"

"He said you were pregnant. He called you my pregnant wife."

"Who? Who who who who?"

"I don't know who. A homeless man. I gave him a ride home. I gave him a ride *here*."

"You let a homeless man into our house?"

"Not our house, I dropped him off at the bend. But it was crazy. I did whatever he wanted. I *wanted* to do it. He *made* me want to. I was thinking he hypnotized me."

"Well this isn't hypnosis, is it," said Nadine. "It hurts, By." Then her body tautened. "Merciful Savior make it stop!"

Byron realized his hand was cold and wet. "Baby, I think your water broke."

"What water!" she hissed. "I'm *not pregnant!*"

But her legs were parted and when he looked he could see a baby crowning, its head pushing to get through her fully dilated cervix.

"Just hold still, baby, and push this thing out."

"What thing!"

"It looks like a baby," said Byron. "I know it's impossible but I can't lie about what I see."

"It's not a baby," said Nadine as she panted. "Whatever it is. It's not a *baby*. Babies don't. Come this. Fast."

But this one did. Like popping a pimple, it suddenly squished out right into Byron's waiting hands. A little boy. Smaller than any of their real children had been.

Not that this baby didn't *look* real. It had the arms and legs and fingers and head of a genuine baby, and it was slithery and streaked in blood.

"It was nice of him to let you deliver this one without an episiotomy," said Byron.

"What?" asked Nadine, gasping as her body convulsed to deliver the afterbirth. The bed was soaked in blood now.

"He didn't tear you. Coming out."

"What?"

"I've got to cut. The cord. Where are there any scissors? I don't want to go clear to the kitchen, don't you have scissors here?"

"Sewing scissors in the kit in the closet," she said.

The afterbirth spewed out onto the bed and Nadine whimpered a couple of times and fell asleep. No, fell *unconscious,* that was the right term for it.

Byron got the kit open and took out the scissors and then found himself hesitating as he tried to decide what color thread to use. Until he finally realized that the color didn't matter. It was insane to even worry about it. Except what was sane about any of this? A woman who wasn't pregnant this morning, she gives birth before dinner?

He tied the umbilical cord and then tied it again, and between the two threads he cut the springy flesh. It was like cutting raw turkey skin.

Only when he was done did he realize what was wrong. The baby hadn't made a sound.

It just lay there on its back in a pool of blood on the bed, not crying, not moving.

"It's dead," whispered Byron.

Well, what did he expect?

How would they explain this to the police? No, we didn't know my wife was pregnant. No, we didn't have time to get to the hospital.

And something else. Nadine still had her legs spread wide, and she was smeared with blood, but her belly wasn't swollen anymore. She had the flat stomach of a woman who takes her workouts seriously. There was no sign that a few moments ago she was nine months pregnant with this dead baby.

There was a knock on the door.

"What?"

"Man here to see you," said Word.

"I can't see anybody right now, Word," said Byron.

The door opened and Byron moved quickly to hide his wife's naked body. But it wasn't Word in the doorway. It was Bag Man.

"You," said Byron. "You son-of-a-bitch. What have you done to my wife?"

"Got that baby out already? That was quick." He looked downright cheerful.

"I got news for you," said Byron. "The baby's dead. So whatever you're doing to us, you blew it. It didn't work."

Bag Man just shook his head and grinned. Byron hated that grin now. This man virtually carjacked him tonight, and somehow made him *like* it. Well, he didn't like it now. He wanted to throw the man against the wall. Knock him down and kick his head.

Instead he watched as Bag Man shambled past him and picked up the baby. "Look at him," said Bag Man. "Ain't he as pretty as can be?"

"I told you," said Byron. "He's dead."

"Don't be silly," said Bag Man. "Baby like this, it can't die. How can it die? Ain't alive yet. Can't die less you been alive, fool."

Bag Man held the baby like a football in one arm, while he snapped open a plastic grocery bag with the other hand. Then he slipped the baby into the bag. It fit nicely, with its legs scrunched up just like it must have been in the womb. That was the first time it occurred to Byron that all those grocery bags were exactly womb-sized. He wondered if that's how they decided how big to make them.

"He'll suffocate in that bag," said Byron.

"Can't suffocate if you ain't breathing," said Bag Man cheerfully. "You kind of slow, ain't you, Byron? Anyway, nobody suffocates in my bags." He looked at Nadine's naked unconscious body and Byron hated him.

"Why don't I just kill you right now?" said Byron.

"For looking at your wife naked?"

"For putting that dead baby in her."

"I didn't do it," said Bag Man. "You think I got the power to do this? Drop dead, fool, this ain't my style." He grinned when he said it, but this time Byron refused to be placated.

"Get out of my house," said Byron.

"That's what I was planning to do," said Bag Man. "But first I got a question for you."

"Just get out."

"You want to forget this, or remember?"

"I'm never gonna forget you and what you did. If I see you in the street, I'll run you down."

"Oh, don't worry, *you* ain't gonna see me, not for a long time, anyway, but go ahead and run me down if you can."

"I told you to get out."

"So . . . one for remembering, the rest for not," said Bag Man. "Your order will be ready in a minute, sir." Bag Man winked and went back out the door, carrying the dead newborn in the plastic bag.

Is this where those dumpster babies come from? Not pregnant teenagers at all.

And those really fat women who give birth without ever knowing they were pregnant. Nadine once said, How can they not know? Well, what if it was like this? What if some voodoo man did it?

Or maybe he really was a hypnotist. Maybe none of this happened. Maybe when I wake up it'll turn out not to be real.

Except when he touched them, the sheets were wet with amniotic fluid and blood.

He got Nadine awake enough to move while he got the sheet and mattress pad out from under her. As he feared, it had gone clear through to the mattress. It was never coming out of *there*. They'd have to buy a new one.

And these sheets? They weren't going in the laundry. He got a plastic garbage bag from the cabinet under the bathroom sink and stuffed the bottom sheet and the mattress pad into it.

As he went back into the bedroom, Nadine padded by him toward the bathroom. "That's a good idea," she murmured.

"What?" said Byron. "Soon as I get clean sheets you can go back to—"

"Washing the sheets. Time to change the sheets," she said. "Did you get dinner?"

"I Cugini, as ordered," he said. Could she really be this calm?

"Mmmm," she said. "I'm gonna shower now, By. Let's eat when I get out."

She didn't remember. She had no idea that any of this had happened.

"You were real sweet, baby," she said.

She thinks we made love, thought Byron.

Well, if a woman can give birth, fall asleep, and wake up five minutes later thinking all she had was great sex, that was some kind of hypnotism, that's for sure.

If it happened at all.

I've got the bloody sheet in this bag, he told himself impatiently.

He opened the garbage bag again just to be sure. Bloody all right. And wet. And slimy. A mess.

He heard the shower start. He tied the bag again and carried it out of the room and through the kitchen, on his way to the city garbage can in the garage.

"Dad," said Andrea, the oldest. "Is Mom okay?"

"She's fine," said Byron. "Just a little sick to her stomach, but she's feeling better now."

"Did she puke?" asked seven-year-old Danielle. "I always feel better if I'm sick and then I puke. Not during the puke, after."

"I don't know if she puked," said Byron. "She's in the bathroom with the door closed."

"Puking's nasty," said Danielle.

"Not as nasty as licking it up afterward," said Word.

Byron didn't tell him off. The girls were saying Gross, Disgusting, You're as funny as a dead slug: the koine of intersibling conversation. Byron only wanted to get to the garbage can and jam this bag of bloody sheet and mattress pad as far down into it as possible.

What was the old man going to do with that dead baby? What was this all about? Why did this witch doctor or whatever he was pick *us*?

He came back in and washed his hands with antibacterial soap three times and he still didn't feel clean.

"The food's not very warm," said Andrea. "Want me to nuke it?"

"Not the salads."

Andrea rolled her eyes. He could hear her muttering as she heated up the warm dishes. "Think you have to tell me not to nuke a salad, I'm not retarded, I think I know lettuce sucks when it's hot."

Byron supervised the setting of the table. And as they were finishing, Nadine came in.

"Well, I feel a lot better," she said. "I just needed to rest a minute and then wash off the troubles of the day."

She really was clueless. For the first time it occurred to Byron that this meant there was no one on God's green earth he could ever tell about what happened. Who would believe him, if Nadine didn't back him up? Miz Nadine, your husband said you swoll up and gave birth all in one hour and a homeless man come and took it away in a grocery bag, is that so? And Nadine would say, That's just sick, if my husband said that he's making fun.

"By," she said, "you look green as a ghost. Are you ill?"

"Bad traffic on the ten," he said.

"I thought you said only a fool takes the ten, you've got to take Olympic."

"So I'm a fool," he said.

Why didn't the old man come with me all the way to our house, if he was here to pick up the baby? Why did he go into that fenced-off park?

And when did they put a gate in the fence? There was no gate in the fence.

Wait a minute. There's no fence. There is no damn fence around that park.

"Really, By, are you sure you shouldn't just go to bed? You look pretty awful."

"I suppose I just need a shower, too."

"Well, right after dinner, and I'll give you a neck rub to wipe out all that tension, see if I don't."

"I sure hope you *can*," said Byron.

"Of course I can, darling," she said primly. "A woman like me, I can do *anything*."

"She is *woman!*" intoned Word. "She rocks!"

"Now *that*," said Nadine, "is one well-raised boy."

"Well-raised *man*," said Word.

"You got a driver's license?" said Nadine. "You got a job?"

"I'm ten," said Word.

"Don't go calling yourself a man, then," said Nadine. "Man's not a man till he earns money."

"Or drives a car," said Danielle.

What a thing to teach the children. That a man's not a man if he isn't making money. Does that mean that the more you earn, the more of a man you are? Does that mean if you get fired, you've been emasculated?

But there was no point arguing the point. Word *wasn't* a man yet, and when he was, Byron would make sure he got a man's respect from his father, and then it wouldn't matter what the boy's mother said. That was a power a father had that no woman could take away.

While the rest of the family bantered, Byron's thoughts turned again to that baby. If it was real, was it a child of Nadine's, or some kind of magical changeling? If it *was* her child, then who was the father? Byron? Was it *our* son that freak toted out of our bedroom in a grocery sack? Word's little brother, now bound for some miserable grave in a dumpster somewhere?

Is he really dead? Or will the old man's magic find some spark of life inside him? And if he does, could I find him? Claim him? Bring him home to raise?

And now Byron realized why Bag Man hadn't given Nadine a choice about whether to remember or not. If the mother didn't believe she had given birth, then how could the father go claiming paternity? Nobody gave maternity tests to *mothers*.

If that's our baby, that old man stole it from us.

I should have told him to let me forget.

But that was wrong, too, and Byron knew it. It was important for him to know—and *remember*—that such a thing as this was possible in the world. That his life could be taken over so easily, that such a terrible thing could happen and then be forgotten.

And now this man knows where we live. This man can do whatever he wants in our neighborhood.

Well, if magic like this is real, then I sure as hell hope that God is also real. Because as long as Bag Man is walking around in Baldwin Hills with dead babies in his grocery sacks, then God help us all.

Please.

2

URA LEE'S WINDOW

Ura Lee Smitcher looked out the window of her house on the corner of Burnside and Sanchez as two boys walked by on the other side of the street, carrying skateboards. "There's your son with that Raymond boy from out on Coliseum."

Madeline Tucker sat on Ura Lee's couch, drinking coffee. She didn't even look up from *People Magazine*. "I know all about Raymo Vine."

"I hope what you know is he's heading for jail, because he is."

"That's exactly what I know," said Madeline. "But what can I do? I forbid Cecil to see him, and that just guarantees he'll sneak off. Right now Ceese got no habit of lying to me."

Ura Lee almost said something.

Madeline Tucker didn't miss much. "I know what you going to say."

"I ain't going to say a thing," said Ura Lee, putting on her silkiest, southernest voice.

"You going to say, What good if he tell you the truth, if what's true is he's going to hell in a wheelbarrow?"

She was dead on, but Ura Lee wasn't about to say it in so many words. "I likely would have said 'handbasket,' " said Ura Lee. "Though truth to tell, I don't know what the hell a handbasket *is.*"

And now it was Madeline's turn to hesitate and refrain from saying what *she* was thinking.

"Oh, you don't have to say it," said Ura Lee. "Women who never had a child, they all expert on raising other women's children."

"I was not going to say that," said Madeline.

"Good thing," said Ura Lee, "because you best remember I chose *not* to give you advice. You just guessed what I was thinking, but I refuse to be blamed for meddling when I *didn't* say it."

"And I refuse to be blamed for persecuting you when I didn't say it either."

"You know," said Ura Lee, "we'd get along a lot better if we wasn't a couple of mind readers."

"Or maybe that's why we get along so good."

"You think those two boys really going to hike up Cloverdale and ride down on those contraptions?"

"Not all the way down," said Madeline. "One of them always falls off and gets bloody or sprained or something."

"They didn't walk like boys looking to have some innocent fun with a hill and some wheels and gravity," said Ura Lee.

"They a special way to walk for that?"

"Jaunty," said Ura Lee. "Those boys looking sneaky."

"Ah," said Madeline.

"Ah? That's all you got to say?"

Madeline sighed. "I already raised Cecil's four older brothers and not one of them in jail."

"Not one in college, either," said Ura Lee. "Not to criticize, just observing."

"All of them with decent jobs and making money, and Antwon doing *fine.*"

Antwon was the one who was buying rental homes all over

South Central and making money from renting week-to-week to people with no green card so they couldn't make him fix stuff that broke. The kind of landlord that Ura Lee had been trying to get away from when she saved up and bought this house in Baldwin Hills when the real estate market bottomed out after the earthquake.

They'd had this argument before, anyway. Madeline thought it made all the difference in the world that Antwon was exploiting Mexicans. "They got no right to be in this country anyway," she said. "If they don't like it, they can go home."

And Ura Lee had answered, "They came here cause they poor and got no choice, except to look for something better wherever they can find it. Just like our people getting away from sharecropping or whatever they were putting up with in Mississippi or Texas or Carolina, wherever they were from."

Then Madeline would go off on how people who never been slaves got *no* comparison, and Ura Lee would go off on how the last slave in her family was her great-great-grandmother and then Madeline would say all black people were *still* slaves and then Ura Lee would say, Then why don't your massuh sell you off stead of listening to you bitch and moan. Then it would start getting nasty.

Thing about living next door to somebody for all these years is, you already had all the arguments. If you were going to change each other's minds, they'd already be changed. And if you were going to feud over it, you'd already be feuding. So the only other choice was to just shut up and let it go.

"So you saying you going to cut them a little slack even though you know they scored some weed and they going up to that open space at the hairpin turn to smoke it," said Ura Lee.

"Up to the 'slack,' that's what I'm saying. How you know they got weed?"

"Cause Ceese keeps slapping his pocket to make sure something's still there, and if it was a gun it be so heavy his pants fall down, and they ain't falling, and if it was a condom then it be a girl with him, and Raymo ain't no girl, so it's weed."

"And you see all that out this magic window."

"It's a good window," said Ura Lee. "I paid extra for this window."

"I paid extra for the rope swing in my yard," said Madeline. "You know how fast boys grow out of a rope swing? About fifteen minutes."

"So I got the better deal."

"And you sure they going up to that nasty little park at the hairpin turn."

"Where else can kids in Baldwin Hills go to get privacy, they can't drive yet?"

"You know what?" said Madeline. "You really should be somebody's mama. Your talent being wasted in this one-woman house."

"Not wasted—I'm here to give you advice."

"You ought to get you another man, have some babies before too late."

"Already too late," said Ura Lee. "Men ain't looking for women my age and size, in case you notice."

"Nothing wrong with your size," said Madeline. "You one damn fine-looking woman, especially in that white nurse's uniform. And you make good money."

"The kind of man looks for a woman who makes good money *ain't* the kind of man I want raising no son of *mine*. They enough lazy moochers in this world without me going to all the trouble of having a baby just to grow up and be another."

"Thing I appreciate about you, Ura Lee, you live next door to my Winston all these years and you never once make eyes at him."

Madeline seemed to think everybody saw Winston Tucker the way she did—the handsome young Vietnam vet with a green beret and a smile that could make a blind woman get a hot flash. Ura Lee had seen that picture on the wall in the kitchen of their house, so she knew all about what Madeline had fallen in love with. But that wasn't Winston anymore. He was bald as an egg now, with a belly that was only cute to a woman who already loved him.

Not that Ura Lee would judge a man on looks alone. But Winston was also an accountant and a Christian and he couldn't understand that not everybody wanted to hear about both subjects all the time. Ura Lee once heard Cooky Peabody say, "What *does* that man talk about in bed? Jesus or accounts receivable?"

And Ura Lee *wanted* to answer her, Assets and arrears. But she didn't know a single person well enough to tell nasty puns to. So she still had that witticism stored up, waiting.

Anyway, Madeline thought her husband was so sexy that other women must be lusting after his flesh, and she'd be the one to know. They were lucky they had each other. "A woman's got to have self-control if she expects to get to heaven, Madeline," said Ura Lee.

"The Lord sometimes puts temptation right next door," said Madeline knowingly, "but then he gives us the strength to resist it, if we try."

"Meanwhile your boy Ceese is going to have his first experience with recreational herbology."

"If heredity is any guide, he'll puke once and give it up for good."

"Why, is that what happened to Winston when he tried it?"

"I'm talking about me," said Madeline testily. "Cecil takes after me."

"Except for the Y chromosome and the testosterone," said Ura Lee.

"Trust a nurse to get all medical on me."

"Well, Madeline, I say it's nice to have some trust in your children."

"Trust, hell," said Madeline. "I going to tell his daddy when he gets home, and Cecil's going to be sitting on one butt cheek at a time for a month."

She got up from the couch and started for the kitchen with her coffee cup. Ura Lee knew from experience that the kitchen was worth another twenty minutes of conversation, and she didn't like standing around on linoleum, not after a whole shift on linoleum in the hospital. So she snared the cup and saucer from Madeline's hand and said, "Oh, don't you bother, I want to sit here and see more visions of the future out of my window anyway." In a few minutes the goodbyes were done and Ura Lee was alone.

Alone and thinking, as she washed the cups and saucers and put them in the drying rack to drip—she hardly ever bothered with the dishwasher because it seemed foolish to fire up that whole machine just for the few dishes she dirtied, living alone. Half the time she nuked frozen dinners and ate them right off the tray, so there was nothing but a knife and fork to wash up anyway.

What she was thinking was: Madeline and Winston have about the best marriage I've seen in Baldwin Hills, and they're happy, and their boys are still nothing but a worry even after they get out of the house. Antwon, who is doing *fine,* still had somebody shoot at him the other day when he was collecting rent, and twice had his tires slashed. And the other boys had no ambition at all. Just lazy—completely unlike their father, who, you had to give him credit, worked hard. And Cecil—he used to be the best of the lot, but now he was hanging with Raymo, who was studying up to be completely worthless and had just about earned his Dumb Ass degree, summa cum scumbag.

Last thing I want in my life is a child. Even if I was good at it— no saying I would be, either, because as far as I can tell *nobody's* actually good at parenting, just lucky or not—even if I was good at mothering, I'd probably get nothing but kids who thought I was the worst mother in the world until I dropped dead, and then they'd cry about what a good mama I was at my funeral but a fat lot of good that would do me because I'd be dead.

Of course, maybe I'd have a daughter like me, I was good to my mama till she got herself smashed up on the 405 the very day

I had finally decided to take the car keys away from her because her reaction time was so slow I was afraid she was going to kill somebody running a stop sign. If I *had* taken the keys away from her, then she'd be alive but she'd hate me for keeping her from having the freedom of driving a car. What good is a good daughter if the only way she can be good to you is make your life miserable?

Not to mention how unhappy it made Mama when Ura Lee up and married that ridiculous Willie Joe Smitcher, who thought he was born with a golden key behind the zipper of his pants and had to slide it into every lock he could get near to, just in case it was the gate of heaven. And people wondered why Ura Lee didn't have kids! Knowing, as a nursing student, just what the chances were of Willie Joe picking up something nasty, she had no choice but to protect her own health by keeping that golden key rubber-wrapped at home. She told him that when he was faithful to her for long enough that she could be sure he was clean, the wrapping could come off, but he chose the other alternative and they went their separate ways with the government's permission before she even got her first job as a nurse. And, give the boy credit, he never came back to her asking for money. He wasn't a mooch, he was just a man who thought he had a mission to perform, like Johnny Appleseed, except for the apples.

It only means that I'll never have a son like him, or a daughter foolish enough to marry a man like him, and that makes me about as happy a woman as lives on Burnside, and that's saying something, because by and large this is a pretty happy street. People here got some money, but not serious money, not Brentwood or Beverly Hills money, and sure as hell not Malibu beachfront money. Just comfortable money, a little bit of means. And only a block away from Cloverdale, and that street have *real* money, on up the hill, anyway.

She only got into Baldwin Hills herself because the earthquake knocked this house a little bit off its foundation and her mama left her just enough money to get over the top for a down payment—a fluke. But she was happy here. These were good people. She'd watch them raise *their* children, and suffer all that anxiety all the time, and thank God she didn't have such a burden in her own life.

3

WEED

Ceese saw Miz Smitcher looking out her window at him and saw how she was talking to somebody, and he knew without even thinking about it that the person she was talking to was his mother.

"Maybe this ain' such a good idea, Raymo."

"What you saying, Ceese, you just getting scared."

"You never seen my daddy when Mama gets mad at me."

"Your daddy don't care if you smoke a little weed."

"He care a lot my mama gets upset. Whole house jumpy when mama get mad."

"So go on home to mama."

That's the kind of thing Raymo always said. Instead of answering Ceese, he just said, You don't like how things are, you go away. "I'm just saying I think my mama knows."

"Knows what? That you and me walking up the street with skateboards? Anybody want to look out they window, they know that. Ain't against no law."

"Miz Smitcher, she know."

"You tell her? That how she know?"

"You know Miz Smitcher! She just look at you, she know what you been doing for the last three days."

"Everybody know what you been doing, you been hiding under your bed, slapping the monkey."

"That's just dumb."

"You haven't figured out how to do it yet?"

"Too much stuff under my bed, nobody can get under there."

They laughed about that for a moment.

"I think Miz Smitcher, she call the cops," said Ceese.

"She call the cops on us, I just have to pay her a visit later."

Raymo always talked that way. Like he was dangerous. And grownups took him at his word—treated him like he was a rattler ready to strike. But in the past few months since Raymo's mom moved into one of the rental houses owned by Ceese's brother Antwon, they'd been together enough that Ceese knew better. Truth was, it surprised him that after all his brag, Raymo actually *did* score a bag of weed.

That was Ceese's problem now. It was easy to tell Raymo that if he scored some weed, Ceese would smoke it with him, because he thought it was like the girls Raymo was always bragging about how they liked him to slip it to them in the girls' bathroom at school or behind the 7-Eleven. All talk, but nothing real. Then he shows up with a Ziploc bag full of dry green leaves and stems, along with some roll-your-own papers, and what was Ceese supposed to do? Admit it was all fronting?

So now he had to think, was Raymo putting on when he threatened to do something bad to Miz Smitcher?

"Look, Raymo, Miz Smitcher, she okay."

"Nobody okay, they call the cops on me."

"Let's just ride down Cloverdale before the cops come and do the weed another time."

"You got it in your pocket, Ceese. You decide," said Raymo. But his smirk was saying, You chicken out this time, you ain't with me next time.

The smirk bothered Ceese. "Ain't like it's real weed," he muttered.

"I heard that," said Raymo.

"You spose to," said Ceese.

"You telling me I can't tell weed from . . . weeds?"

That's what I'm telling you all right. "No," said Ceese. "How would I know?"

"So you don't get high, you going to start telling everybody I couldn't tell weed from daffodils?"

"You can't help it, you buy fake weed."

"Just give me the bag and fly on home to Mama," said Raymo. "Dumb little—"

"No, I'm okay with it, I'll smoke it with you."

"I don't want you to," said Raymo. "You a virgin, I don't want to be your first time."

Ceese hated it when he twisted everything to be about sex. "Let's just smoke it," said Ceese, and he started walking through the wildflowers growing profusely between the road and the lawn.

"Not here," said Raymo. "Somebody pack your head with stupid?"

"You said we going to smoke the weed up by the pipe."

"On the way back down the hill."

"We got to walk all the way up to the top?"

"When your daddy call somebody to see if you really go to the top, they say yes, they saw us go up there, we rode back down."

"My daddy don't know anybody higher up Cloverdale than his own house."

Just then an old homeless man came out of one of the houses on the downslope side of Cloverdale, carrying a bunch of grocery bags, some full, some empty. The old man winked at them and Ceese couldn't help it, he waved and smiled.

"You know that guy?" asked Raymo.

"He told me he your long-lost daddy, come to see how you turn out, decide if your mama be worth—"

"Shut up about my mama," said Raymo.

But Ceese knew what he was mad about was joking about his

daddy. That was a sore spot for Raymo, what with his mama not actually knowing who Raymo's daddy was. Not that Raymo ever admitted that—Ceese only knew because his own mama told Miz Smitcher once.

They walked farther up the hill.

Word Williams was standing at the curb, looking down the street.

"Look at that kid, wishing he was us," said Raymo.

"He ain't even looking at us," said Ceese.

"Is so."

But he wasn't. As they got closer, he moved back onto his yard so he could look around them, down the hill.

"Whazzup, Word?" said Ceese.

Word looked at him like he'd seen him for the first time that moment.

The door to Word's house opened and his older sister Andrea leaned out and called to him. "Get in here, Word, it's time to eat."

Word looked back down the road, then glanced at Ceese as if he wanted to ask a question.

"Word!" said Andrea. "Don't act like you don't hear me."

Word turned and walked back toward the house.

Raymo was a half-dozen steps ahead. Ceese ran to catch up.

"What you talk to that boy for?"

"Look like he was having some kind of problem," said Ceese. "Just a little kid."

"My mama used to tend him and his little sister in the summer," said Ceese.

"She ever tend that older sister?" asked Raymo. "She *hot*."

"She wasn't then," said Ceese. It was weird to think of Andrea being "hot." Or maybe it was just that Raymo never thought that any girl was too rich or too smart or too pretty for him. Nothing out of reach for Raymo.

"Keep up," said Raymo.

Ceese hated it when Raymo treated *him* like a little kid. Giving him orders. Talking down to him. But mostly he didn't do that, and usually it was when he was a little bit mad. It beat getting shoved around or cussed at. And he *did* let Ceese carry the bag of weed. Though that might have been so Ceese would be the one carrying, if they got caught.

They got to the top of the hill but Raymo insisted they walk right to the end of Cloverdale, where a fence blocked the road off from the upper part of Hahn Park. You could see the place where the golf course bottomed out, like a big green bowl. Or more like a green funnel, because at the lowest point you could see where a big culvert split the grass to capture all the runoff from the rain. Ceese didn't know if that water was piped down to the little valley by the hairpin turn where the drainpipe stood up like a totem pole. So he asked Raymo.

"How could it?" said Raymo.

"It's got to go somewhere."

"They got that huge drainage up there, you think they dump it down in that little valley so that one little pipe carry it all away? *That* little pipe just for the runoff from below the park."

Like you know everything, thought Ceese. But he didn't say it, because there was no reason to make Raymo mad, and besides, he was probably right.

"All right," said Raymo. "People seen us up here. Now they see us ride down."

"You know I can't make that hairpin turn."

Raymo looked at him like he was the stupidest kid in the world. "We don't *want* to make the hairpin turn, *Cecil*. We want to get off the road and onto the grass and up into the trees to smoke that *weed* you're carrying. Or did you think you just started *growing* weed in your pants?"

"I just don't want to fall down on the asphalt," said Ceese. "Scrape myself all up."

"Well, here's what you do," said Raymo. "You go real slow, back and forth across the road. And then tomorrow, when you get down to the hairpin, you can wake me up and we'll go smoke the weed for breakfast."

With that, Raymo pushed off and scooted along the level part of the road until he could turn and start down the slope of Cloverdale.

Ceese was right behind him. Hating every minute of it. Not because he didn't like the exhilaration of speed, or the rumble of the asphalt under his skateboard wheels. What he hated was Raymo going faster than Ceese ever could, while waving his arms and squatting down and standing up and even raising one leg like a stork, all the while whooping and calling out to Ceese. And though Ceese could never understand the words, since Raymo was facing away and his voice was mostly lost in the noise of the skateboard, he got the message just fine: You always a loser compared to Ray-*mo*.

He only want me around so they somebody to watch him be cool.

Why can't he ever do something just because it's fun?

Why can't he ever have me with him cause he likes me?

Son of a bitch. I'm going to stop hanging with him. Smoke this weed, that's it, I find somebody don't think I'm dumb.

Of course, Ceese had made this resolution before, about a dozen times, but so far he'd never actually gone so far as to say no when Raymo showed up and told him what they were going to do that day.

Ceese never even *hesitated*. That's what his decisions were worth.

I got no spine. Had me a spine, I'd be cool too. Not cool like Raymond, my *own* kind of cool. The guy who didn't need nobody. Stand alone, stand tall. Stead of tagging along like a little brother.

That's what I am. Always somebody's little brother. Got plenty of brothers, but what do I do? Go and find me another.

By the time Ceese got to the hairpin, Raymo was nowhere in sight.

This was the part that Ceese always dreaded: stopping. He liked the kind of hill where at the bottom the road just goes straight for a long time. He liked going for the *distance*. But here, that wasn't possible. One way or another, he was going to end up off these wheels. He could do it all splayed out in the street like roadkill, or he could do it by running up into the grass and falling all over himself like a dumbass.

Better to be a dumbass on grass than . . . than . . .

He searched for a rhyme, even as he steered toward the place where the grass looked softest.

Than a toad in the road.

His board hit the edge of the road and flipped on the rocks before reaching the grass. Which meant that he was off the board before he had a chance to jump high enough to make sure he landed on the grassy slope. This was not going well. All he could do was try to stay airborne and roll when he hit, so he didn't come home grass-stained. Better bloody than grass-stained, he learned *that* long ago. Grass stains got you whipped, but blood got bandaids.

He landed on his face in the grass and flipped kind of sideways, twisting his neck so that when he finally stopped rolling down in the tall grass, he lay there for a few seconds, wiggling his toes to make sure his neck wasn't broke. He wasn't sure why that worked, but that's what the guy at school said, *Don't* move your neck, that just makes it worse. Instead, wiggle your toes to make sure you can.

"Look like you trying to mow the grass with your chin, fool," said Raymo.

"Where were *you*?" asked Ceese.

"Lying behind the hill. You sailed right over me."

"Like the Goodyear blimp," said Ceese.

Raymo broke up laughing. "I can't believe you. Complete klutz, can't ride, can't even *fall* right, damn near broke your neck, but you still funny. That why I hang with you."

"Yeah, but why do I hang with *you*?" said Ceese.

"Cause I'm cool as you wish you was," said Raymo.

"Guess that's it," said Ceese.

"You hang on to any of that weed?" asked Raymo.

Sure enough, it wasn't in Ceese's pocket. He leapt to his feet, discovering just how sore his elbows and knees were—and fully grass-stained. He was already back at the slope heading up to see if the bag had fallen out of his pocket where his board hit the gravel, when he realized Raymo was laughing. He turned around, and there was Raymo, holding up the bag.

Ashamed, both of his panic and that he lost the bag in the first place, Ceese sauntered back toward the older boy. "Who needs weed when I can get high on inertia?"

Raymo cocked his head and made his eyes go buggy. "Inertia? In-*er*-she-ah! You already been to college or something?"

"You took that class," said Ceese. "You learned about inertia."

"I learned about it for the *grade*, I didn't work it into my conversation to show off how smart I am."

"Sometimes I get tired, you calling me dumb."

"I didn't call you dumb," said Raymo.

"You always call me dumb."

"I call you a dumb-*ass*. But not just plain *dumb*."

Ceese was angry and ashamed and he hurt all over and he was going to catch hell for all these grass stains. But he couldn't afford to answer the way he wanted to, because then Raymo would beat the hell out of him and, worse, stop being his friend.

So Ceese stood there and looked at the only thing sticking up out of the grass that wasn't Raymo: the rusted-up drainpipe.

There was something moving at the base of the pipe.

His first thought was that it was some kind of animal. There were squirrels everywhere, but this looked taller, and a different color. And shiny. What kind of animal was shiny? An armadillo? A really huge wet toad?

Ceese jogged down the slope and right past Raymo.

"Where you going?"

Ceese ignored him. What kind of dumbass couldn't see he was heading for the drainpipe?

As he got closer, though, he could say that the thing he spotted from the slope was just a handle of a plastic grocery-store sack.

Then it moved, and since there wasn't any wind and none of the grass was moving, it meant there might be an animal inside it. Maybe a mouse or something. Trapped in the bag.

Well if it was, he'd set it free before Raymo even knew it was in there. Because Raymo was bad with animals.

It wasn't a mouse. It was a baby. The smallest baby Ceese had ever seen. Stark naked, with the stump of the umbilical cord still attached. It wasn't crying, but it didn't look happy either. Its eyes were closed and it only moved its arms and legs a little.

"What you got?" asked Raymo.

"A baby, looks like," said Ceese. "But it's too small to be real."

"Ain't even human," said Raymo, looking down at it. "You going to smoke or not?"

"Got to do something about this baby."

"Smoke first."

Ceese knew that was wrong. "My brother told me that weed makes you forget stuff and not care. We got to do something about this baby while we still remember it's here."

Raymo stuffed the Ziploc bag into his pocket. "You want to take it somewhere, you do it without old Raymo. I don't want nobody thinking I the daddy."

Ceese wanted to say, Only way you be the daddy is if the mama be an old sock you hide under your bed. But he didn't say it; Raymo didn't like getting teased. He could dish it, but he couldn't take it.

"I don't want nobody asking me questions, I got a bag of weed on me," said Raymo.

"It's probably nothing but parsley and broccoli or something anyway," said Ceese. "Nobody gives you good weed for free." Ceese leaned down and picked up the grocery bag by the handles.

"What you going to do with that thing?"

"Take it to Mama," said Ceese. "She know about babies."

"Not much," said Raymo. "She made *you*, didn't she?"

The baby was lighter than Ceese expected. But it still felt wrong to hold it by the handles of the sack. What was he going to do, walk along swinging it like a dead squirrel?

He lifted it higher, to cradle it in his arms. That's when he saw that the baby was covered with ants inside the sack. And the outside of the sack was swarming with them. A lot of them were already racing up his arm.

Ceese set down the sack and started brushing the ants off his arms.

"What you doing, you dumbass?" said Raymo. "You doing some kind of wacko I-got-a-baby dance? Or you got to pee?"

"Baby's got ants all over it."

"I heard babies sometimes eat ants cause they need it in their diet."

"Was that on Discovery Channel or Animal Planet?" asked Ceese. The last of the ants was off him. He peeled back the sack and lifted the baby in his hands, holding it far away from his body. "Come here and brush the ants off this baby."

"Don't go telling me what to do," said Raymo. "You don't tell me what to do."

"We got to get the ants off this baby. You want to hold it while I brush, that's just fine with me."

"I ain't holding no baby. Get my fingerprints on it? No way."

"Then brush off the ants." And then, in deference to Raymo's superiority, Ceese turned it from a demand into a request. "Puh-leeeeeeze."

"Well, since you asked like such a polite dumbass." Raymo brushed off the baby's naked limbs and trunk.

"Careful with the top of his head, babies got a soft spot."

"I know that, *Cecil*," said Raymo. Then he suddenly backed away, looking scared.

"What!" demanded Ceese.

"Ant come out of his *nose!*" said Raymo.

"Brush it off! It won't bite you."

Raymo steeled himself for a moment, then came back and flipped the ant off the baby's cheek. "Freak me out, that's all."

"Ants probably in there eating the baby's brains," said Ceese. "Baby probably retarded now, they ate so much."

"Shut your mouth," said Raymo. "You making me throw up."

The baby wiggled and made a mewing sound. Just like a kitten.

Thinking of a kitten made Ceese pull the baby back from Raymo, because of that time Raymo took a baby kitten and stepped on its head just to see it squish. Raymo called it a "biology experiment." When Ceese asked him what he learned from it, Raymo said, "Brains be looser than liver, and wetter, and they kind of splash." Ceese didn't want Raymo to start thinking scientifically about this baby.

"Just leave it," said Raymo. "Girl who left it there, she want it dead."

"How do you know it was a girl?"

"Boys don't have babies," said Raymo. "Surprised you didn't know."

"Maybe she hoped somebody find it."

"You want somebody to find it, you leave it on they doorstep, buttgas."

"Buttgas?"

"Worse than a dumbass," said Raymo.

"Well we *did* find it, and I'm not going to let it die."

"No," said Raymo. "Not *let* it die."

That was it. Ceese clutched the baby as close as a football and started for the edge of the grass. Raymo just laughed at him, but Ceese was used to that.

"Hey, buttgas!" called Raymo. "You know who owns this skateboard?"

Ceese looked back. Raymo was standing at the edge of the

road, right at the hairpin turn, where Ceese's skateboard had flipped to. Ceese was clear down by the fancy white house at the end of the little valley.

"You know it's mine!" called Ceese.

"Don't see nobody's name on it!" called Raymo.

Ceese didn't know for sure what Raymo was about, but either he was trying to provoke Ceese into walking all the way up the steepest part of the road to get his skateboard, and then probably trying to goad him into riding it home while holding the baby—or he was planning to steal the board and taunt Ceese while he was doing it, just so Ceese would feel helpless and small.

But standing there with that baby in his arms, Ceese wanted with all his heart to be free of Raymo and everybody else like him, all the bullies who kept looking for nasty stuff to do, and always had to have an audience for their nastiness, and didn't care much about the distinction between audience and victim.

So Ceese just turned his back and kept walking down Cloverdale. It was steep, and he walked extra careful, to keep from jostling the baby too much. Before too long, he could hear the sound of a skateboard coming up behind. Knowing Raymo, it was possible he'd deliberately crash into Ceese to make him drop the baby. So Ceese made a run for the front yard of one of the houses and got behind a hedge.

Sure enough, Raymo had been heading right for him. But he wasn't going to crash into a hedge just for a lame joke.

So he hooted at Ceese and got back out on the road. "Mama Ceese got herself a widdo baby!" He was holding his own skateboard and riding Ceese's. Of course.

Ceese didn't say anything. Just watched him go.

Why've I been hanging with that vienna sausage anyway? Makes no sense. Sure thing I got no desire ever to see him again. Why did I put up with all his crap for so long?

Right up to the minute I found this baby, and not a minute longer.

Ceese's face burned with—what, embarrassment? Or the flush of sudden realization?

Maybe he had spent all this time with Raymo, making his mother all worried and coming close to getting into trouble a dozen times, just so he'd be at the drainpipe today, to find this baby.

That was just crazy. Who could arrange something like that, God? And God sure as hell wasn't going to use a dipstick like Raymo as an instrument of his divine will. That would be like the devil sending Gabriel to fetch his laundry, only in reverse.

When Ceese got to Du Ray, Raymo was nowhere to be seen. No surprise there. Ceese took the left on Du Ray, then the next left on Sanchez. It wasn't far. And when he got to the front door, Mama was there, holding it open behind the screen.

"Just tell me that what you got ain't yours," she said coldly.

"Don't know whose it is," said Ceese.

"You mean you don't *know* if you're the daddy?" There was real menace in her voice.

"I mean I found it. I don't know who the mama is. And I *sure* know I ain't *no* baby's daddy. Less it can happen by looking at pictures."

Mama gasped. So did Ceese. He'd never talked like that to his mama in his life. Which, he was sure, was the only reason he was still alive. And from Mama's face, that was about to come to a quick end.

At that moment, the baby cried softly. Which was about the only thing that could have changed the subject from how Ceese had just said his last words.

"You really find this?" The screen swung open.

"Inside a Lucky's bag and covered with ants," said Ceese. "It's a boy. He's alive."

"Seeing how I'm not blind and stupid, I already knew that."

"Sorry, Mama." He said it fervently enough that it might cover for what he said before.

"Before you ask, no, you can't keep it."

"It's real little, Mama."

"They get bigger."

"I don't want to *keep* it, Mama, I just don't want it to *die*."

"I know that," said Mama. "I'm thinking. Okay, I've thought. Take it over to Miz Smitcher. She's a nurse."

"Don't you want to take it?" said Ceese.

"No, I don't," said Mama. "That baby was conceived in sin and left to die in shame. Don't want no sin or shame in my house."

Ceese wanted to yell at her that the baby didn't commit any sins and the baby had nothing to be ashamed of, and what about "Even as ye have done it unto the least of these my brethren" and "suffer little children to come unto me"? But he wasn't so stupid as to throw Bible verses into Mama's face. She'd have ten more to answer him with, and no supper as punishment for blasphemy or whatever religious felony she convicted him of. The most common one was failing to honor his father and mother, even though he was the politest kid he knew of. Or maybe just the most beatdown.

Not wishing any further argument with Mama, Ceese walked to the gap in the fence they always used to get between Miz Smitcher's house and their own. It wasn't a gate—it was just a gap where two separate fences had sagged apart. And now that he was there, he realized that holding a baby made it a lot harder to squeeze through. He ended up holding the baby ahead of him in one hand, and he near dropped it.

He got through just in time. Miz Smitcher was a night-shift nurse, and she was heading out the front door to her car when Ceese started banging on the back.

"What is it?" she said. "I got no time right now for—"

Seeing the baby changed her whole attitude. "Please God, let that not be yours."

"Found it," said Ceese. "Covered with ants up in that little valley on Cloverdale. Mama said take it to you."

"Why? Does she think it's *mine?*" said Miz Smitcher.

"No, ma'am," said Ceese.

Miz Smitcher sighed. "Let's get that baby to the hospital."

Ceese made as if to hand the baby to her.

She recoiled. "I got to *drive,* boy! You got a baby seat in your pocket? No? Then you coming along to *hold* that child."

Ceese didn't argue. Seemed like once he picked that baby up, he couldn't get nobody else to take it no matter what he said or did.

4

COPROCEPHALIC

I t irritated Ura Lee, the way folks just assumed that because she was a nurse, she'd take care of their problems, no matter what. Found a baby in a field? Why, give it to the nurse lady! Never mind that she's never had a baby in her life and never worked with newborns on the job.

Only people I ever diapered were Alzheimer's patients and stroke victims. Madeline Tucker, now, *she's* taken care of four sons, *she's* got diapering down to a science, not to mention bathing and feeding babies. She's got a car at home, no job that she's already running late for, and it's her boy found the baby. But it never crosses her mind to take the baby to the hospital herself, does it? Because Ura Lee Smitcher is a nurse, so it's *her* job.

"Fasten your seat belt," she told Ceese.

When he didn't obey, she glared at him. He was moving his head and shoulders in a weird way. It finally dawned on her that he was trying to snake his head through the shoulder strap.

"Use your hands, child, or do you think God stuck them on the ends of your arms so you could count to ten without getting lost?"

"I'm holding the baby!" Ceese protested.

"Your *lap* is holding the baby," said Ura Lee. "Use your head."

"I *was*," Ceese murmured as he let go of the baby and pulled the seatbelt across his middle.

Of course, the baby's head flopped down and hung like fruit from a tree. Ura Lee reached over and supported the head. "You don't just let go of the head, you want to break its neck?"

"You said to . . . I was just . . ."

"What were you doing with Raymo? Smoking something made you stupid?"

"No," said Ceese angrily. "I'm stupid without any weed."

At first she thought he was being smart-mouthed and she was about to smack him when she saw that his eyes were glistening. It occurred to her that maybe this boy had been called stupid a few times too often.

His seatbelt fastened, he got his hand back under the baby's head, and she was free to shift into gear. She backed the car out of the carport and onto Burnside, then headed for Coliseum and then La Cienega. She drove gently, because she wasn't sure this boy could hold on to the baby. It looked like he was being so gentle that he couldn't get a decent grip on it.

"You sure you got no idea where that baby comes from?" she asked.

"I know exactly where it came from," said Ceese coldly.

"All right then," she said. "Who's the mother?"

"How should I know?"

"You said—"

"They showed us a movie in P.E.," said Ceese scornfully. "But it didn't tell us how to figure out who's the mother of a naked ant-covered baby you find in the grass by a rusty old drainpipe. I guess they only teach that to nurses."

Well, that was an interesting reaction. Seemed like young Ceese Tucker didn't take crap from anybody. Maybe there was more to the boy than tagging along after Raymo Vine.

At a light, she reached into her purse, pulled out her cellphone, and called work to tell them she was late because she had to bring a baby to the emergency room. She was explaining it for the second time to her supervisor, who seemed to think Ura Lee was so stupid that this is the kind of excuse she'd invent for being late to work, when she realized that the car in front of her was stopping suddenly. She jammed on the brakes and saw the baby fly forward out of Ceese's arms. It hit the dashboard—with its naked butt, fortunately, instead of its head—and dropped like a rock onto the floor.

The baby lay there, silent. Not crying, not whimpering, not even squeaking.

"God have mercy on you boy, if you killed that baby!"

"Why'd you stop so fast?" Ceese shouted back at her.

"What did you want me to do, you smart-mouthed little coprocephalic? Run into the car in front of me?"

"He's breathing," said Ceese. "You got so many McDonald's wrappers on the floor it probably saved his life."

"You criticizing how I keep my car, now?"

"No, I'm trying to figure out why you called me a shithead when you're the one slammed on the brakes without warning!"

"I couldn't make the car in front of me disappear!"

"And I couldn't repeal the law of inertia that made this baby fly out of my arms," said Ceese. "What you yelling at me for?"

It was a question to which Ura Lee had no rational answer. "Because you're here and I'm mad," said Ura Lee. "Are you going to pick the baby up or use it as a footrest?"

He bent over and scooped it up. Clumsily, but then it's not the kind of thing people got to practice much, picking up babies off the floors of cars. The baby still didn't make a sound. Hadn't made a sound the whole time, before or after falling on the floor.

Ceese was stroking the baby. Murmuring to it. "You all right? You okay?"

He wasn't careless with this baby. She'd judged him wrong.

"I'm sorry I yelled at you," she said.

He didn't look at her.

"I was just upset and I took it out on you," she said.

"That's okay," he murmured, so soft she could hardly hear him.

"That how you accept an apology?" she asked.

"I don't know," he said. "Nobody ever apologize to me before."

"Oh, now, that's just silly," she said.

"Sorry," he said.

Then again, he was the youngest, with nothing but brothers, and she didn't see Madeline or Winston doing much apologizing to their baby.

"Was that true?" she asked. "Nobody *ever* told you sorry?"

"Sure," he said. "My brothers. All the time. One of them hits me upside the head, he says, 'Sorry.' One of them walks by and knocks me against the wall, he says, 'Sorry.'"

"I get the idea," said Ura Lee.

"One of them comes up to me when I'm playing with a friend and pulls my pants down, undershorts and all, and flips me there where it really hurts and when I'm crying and my friend's run off home, he says, 'Sorry, Cecil.'"

"Well, your life is one long nightmare," said Ura Lee. Thinking maybe he was exaggerating.

"Damn right," said Ceese softly.

"What did you say?"

"Damn right, *ma'am*," said Ceese, loudly this time.

And Ura Lee busted out laughing. This boy was something. Or maybe holding a baby in his arms made him feel like more the equal of an adult. So he could give sass instead of just taking it.

"Is that really what it's like to have brothers?" she asked him.

"That's what it was like to have *my* brothers," said Ceese.

"But if you had a little brother, you wouldn't treat him like that?"

Ceese barked out a little laugh. "Miz Smitcher, I would be the best damn brother any kid ever had. But no way is my mom going to let me keep this baby, so you can forget it."

Ura Lee hadn't been thinking that at all. Hadn't crossed her mind. But now that she was thinking about it, she couldn't imagine why she had said that to him at all. How was he going to have a little brother, indeed?

Of course, one way might be to keep the child herself. Then Ceese would be the next-door neighbor. Not that they'd play much together. But when this baby was first growing up, he'd have Ceese next door as an example of a decent kind of boy. Kind of a protector maybe. Wasn't that what Ceese already was? This baby's protector?

She pulled into the hospital parking lot. For a moment she thought of taking the baby right to Emergency, but then she'd have to come out later and move her car, and it's not like the baby was choking or having respiratory difficulty or diarrhea. It was just naked and newborn and dirty, unless the doctors found something that wasn't visible to the naked eye.

Just take the stray to the vet, have him look it over to make sure it didn't have worms or the mange, and you take it home and voilà! You had yourself a pet!

What in the *world* was she thinking? Keep the child herself! How could she possibly keep a child, what with them locking her up in a mental ward, since taking on some little lost baby would be sure proof that she'd lost her mind?

"*Don't* get out of the car yet," she snapped at Ceese as she brought the car to a stop in the parking space. "Let me come around and take that baby out of your arms."

"How am I going to get home?" asked Ceese.

She slammed her own door and walked around the back and opened his door. As she took the baby, she answered his question. "I'm gonna give you money for the bus."

"I don't know the bus route."

"Then I'll tell you the bus route."

"What if I get off at the wrong stop?"

"Here's an idea: Don't get off at the wrong stop."

By now he was out of the car, tagging along behind her as she carried the baby toward Emergency. "Why can't I just stay here?"

"Because this is a working hospital and there isn't a soul to look after you."

"I could work. I know how to clean stuff. I help Mom with the housework all the time."

"You don't know how to do hospital clean, boy," said Ura Lee. "And they got people *paid* to do that anyway."

"Don't they have magazines? Like the doctor's office? I could read magazines."

It dawned on her that maybe this boy was really attached to the baby he'd found.

Or maybe he was just bored silly with life in the summertime, and he figured hanging around a hospital was better than walking up Cloverdale to ride down it on his skateboard.

"Tell you what," said Ura Lee. "They're going to tie me up with paperwork for an hour at least. So I'm already missing half my shift. I'll take you home. *When* I got this baby admitted."

"Cool," said Ceese.

She was about to launch into a long list of warnings about don't talk and don't wander around and don't pick stuff up and for heaven's sake don't open drawers or cupboards or somebody's going to assume you looking for drugs.

Only before she said any of it, she remembered that this was a pretty good kid. Gotta give him a chance to prove he's an idiot or a criminal before you treat him like one.

This kid knew about Newton's laws of motion, which meant maybe he actually paid attention in school. Bill Cosby would be downright proud of this boy!

More than that, Ceese actually understood that *coprocephalic* meant "shithead." That made him so smart it was almost creepy.

She was going to have to *watch* this boy.

5

BABY MACK

It was all grown-up stuff, what Miz Smitcher was talking about with the people at the desk. Meanwhile, there sat Ceese, holding the baby on his lap.

The kid had a diaper now, which it got right after its bath. Miz Smitcher did that herself, in about an inch of water, not ever scrubbing very hard, but still getting all the stains and dirt off the kid, right down to pulling on its little pud and washing it all over. Ceese was embarrassed at first, and Miz Smitcher must have seen how he felt, because she said, "As long as it ain't yours I'm washing, there's nothing to be embarrassed about."

Which embarrassed him way more than he already was—no doubt that's what she had in mind. But he didn't go away, he kept watching, right through the diapering. Ceese had never seen anybody diapered before, being the baby of the family. It looked easy enough. He said so.

"That's cause we have these little sticky tabs on a paper diaper," said Miz Smitcher. "Not all that long ago, diapers were made of cloth, and you had to pin them into place, and like as not you'd stick the baby or your own finger and then there'd be screaming and cussing like you wouldn't believe. And then when the diaper's all covered with feces or soaked with urine, you got to take it to the toilet and rinse it off and then load it all into the washing machine. Up to your elbows in piss and poop, that's what it was like to have a baby in the old days. Up to about thirty years ago."

"Man," said Ceese. "Was that back when they still fed babies out of bottles, or did they already invent the tit by then?"

Oh, the glare she gave him. But he could see from the way she clenched her lips to keep from smiling that she wasn't really mad.

And when the baby was clean and diapered and in a little undershirt that looked like doll clothes, back he goes into Ceese's arms while Miz Smitcher sees to the paperwork about getting the baby turned over to state custody.

Ceese couldn't hear much from where he was, but he could see that Miz Smitcher was getting angrier the longer it took. Not only that, but three times somebody came down from wherever it was that Miz Smitcher was supposed to be on duty, telling about how they needed her up there *right now.*

So he got up and walked over to her, holding the baby. "Miz Smitcher, I can stay here all day if you just call my mom and tell her I'm with you. That way you can go do your shift and then they can get all their paperwork done and we can take the baby home then."

Miz Smitcher looked at him like he was insane. "I'm *not* taking this baby home."

The woman behind the desk said, "They'll find a foster home in a few days, it just takes time."

"Then the baby stays *here* in the neonate unit," said Miz Smitcher.

"But the baby isn't sick and the baby wasn't born here, so as I've told you, Ura Lee, there ain't no way in hell the hospital is going to admit that baby because who's going to pay for it?"

"I am!" said Miz Smitcher.

"Well if you're going to pay hospital rates for babysitting," said the desk lady, "why don't you just take the baby home and let this boy here babysit for you? Just till they get a foster family for it."

"Him," said Ceese.

"What?" said the desk lady.

"Baby's a him, not an it."

"Baby doesn't understand a word we're saying, so I doubt that I have offended it or negatively affected its gender-role identification process," said the desk lady.

"He's a boy," said Ceese. "He's alive. I found him."

The desk lady pursed her lips and looked at the papers on her desk.

Miz Smitcher jabbed him in the arm, but not so hard as to hurt. Ceese looked up at her. She was doing all she could to keep from grinning.

"Seems to me," the desk lady said, "this stubborn young man here has offered you the best solution. You might as well get paid for part of this day, and he seems to be quiet enough."

"Baby's going to need feeding," said Miz Smitcher.

"You're bound to be right about that," said the desk lady.

"They got bottles and formula up in neonate," she said.

The desk lady sighed. "Miz Smitcher, now you're just trying to make me tired. You know perfectly well that I can't admit that baby. But you also know perfectly well that if you take that boy up to neonate and let those nurses coo over that baby for a while, a bottle or two is bound to fall off the cart at feeding time. Along with a few clean diapers now and then."

Miz Smitcher grinned. "I always like hearing practical advice."

The desk lady went on muttering as they walked away. "Make me say it out loud. Knew it perfectly well from the start. Stubborn . . ."

"I hope you were serious about what you offered," said Miz Smitcher, "cause everybody in this hospital got work to do, and you just need to hold that baby and don't bother nobody unless the baby's wet or stinking or crying."

"This baby don't cry," said Ceese.

"Give him time," said Miz Smitcher, "he'll figure out how."

"Should I try to teach him?"

She barked out a laugh. "Now, that'll be a first. Teaching a baby to cry. What you want to do next, teach clouds to float? Teach the sun to shine?"

"I just want to do right," said Ceese.

She gave him a quick one-armed hug as they walked along, which almost made him drop the baby, since it took him kind of by surprise. "I know you do," she said.

The rest of the morning and all afternoon he spent in neonate. The desk lady was right—the neonate nurses were all coos and babytalk, as much to him as to the baby. And by the end of the day, Ceese felt like an expert at diaper changing and baby feeding. Not only that, but one of the nurses bought him a sandwich out of a machine and a carton of milk for his own supper. And then later in the evening, a Coke.

Along with a warning not to try to give any of that Coke to the baby. Till she said it, Ceese never would have thought of feeding any to a baby, but after the warning, it was the only thing he could think of. How easy it would be to pour half the can into one of those formula bottles. Maybe the bubbles would tickle the baby's nose. Or make him burp. Babies were supposed to burp, weren't they? And except for the bubbles, wasn't Coke just sugar water? Well, and caffeine, but a few swallows of caffeine might be just what this baby needed, to wake him up.

So Ceese did the only thing that made sense. He drank the rest of the Coke right down, so there wasn't even a drop left. Then he burped so hard it made his eyes sting. But he still felt like a hero.

A really stupid hero, since the only danger the baby was in was from the hero himself. But hey, he thought of a bad thing and he didn't do it, and wasn't that what it meant to be good? Wasn't nothing good about not doing bad stuff you didn't even think of. Pastor Sasquatch never mentioned anything about how you can't be good unless you have bad thoughts. But it was true just the same, Ceese was sure of it. And now he was kind of proud of himself, because he had bad thoughts all the time, and he didn't do anything about any of them. Well, almost any.

Ceese got up every now and then during the afternoon and walked the halls with the baby, partly so his butt didn't get so sore from sitting, and mostly because it was something to do, and there wasn't many things as boring as sitting there holding a quiet baby while your arms went to sleep.

Only when he got up after finishing the Coke, he didn't go down the halls. Or to the elevator. He went to the door with the EXIT sign over it and pushed through it and found himself on a landing, with stairs going up and stairs going down.

At the railing, there was a gap between the flights of stairs that went right down to the bottom. It wasn't very wide. Ceese figured that when he dropped the baby, it wouldn't go straight down, it'd bounce off one of those railings and then land on the concrete stairs somewhere instead of smacking into the basement floor.

I'm not dropping this baby! Ceese told himself. What put an idea like that into his head?

He *could* just set the baby on the top step and give him a little push and let him roll down. Maybe he'd go right down to the bottom, but probably it'd be like when Ceese rolled down one of the grassy hills in the park, he always veered off till his head was pointed down the hill. Baby'd probably do that and end up bouncing down the stairs on his squishy little head. Ceese could say he dropped it. Nobody'd be too mad at him. It's not like the baby belonged to anybody, and people expected kids to be clumsy.

"Is that what you really want to do?"

Ceese snapped out of his concentration. Down at the bottom of the next flight of stairs, and coming up toward the opposite landing, was a big woman in black leather and a motorcycle helmet.

"I'm talking to you, boy," said the motorcycle woman. "I'm saying, you really want that baby dead?"

"No," said Ceese. "What you talking about anyway? Who are you?"

She stopped at the landing ten steps below Ceese, her head haloed by the light from the window. "I'm just saying, before you kill somebody, you need to think real careful. Because when you change your mind, they're still dead."

"I ain't killing nobody."

"I'm glad to hear it," said the motorcycle woman. "Killing people is a serious responsibility. I hardly ever do it myself, and it's my job."

Ceese didn't doubt for a minute that she was telling the truth.

A thought occurred to him. "You this baby's mama?"

"Baby like that got no mama," said the motorcycle woman. "And a good thing, too. He'll be nothing but trouble, you'll see. Dark trouble for everybody around him. Give him to me, I'll send him home."

"No," said Ceese.

"You can tell them that a sexy-looking woman in black leather come and kissed you and you couldn't tell her no."

Kiss him? She was going to kiss him?

She laughed. "Or you could say an evil-looking alien with a space helmet came and carried the baby off to heaven in a UFO."

"Like they'd believe that."

"I'd make sure the nurses saw me running with the baby. They'd believe you all right. I'm not here to cause you trouble. I'm here to save you from a lot of sadness and woe."

"You're one of them wacko women that steals other people's babies from the hospital cause they can't have any of their own."

"I could have a hundred babies if I wanted to," she said. "Want me to have *your* baby? You that hungry to be a papa?"

She was halfway up the steps, and he hadn't even noticed she was climbing. All he had to do was stay there, and she'd come and take the baby out of his arms.

For a moment, that sounded to him like the most natural thing in the world.

Then he knew that it was the most terrible thing he'd ever

thought of. Because if she ever got control of this baby, she'd stuff his tiny body down the drainpipe in that little park and he'd never be seen again. Maybe she meant to do that all along, and the only reason she couldn't was that he found the baby and carried him away.

"I saved this baby," said Ceese. "I don't want him dead."

"You don't?" she asked. "Not even a little curious about what it's like to watch the life go out of something?"

She was two steps down, and her head was almost even with his, and if she wanted to take the baby from him, she had only to reach out. But she didn't reach.

"I don't like you," said Ceese.

"Nobody does," she said. "It's a lonely life, being too cool for this world."

And at that moment, the baby started making noises. Not crying. Little soft cooing babbling noises. Like he was trying to talk babytalk to them.

"Except this little baby," she said. "He likes me fine. He knows me."

"You *are* his mama," said Ceese.

"Maybe I'm his girlfriend, you ever think of that? Or maybe he's my papa. You just never know how people are going to fit together in this world. Give him to me, Cecil. Your mother would tell you to do it."

He wanted to. He could feel it, this longing to hand the baby to her, rising in him like hope. And yet he knew it was wrong, that it would be the death of the baby to hand him over. "I won't do it," he said. "Don't you worry."

"I wasn't worried," she said. "Just hoping."

"I was talking to the baby," he said. "I'm not going to let you have him."

The door behind him opened. It was one of the neonate nurses. "Who you talking to out here?" she asked.

Ceese was going to say, Her, but when he turned back around

the motorcycle woman wasn't on the second step down anymore. For a second he thought she was entirely gone, but then he looked down and she was at the bottom of the next flight of stairs, where if he called to the nurse to come and see, the motorcycle woman would be gone before she could get there to look.

So Ceese said, "Talking to the baby."

"It's dangerous by these steps," said the nurse. "What if you dropped him?"

Below him, the motorcycle woman held out her arms. But despite her promises, Ceese knew that if he tossed the baby to her, she would step back and let the baby hit the stairs and spatter his brains everywhere and she'd be gone and they'd think Ceese went crazy and killed the kid and they'd lock him up until he admitted that there was never no motorcycle woman holding out her arms.

"I won't drop him," said Ceese.

"Still, come away."

"Sure," he said. "Wanted to look out the window is all."

"All that's out that window is a parking lot and a lot of hot asphalt trying to cool off in the darkness," said the nurse. "Want another Coke?"

Yes he did. So he could get the baby to drink it.

"No thank you," he said.

Was this what it was like for everybody? Did they all keep thinking of ways to poison or drop or otherwise kill their babies?

Not my baby, he reminded himself. Not mine at all. But that means, not mine to hurt, either. Not mine to give away to motorcycle women. Not mine to kill.

He belongs to himself, that's what. And nobody's got a right to steal his whole future from him.

Am I crazy, to think of ways for this baby to die? Was there really a motorcycle woman on those stairs? How would she know my name was Cecil? She called me Cecil and she didn't make a sound when she went down those stairs in a couple of seconds when my back was turned.

He sat on the bench between the elevators for the rest of the shift. When Miz Smitcher came to him and woke him, the baby was still in his arms, and still alive. And sure enough, even though a different desk lady had lots of things to sign at the desk when they got there, none of them gave Miz Smitcher permission to turn the baby over to the hospital. She had to take the baby home.

"All right then," said Miz Smitcher, "if I'm going to be his foster mother, I'm going to name him."

"Might as well," said the new desk lady. "Got to call him something."

"Mack," she said.

"First name or last?" asked the desk lady, poised to write something on a form.

"First name."

"Short for something?"

"That's the whole name. The whole first name."

"Last name Smitcher?" asked the desk lady.

"No way in hell," said Miz Smitcher. "Bad enough I'm stuck with Willie Joe's name, I'm not going to impose it on a poor little baby who with any luck will never meet him. Last name *Street*, that was my name when I was growing up. My daddy's and mama's name."

"Mack Street," said the desk lady.

"Just like that?" asked Miz Smitcher. "Don't need permission?"

"There's countries where you can't give a baby a name without the government's okay, but here, you just pick a name."

"What if this baby already had a name?"

"The person named him went and left him in a field somewhere," said the desk lady. "I'm betting there's no birth certificate. He still had amniotic fluid on him, the doctor said. He was born and laid in that grass and that was it. So this is the first name he ever had, count on it."

Miz Smitcher turned to Ceese. "What do you think? Mack Street okay?"

"Mack's an okay name," said Ceese. "Better than LeRoy or Raymo," he said.

"I agree with you there."

"Way better than Cecil."

"Cecil's a good name," said Miz Smitcher. "Every Cecil I knew was a fine man."

Not all. Not if you knew the sick crap that was going through my head this afternoon.

"But we got a Cecil in the neighborhood," said Miz Smitcher. "Near as I can tell, we got no other Mack."

"Mack Street is a good name," said Ceese.

And then it was done. Papers signed. And in a few minutes, Ceese was sitting in the car beside Miz Smitcher, holding little Mack Street in his arms.

They went home by way of a Kmart, where Miz Smitcher bought a baby seat and some cans of formula and some baby bottles and baby clothes and disposable diapers. "Stupid waste of money when the baby's going to live with somebody else in a couple of days," she said.

"So keep him," said Ceese.

"What you say?"

"Nothing," said Ceese.

"I know what you said."

"Then why did you ask?"

"Wanted to see if you had the balls to say it twice."

"Keep him," said Ceese. "You know you want to."

"Just because *you* want to doesn't mean everybody else does. He's an ugly little baby anyway, don't you think?"

Ceese just stood there watching while she finished belting the car seat into place. By the time she was done, she was dripping with sweat. "Give him to me now," she said.

Ceese handed the baby in to her.

"More trouble than you're worth, that's what you are," she

cooed to the baby. "Use up all my savings just to put food in one end and out the other."

Ceese looked out across the parking lot toward the street. Under the bright streetlights there was a homeless man standing on the curb, watching him, or at least looking toward Kmart.

Ceese heard again the thing that must have made him turn and look: the sound of a motorcycle engine revving.

A black-clad woman bent over the handlebars of a black motorcycle that rode along the street. She wasn't looking where she was going, she had her head turned toward Kmart, and even though there was no way to see her eyes, Ceese knew exactly who she was and what she was looking at.

The homeless man stepped into the street in front of her.

She screeched to a stop, the front wheel of her bike between the homeless man's legs.

The homeless man flipped her off.

She flipped him back.

He didn't move.

She walked her bike backward a couple of steps, then revved up and drove around him, flipping him off again.

He double-flipped her back, then strode back to the sidewalk.

"You gonna live here at Kmart, or you coming home with me?" asked Miz Smitcher.

"Home with you," said Ceese.

"Then get in the car."

He did. By the time they got to the street, neither the motorcycle nor the homeless man were anywhere to be seen.

At home, Mother was strangely nice about his being away all afternoon and half the evening, and when Dad got back late from work, he didn't say much, either. "Well, it's nice that Miz Smitcher will have a child to look after," Dad said.

"She didn't sound too happy about it," said Ceese. "I'm going to be helping her by tending him during the day."

"That'll keep you out of trouble," said Dad, laughing a little. And then it was on to other topics with Mom, as if finding a baby happened every day in their neighborhood.

It was all sort of anticlimactic. There was nobody to tell about the motorcycle woman or the homeless man. Nobody who even wanted to hear more about finding the baby. It was all just . . . done. Over with. It'll just be Miz Smitcher's little boy growing up next door, and everybody will forget that I found him and diapered his little butt and fed him and didn't throw him down the stairs.

He ate a late supper and went to bed and lay awake for a long while. The last thing he thought was: I wonder if Miz Smitcher is going to smother little Mack in his sleep.

6

SWIMMER

Mack Street grew up knowing the story of how Ceese found him in a grocery bag and Miz Smitcher took him in. How could he avoid it, with neighborhood kids calling him by nicknames like "Bag Boy" and "Safeway" and "Plasticman."

Miz Smitcher wouldn't talk to him about it, even when he asked her direct questions like, Why don't you let me call you Mama? and, Was I born or did you buy me at the store? So he got the straight story from Ceese, who came over every afternoon at four-thirty to take care of him while Miz Smitcher went to work at the hospital.

Mack would ask Ceese questions all the time, especially when Ceese was trying to do his homework, so Ceese made a rule: "You get one question a day, at bedtime."

Mack would store up his questions all day trying to decide which one would be tonight's bedtime question. A lot of times he had one that he knew was great, the most important question ever, but by the time bedtime came around he had forgotten it.

So as soon as he thought of a great question, he asked Ceese to write it down for him. "So you're still interrupting my homework with your question," said Ceese.

"You don't got to answer it now," said Mack. "Just write it down so I don't forget."

"Write it down yourself."

"I can't," said Mack. "I'm only four."

"If you can't remember it and you can't write it down, that's not my fault," said Ceese. "Now let me do my homework."

So that night, Mack's question was, "Will you teach me to read?"

"That's not a question," said Ceese.

Mack thought for a minute. What *was* a question, anyway? "I don't know the answer and you do."

"That's a *request*."

"If that one doesn't count, then I get to ask you another."

"Hit me."

Mack hit him.

"Ow!" said Ceese. "When somebody say 'Hit me' it means 'Go ahead.' "

"What would you say if you wanted somebody to hit you?"

"Nobody wants somebody to hit them. And that's your question, and that's my answer, go to sleep."

"You're mean!" called out Mack as Ceese went back into the living room to watch TV till he fell asleep on the couch, which is where he spent every night that he tended Mack.

"I'm the meanest!" called back Ceese. "Miz Smitcher specially picked me to tend you cause I'm the most wicked boy in Baldwin Hills!"

That was why Mack Street started teaching himself how to read when he was four years old, by copying out letters, not knowing what they said, and then asking Miz Smitcher to tell him what the letters spelled. She could always answer when he copied them down in the same order as on the page, but when he changed the order she'd say, "It doesn't say anything, baby." Finally she gave up and taught him the sounds of the letters, and pretty soon he was sounding out words for himself.

But by that time he had already asked Ceese the most important and worrisome questions.

Who's my daddy? Who's my mama? To which the answer both times was "Nobody knows, Mack, and that's the truth."

How come they sometimes call me Ralph's? "Cause it's the name of a grocery store. Like Safeway."

Well, why do they call me grocery-store names? "That's a second question so you better save it till tomorrow."

Next night, he remembered and got the answer. "Cause when you was found, Mack, you was a naked little baby in a plastic grocery bag, covered with ants and lying in a field."

The next night: Who found me? "Me and Raymo, only Raymo wanted to kill you like a cat and I wanted to save you alive."

Bit by bit Mack got the story from Ceese. He wasn't sure he believed it, so one of his questions was, "Is that all true? Cause if it ain't, when I'm bigger I'll beat the shit out of you."

"Who taught you to say shit?" demanded Ceese.

"Is that your question for tonight?" said Mack.

"My *answer* to your question, before you said a nasty word that Miz Smitcher going to wash out your mouth with soap, my answer is Yes."

But thinking about what Miz Smitcher might do drove out what he'd asked. "What was my question?"

"That's *another* question, which I don't have to answer, nastymouth baby."

"Shit shit shit shit shit."

"I'm going to get the stapler and fasten your tongue to your nose and see if you want to say any more nasty words."

"If you do I'll bleed on your shirt!"

"You bleed on my shirt, I'll pee on your toys."

Mack loved Ceese more than any other human on earth.

In good weather, which was most afternoons, Ceese took Mack out to play in the neighborhood before dinner. Ceese was way older than any of the children Mack played with, so he always brought along a book so he could read, but then most of the time Ceese would get involved in the kid games they played, sometimes cause there was a fight and Ceese had to break it up, but mostly cause kid games were more fun than the books Ceese had to read for school.

"Mack, if you happen to live to be my age and somebody tells you you going to have to read *The Scarlet Letter* I recommend you just kill yourself right off and get it over with."

"What's *scarlet*?" asked Mack.

"Ask me at bedtime."

Mack didn't know he was having a great childhood. Ceese tried to tell him one time. About how rich kids grew up in big empty mansions and never saw anybody except servants and nannies. And poor kids grew up in the ghetto where people were always shooting bullets into their house so they never slept at night and they got beat up every day and stabbed if they went out of their house. And kids from in-between families lived in apartments and never had anybody to play with but mean ugly kids at day care.

"But you, Mack, you got a whole neighborhood full of kids who know who you are. You're famous, Mack, just for being alive."

Mack didn't know what famous was. So what if everybody knew who he was? He knew them right back. Was everybody famous?

Okay, so everybody thought he was special or weird because he was found instead of being born or adopted. But that wasn't what made Mack different, he knew.

It was the cold dreams.

He tried to talk about it to Ceese one time. "I had a really bad cold dream last night."

"A what?"

"A cold dream."

"What's that?"

"Where you dream and it's really *real* and you want it so bad, and when you wake up from it you're shivering so hard you think it's going to break your teeth."

"I never had a dream like that," said Ceese.

"You didn't? I have them sometimes when I'm not even asleep."

"That's just crazy. You can't have a dream when you're not asleep."

"It comes in front of my eyes and I just stop and watch and when it's done I'm shivering so hard I can't even stand up."

"You crazy, Mack Street."

Ceese must have told Miz Smitcher because the next day she took him to a doctor at the hospital who stuck things all over his head and then a bunch of metal rods made squiggly lines on a moving paper and the doctor just smiled and smiled at him but he looked all serious when he talked to Miz Smitcher and then they glanced at him and closed the door and kept talking where he couldn't hear.

After that he decided that having cold dreams wasn't normal and just got him in trouble, so he didn't talk about them anymore.

But the cold dreams scared him. They were so intense. And strange. His regular dreams, even his nightmares, they were about things in his life. His friends. Miz Smitcher. Ceese. Grocery bags and ants. But the cold dreams would be about grownups most of the time, and more than once it happened that he'd see a grownup for the first time in his life, and it would be somebody from a cold dream.

"Miz Smitcher," said Mack, "I know that man."

"You never met him before in your life."

"He all the time sees this woman naked."

She was furious. "Don't you say such things! He's a deacon at church and he does *not* see women naked and how would you know, anyway?"

"It just came into my head," said Mack, which was true.

"You're too young to understand what you're saying, which is why I don't beat you till your butt turns into hamburger."

"Better than my butt turning into a chocolate milkshake."

"How about beating your butt into french fries?"

"That doesn't even make sense," said Mack.

"Don't go talking about men seeing women naked," said Miz Smitcher.

"I was just saying that I know that man."

"You don't know him. *I* know him and he's a good man."

But then came a day when Miz Smitcher sent him out of the room when Ceese's mama came over and the two of them talked all serious and after Ceese's mama left Miz Smitcher came in to Mack's room and sat down on the floor and looked him in the eye.

"You tell me, Mack Street, how you happened to know about Deacon Landry and Juanettia Post."

"Who are they?"

"You met Deacon Landry and you told me you saw him looking at a naked woman."

From the look in her eye, Mack knew that this was something really bad, and he wasn't about to admit to anything. "I don't remember," he said.

"I'm not mad at *you,* baby. You just tell me what you saw and when you saw it."

"I don't know, Miz Smitcher," said Mack. "I don't know nothing about naked women. That's nasty stuff."

She searched his eyes but whatever she was looking for, she didn't find it. "Never mind," said Miz Smitcher. "You *shouldn't* be thinking about naked women anyway, I'm sorry I brought it up."

But she paused in the door of his room and looked at him like he was something strange, and he decided right then that he'd never tell anybody about those cold dreams, not ever again.

And he probably would have kept that promise if it wasn't for Tamika Brown.

Tamika was older than him and he only knew her because of her little brother Quon who was Mack's age, and they played together all the time cause the Browns only lived a few doors down. Mack even went into their house sometimes because Quon's mama wasn't one of those women who wouldn't have a grocery-bag baby in their house. But he didn't see Tamika except when she was just going out the door or running around getting ready to go out the door. And she was always wearing a bright red swimming suit because that's what Tamika did—she was a swimmer.

Quon said she was in competitions all the time, and she outswam and outdived girls two years older than her and people said she was a mermaid or a fish, she was so natural and quick in the water. "She just lives to swim."

And one time Miz Brown told a story about when Tamika was a baby. "My husband Curtis and I had her in the pool, with those bubble things on her arms, and she wasn't even two years old yet, so we were both holding on to her. But she was kicking so strong, like a frog, that I thought, I'm just holding her back, and Curtis must have thought the same thing at that very moment because we both just let go, and she takes *off* like a motorboat through the water and we knew right then that she was born to swim. Didn't have to teach her none of the strokes, she just knew them. Curtis says there's a scientist who thinks humans evolved from sea apes, and the way Tamika took to the water, I could believe it, she was born to swim."

So when Tamika showed up in one of Mack's dreams, he would have thought it was just a regular dream about people he knew. Except that he woke up shivering so bad he could hardly climb out of bed and go to the toilet without falling over from the shaking.

In the dream she was Tamika, but she was also a fish, and she swam through the water faster than any of the other fish. They swam around her when she was holding still, but then she'd give a flick with her back and just like that, they'd be far behind her. She swam to the surface and flipped herself out and flew through the air and then dived back in and the water felt delicious to her, and she didn't ever, ever have to come up because she was a fish, not a girl. She didn't have legs, she had big flippers, and in the water there was nothing to slow her down or hold her back.

"Why would a girl want to be a fish?" Mack asked Ceese one day.

"I know a lot of girls like to *eat* a fish," said Ceese. "Maybe some want to *meet* a fish. And if they cooking they got to *heat* a fish."

"Get mad and they want to *beat* a fish," said Mack, playing along.

"Playing cards they might want to *cheat* a fish," said Ceese.

But Mack was done with the game. "I'm not joking."

"Whazz wet?—that's how you *greet* a fish."

"Tamika Brown, she really wants to be a fish."

"She likes to swim," said Ceese. "That doesn't mean she's crazy."

"She wants to get down in the water and never have to come up."

"Or maybe *you* crazy," said Ceese. "Give it gummy worms, that's how you *treat* a fish."

"I dreamed about her," said Mack. "No arms and legs, just fins and a tail, living in the water."

"You way too young to be having *that* kind of dream," said Ceese, and now he was laughing so hard he could hardly talk.

"I'm not joking."

"Yes you are, you just don't *know* you joking," said Ceese.

Mack wanted to tell Ceese about the cold dream he had about Deacon Landry and how it came true in the real world, with Juanettia Post, and nobody liked how it turned out. What if Tamika's dream came true, too? Quon wouldn't want no fish for a sister.

Ceese would just laugh even more, maybe die from laughing so hard, if Mack told him that he was worried about a girl turning into a fish.

That's because nobody but Mack ever seemed to have dreams like his. Nobody else knew how real they were, how strong, how they gripped him with desire.

You don't know, Ceese, how it feels to want something so bad you'd give up everything if only it could happen. But in a cold dream, that's how it feels the whole time, and then it leaves me shaking when I wake up out of the wish.

CURTIS BROWN WOKE UP on that hot August night, covered with sweat and needing to pee. Happened a lot, sleeping on a water bed. The motion of it sort of alerted his bladder. Either that or he was getting old—but he and Sondra were still young. Their oldest, Tamika, was only ten. Curtis was a long way from being some-body's grandpa who had to get up and go to the toilet three times a night.

It was Curtis's daddy who stalked through his house late at night, flipping lights on and off and cussing under his breath about how it didn't make no sense that he feels like he's got to pee but he can't get anything out. And when Curtis says to him, Daddy, that means you got to get your prostate checked, Daddy just looks at him and says, You think I'm going to let some doctor stick his fin-ger up my anus and smear jelly all inside my rectum? *You* get your ass reamed out, you think it's so fun. You the crazy one, not me, sleeping on a water bed like a yuppie, you need your head exam-ined, don't go telling me to have my ass examined, at least my head ain't *up* my ass like you. And then he laughed and kept saying to anybody who'd listen, Curtis gone to the proctologist to have his head examined, cause you got to go through his ass to get to his head.

Never going to be an old man like my daddy, Curtis told himself all the time. Never going to make my kids wish I was already dead.

Curtis lay there on the bed, wondering if he really had to pee so bad he couldn't just go back to sleep, cause if he got up then when he got back to bed the sheets would be cold and clammy unless he stayed up long enough for them to get dry and then . . .

Something bumped him.

Bumped him from *underneath.*

He was out of that bed in a second, standing beside it, looking down. It was still undulating from his getting up. But Sondra lay there peaceful as could be, snoring just a little the way she did, even as she rocked slightly from the bed's movement.

I'm going crazy, thought Curtis as he stumbled to the bathroom. Either that or the chemicals in the bed ain't doing their job and the algae gone and growed into the Blob. Now that's the kind of nightmare would have kept him awake all night, back when he was a kid. Except they didn't even have waterbeds then. No, wait, yes they did. There was that 1970s movie where the cop—Eastwood? Some white cop, anyway—busts into some black pimp's room where he's lying with some girl on his waterbed, and when he's done asking questions the white cop shoots the bed for no reason at all, just to be mean and make it leak all over.

When he was done he didn't wash his hands, because he was tired and he hadn't got any on himself and besides, urine was mostly uric acid so it was cleaner than soap, or that's what that guy said at that spaghetti dinner at the Masons' house on Memorial Day, so it didn't matter if you washed your hands after you peed, you could eat a banana with your bare hands and be perfectly safe. It was wiping yourself that made it so you needed to wash, that's where diseases came from. Little-known facts, Curtis said to himself. That's all I got in my head, is little-known completely useless facts.

He padded down the hall to look at the kids' rooms. The boys had kicked their covers off and Quon, as usual, was asleep with his hands inside his underpants, what were they going to *do* with that boy, couldn't stop playing with it like he thought it was made of Legos or something. Tamika, though, her covers were all piled up on top of her. How could she sleep like that? Too hot for that, she was going to sweat to death, if the pile of blankets didn't smother her.

He pulled the blankets back and she wasn't under them.

He looked around her room to see if maybe she had fallen asleep somewhere else. He went back into the hall and she wasn't in the kids' bathroom and she wasn't in the kitchen or the living room and then he knew where she was, he knew it was impossible but didn't she say she wished she could live underwater like a fish, live there all the time?

No way she could be inside the waterbed. But she wasn't anywhere else, and *something* bumped him, he didn't imagine it, it was real. Something bumped him and if it was Tamika she had already been under the water way too long.

He was halfway down the hall when he realized that he'd need something to cut through the plastic. He ran to the kitchen, got the big, sharp carving knife, and ran back to the bedroom and started yanking the sheets off the bed.

"What you doing, baby?" said Sondra sleepily.

"Get up," said Curtis. "There's something inside the water-bed."

She got up, dragging the top sheet with her. "How can there be something inside there? You sleepwalking, baby?"

His only answer was to plunge the knife into the plastic—but near the edge, where he wouldn't run a risk of stabbing Tamika, if she was really under there, if he wasn't completely insane. The knife went in on the second try, and then he sawed and tugged at the plastic and the stinking water splashed into his face and now the opening was wide enough and he reached down in, reached with both hands, leaned so he could feel deep into the bed and there was an ankle and he grabbed it and pulled, and when he got the foot out of the bed Sondra screamed.

"Hold on to her," said Curtis, and he fumbled around and found Tamika's other leg and now they could pull her out, like she was being born feetfirst with a huge gush of water. They pulled her right over the edge of the waterbed frame and she flopped onto the floor like a fish.

She looked dead.

Curtis didn't waste a second except to say, "Call 911," and then he was pushing on Tamika's chest to get the water out and then breathing into her mouth, trying to remember if there was something different about CPR if it was from drowning instead of a heart attack or a seizure. When he pushed on her chest water splashed out of her mouth but did that mean he had to get all the water out before breathing into her lungs and was he still supposed to pump at her chest to get her heart started?

He did everything, sure that whatever he was doing had to be wrong but doing it anyway. And when the EMTs got there, they took over, and before they got her onto a cart she had a tube down her throat and they assured him that her heart was beating and she was getting air.

"How long was she underwater?" asked one of the guys.

"I don't know," said Curtis. "Took me a while to realize she was in there."

"You expect me to believe she cut through waterbed plastic herself, a little girl like that?" asked the guy.

"No, I cut it open to get her out," said Curtis.

"Right," said the EMT. "So how did she get *in?*"

"Come on!" demanded the other guy and they were out the door with Tamika, rushing her to the hospital. And Curtis and Sondra woke up Azalea Mason and she came over and stayed in the house so the boys wouldn't wake up to no grownups there, and then they went to the hospital to find out if the light of their lives had gone out on this terrible, impossible night.

URA LEE POURED COFFEE into Madeline Tucker's cup.

"I don't know why he even sticks with such a story," said Madeline.

"Sondra says that's how it happened," said Ura Lee Smitcher.

"Well she *would,* wouldn't she, seeing how she doesn't want her husband to go to jail."

"I'd want *my* husband to go to jail if he stuck my daughter inside a waterbed so long she was brain-damaged. That's if I didn't kill him with the knife he used to cut through the plastic."

"Well, that just shows you are not Sondra Brown. She is loyal to a *fault.*"

"I suppose that's easier to believe than thinking Tamika could somehow magically appear inside a waterbed," said Ura Lee. "It's just a completely crazy thing. The Browns are good people."

"Those child abuser wackos always *look* like good people."

"My Mack plays there all the time with their boy Quon, he'd know if they were abused children. Abusers live in secrecy, and their kids are shy and closed-off."

"Except the ones who don't and aren't," said Madeline.

"Well, I guess they better hope you aren't on the jury, since you already got that man convicted."

"Reasonable doubt, that's the law," said Madeline. "When he tells people she was inside the waterbed and there wasn't a break in it anywhere until he cut it open to get her *out,* then he better plead insanity because ain't no jury in this city, white *or* black, that would let him off. He ain't O. J. and ain't nobody going to believe him if he starts talking about the LAPD framing him, not even if he got Johnnie Cochran and a choir of angels on his defense team."

"Johnnie Cochran ain't taking this case anyway," said Ura Lee, "cause the Browns don't have that kind of money and besides, Tamika isn't dead."

"Brain-damaged so she might as well be dead. Poor little girl."

Ura Lee looked over at the hallway and saw Mack standing there. "You need something, Mack?"

"Did Tamika go into the water last night?" he asked.

"Little pitchers have big ears," said Madeline Tucker.

"It's not like we were talking soft," said Ura Lee. "Mack, don't you have homework?"

"I'm five."

"No reason to treat you like babies," said Ura Lee.

Mack and Madeline both looked at her like she was crazy.

"That's why I don't tell jokes," said Ura Lee. "Nobody ever laughs."

"Nobody thinks you're joking, that's why," said Madeline.

"Yes, Mack, the Browns' little swimmer almost drowned and she was without air for so long it hurt her brain."

"She isn't dead?"

"No, Mack, she's alive. But there's things she won't be able to do anymore. Doctors don't know how bad the damage is yet. She might get some of it back, she might not."

Mack had tears in his eyes. He was taking it harder than Ura Lee would have expected.

"Mack, this kind of thing happens sometimes. Accidents that hurt people. All you can do is pray that it doesn't happen to someone you love, and then pray for strength to deal with it if it does."

"I should have told her," said Mack.

"Told her what?"

"To stop wishing she could be a fish."

"Mack, honey, this doesn't have a thing to do with you."

But Madeline was intrigued now. "She told you she wanted to be a fish?"

Ura Lee didn't want Madeline to start making something out of this. "It wouldn't matter if she did."

"Well it would too, if it would show she had a motive for getting into that waterbed."

"Motive or not, she can't fit down the hose hole in a waterbed, and that was the only way she could have got in."

"If Mack knows something," said Madeline stubbornly, "then he's got to tell."

"He's five years old," said Ura Lee. "Nobody is going to accept his testimony, especially since there's no way Tamika could have got in that waterbed except through the gash Curtis Brown cut in it."

Madeline leaned closer to her. "Did you see it? Did you go over there and see the gash?"

Ura Lee turned to Mack. "Mack, this is a grownup conversation. Tamika's going to be fine in the end, I'm sure of it. It's sweet of you to care what happens to your friend's big sister. But now you need to let us talk."

Mack turned around and went back up the hall. Madeline was about to talk again, but Ura Lee held up her hand till she heard the door close. Then she got up and walked to the hall and looked down to make sure Mack wasn't faking being out of earshot.

"Well?" asked Madeline, when Ura Lee returned to the living room.

"Well I did *not* go over there to spy on them. I think you want to talk to Miz Ophelia for that kind of thing."

"Oh, she wouldn't go in that room, she called it the death room and said it had some powerful curse on it."

"Well, if you're reduced to asking *me* for gossip, Madeline, you are at the bottom of the barrel, cause nobody tells me anything and I wouldn't remember it if they did."

IN HIS BEDROOM, Mack was afraid to go to sleep. What if he dreamed again, and someone else had something terrible happen to them? So many cold dreams. A whole neighborhood full of them. And when they came true, it wasn't ever going to be like the dreamers hoped.

He stayed awake forever, it felt like. And then he woke up and it was morning and he knew that he'd have to find another way to stop the cold dreams from coming true.

7

NEIGHBORHOOD OF DREAMS

The older Mack got, the more he lived outside the house. Nothing against indoors. That was the place of breakfast, of sleep, of Miz Smitcher's hugging and kissing and scolding. It was a good place and he was glad to go back there when Ceese called to him at night.

But he grew up on the streets, more or less. Once school started for him, he'd go, and try to concentrate while he was there. But for him the *real* day was that morning run to the bus stop to hang out with the other kids from the neighborhood, and it started up again after school when the bus finally let him go in the afternoon. Summers were only different because he got to get lunch at the house of whatever kid he was playing with.

Ceese, who was in high school now, mostly gave up trying to make supper for him—it was hard enough for Ceese to find him in the evening. Mack didn't hide from him, and the moment he heard Ceese's voice calling from up or down the block somewhere, Mack would drop what he was doing. He never pretended not to hear. But Mack could be most anywhere, on any given day, so Ceese might lose half an hour of homework time walking up and down Cloverdale or Sanchez or Ridgeley or Coliseum, calling out, "Mack! Mack Street! Get home now, boy!"

"That boy getting himself a powerful set of lungs calling out for you," Miz Dellar said one evening. Mack had eaten dinner with Tashawn Wallace's family, and Miz Dellar was Tashawn's great-grandma, about the oldest person Mack knew in person. Her teeth hurt her, so she only wore them at supper, and Mack liked to watch her put them in.

"He knows I always come home," said Mack.

"He cares about you, boy," said Miz Dellar. "That's worth more than a day's pay in this day and age."

"Day's pay for me is the same as a week's pay," said Mack. "Nothing."

"That's cause you lazy," said Tashawn. She liked Mack fine, but she always said things like that, dissing him and only pretending it was a joke.

"He can't be lazy," said Miz Dellar, "cause he stinks like a sick skunk."

"That means he's dead," said Tashawn.

"Do we *have* to have a conversation like this while people are trying to eat?" said Mrs. Wallace, Tashawn's mother.

"Mack's lazy," said Tashawn. "He doesn't do any work."

"I do homework," said Mack.

"Not so anybody'd ever know it," said Tashawn. "He always says he forgot to do it."

"No, I forget to *bring* it. I *did* it, I just didn't have it at school."

"Tashawn, let up on the boy," said Mrs. Wallace.

"Oh, that's just how Tashawn shows love," said Miz Dellar.

Tashawn made gagging noises and bent over her plate.

"Thanks for supper," said Mack. "It was delicious but I got to go or Ceese will think I died."

"If he smells you he'll *know* you died," said Tashawn.

"I wish you hadn't mentioned his smell," said Mrs. Wallace to Miz Dellar.

"He just smells like a child who's been running around all day in the sun," said Miz Dellar. "It's one of the few odors strong enough I can still smell it, so I kind of like it."

Mack stood in the doorway, listening to them for a moment. To him, conversation like that sounded like home.

But then, *all* the conversations in *all* the houses sounded like home to him. There was hardly a door within three blocks of Miz Smitcher's house that Mack hadn't passed through, and hardly a table he hadn't sat down at, if not for supper then at least for milk or even for a chewing out because he did something that annoyed some grownup. Some of those houses, he wasn't welcome at first, being, as they said, "fatherless" or "that bastard" or "a son of a grocery bag." But as time went on, there were fewer and fewer doors closed to him. He belonged everywhere in the neighborhood. Everybody working in their yard greeted him, even the Mexicans who did the gardening for the really rich people up on the higher reaches of Cloverdale and Punta Alta and Terraza. They'd call out to him in Spanish and he'd answer with the words he'd picked up and come and work beside them for a while.

Cause Tashawn was wrong. Mack worked hard at whatever task anyone set him. If a Mexican was trimming a hedge, Mack would pick up the clippings and put them in a pile. If one of his friends had to stay in and do chores, Mack would work alongside without even being asked, and when his friend got lazy and wanted to play, it was Mack who kept working till the job was finished.

At home, too, whatever Ceese or Miz Smitcher asked him to do, he did it, and kept right at it till it was done. Same with his homework—when somebody reminded him to do it.

That was the problem. Mack didn't think of any of the work he did as *his* work, just as he didn't think of any of the houses he went to as *his* house or any of the friends he played with as *his* friends. If there was a job and someone asked him to do it, he did it, but he never remembered to do any of the chores Miz Smitcher or Ceese assigned to him. They had to remind him every time. Had to remind him to do his homework, and then in the morning had to remind him to *take* his homework, and if they didn't remind him to take his lunch he'd leave that behind in the fridge, too.

He just wasn't much for finding patterns in his life and holding on to them. He never thought: It's nearly seven-thirty, time to grab my lunch and my homework and head for the bus stop. He never thought: It's getting late, Ceese will be looking for me.

If Ceese didn't call him home, Mack would stay wherever he was till they kicked him out or reminded him to go home, and if they didn't ever do those things, well then he was likely to spend the night, lying down wherever he got tired and sleeping there until he woke up. That happened most often when he was playing up in Hahn Park, which crowned the heights above Baldwin Hills. The park employees were used to finding him when they came to work in the morning, and one of the gardeners warned him, "You best learn to snore real loud, boy, or someday I'm going to mow right over you and never know you was there till your bones get chipped up and spat into my grass bag."

When he *did* spend the night in the park, though, there was so much trouble at home. Tears from Miz Smitcher, real anger and cussing from Ceese. "We thought you were dead! Or kidnapped! Can't you come home like a normal child? When I get home from work I want to find you *here*."

Ceese was even worse. "Miz Smitcher trust me to take care of you, and you make it look like I don't even look out for you. That shames me, Mack. You make me ashamed in front of Miz Smitcher."

Eventually, though—about the time when the police informed Miz Smitcher that they were *never* going to help her search for

Mack again—they just gave up and recognized that Mack hadn't come to harm yet, and the whole neighborhood looked out for him, so if calling him through the neighborhood didn't bring him home, well, he could spend the night out. It's not like they had any choice.

"Maybe it comes from being abandoned as a baby," Mack heard Miz Smitcher say to Mrs. Tucker.

"Maybe he's just like his daddy," said Mrs. Tucker. "Men like that, they don't ever sleep in the same bed twice."

Which made Mack think that Mrs. Tucker must know who his daddy was, till Ceese set him straight. "My mama was just imagining your daddy, Mack. Nobody knows who he is. But my mama sure she knows everything about people she never met. Just the way she is."

The only struggle Ceese won was teaching Mack that he had to use a toilet to pee or poop in *every* time, and not just when one happened to be close when he felt the need. Till that battle was finally over, Mack was as likely to squeeze a turd onto the sidewalk as a puppy was. It was only when Ceese made him go and pick up his turds with a Glad bag and carry them home in front of the whole neighborhood that Ceese finally got the right habit. "You nothing but a barbarian," Ceese told him. "A one-boy barbarian invasion. You a Hun, Mack. You a Vandal."

But it wasn't really true. There was nothing destructive in Mack. When he was little and Ceese tended him by building towers of blocks, it was Ceese who had to knock them down—Mack wouldn't do it. Not that he objected to the noise and clatter of the falling blocks. It's just that to Mack, when something was built, it ought to stay built.

Except for Mack's own body. With his personal safety, Mack was reckless. The neighborhood kids soon learned that he would take almost any dare. Climb up on the roof. Jump off. Walk along the top of that high fence. Climb that tree. Drink that murky brown liquid. One of Ceese's main jobs in tending Mack was to keep the other kids from daring Mack to do something truly suicidal.

It didn't always work out well. Mack was pretty deft for a little kid, but he fell off a lot of high places. The miracle was he never broke his neck or his head or even his arm. Sprained his ankle once. Lots of bruises. And cuts? Mack left blood scattered all over Baldwin Hills from his various scrapes and slices and gashes and punctures. Miz Smitcher made sure his tetanus shot was up to date.

By the time Mack was in school, though, the daring had stopped. Most of the kids realized that it was wrong to dare Mack to do stuff, because he'd do it almost by reflex, so when he got hurt it was their fault. And Mack gradually came to realize that he didn't have to do stuff just because people said so.

When he took those dares, it wasn't because he felt a need to prove that he was brave, or to impress the other kids, or because he feared being excluded from the group. He wasn't particularly aware of whether or not he belonged to a group of friends or not. Whoever was there, he'd play with; whoever wasn't, he wouldn't. If there was nobody around and he wanted company, he'd go off by himself until he ran into somebody interesting.

So when he took all those dares, it was simply because once an idea was suggested to him, he assumed he ought to do it. At least until something happened to make him change his mind—like Ceese yelling "Are you out of your mind, you crazy kid!"

But by school age, he was learning not to do whatever came to mind. He was taking control of what happened to him.

It was because of those cold dreams. After he saw what happened to Tamika Brown, he'd feel a cold dream coming on and he'd try to get out of it. He didn't feel like he was just a watcher. But he also didn't feel like he exactly *was* the person making the wish, either. It was more like he joined on to that person, got inside them, and as he remembered the cold dream of Tamika swimming, it felt to him like it became real only when *he* began to wish for the dreamer's wish. Like he made it come true.

When he asked Ceese at bedtime one night, "Can one person make another person's wish come true?" Ceese's answer was true enough.

"Course you can. Person wishes for money, you give him a buck."

And that was the question for that night. By the next day, Mack had figured out that Ceese couldn't answer his question anyway. How would he know? Mack was the only one in the world had these cold dreams. Cause if he wasn't, then somebody else would have talked about it. They talked about everything else. "I had a cold dream last night and made your wish come true! You wished to pee, and I made you wet the bed!"

And even if he wasn't the one making the dreams turn real, he still didn't want to be there to watch them. Some of the dreams were ugly; some of them were mean; a lot of them he didn't even understand. And even the good ones—he just didn't want to know about them.

Because he always knew who the dreamer was. Oh, not during the dream, necessarily. But later, the next day or the next month or the next year, he'd run into somebody and he'd just know, looking at them, that he'd seen their dream.

How do you get out of a dream? It's not like you could make yourself wake up. Even in his own dreams, whenever Mack dreamed of waking up, it turned out that the waking up was part of the dream. He could dream himself woken up three times in the same dream and it didn't happen.

And it's not like he did his clearest thinking in his sleep. He'd be in a cold dream but he wouldn't say to himself, This is a cold dream, I've got to wake up—heck, having that thought would mean he already *had* woken up. Instead, he just felt a strong desire to get out of there.

So in his dream, instead of waking, he'd start running.

And then a funny thing would happen. Instead of running, he'd be riding in a car. Or an SUV or something, because regular cars couldn't drive on such rough roads. He always started out on a dirt road, with ragged-looked trees around, kind of a dry California kind of woods. The road began to sink down while the ground stayed level on both sides, till they were dirt walls or steep hills, and sometimes cliffs. And the road began to get rocky. The rocks were all the size of cobblestones, rounded like river rocks, and the vehicle hurtled along as if the rocks were pavement.

The rocks glistened black in the sunlight, like they'd been wet recently. The cobbly road started to go up again, steeper and steeper, and then it narrowed suddenly and they were almost jammed in between high cliffs with a thin trickly waterfall coming from the crease where the cliffs joined together.

He always knew that they'd done it again—him and whoever it was in the vehicle beside him. They'd missed the turn. They hadn't been watching close enough.

So they backed out—and here was where Mack absolutely knew it wasn't him driving, because he didn't know how to back a car. If it was a car.

Backed out and headed down until the canyon was wide enough that they could turn around, and then they rushed along until they found the place where they had gone wrong. When the road reached the lowest point, there was a narrow passage off to the left leading farther down, and now Mack realized that this wasn't no road, this was a river that just happened to be dry.

The second he thought of that, he heard distant thunder and he knew it was raining up in the high hills, and that little trickle of a waterfall at the dead end was about to become a torrent, and there'd be water coming down the other branch of the river, too, and here they were trapped in this narrow canyon barely wide enough for their vehicle, it was going to fill up with water and throw them down the canyon, bashing against the cliffs, rounding them off just like one of the river rocks.

Sure enough, in the dream here comes the water, and it's just as bad as he thought, spinning head over heels, getting slammed this way and that, and out the windows all he can see is roiling water and stones and then the dead bodies of the other people in the vehicle as they got washed out and crushed and broken against the canyon walls and suddenly . . .

The vehicle shoots out into open space, and there's no cliffs anymore, just air on every side and a lake below him and the vehicle plunges into the lake and sinks lower and lower and Mack thinks, I got to get out of here, but he can't find a way to open it, not a door, not a window. Deeper and deeper until the vehicle comes to rest on the bottom of the lake with fish swimming up and bumping into the windows and then a naked woman comes up, not sexy or anything, just naked because she never heard of clothes, she swims up and looks at him and smiles and when she touches the window, it breaks and the water slowly oozes in and surrounds him and he swims out and she kisses his cheek and says, Welcome home, I missed you so much.

When Mack got old enough to take psychology, it was easy to guess what *this* dream was about. It was about being born. About getting to the lowest point, completely alone, and then he'd find his mother, she'd come to him and open the door and let him come back into her life.

He believed his dream so much that he was sure he knew now what his mother looked like, skin so black it was almost blue, but with a thinnish nose, like those men and women of Sudan in the *African Peoples* book at school. Maybe I *am* African, he thought. Not African-American, like the other black kids in his class, but truly African without a drop of white in him.

But then why would his mother have thrown him away?

Maybe it wasn't his mother's idea. Maybe she was drugged and the baby was taken out of her and carried off and hidden and she doesn't even know he was ever alive, but Mack knew he would find her someday, because the dream was so real it had to be true.

He knew it was about his mother because he wished so hard to be able to reach out and touch her, but instead he was under water, swimming up to the surface, up for air, only the bright sky seemed to dim and the surface got farther and farther no matter how hard he swam and he knew this was because cold dreams could come true, but not *his* dreams.

And that was fine with him. Because the cold dreams he couldn't get away from, he didn't like the way they came true. It was like somebody always turned the granting of a wish into a dirty trick. So the last thing he wanted was to have his dream of escape turn into a wish, too. He didn't want any such trick played on *him*.

Though he did wish he knew who it was in the vehicle beside him.

Such was the landscape of his dreams—the same road every time, the same canyon, the same lake. And he only got there when he was fleeing from someone else's deepest wish.

Was that the water that chased him down the canyon? A flood of other people's desires?

Their desires were part of his map of Baldwin Hills. He knew the streets, he knew the houses, but it wasn't by the addresses or the names. It was by a memory of the dreams that came from there.

There was Ophelia McCallister, a widow who longed only to be reunited with her husband, who had died of a heart attack right after he completed a merger that left her wealthy. Mack hated that hunger of hers, because he dreaded every way he could think of for her wish to be granted.

Same with Sabrina Chum, who hated her huge nose and longed to be rid of it. And his own friend Nathaniel Brady, whose conscious dream of slam-dunking baskets was born, at the deepest level, of a wish to fly.

Professor Williams's deep hunger to have his poetry read far and wide seemed harmless enough. But Mack knew better than to think that any longing in a cold dream could be fulfilled without some evil twist.

Like Sherita Banks, who simply wanted men to desire her. Didn't she know how easily such a wish could be granted *without* magic? It didn't have to be *longed* for, inviting the perverse joke of whatever malevolent force ransacked Mack's dreams and destroyed his neighbors' lives.

It was like that fairy tale Ceese read to him once, about the fisherman who caught a fish that granted him three wishes. Without thinking, he wished for a big pudding. And when his wife scolded him for wasting a wish, in fury he wished it would stick to her nose. It took the third wish to make it all go away.

When Mack saw Sondra Brown pushing Tamika in her wheelchair, with all the pads and straps and braces that held the girl's spastic body upright, he thought: Where's the third wish, the one I can use to undo it all?

After Ceese and he watched the DVD of *Darby O'Gill and the Little People,* Mack walked around for weeks, whispering to himself whenever he wasn't paying attention, "Fourth wish and all is gone."

But there had been more than four wishes granted in this neighborhood. Besides, how would "all is gone" work with Romaine Tyler's architect father, who was crippled by an I-beam dropped from a crane on the construction site of his newest building, granting her wish that he could be home all the time, so she could see him whenever she wanted? Now she saw him in constant pain, his back and shoulder so shattered he survived in a haze of drugs and never rose from his bed.

Would "all is gone" make him healthy again, back to work but so busy he was never home to see his lonely little girl? Or would it simply let him die, granting *his* heartfelt wish, so deep that he never saw it himself, certain as he was that he believed that Jesus saved his life in that accident for a reason.

It's not Jesus, Mr. Tyler. It's the sick dreams of the son of a grocery bag, who ate at your table and didn't mean to let this happen to you.

Mack saw Romaine at school all the time, and he kept thinking, Why did you have to come into my dreams so often? I tried to get away from your longing, but I can't resist a dream like that forever. It's not my fault.

And, underneath, the truer belief: It's all my fault.

Yet when he left his neighborhood, haunted as it was by all the wishes Mack had dreamed, he felt vaguely lost. Going north on La Cienega or La Brea toward the freeway, or eastward to the failing mall and the increasing poverty, or south into the land of oil wells, the buildings seemed emptier and emptier to him. Still plenty of people, but they were strangers who had never hungered in his dreams. Much as he dreaded the cold dreams, at least he knew the dreamers.

And so the years passed. To an adult, his childhood would have seemed idyllic. Like something out of *Dandelion Wine*. Freedom all summer, friends to gripe with about school. Adventures in Hahn Park and in the rough woods above the runoff pipe or scrambling up the wild brush of the hillsides. The older he got, the more freedom he had—even though he always seemed to have all the freedom he wanted. Ceese graduated from high school and then college and by then Miz Smitcher knew there'd be no point in replacing him. The whole neighborhood looked out for Mack now.

Mrs. Tucker, Ceese's mom, kept talking about how it was time to move into someplace small, since the last of her kids was gone, but she was still there day after day, year after year, whenever Mack stopped in. Sometimes Ceese was there, but not often; he was busy all the time now, working for the water department doing some computer thing while he went to graduate school to learn engineering. Mack was more likely to run into one of Ceese's older brothers, who always seemed to be recently divorced or freshly out of work or coming over full of advice about why whatever Mrs. Tucker was doing, she was doing it all wrong.

And Miz Smitcher was older, too. It was a thing that Mack only noticed from time to time, but he'd look up at her and see that there was steel grey in her hair now, and the skin of her face sagged, and she groaned more when she got her shoes off; and she had enough seniority that there was no more nonsense about late shifts, unless she was filling in for somebody.

Mack never tried to put a word to what he felt for her. He knew she had taken him in when he might have been put into foster care. And even though it was mostly Ceese who raised him when he was little, he knew he was attached to her in such a way that he would never leave her, would never want to leave; no matter how old he got, no matter how widely he roamed the neighborhood, he'd come home to her.

Because that was her wish. He was her wish. To have him as her son.

There were times he even wondered if she had conjured him up in her own cold dream. If he just magically appeared at that drainpipe at the hairpin turn of Cloverdale, swept out of his real mother's arms and into the place where he would be found and brought to Miz Smitcher, exactly the way Tamika Brown had been pulled from her sheets and plunged into the waterbed beneath her sleeping parents. In answer to a wish so deep that it could not be denied.

He knew her cold dream, too. It was of herself, lying in a hospital bed, surrounded by the very same equipment that she monitored for strangers. Nurses and doctors moving around her, murmuring, none of their words meaning anything, because the only thing that mattered was: When she opened her eyes, there was Mack Street, a grown man now, holding her hand, looking into her eyes, and saying, "I'm here, Miz Smitcher. Don't you worry, ma'am, I'm here."

8

SKINNY HOUSE

The summer he turned thirteen, Mack was getting taller—fast enough that Miz Smitcher grumbled about his wearing jeans one day and then she had to give them to Goodwill and buy him a bigger pair the next. And his voice was changing, so when he talked he kept popping and squeaking.

He didn't find so many kids when he walked the neighborhood these days. Or rather, not the familiar ones, not the ones his age. They were all indoors, online, playing games or chatrooming, or hanging somewhere that other kids could look at them and size them up and decide they were cool.

A lot of the boys had decided they were ghetto now, talking like they came from the mean streets of Compton or South Central, putting on the walk and the clothes and the jive they saw in the movies instead of talking like the upper-middle-class California boys they really were.

Mack didn't mind and still talked to them like normal, but he didn't put on attitude like that himself, not the talk or the clothes or even the walk, so it left him as an outsider, looking somehow younger than his friends. Or older, if you looked at it another way, since he showed no sign of caring whether he was part of any group or not.

Even his grades at school stayed pretty good, since the teachers asked him to study hard and learn, and so he did. But nobody gave him any crap about "acting white" or thinking he was better than them when he got good scores on the test and always had his homework to turn in. He was just being the same old Mack. No threat to anybody. Always a good companion, if he happened to be there. But not somebody you thought to call up if he wasn't. So it never seemed he was in competition with them, not about grades, not about girls, not about anything.

Now when he walked the neighborhood, it was younger kids he saw. But fewer and fewer of them. Baldwin Hills was the kind of neighborhood where, once a black person bought a house there, that was it. If they had wanted to move "up" to a white neighborhood, they'd already have moved there. A house in Baldwin Hills was like tenure at a university. Once you got it, you weren't going anywhere. You weren't going to move just because your kids were gone. Even if, like Mrs. Tucker, you kept saying you were. So when the kids grew up, the houses didn't fill up again with new babies and toddlers and schoolkids, unless grandchildren came to visit.

Baldwin Hills was getting old. Eventually, as people died or went to nursing homes, new families would move in. But right now, as Mack wandered the streets of his neighborhood, it was just a little . . . emptier.

And when Mack got the notion to drop in on somebody at mealtime, they didn't turn him away. They just weren't home. Too busy.

He wasn't *close* to anybody—not at school, not at home. He hadn't realized that no one confided in him. He never asked questions because, by and large, he already knew. And he never confided in anyone else about anything deeply important to him because he couldn't. The things most important to him had to be kept secret for the sake of the people who would feel betrayed if he broke that rule.

So his walks and runs through the neighborhood were more and more likely to be solitary, or with younger kids trailing after him. And that, too, was all right with Mack. He liked being alone. He liked the younger kids.

What he didn't like was walking past one particular spot on Cloverdale, just a few houses up from Coliseum. And he didn't know why he didn't like it. He'd just be walking along, thinking his thoughts or looking at whatever he looked at, and then, just as he passed between Missy Snipe's house and the Chandresses', he'd suddenly feel distracted and look around him and wonder what he had just seen. Only he hadn't seen anything. Everything looked normal. He'd stand there on the sidewalk, looking around him. Nobody doing anything, except perhaps some neighbor in another yard looking up at him, probably wondering why Miz Ura Lee Smitcher's strange boy was standing there dazed like somebody smacked him in the head.

He always shrugged it off, because he had someplace to go. And yet he remembered it, too, and walked on the east side of the street as often as not, sometimes even crossing over, going out of his way to avoid it, only to cross back again afterward.

What am I afraid of? he asked himself.

Which is why, on one day in that hot summer of the year he turned thirteen, instead of avoiding that spot on the west sidewalk of the lower part of Cloverdale, he made straight for it, made it his destination, and found himself standing there wondering what it was that had bothered him so many times before.

He still couldn't see anything. This was stupid.

He decided to go home.

He took a step.

And there it was again. That moment of startlement. He'd *seen* it. Out of the corner of his eye.

But when he turned to look, there was nothing. He side-stepped, looking between the houses, going up and down the sidewalk, and there was *nothing*.

Again he decided to go home.

Again, as he passed the same spot, out of the corner of his eye he saw . . .

It was out of the corner of his eye.

Instead of sidestepping, he now turned his face resolutely southward, looking up Cloverdale toward the place where it jogged to the west at Sanchez Drive. Without turning his eyes to left or right, he took a few steps backward, then forward, and both times he saw it, just a little flash of something to the right, directly between the houses, right at the property line.

Finally he got it exactly right and stopped, right there, with whatever it was holding steady at the corner of his eye.

He knew better now than to try to look right at it—it would surely disappear. Instead, keeping his gaze southward, he took a step onto the lawn between the houses. And another.

The shimmer became a vertical line, and then it became thicker, like a lamppost or a telephone pole—how much could he see, really, out of the corner of his eye? With each step it widened out, shoving the other houses aside.

Another step and it was as wide as any house in the neighborhood. A whole house, directly between Snipes' and Chandresses', and nobody but him knew it was there, mainly because there was no way in hell it could possibly be there. A whole house that was skinny enough to fit between two houses taking up no space at all.

He reached out a hand and touched a bush growing in the nonexistent front yard. He sidled closer to the house and in a few moments he had his hand resting on the door handle and it was as real and solid as any door handle in the neighborhood.

So he slowly turned his head and this time it didn't disappear. It stayed right where it was.

A whole secret house.

Somebody else might have doubted his sanity. But Mack Street knew he lived in a neighborhood where young swimmers could wish themselves inside a waterbed.

He rang the doorbell.

In a little while he heard someone moving inside. He rang again.

"Don't keep pestering the doorbell," a man called out.

Mack let go of the doorbell and the doorknob and the house didn't disappear, as he had feared it might. Instead, the door opened and there stood a black man in Lakers basketball uniform, except he was barefoot and had a can of beer in his hand and a big filthy rasta do like he'd been homeless for a couple of years.

"Can I use your toilet?" asked Mack.

"No," said the man. "Go away."

But Mack ignored him because he knew that the man didn't really mean it. He walked past him and found the bathroom behind the first door he tried.

"Can't you take no for an answer, boy?" asked the man.

"You want me peeing on your floor?" asked Mack.

"I don't even want you *walking* on my floor. Who do you think you are?"

"I think I'm the only person in Baldwin Hills who knows this place even exists." Mack finished peeing and flushed and then, being a nurse's son, he washed his hands.

"Doesn't do any good to wash your hands," the man said from outside the bathroom. "The towel's filthy."

"I don't know how it could be," said Mack. "It ain't like *you* ever use it."

"Not all the company I get is as tidy as you."

"How do you ever get company at all, being how your house is only visible out of the corner of your eye."

"Depends on where you're coming from. The Good Folk find it whenever they care to come and visit."

"I don't know that I'm such bad folk. I think the folk of Baldwin Hills are maybe a little better than average."

"Well, nobody would know that better than you, Mack Street," said the man. "But the Good Folk I was referring to aren't *from* Baldwin Hills."

"You got any peanut butter?" asked Mack.

"I'm not here to feed *you*," said the man.

"How did you know my name?" asked Mack, now that he realized that's what the man had just done.

"Everybody knows your name, Mack Street. Just like everybody knows my house."

"You mean all of the . . . Good Folk."

"They know my house because I'm right on the shore of the strongest river of power the world has seen in five hundred years. And they know your name because that river started flowing the day that you were born. It's like your birth sort of popped the cork and let it rip. Like lava from a volcano. Power flowing down Magic Street and on through the whole neighborhood."

"I don't know what you're talking about."

"You know exactly what I'm talking about, Bag Baby," said the man.

"What do you know about the day I was born?"

"Everything," said the man. "And everything about your life since that happy day. The woman who tried to get you killed that very first day of your life. The boy who almost did it and then spent years of his life in penance for having even entertained the thought."

"You talking about Ceese?" asked Mack. "You expect me to believe Ceese almost killed me?"

"In fairness, no. He didn't almost *do* anything. He fought off the desire. Do you have any idea how strong he must be, to resist *her*?"

"I might if I knew who *her* was."

The man smiled benignly and passed a hand over Mack's nappy head, which Mack always hated but never complained about. "So you're thirteen now. Your lucky year."

"Doesn't feel all that lucky so far."

"Well, it wouldn't to *you*, being a child, and therefore incapable of taking the long view of anything."

"How do you keep your house invisible?"

"It's perfectly visible," said the man. "It just takes a little work. There's a lot of things in the world like that. Most people just don't take the time to look for them."

"What's your name?" asked Mack.

"Why, do you plan on opening a bank account for me? Send me a Christmas card?"

Mack didn't like evasiveness. He liked it when people answered plain, even if it was to say, None of your business. "I'll call you Mr. Christmas."

"You don't *get* to pick names for strangers, not in *this* place, boy. I'm master of my own house!"

"Then give me something to call you."

"I don't want you to call me," said Mr. Christmas. "I've been called enough in my life, thank you kindly."

"I'm betting this isn't your house at all," said Mack. "I'm betting you're a squatter, and you're mostly crazy or at least half, but somehow you made it so the neighborhood thinks this street goes from Chandresses' house to Snipes' with nothing in between."

"I can't help what ignorant people think. The house is mine and it don't take no deed to prove it."

"I'm hungry," said Mack. He was tired of talking to somebody who wouldn't say anything useful.

"I'm sorry to hear that," said Mr. Christmas.

So he wouldn't even share food with a visitor. "What you got here that's so important you got to hide from the world."

"Me," said Mr. Christmas.

"Why you hiding? You kill somebody?"

"Only now and then, and it was a long time ago."

"You planning to kill me?"

"This isn't Hansel and Gretel, Mack. I don't eat children."

"Didn't ask if you planning to eat me."

"Believe me, Mack, I don't want you dead." He laughed.

"What's so funny?"

"Humans."

"As if you wasn't one yourself." Mack walked out of the living room and into the kitchen. It was right where it was supposed to be. He went to the fridge and opened it. There was plenty of food inside. Everything he liked to snack on. Milk. Juice. Grapes. Lunchables. Salami. Bologna. Even a leftover mess of beans that looked just like Mrs. Tucker's recipe for burn-your-head-off chili.

Mack took the chili out of the fridge and opened a drawer and took out a spoon.

"Where's the microwave?" he asked

"Do I have one?" Mr. Christmas asked in return.

Mack looked around. The microwave was on the counter right beside the fridge, exactly where it was in Mrs. Tucker's kitchen. He put in the chili, set it for two minutes, and started it going.

"Well, who knew," said Mr. Christmas.

"Who knew what?"

"That I had a microwave."

"You telling me this is a rental and you just moved in?"

"I guess my house just bound to give you whatever you want."

"I want answers."

"Ask the house," said Mr. Christmas.

Mack was sick of this. He rocked his head back and shouted at the ceiling, "Who this brother! I want his name!"

There was a clattering only a couple of feet away. Mack whirled and looked. In the middle of the kitchen floor there was a thick disk of plastic, bright orange. "What's that supposed to be?"

"A pile of flop from a plastic cow?" said Mr. Christmas. "A traffic cone had a baby?"

Mack leaned his head back again and shouted, "What's this thing supposed to be?"

Another clatter. Now, lying beside the plastic thing on the floor was a crooked stick.

"What is this," said Mack. "ESPN in Middle-earth? I don't want to play hockey."

"This is getting funny," said Mr. Christmas.

The microwave dinged. Mack opened it, took out the chili. It wasn't burning hot, but it was warm enough to eat. He dug in with the spoon.

It didn't just look like Mrs. Tucker's chili, it *was* her chili. Mack jumped up and whooped just like he did when he ate at Tuckers' house. The first bite of chili always made him dance, it was so spicy.

"You eat that on purpose?" asked Mr. Christmas. "Even though it burns?"

"It doesn't *really* burn," said Mack. "It stimulates the nerves in your mouth."

"I guess I accidently asked Mr. Science."

"It also stimulates the nerves in your butt on the way out. I mean, that's *chili.*"

"You telling me more than I want to know, boy."

"You telling me nothing, so I guess on average we having a conversation."

"Eat your chili," said Mr. Christmas.

"Did you buy this house? Or build it? Or just steal it and then hide it from everybody?"

"Are you doing a research paper for school or something? Writing a children's book? *The Skinny House on the Cheap End of Cloverdale.*"

"*The Skinny House Out of the Corner of Your Eye.*"

"*The Skinny House Where Strange Boys Come and Ransack the Fridge.*"

"*The Skinny House of Lies and Secrets,*" said Mack.

"*The Skinny House of the Fairy,*" said Mr. Christmas.

"Now who's telling more than the other person wants to know?"

"I finally tell you the truth, and you won't believe me," said Mr. Christmas.

"You think I believe a single thing that's happened here this afternoon?"

"You eating that chili."

"I'm pretending you polite enough to offer me food."

"You sure take magic in stride, boy."

"I already seen too much magic in my life," said Mack. "And it's all ugly."

"I'm not the architect, Mack. This house just like the others in this neighborhood. I don't know why people so thrilled to live in Baldwin Hills. I don't think this house is so much."

"The houses up the hill are just fine," said Mack. "But even houses down here in the flat better than what everybody used to have, in Watts."

"Your mama tell you that?"

"Miz Smitcher did," said Mack. "I don't know my mama."

"I do," said Mr. Christmas.

Mack took the last bite of chili. "She living or dead?"

"Living," said Mr. Christmas.

"She live around here?"

"Right up Cloverdale."

"That's such a lie," said Mack. "You think a girl could get pregnant and have a baby around here and the whole neighborhood don't know it?"

"People kind of forgetful sometimes," said Mr. Christmas.

Mack ignored him. He got up and washed the dish and the spoon and put them to dry. Mr. Christmas said nothing till Mack was done. "You downright tidy," he said. "Convenient to have around the house."

"I just felt like washing it," said Mack.

"And you do whatever you feel like," said Mr. Christmas.

"Mostly."

"But ain't it convenient that what you *feel* like doing is just exactly what other people want you to do."

"I try not to be a bother."

"You do your homework, get good grades, you don't steal anything but you don't tell on your friends that do, you go everywhere and see everything but you don't gossip and you don't take anything or damage anything and you don't even drop a candy wrapper on the ground, you take it home and put it in the garbage."

"You been spying on me?"

"I guess you just a civilized boy, that's all," said Mr. Christmas.

Mack wasn't interested in this man's opinion of him. "So what's your back yard like? Does it just disappear again, like in front?"

"Look and see," said Mr. Christmas. "I don't go back there much."

Mack went to the back door and opened it and looked out onto the patio. There was a rusted barbecue off to one side, and an old-fashioned umbrella-style clothesline with a few clothespins hanging on it like birds perched along a wire. Behind the patio a couple of scraggly-looking orange trees were covered in fruit that had been pecked at by birds or gnawed by squirrels. And the scruffy, patchy, weedy lawn was dotted with rotting fruit.

"All the cheap Mexican labor in LA," said Mack, "and you can't even hire a gardener?"

"You call this a garden?" asked Mr. Christmas.

"Don't you even want to eat these oranges before they rot or the birds and squirrels get them?"

"I've had oranges before. They ain't so much."

"What *do* you eat?"

"Got a taste for See's Candies," said Mr. Christmas.

"I'm surprised you don't have them growing on trees, the way this house goes."

"I got me a box a few years back. It hasn't run out yet."

"Either that was a big box, or you don't eat much."

"Thirteen years," said Mr. Christmas. "As a matter of fact, I got that box as a birthday present."

"When's your birthday?"

"It wasn't for *my* birthday," said Mr. Christmas. "You jump to a lot of conclusions."

Mack was tired of riddles. He walked out onto the patio.

Did the trees grow taller?

He stepped back. The orange trees were definitely smaller again.

"I see," he said. "Your front yard gets smaller and smaller till your house just disappears. But the back yard gets bigger and bigger."

"It does what it does," said Mr. Christmas.

Mack walked back toward the trees. Right to the edge of the patio. Curiously, the patio had shrunk down now to a brick path, and when he turned around, the house was farther away than it should have been, and was half hidden among trees and vines that hadn't been there when he crossed the patio. Mr. Christmas stood in the doorway, but he was no longer dressed the way he had been. Nor was he quite the same man. He was thinner, and his clothes fit snugly, and he looked younger, and his hair was a halo around his head, not filthy dreads at all.

"Who *are* you?" called Mack.

Mr. Christmas just waved cheerfully. "Don't let anything eat you back there!" he called.

Mack turned back toward the forest—for that's what it was now, not a lawn with trees, but a track through a dense forest and not an orange in sight, though berries grew in profusion beside the path, and butterflies and bees and dragonflies fluttered and hovered and darted over the blossoms of a dozen different kinds of wildflower.

It didn't occur to Mack to be afraid, despite Mr. Christmas's warning. If anything, this forest felt like home to him. Like all his wandering through the neighborhood and Hahn Park his whole life had actually been a search for this place. California was a desert compared to this. Even when the jacaranda bloomed it didn't have this sweet flowery scent in the air, and instead of the dismal brown dirt of Los Angeles there was moss underfoot, and thick loamy black soil in the patches where the path hadn't quite been overgrown.

And water. Los Angeles had a river, but it was penned in like the elephants at the zoo, surrounded by concrete and left dry most of the year. Here, though, the path led alongside a brook that tumbled over mossy stones and had fish darting in the waters, which meant that it never went dry. Frogs and toads hopped out of the way, and birds flitted across the path in front of him, and beads of water glistened on many a leaf, as if it had rained only a few hours ago—something that never happened in LA in the summer—or perhaps as if the dew had been so heavy that it hadn't all evaporated yet.

The branches and leaves were so thick overhead that the path grew darker, like twilight. Or perhaps it was twilight in this place, though it couldn't be much later than six o'clock.

Off in the distance, mostly hidden by bushes or vines or trunks of trees, but flashing occasionally as he walked along, there was a tiny light.

Mack left the path and headed toward it. It didn't occur to him at first that he might get lost, once he left the path. He had never been lost in his life. But he had never been in a real forest, either—the open woods of Hahn Park were nothing like this. And when he turned around after only a few steps, he couldn't tell where the path was.

But he could still see the light, flickering among the distant trees.

Now the bushes and branches snagged at his clothes, and sometimes there were brambles, so he had to back out and go around. He found himself on the brink of a little canyon once, and had to turn around and climb down into it, and then search for a place where he could leap over the torrent of water that plunged down the ravine. This place was getting wilder all the time, and yet he still wasn't afraid. He noted the danger, how easily he might get lost, how a person could fall into the current and be swept away to God knows where, just like in his dream, and yet he knew that this wasn't the place or time for his dream to come true, and he would not be harmed here, not today.

Unless, of course, this sense of confidence was part of the magic of the place, luring him on to destruction. Magic was tricky that way, as he knew better than any other soul. What seemed most sweet could be most deadly, what promised happiness could bring you deep and endless grief.

But he went on, clambering up the other side, which was, if anything, steeper than the side that he had climbed down.

When he got to the top again, he could see that there were two lights, not just one, and they were much nearer now. Only a few dozen yards through the bushes and trees—easy passages, mostly—and he was on the edge of a clearing.

The two lights were like old-fashioned lanterns. Glass-sided, with ornate metal lining the panes. Unlike a lantern, though, there was neither base nor roof to the lights, just glass all the way around. Nor were there stands holding them up, or wires holding them suspended from above. They simply hung in the air, flickering.

There was no bulb inside, giving light. Nor a wick of any kind, nor a source of fuel. Just a dazzling point of light drifting around inside each lantern, bumping against the glass and changing direction again.

Mack was going to step out into the clearing and look more closely at the lights, but that was when he heard a growl, and saw that a panther, black as night, slunk from shadow to shadow around the forest verge. Its eyes were bright yellow in the lantern light, and at moments Mack thought he could see a red glow even deeper inside the eyes.

Mack took a step into the clearing.

The panther growled and bounded suddenly to the middle, directly between the two lights.

Mack took just one more step, not because he was so brave that he did not fear the panther, but because it would have been unbearable not to get a closer look at what the panther's front paws rested on.

It was a corpse, flyblown and rotted. The man had been wearing trousers and a longish shirt, though the shirt had been torn by claws. And instead of a man's head, on his shoulders was the head of a donkey, its eyesockets empty, its fur patchy. Mack had seen squirrels in this condition before; he knew that under the collapsing rib cage there would be nothing, the worms and bacteria having done their work.

This panther must have been here a long time, if it was what killed the donkey-headed man, and the clawing the man's clothes had received suggested that it was.

Whatever the two lanterns were, it was clear enough that the panther did not intend to let anyone near them.

And that was fine with Mack. He was curious, but never so curious that he'd die for an answer. Let the globes of light keep their secret, and let the panther go hungry for another while.

Having seen the sources of the light he saw from the path, there was no reason for him to remain here. He started back.

The moment he left the clearing, though, he was plunged into darkness. If it had been twilight before, now it was night, and without the bobbing lantern light ahead of him to guide him, he had to feel his way through the dark like a blind man.

Somewhere ahead of him was a ravine, its sides so steep that he had clung to vines and roots in order to climb. And at the bottom, a torrent that could sweep him away if he misjudged in the darkness and failed to jump all the way across.

"I'm not getting home tonight," Mack said out loud.

Behind him, he heard the deep rumble of a big cat, purring.

He stopped, held still.

A warm sleek-furred body pressed close against him as it slid past, then turned and rubbed itself again on his legs.

A tongue lapped at his hand.

He didn't think this was the way that cats treated their prey.

Wouldn't do any good to climb a tree to get away from a panther, either. And it didn't seem angry.

Mack took another step toward the ravine. Suddenly the cat was in front of him, blocking his way. And instead of a purr, there was a fierce, short growl.

I'm in Narnia, thought Mack. Only it's a black boy's Narnia, so instead of a golden lion there's a black panther. And instead of entering through the back of a wardrobe in England, I got here through the back door and patio of an invisible house on a street in Baldwin Hills.

So what was the deal here? Guys like C. S. Lewis and what's-his-name who wrote *Alice in Wonderland*, were they reporting things they really experienced? Or things they dreamed? Or were they imagining it, but it happened that in the real world the things they imagined really did come true? Or is all this happening because I read their books and so my own mind is finding ways to make their fantasy stories turn real? Or am I crazy and cold dreams are nothing but the ugly nightmares of a wacked out bastard boy whose mind was broken as he lay covered with ants in a grocery bag by a drainpipe at the bottom of Hahn Park?

Either this panther was a black Aslan or a black White Rabbit or . . . or something. Whatever. The main thing was, it only growled when Mack walked in this direction. Or when Mack tried to walk toward the lanterns. And it was dark. Night. Mack had eaten supper, such as it was. The leftover chili. So it's not like he had a compelling reason to go home, except that Miz Smitcher would worry about him, and there was nothing he could do about that, she'd worry a lot worse and a lot longer and to less effect if he pissed off this panther and ended up lying in the woods with claw marks on his clothing and maggots eating his dead flesh.

So he lay down where he was standing. The ground was soft and yielding. He could hear the breathing of the panther near him. He could see nothing at all. Not even the lights in the clearing, now that he was down below the level of the underbrush. If there were snakes or other fearsome beasts near him, he'd never know it; the rustlings and stirrings he heard were bound to be small creatures of the night, but they were none of his business and he hoped they'd feel the same about him.

Lying there, in the minutes before sleep overtook him, Mack thought about Mr. Christmas and all he'd said. He knew Mack's mother. Could that be true? A woman somewhere nearby. In the neighborhood. Was it possible? She gave birth, and everybody forgot she had even been pregnant? If that was so, then Mack really was home here. Or rather, there in Baldwin Hills, since right now "here" was a dark magical wood with a panther lurking nearby.

And what was that business with the hockey stick and the puck that appeared in midair and fell to the floor in the kitchen of Mr. Christmas's Skinny House?

It was the house, answering his question about Mr. Christmas's identity, just as he had asked.

Puck. There was a character named Puck. Mack had heard the name, or read it somewhere. Vaguely the memory came to him: It was a character in Shakespeare. Mack had never read Shakespeare, but somewhere in his schooling, somebody had told or read him the story of someone named Puck. A fairy named Puck. Mr. Christmas *was* a fairy, like he said, only not what guys meant when they called an effeminate kid a fairy. More like an elf. A tall black old elf with a rasta do. Only when Mack had walked into the woods and looked back at him, he had turned back into something more like himself, and what Mack had seen was the fairy, tall and lithe, his hair a halo around his head, his clothes clingy and . . . green. They had been green.

Got to read me some Shakespeare and find out who the hell Puck is. The story of the guy with a donkey head, that was part of it.

It was a play, now he remembered. A group of college students came to their elementary school and put on a play that started with the queen of the fairies falling in love with a guy with a donkey head, and then a bunch of stupid guys acting out a play about a boy and girl who fall in love and then kill themselves because one of them was torn by a lion or . . . or something.

That's all this is. I'm asleep somewhere and dreaming that play they put on for us when I was in fifth grade.

Only he knew that he wasn't dreaming, that he was very much awake.

Until, a moment later, he wasn't.

9

CAPTIVE QUEEN

Mack awoke in the first light of morning, cold and covered with dew, but not uncomfortable, not even shivering except one quick spasm when he first bounded to his feet.

Only when he was standing did he realize that the panther had slept close to him all night, and from the sudden chill of evaporating sweat he knew that the beast had been pressed up close to his back. Now it lazily rose up and stretched and padded away from him, back toward the clearing where two lanterns hung suspended in the air.

Mack wasn't interested in going back there now. Miz Smitcher would worry and he didn't want her to be unhappy or worried, though truth to tell she probably wasn't, since she was bound to assume he had spent the night in somebody's house.

Alone now—for the panther felt to him like more than an animal—Mack did as his body required, stepping right out of his pants in order to empty his bladder and then squat down to hold on to a sapling trunk while he emptied his bowels. It had been a long time since he'd done it outdoors, but his body was so healthy and worked so naturally that his turd came out dry and he didn't even need to wipe himself, though he scooped up some old leaves and made a pass at his butt just to be sure.

Then he stood up and took a step and then snatched back at the sapling, because his foot didn't find the ground, it hung out in the air, and he realized that the trees and saplings here leaned out over the ravine or grew up from inside it. He had slept on the edge of a cliff last night, the cat between him and death, and the turd he laid had fallen down into nothing.

Even holding on to the sapling, he couldn't fully recover his balance. The best he could do was swing around as he slipped, so he was facing the cliff and could grab with his other hand and catch at a root to stop himself from falling all the way down. He caught one, but he couldn't keep his grip, and the vine he clutched with his other hand broke, and down he went, his bare feet finding no purchase, his hands grabbing at this and that, until he landed on the steep grassy bank of the torrent.

It knocked the breath out of him, but not the sense—he knew as he slid down toward the water that he had to stop himself or he'd be caught up in the current and battered to death against the banks and stony bottom of the stream, if he didn't drown first.

He caught a tough root growing right at the water's edge, as his legs went into the water. It was so cold, right up to his waist, that it knocked the breath out of him all over again—not that he'd had even a moment to catch it after the fall—and the shock was so great he almost lost his grip.

But he held on, and even though the water tore at him and held him out almost horizontal in the water, he was able to get a leg up into the roots of another tree and then climb up out of the water.

He sat on the bank, still without his trousers, trembling with the cold of the water and the pain and bruises of the fall and the fear of having come so near death.

Far above him, he knew, were his pants. And his shoes? He couldn't remember if he had been barefoot yesterday when he went to take a look at the strange spot between Chandresses' and Snipes'. He wore shoes more and more these days, and he might have been wearing them, but he couldn't remember taking them off last night when he went to sleep. Main thing was, he was naked from the waist down, and somehow he had to get home, only a block or so but that was a long way when your butt was naked and the neighbors all knew where you lived and how to call and tell Miz Smitcher.

Should he climb back up and get those pants?

The ravine was a lot less steep on the other side. And Mr. Christmas—or Puck, if that was really his name, and why would the house lie to him?—might have something he could wear. At least a towel he could wrap around himself as if he was coming back from somebody's swimming pool.

So he rested a little more, then jumped the stream and climbed up the other side. Then he just walked, trusting that he'd run across the path and know it when he saw it. And sure enough, he did.

It was still that faint light of earliest morning when he saw the back of the Skinny House. Mr. Christmas was no longer standing at the door, of course, as Mack lightly ran along the mossy path until his feet touched brick. And in a few steps the house was itself again, and the patio was concrete with the rusty barbecue and the umbrella clothesline stand and the old screen door that stood just the tiniest bit ajar.

Mack opened it, and turned the knob and the door into the kitchen opened, and there was Mr. Christmas, looking like himself again—or not like himself, depending on which version was really him. The dirty dreads, anyway, and the clothes he was wearing, and he sat at the kitchen table sipping something that wasn't coffee but Mack didn't know what.

"Forget something out there?" asked Mr. Christmas.

"Is your name really Puck?"

"Somebody steal your pants or you give them to a beggar? Or have you decided to go au naturel today?"

So he wasn't going to answer, and Mack wasn't interested enough to keep pushing. "I need something to wear."

"As I was saying."

"Got anything that would fit me?" asked Mack. He looked at Puck's thickish body and said, "Or something that won't fit me unless I tighten a belt really tight and roll up the pantlegs?"

"I got nothing that fits *me*, if you haven't noticed," said Puck. "But you're welcome to look in the closet and see what I got. Seeing how this house responds to you a lot better than it does to me."

Mack walked into a bedroom that didn't look like anybody had ever slept in it, considering that there weren't even sheets or blankets or a pillow on the bed, and the bed was just a bare mattress on the floor.

He went to the closet and slid the cheap sliding door open and there were six pairs of pants hanging there on hooks, each one identical to the pants he had left behind on the wrong side of the ravine. Four of them were clean, but one was damp and muddy, and another was torn as if by savage claws and covered in half-dried blood.

"Guess things might have turned out a few different ways," said Puck.

"But they turned out this way," said Mack. He took one of the clean pairs of pants out of the closet and put them on.

"You know how these pants would have gotten so wet and muddy?"

"I almost fell into the stream at the bottom of a canyon," said Mack.

"So these torn and bloody ones . . ."

"The panther," said Mack.

"Panther?"

"The one guarding the lamps."

"Ah," said Puck. "Lamps."

"They just hanging there in the air."

"Oh, they got something holding them up," said Puck.

"Duh," said Mack. "Magic, of course."

"So if you come close, this panther . . ."

"You never gone there?" said Mack. "You never saw that dead man? With a donkey head?"

Puck chuckled and shook his head. "Once *she* loves you, you never forget, you never give up."

"He ain't trying no more," said Mack. "Whatever it is he was trying to do."

"He was trying to set her free."

"Set who free?"

"The queen."

"I don't know what you talking about. I got to go home now."

"Why you pretending you don't want to know?"

"Cause whatever I ask, you don't tell me nothing. But when I don't ask, you full of information."

"She's the most beautiful woman who ever lived," said Puck. "But her soul's been captured and locked in a glass cage."

"The queen."

"The Queen of the Fairies," said Puck.

"And the dead guy with the donkey head, he was in love with her."

"Shakespeare, that asshole, he never understood anything. About love *or* magic. Always had to 'improve' the story." Puck winked. "He couldn't take a joke."

"You don't like Shakespeare?" asked Mack.

"Nobody likes Shakespeare. They just pretend they do so they look smart."

"I like Shakespeare," said Mack.

"You never read Shakespeare in your life."

"Some college students, they put on a play for us. I liked it."

"Yeah, yeah, cause they *told* you to like it. And cause they didn't put on *Othello* with some white dude with his face painted black."

"So it was Shakespeare locked a queen's soul in a lantern in the woods?"

"No," said Puck scornfully. "Shakespeare wouldn't have the power to pick his own nose, he come up against the queen."

"Who locked her up, then?"

"Himself," said Puck. "If you think I saying his name in this place, you crazy."

"What about the queen. What's her name?"

"She has so many. Mab, some call her, and that's closer to her true name. But also Titania. Shakespeare knew those names but he didn't think she was the same person."

"So why don't you go out into the woods and set her free? Guy can make a whole house disappear from the street, you got to be more powerful than a panther."

"How far off the ground was that lantern?" asked Puck.

Mack held his hand out, about shoulder high.

Puck laughed bitterly. "So he didn't shrink you."

"Shrink me?"

"I step off the bricks into the woods, I shrink down to fairy size. Small enough to ride a butterfly. Only they's no flying across that ravine. You think you had a hard time climbing down and up again? Crossing that water? How hard you think it be, you this high." He held up his hand, his thumb and fingers about four inches apart.

"You? That tall?"

"In those woods."

"And you can't do anything about it?"

"That my natural size," said Puck. "When I'm home."

"Is that home for you, in there?"

"It's part of home. A corner of home."

"So what's it called?"

"Faerie," said Puck. "Fairyland."

"Not Middle-earth, then," said Mack. "Not Narnia?"

"Made-up bullshit, that stuff," said Puck. "There's no lion in that place, making people be good. There's just power, and those who got more of it and those who got less."

"And in that place, you're little."

"I'm little, my house little. That panther, he swallow me whole, if he can. Birds come down and get me if I try to fly. I can't get in to set her free."

"But I could," said Mack. "I'm tall enough."

"But you scared of that panther."

"Only a little," said Mack. "What I'm scared of is dying."

"Same thing."

"Don't care how," said Mack. "Just don't want to do it. Panther no worse than any other way."

"What did she look like?"

"*If* it was her, and you not just shitting me, then she was this little bit of light bouncing around inside the glass. Bright, though."

"Couldn't look right at her, could you."

"Burned a spot in my eye, didn't wear off till morning. Saw her in my sleep."

"Ah," said Puck. "You had her dream?"

Mack shook his head. "Not like that. I just dreamed about that point of light."

"Ah," said Puck, clearly disappointed.

"So who's the other one?" asked Mack.

"Other one?"

"Two lanterns, two lights. One of them might be this queen, but who's the other?"

"A prisoner of love," said Puck, and then he started singing it.

When grownups started singing old rock songs, the conversation was over. Mack had his pants on, and he better get home.

"You going to set her free?" asked Puck.

"You get me a can of panther repellent and a big stick, I get that glass open."

"Is that a lie or a promise?"

"If she's really in one of those jars."

"That's a good point," said Puck. "What if you open the wrong one."

"Who's in the other one?"

"I told you."

"You told me nothing. You always tell me nothing."

"I told you it was Queen Mab in that jar."

"That's probably just another lie."

"I don't lie," said Puck. "These days, I don't even spin." He demonstrated how slowly he moved when he tried to turn himself around.

Mack didn't wait to watch. He headed out of the bedroom and out of the house. When he reached the sidewalk, he turned around to look, and the Skinny House was gone.

Mack reached down into his pants pocket and found the five-dollar bill he carried around in case of emergencies. Like having a magic wand. You have a five-dollar bill and you want a drink or some candy or a bus ride, then you got it. Small magic, but magic just the same.

Puck's magic—now, that was big time. But it seemed to Mack that maybe Puck wasn't the one *did* that magic. He didn't seem all that powerful. Couldn't make Mack do anything. Maybe he was trapped in that house the way that fairy queen was trapped in the lantern in the woods.

If he wasn't lying about what those lanterns were about. Had he really been there and seen the lights? Was he really so small and flightless that he couldn't get to either lantern? When Mack was telling the story, Puck nodded his head like he knew all about it, but then from his questions it seemed like he'd never been there, had no idea what it took to get there from here.

Puck hadn't even known that Mack would have pants in the closet. And did each one of those pairs of pants have his five-dollar bill in the pocket? If he was ever running short of money, could he come back here and get another Lincoln from the extra pants? Or would they be gone if he ever came back?

Mack turned away from the house and looked up the street and then took a step forward, then back, until he saw the house come into view again through the corner of his eye.

Had to make sure the house wasn't gone for good. What if he wanted to go back? Had to make sure he could.

Then he turned and ran home in the predawn light. A few cars out and running. Dr. Marvin heading out to put big tits into some woman or liposuck the fat out. Mack waved at him, and Dr. Marvin waved back.

Miz Smitcher was standing by her car when Mack jogged up to the house. Mack remembered that she was covering the early shift this week.

"Where you been?" she asked.

"Fell asleep in the woods," said Mack. "I'm sorry, Miz Smitcher."

"Don't scare me like that, Mack Street," she said softly. "You all I got."

My mother lives in this neighborhood, Miz Smitcher. Did you know that? Did you keep that from me? You lying to me all my life, or you didn't know?

Out loud, Mack said, "I didn't mean to. I won't do it again."

"Until the next time you don't mean to but it just happens."

Mack hung his head, showing his shame.

She touched the back of his head. Not rubbing his hair, like Mr. Christmas did. Just touching him. Laying her big nurse hand on his head like she laid it on her patients at the hospital. Felt good. Felt like a promise that everything going to turn out okay.

She took her hand away and his head felt cold without it.

"I be home late tonight, kind of working half a double," said Miz Smitcher.

"I'll do my homework the minute I get home."

"Don't wait dinner for me, what I'm saying."

"I won't."

She got in the car and backed out of the driveway and pulled out into the street. He watched her out of sight, then went into the house and took a shower.

When he came out, he heard a voice from the kitchen. "Mack Street, when you get dressed, would you mind coming in here and talking to me?" It was Mrs. Tucker, Ceese's mom. It was plain she knew that Miz Smitcher was gone, so it was Mack she wanted to talk to. She didn't sound agitated—in fact, she sounded downright perky. But it wasn't like adults came calling on him every day. Had to be something wrong, and had to be she thought he had something to do with it or knew something about it, so whatever it was, Mack was probably going to wish it wasn't happening.

Didn't make him dress any faster; didn't make him dress any slower. He'd find out what it was, deal with it as best he could. Mack wasn't one to worry, or at least he didn't go to great lengths to avoid facing whatever was coming at him.

Once he had his briefs on, he paused for a moment before putting on his pants. They weren't too dirty to wear—though they did look as though they had made the passage through the woods. Thing is, he wasn't sure he could trust them. He'd read plenty of stories about magic stuff that disappeared at midnight or some other inconvenient time. But at least he'd have his briefs on, if the pants vanished off his butt. So he pulled on the pants and padded into the kitchen where Mrs. Tucker was sipping tea and looking a little tense.

Ceese was sitting in the chair next to her. Well, that was no big deal, Ceese probably didn't have a morning class.

Mrs. Tucker smiled at him and offered him tea. He thought tea tasted like dishwater and he never drank it. Still, he sat down across from her when she asked him to, and waited for her to get to the point.

"It's just a little thing," she said. "Hardly worth mentioning, but it's been bothering me since it happened last night." And then she stopped.

Mack looked at Ceese, who was staring at the table looking solemn.

"I brought Ceese along because he's going to be a policeman now," said Mrs. Tucker. "Not that I think any crime has been committed!"

"And not that I know a thing about police work yet," said Ceese. "I just signed up to train for the test."

"You're going to be a cop?" asked Mack, fascinated. "You never hit anybody in your life."

"I did so," said Ceese, "but that ain't what decides you on being a cop. The idea is you try *not* to hit anybody, but if you have to, then you know how. Same thing with guns. You hope to be a cop who never has to fire a gun at a person, but if the time comes when you got no choice, then you know how to do it right."

"So why you doing it, Ceese?" asked Mack. "I thought you were going to build bridges."

"I was going to design electronics," said Ceese. "Lots of different kinds of engineering, Mack. But I was bored. Didn't feel like anything I was doing mattered to anybody. Being a cop, now, that matters. You make a difference. You keep people safe."

"Like you looked after me," said Mack.

"Like that."

"So what do you think I done wrong?"

"No," protested Mrs. Tucker. "We don't think you did a thing that's wrong. In fact, if you did it, then it definitely *wasn't* wrong, but I just have to know."

"Know what?" asked Mack.

"What happened to the leftover chili I was heating up for Winston and me for supper last night."

Mack knew at once what happened to it, and it pissed him off. If the magic at Skinny House could arrange for half a dozen copies of his pants to hang from hooks in a closet, why couldn't it simply *copy* Mrs. Tucker's chili out of her fridge instead of stealing it?

But he couldn't very well say so. He could just imagine how they'd react if he said, I ate it, but not from *your* fridge, it got magically transported to the fridge at an invisible house down the street, so when I ate it I didn't know I was eating yours. But it sure was delicious. I did my hot-mouth dance when I ate it.

"What happened to it?" asked Mack.

"That's what we don't know," said Ceese patiently.

Mack just sat there, looking back and forth between them.

"I was preparing dinner," said Mrs. Tucker. "I checked in the fridge to make sure there was enough chili for the two of us, and there was. And then I went to the sink and washed the corn on the cob and cut up some bananas to put with a can of mandarin oranges to make a little fruit salad. And when I came back from the can opener with the oranges to drain off the liquid into the sink, there was the chili dish, freshly washed and still wet, in the drain-dry beside the sink. And a spoon."

"Somebody snuck in and ate your chili and *washed the dish* while you were opening the mandarin oranges?" asked Mack.

Ceese gave the tiniest sigh.

"I'm just so afraid I'm losing my mind," said Mrs. Tucker. "I was hoping you'd tell me that . . . that you perhaps did it as a prank. Meaning no harm. I'd be so relieved to know that it was you, and that I'm not crazy."

"You not crazy," said Mack.

"Then you did it?" said Ceese, sounding calm but also just the tiniest bit incredulous.

Mack shrugged. "I was not in your kitchen yesterday or last night, Mrs. Tucker."

"Where were you?" asked Ceese.

Mack looked at him calmly. "You asking for my alibi, Officer?"

Ceese got a small smile. "I guess so, Mack Street."

"Got no alibi," said Mack. "I was walking around in the neighborhood and in the woods and I slept under a tree last night with a big black cat. I reckon that cat ain't much of an alibi."

"But you didn't eat Mom's chili," said Ceese.

"I was not in your kitchen yesterday."

"I just can't imagine," said Mrs. Tucker, "why somebody would eat my chili and then *wash the dishes.*"

"I think," said Ceese, "we're not quite ready to start an urban legend about a sneak thief called 'Tidy Boy' who steals food from fridges while the cook is in the kitchen, and washes up without a soul noticing he's even there."

Mrs. Tucker could hear the trace of amusement in Ceese's voice and her eyes started swimming with tears. Mack knew that her deepest wish was being young again. He dreaded the evil way that magic would make the dream come true—probably a second childhood brought on by Alzheimer's. But growing old terrified her, and this seemed like proof to her.

Magic always found a way to be cruel. Mack couldn't even have a chili supper without hurting somebody.

"Mrs. Tucker," said Mack, "I can't tell you what happened to your chili, but I can promise you this. You're not going crazy, you're not getting old, something really happened, but if you keep talking about it people going to *think* you crazy. So maybe you better let it go."

For the first time, Ceese got real alert. He didn't say anything, but now he was looking at Mack real steady, and the amusement was gone.

"Do you think so, Mack?" asked Mrs. Tucker. "I know it's silly, you're only a boy, what would you know?"

"I know that the chili was really in your fridge when you saw it. I know you didn't accidently eat it and wash up afterward and then forget you did."

"*How* do you know, Mack?" she said plaintively. "How can I know you really know?"

"Doubt me if you want, but I know everything happened just the way it seemed to you, and you didn't forget anything. That's the best I can do."

She looked at him searchingly, then reached out and clutched at his hands, there on the table. "Mack, you're an angel to say that to me. I know Ceese doesn't believe me, though he's too kind ever to say so. I just needed *somebody* to believe me."

"I do, Mrs. Tucker."

"Well then," she said. "I'll just wash up my cup . . ."

She stood up.

"I'll do that, Mrs. Tucker," said Mack. "I like washing dishes."

"You do? That's very strange of you," she said, and then laughed. It sounded only a little hysterical. "But very nice."

Ceese left with her out the back door, but as Mack expected, he was back before Mack finished drying the cup and saucer and spoon and putting them away.

"All right, Mack, what was all that about?"

"Ceese, why should I tell you?" said Mack.

"Cause I think my mother *is* losing her mind and if you know some reason I shouldn't think that, you better tell me."

"She's not losing her mind," said Mack. He got down a bowl and spoon for his breakfast.

"That's not good enough," said Ceese. "Just your word like that?"

"I ever lie to you, Ceese?" asked Mack.

"Not telling me the whole story, that's the same as a lie."

"Not if I don't pretend that it's the whole story when it's not."

"So you're going to keep it a secret."

Mack laughed. "All right, Ceese, I'll tell you. I went into an invisible house four doors up from Coliseum on Cloverdale, between Chandresses' and Snipes', and in that house I got hungry and opened the fridge and there was your mama's chili in a glass dish. I nuked it for two minutes, ate it, did the warpath dance cause it was so spicy, then I washed the dish and spoon and put them in the dish drain *in that house.*"

Ceese shook his head. "So you're not going to tell me."

"I suppose it's better you think I'm a liar than you think I'm wacked out," said Mack. "Except that if I'm a liar, you're going to think your mama losing it when she ain't. And you also won't trust my word, but I never lied to you, Ceese, and I didn't start now."

"An invisible house."

"It's only invisible from the street," said Mack. "You get closer, it gets bigger."

"Show me."

"I don't know if I can," said Mack. "Maybe I'm the only one can see it."

Ceese shook his head. "Mack Street, I'm going to hold you to this. You going to show me."

"I can try. I just . . . maybe you'll see it, maybe you won't. I see a lot of things I don't tell people about," said Mack. "They just think I'm crazy. Miz Smitcher, she showed me early on that I better not tell what I see. It just makes folks upset."

Ceese's face looked cold and distant. "Let's go now," he said.

Mack led him down to the place and all the time he was half afraid that it wouldn't be there anymore, that weird spot in the sidewalk where you could see Skinny House out of the corner of your eye. But it was there.

"You see that?" asked Mack.

"See what?"

So Mack made him stand exactly where Mack had been standing, and then had him look straight up Cloverdale and then step backward and forward.

"I don't even know what I'm supposed to see."

Mack shook his head. "It's there. But like I thought, you can't see it."

Ceese sighed. "Mack, I don't even know why you doing this. It's one thing to make my mama feel better, I don't blame you for that, but telling this stuff to *me* when it's just us two—"

Mack didn't hear him finish the sentence, because he figured the only proof he had was to have Ceese watch him disappear. That must be what happened when Mack went into Skinny House, so he'd do it when Ceese was watching.

So Mack lined himself up with the thin vertical line of Skinny House and then strode right toward it. As before, it grew wider until it was the full width of a house. He reached out far enough to touch the front door, then turned around.

There was Ceese on the sidewalk, looking around every which way, trying to see where Mack went.

Mack opened the front door and went inside.

There was nobody there. And not a stick of furniture. Nothing in the kitchen, either. No fridge, no dishes in the cupboard, nothing.

But there were five pairs of pants in the closet, hanging from hooks. And when he checked the pockets, five dollars in each of them. Mack took all the bills and put them in different pockets of his pants. Then he went back out the front door and jogged toward the sidewalk.

Ceese was a few paces away, and partly out in the street, still looking for him. Mack called to him, but Ceese couldn't hear him. Not till Mack actually set foot on the sidewalk. Then he whirled around.

"Where were you?" Ceese demanded.

"Watch me carefully," said Mack. "Your eyes right on me."

Ceese watched. Mack stepped off the sidewalk. Skinny House disappeared and Mack clearly did not.

"Shit," said Mack. "All right, look away, but keep me visible in the corner of your eye."

Ceese rolled his eyes, but did as Mack had ordered.

This time when Mack stepped off the sidewalk, Skinny House

grew larger and Ceese whirled around to see what had happened to Mack. Mack walked right back to the sidewalk and reappeared right in front of Ceese's eyes.

"Good Lord," whispered Ceese. "You can disappear?"

"Of course I can't disappear," said Mack. "It's not *my* magic, it's the magic of Skinny House. It's not like I can disappear by stepping off the sidewalk anywhere *else* in Baldwin Hills."

"You been magic the whole time I looked after you?"

"I'm not magic!" said Mack, and now he was getting a little angry. "Or can't you hear me?"

"I hear you, I just don't—I never saw anything like that before."

"You seen it all the time," said Mack. "In movies and on TV."

"Yeah, but they fake it."

"But do you know *how* they fake it?"

"Not exactly, but it has something to do with . . . hell, I don't know."

"You don't know how to do it, it's magic to you." Mack held out his hand.

"What," asked Ceese.

"Take my hand and look up the street. Don't look toward the houses at all. Stand right . . . right *there*."

Ceese obeyed.

"Now, when I pull you, you just follow, but don't look where we're going." When he could see that Ceese was following orders, Mack stepped off the sidewalk and headed toward Skinny House. He half expected to feel Ceese's hand vanish from his, or to have the grass just be the grass between the two visible houses.

But no, Skinny House loomed, and Ceese's hand stayed in Mack's, and in a moment they were standing on the front porch and Ceese was looking back and forth between the neighboring houses and touching the door and the walls, saying, "Good Lord."

"Ceese, I know the Lord got nothing to do with this, and I'm pretty sure that it ain't good."

10

WORD

Mack and Ceese stood on the back porch of Skinny House, looking at the orange trees and the rusty barbecue and the umbrella-style clothesline.

"So that's really a forest back there." Ceese's voice was flat, not the least bit sarcastic, but Mack knew him too well not to recognize the irony in the way he spoke.

"We're standing on the back porch of an invisible house, and you still don't believe me?" said Mack.

"Well, there wasn't a fridge in the kitchen, either," said Ceese.

"Because it was your mama's fridge. It was probably *all* your mama's stuff. I showed you the pants. I showed you the claw marks and the bloodstains. I showed you the five-dollar bills I took out of all the pockets."

"That doesn't prove anything. Lots of people got more five-dollar bills than that."

"But not *me*," said Mack.

"Miz Smitcher didn't up your allowance?"

"Ceese, you gave me the *original* five dollars."

Ceese hooted. "That was three years ago!"

"I don't spend much."

"Mack, I believe you, of course I do. But it takes getting used to."

"What's to get used to? Either it's in front of your face or it isn't. This is, so you got to believe it."

"And if it isn't in front of my face?"

"Then you got to have faith."

"When you have faith in something a lot of other people believe, then you a member of the church," said Ceese. "When you have faith in something nobody believes, then you a complete wacko."

"Well, I believe it and so do you, so between us, we half a wacko each."

"And you been keeping secrets like this your whole life?"

"Nothing like *this*. I only found this place yesterday."

"And there was a man in the house."

"I call him Mr. Christmas." For right now, Mack wasn't interested in bringing Puck's real name into the conversation. He had a feeling that might make things too strange for Ceese.

"Cause he looks like Santa Claus?"

"He looks like Bob Marley only not dead."

"Well, then, the name 'Mr. Christmas' make perfect sense. I always think of Bob Marley at Christmastime."

"I wish I knew where he was," said Mack. "He could explain things to you a lot better than me. Except that he lies all the time."

"*All* the time?"

"No. He tells the truth just enough to keep you from knowing what's what."

"Well, then, I can't wait to meet him. I don't have half enough liars in my life."

"Come on out into the woods with me. Just a little way," said Mack.

"Why?"

"For one thing, so you can see that I'm not making it up."

"I really do believe you now, Mack. I really do."

"You scared of the woods?"

"I'm scared of that panther. He likes *you* fine, but I don't want to test to see if my pistol can kill a magic cat. Besides, a cop shooting a Black Panther is such a stereotype."

"Ha ha," said Mack. "It ain't that kind of panther, and you no kind of cop at all, yet."

"I don't even have a *gun* yet," said Ceese.

"Then why you worried about whether you can shoot a panther?"

"Thinking ahead."

Mack took him by the hand and dragged him to the edge of the patio. But the cement didn't turn to brick under their feet, and when they stepped off into the grass they squished rotting oranges, which was fine for Ceese, wearing shoes as he was, but pretty icky for Mack, whose feet were bare.

"I guess I don't have permission to enter Fairyland," said Ceese.

"Then why were you able to get into the house?"

"Maybe halfway is as far as I can go."

"No, let's try getting you in sideways."

They tried crossing the patio with Ceese's eyes closed, and with Ceese walking backward, but there was no woods and no brick path and finally it occurred to Mack that maybe the problem wasn't Ceese.

"Let me see if it's still there for *me*," said Mack. He let go of Ceese's hand and jogged across the patio and sure enough, there was brick under the orange-sticky soles of his feet, and then moss and dirt. He took only a couple of dozen steps into the woods and then looked back.

Where Puck had turned small and slender and green-clad, Ceese had changed in an entirely different way. It was as if the house had shrunk behind him. Ceese was at least twice as tall as the house, and he looked massively strong, with hands that could crush boulders.

Now I know where all those stories about giants come from,

thought Mack. Giants are just regular people, when they come into Fairyland.

Except Ceese *can't* get in. And what about me? I'm regular people, and I'm just the same size I always am.

"Mack!"

The voice was faint and small, and for a moment Mack thought it was Ceese calling him. But no, Ceese was looking off in another direction and anyway, a man that big couldn't possibly make a sound that thin and high.

Mack looked around him there in the woods, and finally found what he was looking for. Down among the fallen leaves, the grass, the moss, the mushrooms, with butterflies soaring overhead, was Puck. Not the big man with the rasta do, but the slender green-clad fairy he had glimpsed last evening on the porch of Skinny House.

He looked dead. Though he must have been alive a moment ago to call to him. Maybe it took the last of his strength. Maybe his last breath.

Puck was bloody, and his wings were torn. His chest looked crushed. One leg was bent at a terrible angle where there wasn't supposed to be a knee.

Mack gently scooped him up and started carrying him toward the house.

Trouble was, Puck grew larger in his hands. Heavier. More like his human Rastafarian self. Too big for Mack to carry safely.

At first he tried to carry him over his shoulder, but that worked for only a few steps before Mack collapsed under the weight of him. Then he got his hands under the man's armpits and dragged him. But it was hard work. His shoes kept snagging on stones and roots. Mack's heart was beating so fast he could hear it pounding in his ears. He had to stop and rest. And in the meantime, he knew Puck was still bleeding and probably dying even deader with every jostle and every minute of delay.

If only Ceese could enter the forest of Fairyland, he could pick Puck up like a baby and carry him.

And then it dawned on Mack why it was Ceese couldn't get in.

He let Puck sag back onto the path and ran the rest of the way to the patio. "Ceese," he called.

"What?"

"Mr. Christmas is in there, hurt bad, and I can't drag him out."

"Well I can't get in."

"I think maybe the reason you can't is that the passageway into Fairyland isn't *tall* enough for you."

"I'm not all that tall," said Ceese.

"In Fairyland you are. I saw you from inside the woods, and you're a giant, Ceese."

Ceese laughed at that—he wasn't all that tall a man, just average—but soon he was doing as Mack suggested, crawling on hands and knees while holding on to Mack's ankle and looking off to the side, and whether all of that was needed or it was just the crawling, he made it onto the brick path—which was no pleasure, on his knees like that—and then onto the mossy path.

"Open your eyes," said Mack.

Ceese did, and he truly was a giant, looking down at Mack like he was a Cabbage Patch doll. And there, two strides away, was a grown black man in a rasta do, just like Mack described him.

"How come I'm a full-grown giant and he's not a tiny fairy, this far into the woods?"

"How do you know you're full-grown?" asked Mack.

He didn't, and he wasn't. In the two strides it took him to reach Mr. Christmas, Ceese grew so tall that his head was in the branches of the trees and he had to kneel back down just to see the path.

He scooped up Mr. Christmas just the way Mack had done and then, a few steps later, he had shrunk enough he had to set him down again and carry him in a fireman's carry. By the time they got to the back door, with Mack holding the screen open so Ceese could get inside, the man was so heavy and huge that Ceese was panting and staggering.

But he remembered how it felt to be so huge, and he kind of liked it.

Now the house was full of furniture again. Ceese took this in stride and laid Mr. Christmas out on the sofa. Now he was able to check his vital signs. "He's got a pulse. I don't suppose there's a phone."

"I wouldn't count on it," said Mack.

"Let's get him outside then, out to the street where somebody can see us, and try to get him to a hospital."

"I was hoping his own magic could heal him."

"You see any sign of it? You willing to bet his life on that happening?"

Mack helped Ceese get him up onto his back again, the old man's arms dangling over Ceese's shoulders. "Get the door open, Mack, and then run out into the street and flag somebody down."

Mack obeyed. First car that came was a nice big one, driven by Professor Williams from up the hill. He pulled right over when Mack flagged him.

"We got a man needs to get to the hospital!"

"I'm not that kind of a doctor," said Professor Williams. "I'm a doctor of literature."

"You the driver of a big car," said Mack, "and you can get this man to the hospital."

By now, Ceese had staggered to the curb, so he was visible.

"That man looks hurt," said Professor Williams.

"That be my guess, too," said Mack.

"He'll bleed all over my upholstery."

"That going to stop you from helping a man in need?" asked Mack.

Professor Williams was embarrassed. "No, of course not." A moment later, he had the back door open and then helped Ceese get the man into the car without dropping him or banging his head against the door or the car roof. It wasn't easy.

And at the end, when Mr. Christmas was laid out on the seat, Professor Williams took a good long look at his face. "Bag Man," he whispered.

"You know this guy?" said Ceese.

Professor Williams handed his keys to Ceese. "You take my car to the hospital. I'll walk back home and get my son Word to drive me to work."

"You sure you trust me with a car this nice?" said Ceese.

Professor Williams looked from Mr. Christmas to Mack and then back to Ceese. "I'm never riding in a car with that man again," he said. "If you're determined to save his life, then go, I won't stop you."

"I just hope I can get to the hospital in time. Unless you got a siren in your car."

Professor Williams gave a bitter little laugh. "I have a feeling you'll have green lights all the way, son."

MR. CHRISTMAS DIDN'T WAKE UP at all, not on the way to the hospital, and not when the orderlies came out and hauled him out of the car and laid him on a gurney and rolled him into the emergency room.

Ceese knew enough about how things worked to tell the hospital people, "No, we don't know his name. No, we don't know who he is. He was lying on the sidewalk when Professor Williams saw him and he didn't have time to take him here so he lent us his car to do it."

That caused some raised eyebrows, and when they signed Mr. Christmas in as a John Doe, Ceese turned to Mack and said, "You watch, they'll have a cop coming by here to ask us if we the ones who beat this man up."

"Why would they do that?"

"Take a look at the color of your skin."

Mack grinned. "This just a suntan, Ceese. You know I spend all day outdoors in the summer."

"What I'm saying, Mack, is, let's go home. Let's not be here when the cop shows up."

"I can't do that," said Mack.

Ceese shook his head. "What is this man to you?"

"He's the man in Skinny House," said Mack. "He's the man who led me into—"

"Don't say it."

"Don't say what?"

Ceese lowered his voice. "Fairyland. Makes you sound two years old."

"*He's* more than two years old, that's what *he* called it."

"So don't you wonder how he got so beat up?"

"It could have been anything, he was so small."

"How small was he?" asked Ceese.

"You know how small he was in your hands when you picked him up?"

"Yeah, but that's because I was . . ." Ceese looked around at the other people in the emergency waiting area. "Well, I was what I was right then."

"That's how big he was to *me,* and I was normal size."

Ceese turned himself on the couch and leaned close to Mack's ear. "That's something I want to know. I got big, and that old bum got small, but nothing happened to you at all."

"So what?"

"So, *why?*"

"I didn't read the instruction manual, I guess."

"I'm just trying to think it out and make some sense out of it."

"It don't *make* sense, Ceese."

"I mean, if humans turn into giants, and . . . whatever he is . . . gets small, what are you?"

"I wish I knew," said Mack. "I never met my mother. Maybe she was regular size, too."

Ceese looked away, then turned to face front. "I wasn't saying about your parentage. Don't get sensitive on me all of a sudden."

"I'm not," said Mack. "I just don't know. I could be anything. I mean, if a regular-looking homeless person with a rasta do can be a fairy."

A new voice came out of nowhere. "Is that why you boys beat him up? Cause you thought he was gay?"

It was a cop standing ten feet away, so his voice carried through the whole room. Mack had never been rousted by a cop, though he'd heard plenty of tales and he knew the rules—always say sir and answer polite and don't ever, ever get mad, no matter what stupid thing they say. Did it make a difference that this cop was black?

"We didn't beat him up, sir," said Ceese. "And we were honestly not referring to anyone's sexual orientation, sir."

"Oh, so you were telling fairy stories to your little friend here?"

Mack didn't think he was so little anymore. Then he realized the cop was being sarcastic.

"As it happens, sir, I used to tend this boy when he was little. I was his daycare while his mother, who is a nurse in this very hospital, worked the evening shift. So I've read him a lot of fairy tales in my time."

The cop squinted, not sure if he was being had. "I've heard a lot of fairy tales, too."

"Not from me, sir."

"So you really did just find that unconscious man by the side of the road," said the cop, "and you happened to flag down the only man in the universe who would hand you his car keys and let you drive his fancy car to the hospital with a dirty bleeding old bum with a broken leg and five broken ribs and all kinds of contusions and abrasions bleeding all over the nice leather interior."

"Well, sir, that's pretty much what happened," said Ceese.

"Except," said Mack.

Ceese turned to him, looking as casual and politely interested as could be, but Mack knew his look *really* meant, Don't touch my story, boy, it's the best one we got.

"He wasn't unconscious when we found him," said Mack. "When I found him, I guess I mean. I heard him. Calling out for help. That's why we found him in the bushes and we dragged him to the street and that's how we knew we couldn't carry him, and maybe we caused him more pain because he was unconscious after that. But we didn't know what else to do."

"Could have called 911," said the cop, "and not moved him."

"We didn't know how bad hurt he was at first," said Ceese. "We thought maybe he was just drunk on the lawn."

"Where was this?" asked the cop, and from then on he was all business, taking notes, and then taking their names and addresses. When it was all done, and he was about to leave, he said, "You know why I believe your story?"

"Why?" asked Mack sincerely, since he didn't think he'd believe it himself.

"Because you'd have to be six kinds of stupid to make that shit up. Cause it's going to be so easy to check. First call is to this Professor Williams."

"We don't know his number at Pepperdine, sir," said Ceese.

"I'm a policeman, a highly trained professional. I am going to use that subtle instrument of detection, directory assistance, and find out the number at Pepperdine, and then I'm going to ask the nice lady who answers the telephone to connect me with Professor Williams. Meanwhile, I think I'll hold on to these car keys, since they might be evidence if things turn out wrong."

"So you don't believe us," said Ceese.

"I mostly believe you," said the policeman.

"If you take the keys, how will we get home?"

The cop laughed.

Ceese explained. "If he doesn't get the right answer from Professor Williams, then we won't be going home."

The cop winked and they followed him out into the corridor, where he pulled out a cellphone and called directory assistance and then talked to the Pepperdine switchboard and then must have got voicemail because he left a message asking Professor Williams to call him about a matter concerning his Mercedes automobile and then he said the license plate number.

"Bad luck for you, boys," he said. "Professor Williams doesn't answer his phone."

"Of course not," said Ceese. "He's a professor. He's in class, not in his office."

"But where does that leave me?"

"Well, you could ask Miz Smitcher," said Mack.

"Who's that?" asked the cop.

"His mother," said Ceese.

"He calls his *mother* 'Miz Smitcher'?"

"He's adopted," said Ceese. "And Miz Smitcher was never one for taking a title she hadn't earned. So she taught him to call her Miz Smitcher like all the other neighborhood kids."

The cop shook his head. "The things that go on in Baldwin Hills." He got a little simpering smile on his face. "I didn't grow up with money like that."

"Neither did we," said Ceese. "We grew up in the flat of Baldwin Hills."

"That like the flat of Beverly Hills? Half a million's still a hell of a lot more than I had, growing up."

"So that's what this is about," said Ceese. "You're giving us a hard time after we brought a crime victim to the hospital, not because you think we did anything wrong, but because you don't like our address. How is that different from rousting us because we're black?"

The cop took a step toward him, then stopped and glared.

"Well, I guess we're definitely having a ride to central booking and getting your names down in the records. The kid, he's a juvenile, but you—Cecil, is it?—I guess you'll be just another black man with an arrest sheet."

"So you get a little power," said Ceese, "and it turns you white."

"All that race talk, that's not going to help you much in the county jail, my friend," said the cop. "Everybody we arrest has a master's degree in victimization."

And that was the moment when Word Williams showed up. "Sir," he said.

The cop whirled on him, ready to be furious at just about anybody. "Who the hell are you?"

"I believe you're holding the keys to my father's car," he said. The way Word talked, like an educated white man, made the cop's attitude change just a little bit. Less strut, more squint—but not a speck nicer.

The cop tossed the keys in his hand. "I wouldn't know," he said. "Who's your father?"

"Dr. Byron Williams, a full professor at Pepperdine University and a noted poet. He called me on his cellphone and told me that Ceese and Mack were taking an injured homeless man to the hospital in his car. He asked me to trade cars with them and get his car cleaned."

"There wasn't too much blood on the upholstery," said Ceese, "and I wiped it up as best as I could."

The cop had that smirk again. "So I guess everybody in Baldwin Hills is really close friends with each other."

Ceese rolled his eyes.

But Mack answered him sincerely. "No, sir, most people only know their neighbors. I may be the only one who knows everybody."

The cop just shook his head. "Why am I not surprised by anything anymore?"

"Perhaps you'd like to call my father," said Word.

"I already did, but he didn't answer his phone."

"His cellphone?"

"How will I know it's really him?"

Word looked at Ceese. "You must have really pissed this man off. Look, I'll give you his cellphone number. But call the Pepperdine switchboard, ask for the chair of the English department, and then ask *her* if this is indeed Professor Williams's cellphone number. You'll know she's really the department chair, she'll confirm the number, and then we'll be square, right?"

"Just give me the number," said the cop. He dialed it, without bothering about the switchboard and the department chair. After a minute of listening to Professor Williams, he handed the keys over to Word, with a faintly surly thank you. He didn't so much as say goodbye to Mack and Ceese.

When the cop was out of earshot, Word turned to them and said, "That's how people with petty authority always act. When they're caught being unjust, the only way they can live with themselves is to keep treating you badly because they *have* to believe you deserve it."

"He was nice enough at first," said Mack.

"No he wasn't," said Ceese. "He just *acted* nice."

"But that's what being nice is," said Mack. "Acting nice. I mean, if you're really nice, but you act mean, then you *aren't* really nice, you're really mean, because nice and mean are about how you act."

"Is he going to law school nights?" asked Word.

"No, he's so young he thinks the world ought to make sense," said Ceese. "So you want me to drive home whatever car you drove here?"

"I had a friend drop me off," said Word. "I mean, I can't drive two cars home."

"How *we* going to get home?" asked Mack.

"Your mom, I guess," said Ceese.

"She doesn't get off till late in the afternoon," said Mack.

"I'll find your mom, get her keys, drive her car, and then come back and pick her up after work," said Ceese.

"No, no," said Word. "Let *me* take you. We're practically neighbors."

Mack didn't know why that felt wrong to him, but it did. Something about Word made him uncomfortable. Which was crazy because nobody ever spoke ill of Word.

Ceese had his own reasons for declining. "We kind of want to stay long enough to find out what's happening to Mr. . . . the guy we brought here."

"Mr. what?" asked Word, smiling. "I thought he was a homeless guy. You know his name?"

"No," said Ceese.

"We had to call him something," said Mack. "So I started calling him Mr. Christmas."

"He look like Santa Claus?"

"More than Tim Allen does, yes sir," said Mack.

Word laughed and slapped Mack lightly on the shoulder. "Mack Street. I've seen you walking through the neighborhood your whole life, but I don't think I ever heard you say a word."

"I say lots of them," said Mack. "But mostly when people ask me questions."

"I guess I never thought you knew something I needed to find out," said Word. "Maybe I was wrong."

What Mack was thinking was: You never heard a word from me, and I never felt a dream from you.

That wasn't so unusual—there were plenty of people in Baldwin Hills who never had a wish so strong it popped up in a cold dream. But there was something about Word that said he had a lot of strong wishes, a kind of intensity about him, especially when he looked at Mack. Like he was just the tiniest bit angry at Mack but he was holding it inside. Or maybe he was really angry, and he was barely holding it in check. Something like that. Something that made Mack wonder why a guy with so much fire inside never showed up in a dream.

"No," said Mack. "You weren't wrong. When people ask me stuff, all they find out is I don't know anything much."

"I think," said Ceese, "a lot of them hope that Mack knows good gossip, wandering around the neighborhood like he does. But see, he doesn't tell stories about people."

But at that moment, Ceese stopped talking and looked over Word's shoulder, down the corridor.

"What?" said Word.

Mack leaned around Word to see what Ceese was looking at. But Ceese grabbed him by the collar and pulled him back, so all Mack caught was a glimpse. It looked like an alien out of a sci-fi book they made him read at school. Like a big ant. Only when he thought about it, he realized it must have been somebody dressed in black, with a black helmet. Like a motorcycle rider.

Word turned around, but too late. When Mack looked, the alien or motorcycle rider was just turning away, so when Word turned, the corridor was empty.

Mack didn't like it when Ceese acted weird, and he was sure acting weird now, gripping Mack's neck so hard it was like he was trying to break a pencil with one hand. So Mack tore away and took off up the corridor the other way, to ask the nurse at the counter what was happening with the man they brought in.

"I don't know if I should tell you," the nurse said. "You're not his next of kin or legal guardian."

"Well, I was sure his guardian when he needed somebody to find him in the bushes and carry him to safety," said Mack.

"You carried him?"

Mack shrugged. Didn't matter whether she believed him or not. "He wouldn't be here if I didn't hear him in the bushes."

"You're Ura Lee Smitcher's boy, aren't you?"

Mack nodded.

She nodded, too, and picked up the phone.

A few minutes later, Miz Smitcher was down there with them and hearing their story. "I guess we just want to know what's happening with the old guy," said Ceese, when they were through telling just enough of the truth to avoid having to spend time with a psychiatrist.

So Miz Smitcher went off and got permission from a doctor, on the basis that these were the boys who found the man, and she'd be with them. Pretty soon they were in a draped-off space gathered around the man's bed. His leg was in a cast and his chest was wrapped up and he had a needle stabbing the back of his hand, connected up by a tube to a bag hanging from a hook.

But the cast and the wrappings and the sheet were all so clean that it was actually an improvement. And seeing him asleep like that made Mack feel safer somehow. Not that he'd felt all that threatened when Puck was awake. But then, maybe he *had* felt a little bit afraid, but just didn't admit it to himself.

They stood there looking at him, nobody saying much because Mack and Ceese were afraid to say anything for fear of giving away some of the strange stuff that happened and becoming the laughingstock of the neighborhood. After a little while Mack's attention turned to Word. Not because he was saying anything— he was silent enough—but because of the way he looked at Puck.

Talk about fire. Talk about intensity. It's like he thought he was Superman and he was going to use his X-ray vision to bore a hole right through the man's head.

"Did you know him?" asked Mack.

It took a moment before it registered on Word that Mack was talking to him.

"Me? No."

"But you saw him before."

Word shrugged.

"Then why do you hate him so bad?"

Word looked at him, startled, and then laughed. "I never heard you were crazy."

"Then you haven't been paying much attention," said Ceese.

Miz Smitcher looked at them like they were all crazy. "Let's leave this poor man alone," she said, and ushered them all out.

Word drove them home, with Ceese sitting in the front seat beside him and Mack in the back, looking for bloodstains, but there wasn't anything at all.

"You cleaned this up pretty good," said Mack.

"There wasn't much to clean," said Ceese. "He didn't bleed much."

"Dad's still going to make me get the car detailed," said Word. "He hates that guy. Wants every trace cleaned off."

"So your dad knows him?" asked Ceese.

Word shook his head. "Nobody *knows* him. But he came to our door once. I let him in. And then he left again."

"You let him in?" Ceese asked. "A guy like that, in your house?"

Word nodded. "My dad thinks I don't remember. Nobody else in the family even remembers. And for a while I didn't—for an hour or so. Then it all came back to me. Mom was sick in the bedroom, and Dad got home and went in there and then that guy came to the door and . . . I let him in."

"What did he do?" asked Mack.

"He went back there. I got ahead of him, to warn them he was coming, but I couldn't stop him. I wanted to, but. No, I didn't want to. I knew I *should* want to. I *wanted* to want to. But no matter what I wanted to want, what I *actually* wanted was to do everything he wanted me to do. I've never felt so helpless in my life." He shuddered.

"I don't get it," said Mack. "If you wanted to stop him, how could you also *not* want to stop him?"

"You can't imagine it till it happens to you. All of a sudden it's like *you* don't even have a vote on what your body does and thinks and feels. You can think about how you don't want to do it, but at the same time, all you want in the world is to please that son of a bitch."

Mack could see Ceese stiffen a little.

"Come on, Ceese," Mack said. "You said 'son of a bitch' in front of me often enough."

Word gave a sharp little bark of a laugh. "Sorry."

"I just didn't realize this man's been around so long," said Mack. "How long ago was it?"

Word laughed again. "How old are you?" he asked.

"Thirteen and two months," said Mack. "Since the day I was found, anyway, and Miz Smitcher says I couldn't have been born very long before that."

"Then that man came to our house thirteen years and two months ago," said Word.

Mack thought about that for a minute. And added into his calculations the way Ceese was glaring at Word.

"So he had something to do with me, too, is that what you're saying?" asked Mack.

"Let's just say that when he came to our house, he had all kinds of empty grocery bags on his belt and in his pockets. But when he left, there was a baby in one of them."

Mack felt a rush of feeling, like his blood was trying to move to different parts of his body all at once. He was a little faint, even.

"And you didn't say anything?" said Ceese softly.

"Nobody would have believed me," said Word.

"Why not?" said Ceese.

"Because my mother wasn't pregnant an hour before," said Word. "But I caught a glimpse of her through the door and her belly was swollen up and . . . who's going to believe that? Especially when *she* didn't remember it even happened, half an hour later? She swelled up, had the baby, and forgot all about it in about two hours. You don't believe it even now."

"Yes I do," said Mack.

"Yeah," said Ceese. "We do."

"Because of him," said Word. "Because of Bag Man."

"Mr. Christmas," said Ceese.

Puck, thought Mack. "So am I your . . ."

"I don't know," said Word. "You might be my brother. Or my half brother. But considering that things like that are impossible in the real world, I'm not altogether sure that you exist." He laughed again, that harsh laugh that said he really didn't think it was funny. "And if you do, what put you in my mother's uterus? Who could I tell? Who could I ask? All I could do was watch. I saw Ceese find you. And soon I heard that Miz Smitcher had taken you in. So you were okay."

"And what if I hadn't found him?" said Ceese. "Or what if Raymo . . ."

"I knew Raymo," said Word. "I wouldn't have let anything happen."

"So you just watched," said Mack. "Like Miriam watching Moses in the bulrushes."

"So you're a Bible reader," said Word.

"I listened in Sunday school," said Mack.

"Exodus. Moses was in danger of being murdered by Pharaoh's men, so they put him a basket and floated him down the river. I suppose today it would be a grocery bag, and he'd be set down in a field by a drainpipe."

"I'm not Moses," said Mack. "And nobody was trying to kill me."

Both Ceese and Word laughed grimly at that, then glanced at each other. Both of them probably wondering what danger the other one had known about.

"Do you read Shakespeare?" asked Mack.

Word shrugged. "My father almost named me William Shakespeare Williams. Instead of William Wordsworth Williams. So I might have been called Shake instead of Word."

"Or Speare," said Ceese helpfully.

"*That* would have guaranteed I never got a date in high school," said Word, and this time his laugh was a little more real.

"What can you tell me about Puck and the queen of the fairies?" asked Mack.

"Puck? Why?"

"Just asking."

"Why? You think that Bag Man's an overgrown fairy or something?"

"Just asking," said Mack. "But if you don't know, I guess I'll have to read about it."

"Good luck on Shakespeare," said Word. "It's written in a foreign language. I heard a black linguist from Berkeley once say that English-speaking people are the only ones who never get to read Shakespeare in their native language. Instead we have to suffer through reading his stuff in the kind of English they were speaking back in 1600."

"I got through Shakespeare okay," said Ceese. "Romeo and Juliet. King Lear."

"High school's one thing. They spoonfeed it to you."

"In college I mean," said Ceese.

"Okay, well, fine," said Word.

"All I want to know is about the Queen of the Fairies," said Mack.

"Titania," said Word. "And her husband is Oberon. They fight all the time. Puck is Oberon's servant, and he plays terrible tricks on people. He takes this guy who's lost in the woods and magically makes him have the head of a donkey, and then Puck gives Titania a love potion and she falls in love with this half-assed guy."

"So Puck is a bad guy," said Mack.

"No, he's a trickster. Like Loki in Norse mythology. He just . . . plays pranks on people. But they're mean tricks. He has no conscience."

They rode in silence for a while.

Then Word glanced back and asked Mack, "So you think this guy is Puck?"

Ceese said, "He's just talking."

"I have a word of advice for you," said Word.

Ceese snorted. "You have a word."

"I know it's a pun on my own name. Don't you think I hear enough of that crap?"

"Your advice?" said Ceese.

"Leave it. Forget about it. My father broods about it. It still poisons him. He watches you from the window. He watches you whenever he passes you in his car. Because he knows. Baby found in a grocery bag, not an hour after Bag Man carried you out of the house. Dad hates that guy. But what good does it do?"

Nobody answered. More silence.

Then Word spoke again. "In the play—in *Midsummer Night's Dream*, that's the play that has Puck in it—what they're fighting about—the queen and the king of the fairies, Titania and Oberon—is a changeling."

"What's a changeling?" asked Mack.

"A little boy. That's all they say. I think there's an old legend that fairies sometimes come and steal away human children and leave fake children in their place. I suppose it's the kind of legend that was invented to explain autistic children. The changeling looks like a perfectly normal child, but he just doesn't respond right."

"Is that what I am?" asked Mack.

"You're not autistic," said Ceese. "Weird, but not autistic."

"How could you be a changeling?" said Word. "There wasn't a baby to swap you for. I don't know what you are. Maybe you're just . . . my magical brother."

"I don't see how you're any kind of brother to him," Ceese said irritably.

"Cecil," said Word, "you're his brother. His real one. Or his father or some combination. Everybody knows that. Everybody in

Baldwin Hills knows you gave up half your own childhood to look after Mack. They love you for it. I'm not making any claim that I mean anything in Mack's life."

"Less than nothing," said Ceese quietly.

"If I had told this story back then, would it have changed anything?"

Silence again, until Ceese finally answered, "They would have locked you up in the loony house."

"He had you in his life. And that was good. What if I had 'found' Mack in that grocery bag? I thought of it. But I couldn't have brought him home. If I had come in that door with that particular baby, I think my dad would have lost it. Might have killed the baby or run out of the house and never come back or . . . I don't know. Dad was crazy. You finding him, that was a good thing, Ceese."

That was the last thing Mack heard for a little while, because right at that moment, he slipped into a cold dream. Didn't even fall asleep first. Just felt himself walking into a hospital room that he had never seen before and firing eight rounds from a handgun right into Bag Man's bandaged-up head. Only the bandages were nothing like the real ones, and the room was nothing like the draped-off area where Mack actually saw Bag Man, and suddenly Mack understood what he was seeing. It wasn't coming out of Mack's memory of the hospital, it was coming out of someone else's imagination. What Professor Williams wanted more than anything else in the world right now, far more than he wanted to be a great poet, was to murder Bag Man.

Mack had never thought of Puck as "Bag Man," but in the cold dream that's absolutely who the man was, what his name was.

Mack tried to force himself out of the dream, but now found himself in his own dream of driving along the road that became a canyon, and he was desperate to get out of the dream but he couldn't until . . .

Until he awoke shivering, with Ceese pinching the skin on his arm.

"Ow," said Mack.

"You fainted," said Ceese. "You were shivering like you were having some kind of fit."

"I was cold," said Mack angrily. "You don't have to punish me for it by pinching like a girl!"

"Just trying to bring you back."

And that's what Mack wanted him to do.

"We okay back there now?" asked Word. "We're almost to your house."

"I had a dream," said Mack.

"In three minutes?" asked Ceese. "That's quick dreaming."

"He's an efficient dreamer," said Word from the front seat. He pulled back into traffic and a moment later turned right on Coliseum and then left on Cloverdale. Both Mack and Ceese looked at where Skinny House was hidden but from the street, of course, they saw nothing.

When they got to the Smitcher house—Mack's house—Word got out of the car to help Ceese get Mack out.

"I'm okay," Mack insisted.

"You just fainted. That suggests you're not exactly okay," said Word.

"I had one of my dreams," said Mack. "Not a sleeping-type dream. A different kind. And somebody was trying to kill Bag Man."

"Who," said Word, laughing. "My dad? I'd believe it!"

Mack just looked at him.

Word stopped laughing. "Oh, come on. I don't *really* believe it."

"Your dad knows which hospital he's in," said Mack.

"My dad's not a murderer."

"I don't want him to be," said Mack. "But the things I see in dreams like this—sometimes they come true."

"Like what?"

"Like Tamika Brown dreaming she was a fish and waking up inside the waterbed."

That knocked them both for a loop. They stared at Mack for a long moment. "You mean Tamika's dad wasn't crazy?" asked Ceese.

"Or lying?" asked Word.

"Like you, Word," said Mack. "Who could I tell?"

"Weird shit's been going on for years, and I never had a clue," said Ceese.

"So you think my dad might just magically appear in Bag Man's hospital room?" asked Word.

"I don't know what might happen," said Mack. "But when these dreams come true, it's always the thing the person wants most in all the world—only it happens in the ugliest way. If your dad gets his wish to have Bag Man dead, then I bet your dad gets caught. Or maybe shot down by the police. And all of us arrested as accomplices, probably. All part of a big setup."

Ceese and Word looked at each other.

"I'm going back," said Word. "It's crazy, but so is everything else. I've got to stay there until . . . or I could call my father."

"No, let's go back," said Ceese. "But not you, Mack. It's too dangerous."

Mack just looked at Ceese with heavy-lidded eyes.

"Oh, don't give me that vulture look," said Ceese. He turned to Word. "But he's right. We got to take him, because he's more in tune with this weird stuff than either of us."

So they piled into the car and headed back for the hospital.

"I'm blowing off an exam to do this," said Word as they pulled into the hospital parking garage.

"So what do we do? Sneak into the emergency room? They know us there."

"He won't be there now," said Mack. "They move them out of there after an hour or so."

"Where will he be?"

"I'll find out."

It was easy, as long as they didn't go through Emergency, where they would all be recognized. Instead, Mack went to an ordinary nurses' station where he was recognized only as Ura Lee Smitcher's boy, and nobody even noticed when he looked up the John Doe who had been admitted to Emergency as an indigent about two hours before—had it already been that long?

Armed with the room number, it was easy enough for the three of them to get to that floor. Mack, knowing the routine and some of the staff on that floor, waited until the ones who might have caused trouble were out of the way, and then led the others on down the hall and into the room.

Mr. Christmas was still asleep, but now he was on a hospital bed and there wasn't a tube anymore.

"So what do we do," said Word. "Wait for my dad to appear?"

Ceese looked around. "Move the old man?"

"This isn't *The Godfather*," said Word. "We can't just move him. They'd notice. And besides, if he comes here by magic, we can't fool the magic, can we? He'll come to whatever room Mr. Christmas is in."

They were interrupted by Mr. Christmas whispering from the bed. "Come here."

They all turned. The man was holding up a feeble hand. He was reaching for Mack. "Hold my hand."

Mack took a step toward him.

"You trust him?" asked Word.

"Don't do it, Mack," said Ceese.

"Help me," said Mr. Christmas.

Mack looked at Ceese and Word, then turned back to Puck. "The doctors already did what you needed."

Mr. Christmas glanced at Ceese and Word, and suddenly they smiled and began pushing Mack gently toward the bed.

"It's all right," said Ceese.

"He needs you," said Word.

And Mack knew right then that Puck was doing to them the thing he had done to Word Williams thirteen years ago. Making them want to do something they didn't want to do. Encourage Mack to obey Puck's command.

The thing was, *Mack* didn't want to do it. Didn't want not to, either. It's as if Puck had no power to make Mack want or not want anything.

"I touched you before," said Mack to the man on the bed. "I . . . carried you. It didn't help you."

Mr. Christmas responded by wiggling his fingers. Give me your hand, his fingers were saying.

Am I doing something I don't want to do? thought Mack as he reached out. Is this what it feels like? But Word's description hadn't made sense to Mack before and he didn't know if he was being Puck's slave or not. So . . . just before touching his hand, Mack stopped, withdrew it, put his hand in his pocket.

Mr. Christmas still wiggled his fingers.

Okay, so I proved I could do it. But now as I take my hand out of my pocket and reach out to him again, is that because I want to or because I . . .

I could keep going back and forth on this all morning, and in the meantime, Professor Williams might pop out of thin air and blast eight rounds into Puck's body.

Mack took the man's hand.

His grip was weak. But the longer he held, the stronger it got. Until Mack said, "You're hurting me."

"Sorry," said Puck. But now he looked stronger. And when he let go of Mack's hand, he sat right up and pulled the bandages off his head and his body. "That really hurt."

"What happened to you?" asked Mack. "Was it the—"

Puck put up a hand to stop him from saying more. Then he stood up and looked down at the cast on his leg.

"Mack," said Puck, "can I lean on you to steady me?"

Mack came closer. The man leaned on him. He took a step. Another.

And then Puck wasn't leaning on him anymore. Mack looked at him, and now he was fully dressed as a homeless man, with grocery bags hanging out of every pocket and looped over his arms. "No reason to hide these from you now," said Puck to Mack. "Now that Word here has told you everything."

And with a nod to Word and Ceese, and a wink to Mack, Puck flung open the door and strode boldly out into the hall. Nobody challenged him.

"You healed him," said Word.

"He healed himself," said Mack. "He's the magical one, not me."

"But he had to hold your hand to do it."

"That's crazy," said Mack.

"And when he was leaning on you," said Ceese, "his cast just disappeared, and he was wearing those clothes."

"So did we save a man's life just now," said Word, "or turn loose a monster into the world?"

"We saved your father," said Mack. "From committing a murder and going to jail for it."

"*If* he was coming."

"Now we'll never know," said Ceese. "But isn't that better than knowing because we *didn't* stop him?"

"Yes, it is," said Word.

"Now let's go home," said Ceese, "before the nurses catch us here and demand to know what we did with the old man."

As they approached the car, Word pushed the button that made the Mercedes give a little toot and blink its lights. "You know what I don't want to do now?"

"What?" asked Ceese.

"I don't want to spend a lot of time trying to figure all this out. I spent years trying to make it make sense and I decided long ago that the best thing for me to do is act as if it never happened, just as my dad does, because there's not a damn thing we can do about it and it's never going to make sense. In fact, not making sense is why we call it magic instead of science, right?"

"Right," said Ceese.

Mack didn't like it. He had finally found not one but two people who believed him, and Word might have even more information about Mack's origins. "I *got* to talk about it," said Mack.

"Fine," said Word. "With each other, not with me. Because if you start telling people this stuff, and they come to me for corroboration, I'll tell them I just drove you guys home in my dad's car and I've got no idea what you're talking about. I'm not letting magic ruin my life."

"I understand," said Ceese. "That makes sense."

"Like hell it does," said Mack.

"Watch your language," said Ceese.

"Yeah, you two got your nice birth certificates and your moms and dads and your damned last names."

Ceese reached over the back of his seat and laid a hand on Mack's head. Mack pulled away.

"Mack," said Word from the driver's seat, "I understand how you feel."

"Like hell," said Mack.

"Mack, don't—" Ceese began.

"Hell hell hell hell."

"You've got to let this boy watch George Carlin and learn more words," said Word.

"Hell," said Mack, toward Word this time.

"The thing is, Mack," said Word, "you already know everything I know. I didn't hold anything back. And I don't want to talk about this or think about it. You've got a family. You even have a mom and dad, if you aren't too picky about standard definitions. Read *Midsummer Night's Dream*. You'll learn more from that than you ever will from me."

This time Mack didn't faint on the way home.

And late that night, after Mack was in bed, he heard Ceese come in and give something to Miz Smitcher. She brought it to Mack as Ceese left the house. It was a big thick book.

"A complete Shakespeare," said Miz Smitcher. "What is that boy thinking? If you read this in bed and fall asleep with that book on your chest you'll suffocate long before morning."

"I won't read it in bed, Miz Smitcher," said Mack.

"Why Shakespeare? Is that summer reading for school? Surely not the whole Works of Bill!"

"He and I were talking about a play I remembered," said Mack. "So I guess he wanted me to be able to read it for myself."

"But why the book?" said Miz Smitcher. "Doesn't he know there are places online where you can get the full text of any Shakespeare play, free of charge? This is so expensive!"

"Ceese is still looking out for me," said Mack.

"He's a blessing in your life, that's for sure," said Miz Smitcher. "But no reading tonight. Plenty of time tomorrow."

Mack thought he'd have trouble getting to sleep, he had so much to think about. But he'd been thinking about it all day, brooding about it, trying to figure out what it all meant and why Puck was living in Skinny House right in their neighborhood and what it might mean to be a changeling and how that might explain why he didn't change size going into Fairyland and . . .

And he was asleep.

11

FAIRYLAND

Ceese knew he couldn't say anything to anybody, yet it troubled him to keep such a thing secret. This wasn't gossip to excite or scandalize people in the neighborhood. This wasn't *entertainment*. From what Mack let slip today, some terrible things had happened in the neighborhood—the worst being Tamika Brown's near-drowning, but there were others, and the danger of more bad things happening. Wishes always being turned against the wisher.

Maybe that was the way of it. All those fairy tales where people got three wishes—they always ended up wishing they hadn't. The whole idea of somebody granting wishes was evil, anyway. I'm the powerful one, and it amuses me to see how ineptly you puny stupid mortals use the few powers that I deign to grant you.

Who was doing it? Or was it simply the way of the world, that all desires exacted their price?

Ceese wanted to talk to somebody about it. But who? Not his mama, that was certain. She'd blab to his brothers, at the very least, and then they'd taunt him for the rest of his life about how he believed in magic and wishes. Dad? He wouldn't even understand what Ceese was talking about.

Ura Lee Smitcher? Maybe. She was a hardheaded woman and not prone to believe in strange things, but she knew how to keep her mouth shut. The only reason not to talk to her was that it would worry her that Mack was tied up in all this. And maybe that was her right, to know what her adopted son was involved in so she *could* worry.

But wasn't it Mack's place to tell his mama what he was going through? Those . . . what did he call them? . . . cold dreams. Skinny House. That big Rastafarian fairy. Man, who could possibly believe that if they hadn't held his tiny body in their hands out in Fairyland? If they hadn't seen his wings?

So Ceese kept it to himself. But he still thought about it.

He read *Midsummer Night's Dream* over and over, at least the fairy parts, and came to the conclusion that he didn't like *any* of the magical creatures. They were vicious and petty and used their power for stupid and selfish things.

Then again, to be fair, ordinary humans did the same thing. Nobody knew how to use power for good.

Not even me. Why do I think I should be given a gun and a nightstick and a badge and sent out onto the streets as a cop? Because I'm so good that I'll never use my power for evil? Isn't that how all the evil people in the world get started?

No. They *know* they're doing something bad, or they wouldn't hide what they did and lie all the time. And when I'm a cop, I'll be protecting the weak people from the powerful ones.

Only how do I protect a kid like Tamika from her own wishes? From the malevolent force that will *twist* those wishes into something dark and terrible?

Over the next few weeks, Ceese started paying attention in church. Then he gave up on the sermons—they were all about working people up to feel the Spirit, but Ceese had seen real magic and he wasn't interested in feelings, he was hungry for understanding. So he spent his time in church reading the Bible, trying to make sense of how Jesus fit into the world that Ceese now understood he lived in.

What *was* Jesus, anyway? The similarities with Mack were obvious. Born to a virgin—well, Mrs. Williams wasn't a virgin, with three other kids already, but she didn't even know she was pregnant. It was a magical birth, for sure, and no way of knowing whether Professor Williams was Mack's daddy or if the boy partook of no mortal's genes. And there was nothing in the New Testament about Jesus being born within two hours of being conceived. But still . . . the Holy Ghost comes over this virgin girl and she gives birth to a magical being who can heal people.

Mack didn't *know* he could heal people, but it was obvious in the hospital that day. He held on to Mr. Christmas or Bag Man or whatever his name was, and the man got better. His bones knitted up, his skin smoothed over without a scar, even his clothes changed. So there was healing in Mack's touch even if he couldn't control it himself. Heck, at the age of thirteen maybe Jesus didn't know what he could do, either. Wasn't that the age when Jesus went and talked with those wise men in the temple? Wasn't thirteen when Jews believed a boy became a man?

So what would that mean, if Jesus and Mack were the same kind of creature? That God the Father was a malevolent fairy king? Ceese thought back to the scary woman on the motorcycle—what was *she,* Satan? Tempting him to kill the boy? But then was it God who played these cruel tricks on people in the neighborhood? What kind of universe would *that* be?

No, these fairies were the opposite of God. Instead of tricks, he healed people. Instead of bringing them grief, he forgave their sins. And if I'm to serve Jesus in this world, thought Ceese, then I have to find a way to fight these fairies.

Except . . . if Mack was the creation of something evil, why was he so good? Why was his heart so full of love and hope and joy? Nothing made sense. Maybe things couldn't be sorted out into good and evil.

So Ceese did nothing, because he couldn't even figure out which side he ought to be on, let alone how he could possibly take on magical beings and defeat them.

And he had this memory: I was a giant in that place.

It had felt so good to be unassailably large. What could hurt him there?

The fairy tales were full of giant-killers.

And if he were a giant *here*, in this world, the real world (though that other one certainly felt real, while he was in it!), he wouldn't be able to help other people using his great size and strength. They'd be terrified of him. They'd shoot him down, like in *King Kong* and *The Iron Giant*.

So Ceese trained to be a cop so he could do some good in the world, and read the Bible to figure out what "good" actually was, and did his best to watch over Mack and make sure nothing bad happened to him.

And now and then he walked past that place on Cloverdale Street, carefully looking straight ahead, but without Mack at his side, he never saw a glimmer of Skinny House, and he never saw either Mr. Christmas or that black-clad motorcycle woman on the street.

WORD GOT RELIGION, TOO. He had seen real power twice in his life now—when Bag Man came out of his parents' bedroom with an impossible baby in a bag, and now in that hospital room when Bag Man was healed just by holding on to Mack Street.

Word thought about Jesus, too, just like Ceese did. Only he saw it from a completely different perspective. He thought: Wouldn't it be cool to have power like that?

It began to haunt his dreams.

. . .

MACK WENT BACK to Skinny House the first chance he got. He wanted to find Puck and ask him all the questions that were burning him up inside. But the house was empty, no furniture, no food, no sign that anyone but Mack was ever there. Mack found that if he brought stuff there, it stayed. Real things that he carried into this passage between reality and Fairyland stayed put and didn't pull disappearing acts. So he kept a notebook there, and wrote down all his thoughts. He also brought food—stuff that wouldn't rot without a fridge. Cans of beans and mandarin oranges and little plastic containers of applesauce. He used his allowance to buy a cheap metal can opener and some plastic spoons.

That way he could take expeditions into Fairyland and carry some food with him. Mack didn't know what was edible and it wouldn't matter anyway—in Fairyland, anything might be poisonous. He didn't want to end up like that donkey-headed man.

Though if something did go wrong, what would happen? If there were six ways he could die, and one way he could live, would the one version of himself that lived come back to Skinny House and find six pairs of pants hanging from the hook again? Or was that splitting of time just a one-shot deal? Did it happen because that's just how things worked, or was it something Puck did, toying with him?

Fairyland was a huge place, Mack discovered, but it followed the terrain of the real world. Mack could sort it out, if he made a rough kind of map and kept his eye on the sun to keep track of east and west, north and south. The mountain of Baldwin Hills and Hahn Park was more forbidding and dangerous than in the real world, but that's because no one had tamed it. There was more water everywhere, too—streams wherever the ground was low, and it rained often when he was there. Right in the middle of summer, he'd come out soaking wet and from the windows of Skinny House he'd see bright sunlight and bone-dry ground.

He ranged far and wide. There were ancient ruins atop the hills of Century City, a huge stone structure with pillars surrounding a central table that was open to the sky. The handiwork looked Greek or Roman, but the arrangement made him think of Stonehenge. It sat right on the crest of the hill that had been cut in two to put Olympic Boulevard through. Only there was no Olympic Boulevard, and so no cut in the mountain, though where the road would have been a spring burbled up from the earth and started a stream that tumbled over clean rounded stones.

Time worked differently in Fairyland. The first time he went in, he slept the night and when he came out it was also morning in the real world. But ever since then, it was different. If he went to Fairyland for a few hours and came out, in the real world only an hour or so would have passed. So for a while he thought that time went half as fast in Fairyland.

Then one day he got permission from Miz Smitcher to sleep over at a friend's house, and then went to Fairyland and walked all the way through the meadows of Santa Monica to the steep terrifying cliffs overlooking a raging sea, and then it was dark and he slept there. The next morning, he foolishly went south along the coast to where the cliffs sank down into the marshes of Venice, and there he saw creatures that he did not imagine could exist in the real world—huge lumbering bright-colored dinosaurs that stood in the swamp, letting the water bear part of their weight, as they browsed and nibbled on the trees that formed a jungle that seemed to go all the way down past Marina Del Rey to the airport.

The trouble with swamps is they're easy to get lost in, and Mack found that out the hard way. He didn't know whether the snakes he met were poisonous or not, but they left him alone, and one time when a gator suddenly appeared out of nowhere, its jaw open and ready to snap at his leg, Mack heard a growl and turned around and there was a panther—maybe *the* panther—threatening the gator. It backed away and fled. But since when was a panther any threat to an alligator? Mack couldn't begin to guess where reality left off and magic began. And as for the panther—was it his friend? Or someone else's friend, ready to help him if it suited that person's purpose, or hurt him, even kill him, if he got out of line?

It took him all day to make his way back up out of the swamp and then he was lost, not sure how far south he had gone. He got confused and thought that Cheviot Hills was Baldwin Hills and that's where he spent his second night, worried to death about how Miz Smitcher was bound to be worried to death. Compared to that, it was hardly even a problem that he had run out of food.

The next morning he found Century City pretty easily, and then struck out southeastward, traversing familiar ground, so it was only noon when he found the path leading to the back yard of Skinny House.

At Skinny House, it was late afternoon.

Mack raced home, desperately trying to think of some plausible lie to tell Miz Smitcher about where he'd been for two whole days.

She was sitting in the living room, having coffee with Mrs. Tucker. "Well, Mack," she said, "did you forget something? Or did you just miss my cooking?"

Mrs. Tucker laughed. "Now, Ura Lee, you are a wonderful woman but you're no kind of cook."

"Mack likes my food just fine, don't you, Mack?"

That's when Mack realized that no matter how long he spent in Fairyland, it was never more than an hour and a half in the real world, though he found through experimentation that it could be much less. The only exception was that first night in Fairyland. And he couldn't think why that time should have been different.

He could bring food and tools into Fairyland—he couldn't resist writing his name with a felt-tip pen on the inside of one of the columns at the Century City Stonehenge—but he couldn't plant anything and have it grow, and when he tried to take things out of

Fairyland, they were transformed. He had thought of trying to get his science teacher to identify some of the berries and flowers he found, but when he came out, they had dried up and crumbled in his pocket so that it was impossible to tell what they had ever been.

He even caught a mouse one time and held it in his hands as he walked back toward Skinny House, watching to see if anything happened. It did. The mouse became very still, and with another step its body became lighter and drier. It was dead, and the corpse was desiccated.

He immediately turned around to try to restore it to life by returning it to Fairyland, but it didn't work. It was still dead. Mack never again tried to carry any living thing back with him from Fairyland.

Yet fairies themselves could make the passage. And anything at all from our world could go the other way.

Or could it?

Mack had never had a problem with any of his tools—a spade, scissors, the Magic Marker, his notebook, his pencils. But he found that he couldn't strike a match in Fairyland. He couldn't set a fire of any kind. He never *saw* a fire there—not even lightning.

So things that depended on fire wouldn't work there. Not guns, not cars. If he wanted a cooked meal, he'd have to bring it with him. If he somehow managed to kill an animal there, he couldn't roast the meat, he'd have to eat it raw.

What did fairies eat? Were they vegetarians? Or could they magically cook their food instead of using fire?

Those were trivial questions, he knew, compared to the big ones: Why did such a place as Fairyland exist in the first place? Were there other lands besides Fairyland and reality? Why was there a connection between the worlds right here on Mack's street? When he hiked through the place, why didn't he ever see an actual fairy? He hadn't seen one since he found Puck, injured.

Who were Puck's enemies? Were they Mack's enemies, too— or was Puck his enemy?

Who was screwing with Mack's neighborhood, and why were they doing it?

Mack struggled through *Midsummer Night's Dream* one time, and couldn't keep track of the lovers and who was supposed to be with whom. Maybe it was easier if you could see actors play the roles so you could tell them apart by their faces. But it didn't matter. The second time through, Mack read only about the fairies. Titania and Oberon. What a pair. And Puck—he seemed to be Oberon's servant but also he enjoyed causing trouble for its own sake.

Again, though, the real question was much more fundamental: This was a play, not history. How could he possibly learn anything from a made-up story?

He went online and learned that *Midsummer Night's Dream* was the only one of Shakespeare's plays that didn't come from somebody else's story. One site said that he probably got his fairies, his "forest spirits," from oral folk traditions.

Fairies cropped up elsewhere in Shakespeare. Changelings and baby-swapping came up in *Henry IV, Part I*. Mercutio talked about Queen Mab—which made Mack wonder if she was the same person as Titania or if there were two queens, or many, and lots of fairy kingdoms, or maybe just one.

The websites talked about how before Shakespeare, everybody thought that fairies were full-sized spirits who hated humans and wanted to cause them harm whenever they could. Supposedly Shakespeare changed all that by making them small and cute.

Only Mack couldn't figure out why they thought Shakespeare's fairies were cute. They weren't evil, either, not exactly. They just didn't care. They had no compassion for humans. People merely amused them. "Oh what fools these mortals be," Puck said— which to Mack sounded like Shakespeare already knew that Puck was a black man, saying "be" instead of "are."

So if the stories Shakespeare heard as a kid were all about full-grown fairies as big as humans who were filled with hatred for the human race, why did he change them to creatures so small that Queen Mab could ride in a chariot made from an empty hazelnut and pulled by a gnat?

But he didn't always make them small. When Puck made Titania fall in love with Bottom while he had a donkey's head, she seemed to be the same size as him.

They all thought Shakespeare was taming the fairies, making stuff up that would make them seem cute instead of dangerous.

Mack knew that when a fairy was in our world, like Mr. Christmas, he was the size of a man. But in Fairyland, he was small. Not so small that he could fit into a hazelnut shell, though. Unless he really *was* that small when he got even deeper into Fairyland. He had already made his way to a point on the path within sight of Skinny House. If he hadn't, if he had still been as tiny as Queen Mab, then Mack would never have found him.

Shakespeare got it right. Shakespeare knew something about how Fairyland worked. Changing sizes. The way fairies mess with humans for fun, but don't actually hate us because they don't care about us.

And if Shakespeare got that part right, then why shouldn't he know about an ongoing rivalry between the king and queen of the fairies? In his day, it was a matter of pranks, arguments over a changeling, love potions. Silly things. But what if it got uglier and uglier as the years passed? What if Oberon somehow managed to imprison Titania in a globe-shaped lantern hovering in a clearing on the far side of a ravine, guarded by a panther?

There were two lanterns there with a fairylight inside. Was the other one Oberon himself? Or maybe some boyfriend fairy that Titania was cheating on Oberon with.

If only Shakespeare had written more.

He was known as the greatest writer in the world. Even people who didn't speak English thought so, just from reading translations of his plays. There was a guy who actually wrote a book that claimed that Shakespeare somehow invented human beings, or something wacko like that.

Was it possible that Shakespeare's brilliant writing had been his *wish*? That he hungered to be the greatest writer in the world the way Tamika had hungered for water to swim in forever. What was it Shakespeare might have asked for? Undying fame. A name that would live forever.

Maybe what he wished for was undying fame in the theatre, thinking that he'd become famous as a great actor, but his wish was granted in an ass-backward way so that yes, he was famous for plays, but never for acting in them. A trick. A catch. Yes, that's why Shakespeare knew how to write about the fairies. He had been granted his heart's desire, but with a catch that made it taste like ashes in his mouth. And then, at the end, even his writing was taken away from him because his hand began to shake so he couldn't even sign his name.

"Shakespeare" indeed. Some prankster fairy—was it Puck himself?—had decided to let Shakespeare's life act out his name. If the pen was his weapon, his spear, then at the end of his career his spear shook so badly that he was unable to keep writing. He hadn't wished for a long career, had he? Nor for happiness in love. He ended up marrying a woman who was years older than he was because he got her pregnant—or somebody did. And then his career was cut off short by his shaking hands—but then, his wish had already been granted, hadn't it? He was already going to be famous forever, so why should he be allowed to keep writing or even keep living long enough to enjoy his fame?

Ha ha, Puck. Very funny.

What fools these mortals be my ass. I heard your teeny weeny little voice, Puck, and dragged you out of Fairyland and took you to the hospital and then you somehow sucked healing out of me then what? Any thanks? Any favors? No, you just disappeared.

Though now that Mack thought about it, maybe not getting a

favor from Puck was the best favor he could think of. Because fairy favors always took away more than they gave.

"Mack, this thing you've got with Shakespeare," said Miz Smitcher one morning, "I'm delighted, I'm happy for you, you're smart as I always thought you were. But you got to *sleep* at night, baby. Look at you, hardly keeping your eyes open. It's a miracle you don't put your Rice Krispies in some other hole."

And because he was tired, Mack answered almost honestly. "I got to find out about him," he said. "He's like me. In a lot of ways."

Miz Smitcher touched his forehead. "Oh, I know, baby. He was white, you black. He had long hair like a white girl, you got hair so nappy your head could rub the paint off a Cadillac. He was English, you American. He was a brilliant writer, you can't spell. He made up plays, you wander around the neighborhood like a stray dog eating at anybody's back door who'll feed you. Who could miss the resemblance?"

Mack sat up straighter and finished his Krispies and didn't talk about being like Shakespeare again.

"I can spell okay," he mumbled.

"I know. But you don't spell like Shakespeare."

"Nobody spells like Shakespeare anymore, Miz Smitcher. He couldn't spell worth . . . spit."

"That's right, baby, you watch your mouth, don't go saying ugly words in front of *me*, I wash your mouth out with special soap from the hospital, tastes so bad it makes you puke."

That was an old game between them, and Mack took it up. "Tastes so bad I got to lick up the puke just so I can have something to puke out again."

"Now you going to make *me* puke," said Miz Smitcher. She got up from the table and started rinsing off her dish to put it in the dishwasher.

So the game was over before it began. Or maybe it never was a game. Maybe she really was mad at him. But why? He didn't actually *say* "shit." So she was probably *really* mad about something else.

About Shakespeare. About Mack reading all the time and staying up late looking stuff up on the web.

Don't you see, Miz Smitcher? This stuff is about me. I'm a changeling myself, and Shakespeare wrote about fairies and changelings because he met them, he must have, he knew the *answers*. Only he's dead and I can't ask him. So I got to find the truth in his plays.

Ariel, for instance, in *The Tempest*. He was a fullsize fairy or spirit because he had been rescued by Prospero and so he was bound to serve him for a certain period of time and . . .

And I rescued Puck. There in the woods, I rescued him, and *he's bound to serve me.*

That's why he's never there at Skinny House. That's why I never see him on the street. He's hiding from me, so I won't realize that he's my slave.

Not that I want a slave.

But if I'm his master, then I can ask him questions and he's got to answer.

But as long as he can't hear me giving him any kind of command, he doesn't have to obey.

Cheater.

That afternoon Mack slipped into Skinny House and out the back door and went to the ruins on the hill above Olympic Boulevard and with spray paint wrote in big letters, one letter per column, PUCK YOU CHEATING FAIRY GET BACK HOME!

Two days later there was a story in the paper that he heard Mrs. Tucker read aloud to Miz Smitcher. "Can you imagine such bigotry in this day and age? Right there in huge letters across the face of the Olympic overpass."

"At least it said 'fairy' instead of 'nigger,'" said Miz Smitcher. "Maybe that's progress, maybe it ain't. The way it used to be for us in this country, I don't wish that on anybody."

Mack heard this and he called Ceese and pretty soon the two of them were parked at Ralph's just down from the overpass, looking at the big letters that said PUCK YOU CHEATING FAIRY GET BACK HOME!

"You wrote that?" asked Ceese. "What did you do, hang upside down over the railing?"

"I wrote it but not *here*. I wrote it in Fairyland. I was sending a message to that lying cheater Puck."

"Puck?" asked Ceese.

"Mr. Christmas. Bag Man."

"You're saying he *is* Puck?"

"I asked the house what his real name was, and it made a hockey puck appear."

"It doesn't look like it says Puck, actually."

"That's what it says."

"That P looks more like an F. See how it's not really a loop there?"

"It says Puck, dammit!" said Mack.

"Don't get excited. But you can see how it got folks talking. They aren't going to think somebody's writing a message to a real fairy named Puck. They're just going to think it's a message from a bigot so dumb he can't make an F right."

"Don't you get it, though, Ceese? I wrote that at a ruined circle of stone columns in Fairyland, and it appeared on the overpass here."

"On both sides, too," said Ceese. "You only wrote it once?"

"Only once."

"So what you do in that place changes things here," said Ceese.

"I've peed and pooped all over Fairyland," said Mack. "You think that stuff pops up in our world, too?"

"Now that's a pretty thought. Right in the middle of somebody's kitchen table."

"Right in the office of some studio bigshot."

"A pool of piss."

"A steaming pile of—"

"You're going to make me puke."

"I puked once there, too."

"You a regular shitstorm, boy. Somebody got to get you under control. I got to find out if there's a serial burglar who breaks into people's houses, takes a dump, and leaves without stealing nothing."

"I'd like to see you prove it."

"We could do DNA testing."

"Shit don't have no DNA," said Mack.

"Did somebody here ask Mr. Science?"

"I wrote that sign in Fairyland," Mack said, returning to the subject. "And come to think of it, stuff that happens here changes the world there, too. I mean, the terrain is pretty much the same. So when we have an earthquake, maybe they have an earthquake, too. Maybe they get mountains because *we* get mountains."

"That's God's business," said Ceese. "Not mine. I'm a cop, not a geologist."

"You not a cop yet."

"Am too. Been a cop for two weeks now."

"And you didn't tell me?"

"I'm still a trainee. Probationary, kind of. I don't want to make some big announcement yet because I still might wash out. But I got a badge and I'm going out on calls."

"You a cop. I can't believe that."

"Now you can't mess with me anymore," said Ceese.

"I never messed with you before," said Mack. "Now I got to start."

"I'll arrest your black ass and give you such a Rodney."

"It takes six cops to give somebody a Rodney."

"It takes six *white* cops," said Ceese. "Takes only one black cop."

"Who the bigot now?"

"Just stating the obvious," said Ceese. "I been practicing Eddie

Murphy's speech from *Beverly Hills Cop*. His 'nigger with a badge' speech."

"Only cop I ever saw was *Baldwin* Hills."

"No, it was *48 Hours*."

"That's one long movie."

"The *name* of the movie is . . . stop messing with me, Mack. I come clear over here cause you want to check out the graffiti they wrote about in the paper, and now you telling me *you* wrote it in Mr. Christmas's back yard."

"It's a big back yard, Ceese."

"Well, I got to give you credit. It's the first graffiti I seen in years that I could actually read. But you can't make a P worth shit."

On the way home Ceese took him to the Carl's Jr. on La Cienega so it turned into a feast, but the whole time, they both knew that something strange and important and maybe terrible was bound to happen one of these days, and they wished they had some idea of what.

12

MOTORCYCLE

So it was that, full of curiosity and dread, Mack Street passed the next four years, living as if it were always summer, passing back and forth between the world of concrete, asphalt, and well-tended gardens in Los Angeles, and the wild, rainy tangle of the forests of Fairyland.

In the one world, he went to high school and learned to solve for n, the causes of the Civil War, how to write a paragraph, the inner structure of dead frogs, and how and why to use a condom. He dropped in on neighbors and ate with them and knew everybody. He took Tamika Brown out in her wheelchair and walked her around to see stuff and learned to understand her when she tried to talk. He broke up fights between neighborhood kids and carried things for old ladies and watched over things, in his way.

In the other world, he wandered farther and farther, climbing higher into the hills, using the tools he brought with him to shape wood and stone. For days at a time he stayed, and then weeks. He built an outrigger canoe and took it out into the ocean, thinking to sail to Catalina, but the currents were swift and treacherous and he used up all his drinking water before he was able to work his way back to shore, south of the barking seals and cruising sharks and killer whales of the rocks around Palos Verdes.

He climbed mountains and wrote notes on the terrain and marked on topographical maps of Southern California. He drew sketches of the creatures that he saw. He traced leaves. He drank from clear streams and looked up to face a sabertooth tiger that merely looked at him incuriously and padded away. He learned that the fauna of Fairyland was impossible. Creatures that could not coexist passed each other on the forest paths or fought each other over carcasses or slept ten yards from each other in the dark of night. Yet whenever he needed to sleep, he lay down in a likely spot and was undisturbed through the night. He was always a visitor here, and even the animals knew it.

His labors were tolerated, his artifacts were undisturbed. But whatever he made or did in Fairyland changed something in Los Angeles.

His outrigger, which he abandoned on a rock-strewn beach where crabs as big around as basketballs were so thick underfoot that he could hardly find a place to walk, became a drug-runner's speedboat that inexplicably drifted to shore, filled with cocaine but with not a hint as to what happened to the crew.

The canvas-roofed shelter he built for himself against the frequent downpours became a roofed bus stop shelter on La Brea where there had been no bus stop.

The melon and bean seeds he planted in a clearing did not grow in Fairyland, but in Koreatown they became a maddening series of ONE WAY and DO NOT ENTER and NO OUTLET signs that made traffic snarl continuously.

His cache of hand tools turned into a huge banyan tree that lifted and jumbled the sidewalk and street at the corner of Coliseum and Cochrane, along with protest signs demanding that the city let this "beloved and historic tree" remain standing. When he took the hand tools out of Fairyland again, the tree remained, but soon died and was cut down and dug out without protest. And when he took the tools back to the same place, instead of a tree, this time there was a seepage of water from a natural spring that caused sewer workers to dig and patch and redig and repatch through Mack's whole junior year in high school.

The one time he tried to carry fire into Fairyland was entirely by accident. Miz Smitcher had taken him to dinner at Pizza Hut and on a whim he picked up a matchbook. He forgot it was in his pocket until he stepped off the brick onto the soft mossy ground of the path in Fairyland, and all at once he felt his leg grow warm, then hot. He tugged at his pants, thinking maybe he'd been bitten by some insect, a spider or fire ant that got into his pants. Then he felt the square of cardboard through the denim and tried to dig the matchbook out of his pocket. It burned his hands. Only then did he realize he had to leave, take the matches back out of the place, back to the patio, where he tossed them on the ground.

He ran back out of Skinny House to the street and then ran around the block to make sure the matches hadn't caused a fire in the real world. He watched the Murchison house for a while, just to make sure. No smoke, no flame. But that would have been too logical. The next day, the story spread through Baldwin Hills about how the Murchisons came home and found that their dog Vacuum, chained up in the back yard, was now missing a leg. Only the vet told them that the dog had obviously never had a right hind leg, since there was no bone, no scar, and . . . the Murchisons quickly realized that the vet thought they were insane and they stopped arguing. At first nobody argued with them about how normal their dog had been the day before, but within a few days it seemed like nobody but Mack remembered that Vacuum had had four legs his whole life until some idiot accidentally carried fire into Fairyland.

Unpredictable. Uncertain. No rules. Mack feared the uncertainty but loved the profusion of life, and wished that he could share it with someone. Ceese did not want to go back there, though. And besides, what kind of companion would he be, towering sixteen or twenty feet in the air? Or taller, for all they knew—maybe Ceese would never stop growing the farther he got from Skinny House, until at the Santa Monica shore he would be so tall he could see over the mountains to the north and look at the Central Valley, or turn eastward and see the Colorado, no longer a thread of silver through a desert, but now a wide stream like the Mississippi.

With all the days and weeks Mack spent alone in Fairyland, which never took more than an hour and a half in the real world, and often less, he felt as if he must be at least a year older than anybody thought. Maybe two years. He had the strong wiry muscles of a man who had hiked from Ventura to Newport Beach, from Malibu to Palm Springs, with only the food he could carry on his back.

As he got older, he also got taller, so each stride took him farther. He grew so tall so fast that for a while he wondered if maybe he was becoming a giant like Ceese was in Fairyland, only slower, and on both sides of Skinny House. It wasn't like he knew of any blood relatives who could show him how tall he was likely to grow. But eventually it slowed down, and while he was tall enough that his loping stride carried him far and fast, nobody would mistake him for an NBA star. Well, maybe a point guard.

His feet were callused so they felt like the skin of the soles didn't even belong to him, they were like hooves. He hated putting shoes on at school—it felt to him like he was in prison, wearing them. And in Fairyland they were more trouble than they were worth, the laces always snagging on something, the soft soles cushioning his feet so that he couldn't feel the earth and learn what it was telling him about the land he was passing through. One pair of shoes was sucked off his feet in the swamp and became a suitcase full of nearly perfect counterfeit hundreds found by a couple of skateboarders in Venice. The newspapers speculated that the bills were part of a terrorist plot to destabilize the economy. No sane person would ever believe that they began as a pair of Reeboks that were sucked off his feet in a mudhole.

And from time to time Mack climbed down into the ravine and up the other side and walked to the clearing where it was always night, and the two globes sparkled with the only lights Mack saw in Fairyland that weren't in the sky. He sat and contemplated the globes, not knowing which was the captured fairy queen, not knowing if she went by Titania or Mab or some other unguessable name.

Sometimes he thought of her as Tinkerbell from the *Peter Pan* movie—a scamp too dangerous to let out into the world. But sometimes she was a tragic figure, a great lady kidnapped and imprisoned for no other crime than being in somebody's way. Titania had saved a changeling from Oberon's clutches. Titania had saved a boy like Mack. So she had to be punished, at least in *Midsummer Night's Dream*. Was it possible that her imprisonment now had something to do with Mack?

"Do I owe you something?" he asked.

But when he spoke aloud, the panther always grew alert and stopped its prowling. If he kept talking, even if it was to the panther and not to the captured fairies, the panther began to stalk him, creeping closer, its muscles coiled to spring at him. So he learned to be silent.

The corpse of the ass-headed man was a collapsed skeleton now, and grass grew over it, and leaves had scattered across it, and before long the ground would swallow it up or rain would carry it away. That's me, thought Mack. Dead and gone, while the fairies live forever. No wonder they don't care about us. We're like cars that whip past you going the other way on the freeway. Don't even see them long enough to wonder who they are or where they going.

And then one day, when Mack came back into Skinny House from Fairyland, his feet covered with mud because it was raining there, he stepped into a kitchen with a table and chairs, a fridge and a stove, and he knew that Puck was back.

Sure enough, there he was in the living room, building a house of cards. Looking like he always looked. Not even bothering to glance up when Mack came in.

"Tread lightly," said Puck.

"Where've you been?"

"Did we have an appointment? Your feet are filthy and you're tracking it all over the carpet."

"Who cares?" said Mack. "As soon as you leave, there won't *be* a carpet."

"You know how this works, Mack," said Puck.

Mack sighed. "Some woman in the neighborhood's going to have to shampoo this carpet."

"It's nice when you're tidy," said Puck. "I try to have some consideration for the neighbors."

"You got towels and soap and shit in your bathroom?"

"Oh, are you suddenly all hip-hop, boy, saying 'shit' like it was 'the'?"

"Nothing hip-hop about 'shit,' " Mack murmured as he headed for the bathroom. There *was* soap, but it was a half-used bar with somebody's hair all over it, and the shampoo was some smelly fruity girly stuff that made Mack feel like he was putting candy in his hair. Couldn't Puck steal this stuff from somebody who kept their soap clean? Rubbing somebody else's little curly hairs all over his own body.

He couldn't stand it, and stood there in the shower picking hairs off the soap and then trying to rinse them off his hand. By the time he got the soap clean the water was running tepid, and it was downright cold when he rinsed.

When he stepped out of the shower, Puck was standing there looking at him. Mack yelled.

"What are you doing? Can't a niggah get some privacy here?"

"You picking up that 'niggah' shit at high school? You grew up in Baldwin Hills, not the ghet-to."

"What are you, my father? And how come *you* get to say 'shit'?"

"I invented shit, Mack," said Puck. "I'm older than shit. When I was a boy, nobody shit, they just threw up about an hour after eating. Tasted *nasty.* Shit is a big improvement."

"I saved your life, asshole, and then you ran off and hid for four years."

"Statute of limitations run out so I'm back," said Puck.

"There's no statute of limitations on owing somebody for saving your life."

"Ain't no lawyers in Fairyland," said Puck. "That's one of its best features."

"We aren't in Fairyland," said Mack.

"Well, your mortal cops and courts sure as hell got no jurisdiction *here,*" said Puck. "But tell me what you want me to do for you, and I'll see if I want to do it."

"I want to know about the queen of the fairies."

Puck shook his head and clicked his tongue three times. "Ain't you got no *young* girls in high school? Why you got to go looking into a woman older than the San Andreas Fault, and a lot more troublesome?"

"So she causes even more trouble than you do?" asked Mack.

"Some people think so," said Puck. "Though maybe it's a tossup."

Mack wasn't going to let the fairy distract him. "Is she named Titania or Mab?"

"I thought we settled that years ago. I don't tell names."

"Then I'll ask the house."

"She ain't here," said Puck. "Won't work."

"I think you're lying," said Mack.

"I'm gone four years, and you call me a liar first thing. You got no manners, boy."

Mack leaned his head back and talked to the ceiling. "What's the name of the queen of the fairies?"

Nothing happened. Mack went back to drying off with the towel.

"Told you so," said Puck.

"Maybe the house just trying to figure out how to show me her name. Her name isn't a word, like yours is."

"Easy," said Puck. "Show you a tit with a tan—plenty of those in Brentwood—then a knee, then some dumb kid standing there saying, 'Uh.' "

"So her name *is* Titania."

Puck made a big show of looking aghast. "Oh, no! I let it slip!"

"So her name *isn't* Titania?"

"Come on, Mack. I'm not going to tell you because it ain't mine to tell."

"All right then, tell me this. Why don't I ever see any fairies in Fairyland?"

"Because this part of Fairyland is a hellhole where nobody goes on purpose. Why else would *he* exile her here?"

"A hellhole?" said Mack. "It's beautiful. I love it here."

"That's because you got protection," said Puck. "In case you forgot, I almost got my ass chewed off in there."

"I *saved* your chewed-off ass, remember?"

"How can I forget, with you always bringing it up like that?"

"I haven't mentioned it in four years!"

"Oh, yeah, congratulations on being a senior. Got AP English this year, too. Not bad for a boy can't figure out how to tie his shoes."

"Are you going to get out of the doorway so I can go out and put on my clothes?"

Puck stepped aside. Mack went into the bedroom and pulled on his jeans.

"Oh, you go commando," said Puck. "No underwear."

"What's the point?" said Mack.

"You ready for *anything,*" said Puck. "Except your pants fall down in the mall."

"I wear underwear when I remember to wash it."

"Good thing you buy tight jeans instead of letting it hang off your butt like those other kids at high school."

"I don't care about being cool."

"Which means you even cooler."

Mack shrugged. "Whatever."

"You want to know why I'm back?" asked Puck.

"I want to know about the queen of the fairies," said Mack.

"I'm back because *he* is about to make his move."

"What do I care?"

Puck laughed. "Oh, you'll care."

"So tell me *his* name, then."

Puck was silent.

"No guessing games?" said Mack.

"Don't even think about his name," said Puck.

"I can't. I don't know what it is."

"Don't think about thinking about it. You might as well have flashing lights and a siren."

"What, he doesn't already know where I am?"

"But you don't want him to notice you *in particular.*"

"I've been tramping all over Fairyland and just asking you his name is going to make him see what he hasn't seen till now?"

"Do what you want, then," said Puck. "Just giving you good advice."

"I'm not afraid of him like you are," said Mack.

"Cause you dumb as a muffler on a '57 Chevy."

"I wouldn't *be* dumb if you'd answer my questions."

"Boy, if I answered your questions you'd probably be dead by now."

"What happened to you, when we took you to the hospital—*he* did that, right?"

"Birds did it."

There was some reason Puck was so scared of him. "*His* birds, right?"

"Who else's? That place is Fairyland, and he *king* of Fairyland."

"Bush is President and American birds don't do what *he* says."

"President ain't king and America ain't Fairyland."

"So why didn't he finish it and kill you?"

"Don't you have someplace to go this morning?" asked Puck. "Like school?"

"Plenty of time to catch the bus. Specially since I didn't have to go home to shower."

"You don't ride with any of the other kids from Baldwin Hills? They all got their own cars, don't they?"

"Not all," said Mack. "Not everybody rich in Baldwin Hills. And even some of the rich ones ride the bus so they don't have to take any shit about their fancy ride when they get to school."

"All about money in your world," said Puck. "Money be *magic.*"

"Yeah, like you're the great social critic," said Mack. " 'What fools these mortals be.' "

"Oh yeah. Will Shakespeare. I loved that boy."

"I thought he was an asshole. According to you."

"Even assholes got somebody who loves them."

"I'm still wanting answers," said Mack. "You going to be here when I get back?"

"I be somewhere. Might be here."

Mack was sick of the dodging. It's not like he was longing for Puck's company the past four years. "Be here when I get back, you got it?"

Puck just laughed as Mack headed out the door.

AS MACK KNEW, it wasn't even seven yet, and his bus wouldn't be by for another fifteen minutes. He had time to stop by the house and pick up his book bag, which would make the day go easier.

Miz Smitcher was eating her breakfast. "Where do you go in the early morning?"

"Exercise," said Mack. "I like to walk."

"So you always say."

Mack pulled up his pants leg and moved his toes up and down so she could see the sharply defined calf muscles flex and extend. "Those are the legs of a man who could walk to the moon, if somebody put in a road."

"A man," she sighed. "Has it really been seventeen years since the stork brought you."

"Not a nice thing to call Ceese." Mack poured himself a glass of milk and downed it in four huge swallows.

"How tall are you now?" asked Miz Smitcher.

"Six four," said Mack. "And growing."

"You used to be smaller."

"So did you."

"Yeah, but you didn't know me when I was little." She handed him ten dollars. "Spending money. Take out a girl for a burger."

"Thanks, Miz Smitcher," he said. "But I got no girl to take out."

"You never will, either, you don't ask somebody."

"I don't ask less I think she say yes."

"So you have somebody in mind?"

"Every girl I looking at, she's on my mind," said Mack. "But they always looking at somebody else."

"I don't understand it," said Miz Smitcher. "Whoever your daddy and mama were, they must have been real good-looking people."

"Sometimes good-looking people have ugly children, sometimes ugly people have beautiful children. You just shuffle the cards and deal yourself a hand, when you get born."

"Aren't you the philosopher."

"I'm in AP English," said Mack. "I know everything now."

She laughed.

In the distance, Mack could hear the whine of a high-powered motorcycle.

Miz Smitcher shook her head. "Some people don't care how much noise they make."

"Wish I had a bike made noise like that."

"Now, Mack, we been over that. You want to drive, you have to have a job to pay for insurance. But if you have a job, your studies will suffer, and if you don't get a scholarship you ain't going to no college. So by not driving you're putting yourself through college."

"Just don't ask me why I got no girlfriend."

"Plenty of girls go out with guys who got no car, baby."

"I don't care, anyway, Miz Smitcher," said Mack. "It's fine as it is." He leaned down and kissed her forehead and then strode to the door, slung the backpack over his shoulder, and started jogging down the street to the bus stop.

He knew the bus driver saw him, but she never waited for anybody. They could have their hand inside the door, she'd still take off when the schedule said. "I run a on-time bus," she said. "So you want a ride, you have yourself a on-time morning."

So he'd jog to school. He'd done it often before. He usually beat the bus there, since he didn't have a circuitous route and a lot of stops, and he could jaywalk so he didn't have to wait for lights.

Only this morning, as he ran along La Brea, the whine of the motorcycle got close enough to become a roar, and then it pulled up just ahead of him. Riding it was a fine-looking black girl in a red windbreaker and no helmet, probably so she could show off her smooth henna-colored do. She turned around to face him.

"Miss your bus?"

Mack shrugged.

She turned off the engine. "I said, miss your bus?"

Mack grinned. "I said:" And then shrugged again.

"Oh," she said. "So you're not sure?"

"So I don't mind walking."

"I'm trying to pick you up. Don't you want to ride my bike?"

"That what you do? Pick up high school boys who miss the bus?"

"Big ones like you, yeah. Little ones I just throw back."

"So you know where my high school is?"

"I know everything, boy," she said.

"You call me boy, I get to call you girl?"

"So tell me your name, you don't want to be boy."

"Mack Street."

"I said your name, not your address."

He started to explain, but she just laughed. "I'm messing with you, Mack Street. I'm Yolanda White, but people I like call me Yo Yo."

"So you like me?"

"Not yet. It's Yolanda to you."

"What about Miz White?"

"Not till my gee-maw dies, and my mama after her."

"May I have a ride to school, Miz Yolanda?" asked Mack in his most whiny, obsequious voice. "I thinks you owes me a ride now, since you stopped me running and now I be late."

"What a Tom," she said. "Next thing you'll be carrying mint juleps to massuh."

For all his bravado in talking sass to her, he wasn't sure about how to hold on, once he was straddling the bike behind her. He put his hands at her waist, but she just grabbed them and pulled his arms so sharp around her middle that he bumped his head into the back of hers and his whole front was pressed up against her back. He liked the way it felt.

"Hang on, Mack Street, cause this is one little engine that *can*."

There was no conversation possible on the way there, because the engine was so loud Mack couldn't have heard the trumpets announcing the Second Coming. Besides which, Mack couldn't have talked, what with all the praying. She took corners laying over on her side and he was sure she was going to put the bike right down, a dozen times. But she never did. Her tires clung to the road like a fridge magnet, and she let him off in front of the school before half the buses had arrived. He kind of wished there were more kids there to see him arrive like this, riding behind a woman so fine. Only it wouldn't matter—they'd just make fun of him because she was driving and he was the passenger. Not that he minded. Those who didn't resent him because he studied hard and got good grades made fun of him because he didn't drive and took long walks and didn't dress cool. "Your mama buy those pants for you?" one boy asked him one day. "Or she sew that out of one of her own pantlegs?"

"No," Mack told him. "I thought you recognize it—these pants your mama's old bra."

Brother wasn't even his friend, he had no right to start talking about his mama. So when he gave Mack a shove, Mack casually shoved him into the lockers hard enough to rattle his teeth and make him sag, and then walked on. Whole different story if he hadn't grown so tall. Lots of things missing in his life, but God was good to him about his size. Guys wanted to get in his face sometimes, cause they thought he was a likely victim, dressing like he did. So he showed them he wasn't, and they left him alone.

You can't have everybody like you, but you can make it so the ones that don't, keep their distance. Not that Mack ever fought anybody. They'd call him out, he'd just ignore them. They say, Meet me after school, and he says, I ain't doing your homework again, you're on your own now. And if they lay in wait for him, he just run on by. He was fast, but not track team fast. Thing was, he could run forever. Nobody ever kept up, not for long. Guys who pick fights, they aren't the kind to do a lot of solitary running.

So Mack Street had a name for himself, and the name was, I'm here for my own purpose, and if you ain't my friend, leave me alone. Senior year, it was okay now, none of the kids his own age would try to pick on him. Anybody taller than Mack was on the basketball team. But even so, there was nobody who'd be all impressed if they saw him on this bike with this woman. Wasn't that a shame. But you got to live out the life you made for yourself. High school was a dry run for the real world, the principal said at least once per assembly. Mack figured in the grownup world, people wouldn't resent him because he was a hard worker and did good. They'd *hire* him because of that. He'd make a living. And then he'd get the right kind of girlfriend, not the kind that went for flash and strut.

"See you when I see you," said Yolanda.

"You said that just like Martin Lawrence," he said.

"You too young to be watching shit like that," she said.

"Old enough to get a ride from a babe on a bike," he said.

"No, you did that cause you 'crazy, de-*ranged.*' "

They both laughed. Then she said it again. "See you when I see you, Mack Street."

She peeled out and was gone. Everybody turned to look, but at her, not at Mack. She might have dropped off anybody.

Why am I suddenly so hungry to be famous at high school? Famous at high school is like being employee of the month at the sanitation department. Famous at high school like being the last guy cut from the team *before* the first exhibition game. Nobody seen you play except at practice.

But the smell of her was on his shirt. Not a perfume, really, like some of the girls dumped on themselves every morning. Nor a hair product, though her hair had given his face kind of a beating, to the point where he wanted to say, You ever think of cornrows, Yo Yo? only the bike was too loud so he kept it to himself.

Mack didn't eat alone—he had a lunch group he sat with—but mostly he just listened to them brag about their prowess in some game or on a date, or talk raunchy about girls they knew would never speak to them. Some of these guys lived in Baldwin Hills and he knew their cold dreams. Not one of them cared about girls or sports as much as they said. It was other stuff. Family stuff. Personal stuff. Wishes they'd never tell to a soul.

Well, Mack didn't tell them any of his deep stuff, so they were even. Only difference was, he didn't talk about girls or sports, either. Only thing he ever talked about at lunch was lunch, because there was no lying about that, it was right there on the tray in front of them. Apart from that and the weather and was he going to the game or the dance, he just listened and ate and when he was done, he threw away his garbage and stacked his tray and tossed his silverware and went to the library to study.

Usually he studied his subject, though sometimes he still went back over the Shakespeare stuff, just to see if maybe he'd understand any of it better now—and he sometimes did.

Today, though, he looked up motorcycles on the internet till he found the Harley that Yo Yo was driving. It was a fine machine. He liked the way it rumbled under him. Like riding a happy sabertooth, purring the whole way as you hurtle over the ground.

13

PROPERTY VALUES

Between his long walks and his cold dreams, Mack once knew everything that was happening in his neighborhood. But now the long walks took place in Fairyland, and he had the skill of shutting down all but the strongest dreams before they were fully formed. So there were things he didn't know about. Nobody was keeping it a secret, he just wasn't there to notice it.

He knew somebody was moving into the fancy white house just below the drainage valley—he heard all about it when Dr. Phelps died and his second wife got the house in the will and sold it. And he saw a moving van come and guys unload stuff.

What he didn't know was who the new owner was. There was no hurry. He was bound to hear, especially because the house was above the invisible line—it was up the hill, where the money was, and so whatever happened there was big news to the people who lived in the flat.

He was eating dinner with Ivory DeVries's family even though Ivory was a year older than Mack and was off at college down in Orange County. Maybe they missed Ivory and Mack was kind of a reminder of the old days, when they both took part in neighborhood games of hide-and-seek. Back when there were enough kids that they could fan out through half of Baldwin Hills.

So Mack was standing at the sink, helping Ivory's sister Ebony rinse the dishes and load the dishwasher. Ebony had always hated her name, especially because she was very light-skinned. "I mean why did my parents choose each other if it wasn't to make sure they had kids that could pass the damn paper bag test. And then they go and name me Ebony? Why did Ivo get to be Ivory? They name the boy the white name and the girl the black black black name?"

"I hate to break it to you, Ebby," said Mack, "but both those names are definitely black names."

"I guess you right, I ain't never going to see no *blond* boy named Ivory, am I?"

Mack and Ebony got along okay, like brother and sister, not that Mack didn't notice how she filled out lately. But she was still in ninth grade and she was so short he could have fit her under his arm. And there was no sign she was interested anyway. So they did dishes together.

He was telling her about teachers he'd had and they were teasing each other about how Ivo always said Mack liked exactly the teachers that he hated most, which Mack insisted on taking as a compliment. That's when the voices in the living room got loud enough to intrude.

"You think it doesn't hurt property values to have that motorcycle roaring up and down the street at all hours?"

Maybe it was the word *motorcycle* that caught Mack's attention.

"It isn't roaring up and down the street, she's just going home."

"She does *not* just go home. She rides all the way to the top of Cloverdale and then *races* down and skids into her driveway. I've seen her do it twice, so it's a habit."

"Woman looks that fine on a bike, it isn't going to hurt property values one bit."

"Now that is just absurd."

"I value my front yard a lot more now there's a chance she might ride by."

"That is the most disgusting—"

"He just a man, what do you expect?"

"It's like mobile pornography, that's what it is, that girl on her motorcycle!"

"I never liked Dr. Phelps's second wife one bit, but now that we've seen this new girl, I wish we had Mrs. Phelps back again."

"She is *not* like pornography, she's got all her clothes on right up to her neck."

"Motorcycle-riding h—whatever."

"The way those clothes fit her she might as well be naked."

"So let's get together a petition that points *that* out to her. I mean, if she's that close to naked, why not—"

"That's enough out of you, Moses Jones."

"Isn't there a noise ordinance?"

Mack and Ebby grinned at each other, and without even discussing it they went to the passage between the dining room and the living room and saw that while they were doing dishes, somebody convened a meeting of the neighborhood busybodies.

Ebby's mama looked at her pointedly. "This is an adult discussion, Ebby."

Ebby just laughed.

"I don't like your tone, young lady," said Ebby's mama.

"We were just wondering," said Mack, "who you talking about on the motorcycle?"

"The *person* who just moved into Dr. Phelps's old house just below the hairpin on Cloverdale."

"Whom I *asked* to keep the noise down late at night, to which she *rudely* replied that her bike was her only ride so how was she supposed to get home when she finished work at three A.M."

"If she can afford that house she can afford a car."

"She's one of those inhibitionists who can't stand it when people aren't noticing her."

"Exhibitionists."

Ebby poked Mack to try to make him laugh, and it nearly worked. To cover his stifled snort, Mack said, "Um, so she got no name at all? Just 'Motorcycle Ho'?"

"Mack Street, I'm telling Ura Lee you use language like that."

"But Mrs. Jones called her—"

"I called her a motorcycle-riding hoochie mama!"

"Her name is Yolanda White," said Moses Jones. "You want her phone number?"

Joyce Jones smacked a sofa pillow into his face. "You better not have her phone number. I got scissors and you sleep naked."

"That's more than we wanted to know, Joyce," said Eva Sweet Fillmore.

"I'm getting Moses some pajamas this Christmas," said her husband, Hershey. Their standard joke: When Eva Sweet found out that Hershey Fillmore was the one leaving those chocolates in her desk in fourth grade, it's like they had no choice but to get married as soon as they got old enough.

"Yo Yo," said Mack.

"What?" asked Ebby.

"If she likes you, she lets you call her Yo Yo."

"Who does?"

"Yolanda White. The motorcycle-riding hoochie mama."

"If you children are just going to make fun!" said Ebby's mama sharply.

"We're back to the dishes!" cried Ebby and she dragged Mack back into the kitchen, though truth to tell, he wanted to stay and listen. Mrs. DeVries made sure he couldn't hear anything from the kitchen, either—she came to the kitchen, gave a child-maiming glare to Ebony, and closed the door.

"That look could dry up a girl's period," said Ebby.

"Make a man's balls drop right on the floor," said Mack.

"I seen her practice that look in a mirror, and it broke."

"She can start cars with that look."

"Homeland Security list that look as a weapon of mass destruction."

From the living room, Mrs. DeVries's voice came loud and clear. "Quiet with that laughing in there or I come back in and look at you both twice!"

In the end, though, when the meeting was over, Mrs. DeVries came to the kitchen where Mack and Ebony were studying, made a cup of coffee, and told them everything. They were going to get Hershey to write a legal-sounding letter—Hershey was a retired lawyer—to scare her that she'd get sued if she didn't quiet down. And Hershey said there might be something in the deed that he was going to look up.

Mack listened to everything and didn't argue, but he knew—as Ebby had already said in their whispered conversation during homework—that this wasn't about the motorcycle noise. It was about Yolanda White being a single woman who might be anywhere from eighteen to thirty-five, nobody wanted to make a bet, who somehow had the money to buy a house like that.

Mrs. DeVries was incensed. "Who does she think she is, buying a house like that? You got to scrimp and save half your life to afford that house. What business a girl that age got with a million-dollar house?"

"Maybe she had a million dollars," said Ebby.

"Or maybe she has a *man* got a million dollars, mark my words, that's how it's going to turn out. He'll get tired of her and suddenly she'll be left high and dry with a place she can't afford. Foreclosure! That's my bet."

"You don't know how old she is, Mom, and she might have earned it. Maybe she invented a cure for cancer."

"Black woman invents the cure for cancer, it's going to be all over the news. Only way that *Yolanda* be on the news is when she

ODs on drugs or holds up a liquor store or gets busted in the front seat of Hugh Grant's automobile on Sunset."

"Or gets lynched in Baldwin Hills," said Ebby.

"We're writing a letter, not finding a rope, Little Miss I-Don't-Have-to-Honor-My-Father-and-Mother."

"How do you know Yolanda White doesn't honor *her* father and mother?" asked Ebby.

"Because I sincerely doubt she knows who her father *is*."

That hung in the air for a long moment before Mrs. DeVries lost her look of triumph and gave a sort of quick glance toward Mack and then suddenly remembered she had to clean up some more in the living room.

As soon as she was gone, Ebby looked at Mack and said, "What was *that* about?"

"She just remembered I don't know who my daddy is, or my mama," said Mack.

"Isn't that just like grownups. It's okay to judge somebody for being a bastard, but *not* if they're sitting at the table with you."

"Actually, these days we prefer the term 'differently parented.' "

"No," said Ebby solemnly, "I am quite certain the term is 'paternity deficient.' 'Differently parented' means your parents are both the same sex, or there's more than two of them in the same house."

They traded politically correct synonyms for *bastard* till Mrs. DeVries came in and sent Mack home so Ebony could go to bed. "It *is* a school night, and not everybody has the stamina to wander through the neighborhood all night and still be up for school in the morning."

So people *did* notice him walking the streets. They couldn't know that for him, the middle of the night might really be morning, because he'd just slept the night in Fairyland. It was like perpetual jet lag for Mack, without the jet.

At the door, Mack finally asked the only question he was still wondering about. "What if Yolanda *does* get rid of the bike? Would you all welcome her to the neighborhood then?"

"Welcome her! What do you mean, bake cookies and cakes and invite her over? Not a woman like that! Not on your life!"

"Well, then, why should she give up the bike for you, if you don't plan to treat her decent even if she *does* get rid of it?"

"She won't be giving up the motorcycle for us. She'll be giving it up to avoid a big ugly lawsuit." And the door closed with Mack outside.

NEXT MORNING, MRS. TUCKER CAME over for coffee while Miz Smitcher and Mack ate breakfast, which was becoming her custom now, with no kids in the house and Mr. Tucker off to work so early every day. Mack usually kept still, but today he had a lot on his mind.

"Over at DeVries they had a meeting last night."

"About Miss Motorcycle," said Mrs. Tucker.

"Motorcycle ain't the problem," said Mack.

"Wakes me up out of a sound sleep every time she goes by!"

"I mean, last night Mrs. DeVries said it didn't matter if Yolanda give up the bike or not, she *still* not welcome here."

"I completely agree," said Mrs. Tucker. "She cheapens the whole neighborhood."

"If she's got the money to buy the house," said Mack, "then what business is it of anybody else's?"

"Got to have respect for the neighborhood," said Miz Smitcher.

"That bike is her ride," said Mack. "Since when do neighbors have the right to tell you what to drive?"

"We not telling her what to drive," said Mrs. Tucker. "We telling her what *not* to drive at three o'clock in the morning."

"Never woke *me* up," said Mack. Though he immediately realized it was probably because he was in Fairyland at the time.

"Might not have the right in law," said Miz Smitcher, "but we have a natural right to protect our property values."

Mack set down his fork and looked at them both in exasperation. "Can you hear yourselves? Property values! They taught us in school that 'property values' was how white people used to excuse themselves for trying to keep blacks out of their neighborhood."

Mrs. Tucker snapped back, "Don't you go comparing racism to . . . to *cyclism.*"

"Not that you were alive in those days, Mack, so you might know what you're talking about," said Miz Smitcher, "but the only reason property values went down when black people moved in was because of racism. If they just stop being racists, then black people moving in doesn't lower property values."

"So if you stop minding her riding her bike . . . ," Mack began.

"Being black doesn't make a loud noise in the middle of the night," said Miz Smitcher. "Neighbors got a right to have quiet. To keep people from being a public nuisance."

"So you're on their side. To treat this girl like a . . . like a *nigger* just cause—"

"That word does not get said in my house," said Miz Smitcher.

"Just cause she's *young* and *cool.* Wasn't anybody in this neighborhood ever young and cool? I guess not!"

Mrs. Tucker looked at Mack and cocked her head to one side. "I don't know that I ever seen this boy mad like this before."

"Say that word in my house," muttered Miz Smitcher.

"I guess I just made your property values go down," Mack muttered back.

"Listen to me, young man. You may be six foot four and too cool to stand, but you—"

"*I'm* not cool, *Yolanda* cool."

"You don't understand anything about what it means to a black family to own a house! White people been owning houses forever, but here in the United States of Slavery and Sharecropping we never owned anything. Always paying rent to the man when he didn't own us outright."

"You never a sharecropper, Miz Smitcher," said Mack, trying to keep the scorn out of his voice.

"My daddy was. Not a homeowner in this neighborhood who didn't have a grandma or grandpa paying rent to some redneck cracker in the South, and a daddy or a mama paying rent to some slumlord in Watts. These aren't the people who made money and moved to Brentwood and pretended to be white, like O. J. These are the people who made their money and moved to Baldwin Hills cause we wanted to have peace and quiet but still be black."

"She black," said Mack.

"We want to be black *our* way," said Miz Smitcher. "Decent, regular, ordinary people. Not *show* black like those hippity-hop rippety-rappers and that girl on her bike."

Mrs. Tucker spoke into her coffee cup. "She's a little bit old to be calling her a girl."

"How do you know she isn't a decent, regular, ordinary person who happens to ride a motorcycle?" demanded Mack.

"And why do you think I didn't go to that meeting last night?" answered Miz Smitcher.

"Well if you're against what they doing, why are you arguing with me?"

"Because you judging and condemning people you don't even understand. What they doing to that girl, you doing to them. Everybody judging and nobody understanding."

"You were talking about property values," said Mack.

"I was explaining why somebody like that comes here, it makes us all feel like we getting invaded. Like the neighborhood maybe starting to turn trashy. Plenty of places for trashy people to live. They don't have to live here. This neighborhood is an island in a sea of troubles. Somebody young and loud like that, she's some people's worst nightmare."

I know what their worst nightmares are, thought Mack. Or at least what they might be, if they got their wishes.

Out loud, he said, "Well, she's not trashy, she's nice."

Both women raised their eyebrows, and Mrs. Tucker set down her cup. "Oh ho, sounds like love."

"She's ten years older than he is if she's a day," said Miz Smitcher.

"It isn't love," said Mack. "But I did something nobody else in this whole neighborhood bothered to do. I talked to her."

"Joyce Jones talked to her and so did Miss Sweet," said Miz Smitcher.

"They did not talk to her, they talked *at* her, told her what she got to do or else."

"Oh, were you there?" asked Mrs. Tucker.

"I'll tell you about Yolanda White. She sees a kid running to school cause the bus driver took off without me like she always tries to do, and she pulls up in front of me on that bike and gives me a ride to school."

Mrs. Tucker gasped and Miz Smitcher looked at him for a long moment. "You been on that bike?"

Only now did Mack realize that they might not take the right lesson from his experience. "My point is that she's a kind person."

But Miz Smitcher wasn't having it. "She's riding along and she sees a schoolboy and she *gives him a ride?*"

"It was a nice thing to do," Mack insisted.

"So you had your arms around her and you were pressed right up against her back and tell me, Mack, did she drive fast and hard so you had to hold on real tight?"

This was not going the way Mack intended. "We were riding a motorcycle, Miz Smitcher, if you don't hold on you end up sliding along the street."

"Oh, I know what happens if you don't hold on to a motorcycle, Mister," said Miz Smitcher. "I see motorcycle accidents all the time. Skin flayed right off their body, these fools go riding in shorts and a t-shirt and then they spill on the asphalt and get tar and stones imbedded in their *bones* and the muscles torn right off their body cause the pavement's like being sandblasted. And that woman took *my* boy and put him on the back of *her* bike so he rubbing up against her and she drove him along the streets like a crazy woman so she put him at risk of ending up in the hospital with a nurse like me changing the dressings on his skinless body while he screaming in spite of the morphine drip—oh, don't you tell me about how *nice* she is."

Mack knew that anything he said now would just make things worse. He dug into his cereal.

"Don't you sit there and eat that Crispix like you didn't hear a word I said."

"He just trying to think of an answer," said Mrs. Tucker.

"Just trying to finish breakfast so I don't miss my bus," said Mack.

"You're not to go near her, you hear me?" said Miz Smitcher. "You think you're friends with her now—"

"I *know* we not friends." They'd be friends when she let him call her Yo Yo.

"Well you're never going to *be* friends because if I ever see you talking to that woman I'm going to kill her or you or both, and if you get on her motorcycle again, I'm kicking you out of this house!"

"So I'd be dead *and* homeless," said Mack.

"Don't make fun of what I'm telling you!"

Mack got up, rinsed out his dish, and started to put it in the dishwasher.

"Don't! Those are clean in there!" shouted Miz Smitcher.

"You're right," said Mack. "Wouldn't want a dirty dish to spoil the property values in there."

"That's exactly my point!" said Miz Smitcher. "That is *exactly* my point. One dirty dish and you have to rewash the whole batch."

"Well, this whole neighborhood better start rewashing, cause

Yolanda White bought that house and I don't think she going to pay any attention to a neighborhood vigilante committee." He stalked off to get his backpack out of his bedroom.

Behind him, he could hear Miz Smitcher talking to Mrs. Tucker. "She already setting parent against child. She is *divisive*."

Mack couldn't let that go. "*She* isn't divisive! *She* just minding her business! You and me the ones getting divisive!"

"Because of her!" shouted back Miz Smitcher.

Mack stood in his room, holding the bookbag. In all his years in this house, this was the first time he and Miz Smitcher ever shouted at each other in anger.

Which wasn't to say that they never disagreed. But up till now, Mack always gave in, always said yes ma'am, because that was how things stayed smooth. Mack liked things to stay smooth. He didn't care enough about most things to yell at anybody about them.

But suddenly he did care. Why? What was Yo Yo, that he should get so mad when somebody dissed her? Why was he *loyal* to her?

He almost walked back into the kitchen and apologized.

But then it occurred to him: About time I stood up for something around here. Always doing what other people want, well maybe I'm ready to fight for something, and it might as well be Yolanda's right to live here and ride a motorcycle and give a lift to a seventeen-year-old *man* who's probably really more like nineteen anyway.

He was ten yards from the bus when the driver started to pull away. She hadn't been stopped there for two whole seconds and he knew she saw him cause she looked right at him. And today he was pissed off, at Miz Smitcher, at the whole neighborhood, and he was not going to take any shit from a bus driver.

He ran, he sprinted. The bus hadn't gone fifteen feet when he took a flying leap and flung himself against the bus driver's window, slapping the glass with his hand. It startled that driver so bad she whipped her head around to look at him before he even slid down to the ground, and she slammed on the brakes without even thinking what she was doing.

Mack landed on his feet and ran directly in front of the bus and stood on the front bumper and yelled through the windshield into the driver's face. "Open the damn door and take me to school like they pay you to do!"

Mack couldn't see his own face but there must have been something new there, because that driver looked at him with real fear in her eyes.

The door opened.

Mack got off the bumper, hoisted his book bag over his shoulder, and *sauntered* to the door. He stepped up, taking his time, and kept his eyes on her the whole time he walked up the steps and past her. She never looked at him once, just kept her eyes straight forward. She closed the door and the bus started forward with a lurch.

Mack turned toward the back of the bus, looking for a seat. All the other kids were looking at him like he was an alien. But not just any alien. He was the alien who had faced down the devil driver. Plenty of them had been left behind, too, over the years, and Mack was the first person to make her stop and wait. So what he saw in the other kids' eyes was awe or delight or amusement, anyway. They were all kids, so they were used to having to take crap from adults whenever the adults felt like dishing it out.

When Mack sat down, Terrence Heck gave him a hood handshake and Quon Brown called out from two rows behind him, in a voice pretending to be a girl, "You my hero, Mack Street."

Mack turned around and grinned. "That be Mr. *Super* Hero to you, Quon."

When they got to school, the bus driver was still fuming, and when he passed her, she muttered, "You want a ride, you get to the bus stop on time."

Mack whirled on her and glared at her and damn if he didn't discover in that very moment that *he* had a look. Just like Mrs. DeVries. He could just focus his eyes on this mean bus driver and she wilted like lettuce in the microwave. "You paid to take children to school," he said to her. "You do your job or lose it."

Then he jumped down the steps like he always did, and behind him the other kids, who had heard the exchange, whooped and laughed and whistled their way past the driver and out of the bus.

I did my own little revolution, thought Mack, and I feel fine.

But that night, when he got back into the neighborhood, it didn't take long for him to hear that Hershey Fillmore had found the perfect way to get rid of Yolanda White. Baldwin Hills had originally been built as a white neighborhood, and as old Hershey suspected, there were covenants in the deeds of a lot of the houses. There was one on the deed to Dr. Phelps's house, which Yolanda White had just purchased.

It seemed that the property could not be sold to a person of color.

"You mean a bunch of black people are going to sue to enforce a racist deed?" Mack asked, incredulous.

"They not going to enforce it, those things don't hold up in court anymore," said Ebby. "No, they going to try to nullify the sale because *she* didn't strike it out of the deed when she bought the house."

"They lost their minds or something? Dr. Phelps didn't strike it out either or it wouldn't have been there."

"Hate is an ugly thing," said Ebby.

"I'll tell you what," said Mack. "Somebody needs to tell that woman what they planning to do."

"And I guess that means you plan to be that somebody?"

"Who else? I already talked to her once."

Ebby was taken aback. "When you talk to her?"

"She give me a ride to school a couple of weeks ago."

"And you didn't mention that last night?" Ebby asked.

"Didn't come up," he said.

"The very woman everybody was talking about in a whole *meeting* and it 'didn't come up'?"

Was Ebby going insane on him? "I told you she went by Yo Yo," said Mack. "So I must have met her. If you asked me how, I would've told you."

"I *thought* we was friends, Mack Street." And she turned around and went back inside her house, leaving him out on the street, feeling, for the first time in many years, excluded from one of the homes in Baldwin Hills.

14

PLAYING POOL

Mack had a cold dream that night, and it was Yolanda White's dream.

In the dream, Yo Yo rode a powerful horse across a prairie, with herds of cattle grazing in the shade of scattered trees or drinking from shallow streams. But the sky wasn't the shining blue of cowboy country, it was sick yellow and brown, like the worst day of smog all wrapped up in a dust storm.

Up in that smog, there was something flying, something ugly and awful, and Yo Yo knew that she had to fight that thing and kill it, or it was going to snatch up all the cattle, one by one or ten by ten, and carry them away and eat them and spit out the bones.

In the dream Mack saw a mountain of bones, and perched on top of it a creature like a banana slug, it was so filthy and slimy and thick. Only after creeping and sliming around awhile on top of the pile of bones it unfolded a huge pair of wings like a moth and took off up into the smoky sky in search of more, because it was always hungry.

It was Yo Yo's job to stop it from eating her cattle.

The thing is, through that whole dream, Yo Yo wasn't alone. It drove Mack crazy because try as he might, he couldn't bend the dream, couldn't make the woman turn her head and see who it was riding with her. Sometimes Mack thought the other person was on the horse behind her, and sometimes he thought the other person was flying alongside like a bird, or running like a dog, always just out of sight.

Mack couldn't help but think: Maybe it's me.

Maybe she needs me and that's why I'm seeing this dream. Maybe her deep wish is not the death of the dragonslug. Maybe what she's wishing for is that invisible companion.

The girl rode up to the mountain of old bones, and the huge slug spread its wings and flew, and it was time to kill it or give up and let it devour the whole herd. Only then did she realize that she didn't have a gun or a spear or even so much as a rock to throw. Somehow she had lost her weapon—though in the dream Mack never noticed her having a weapon in the first place.

The flying slug was spiraling down at her, and then suddenly the bird or dog or man who was with her, he—or it—leapt at the monster. Always it was visible only out of the corner of her eye, so Mack couldn't see who it was or whether the monster killed it or whether it sank its teeth or a beak or a knife into the beast. Because just at the moment when Yo Yo was turning to look, the dream stopped.

It stopped, and not because Mack had been able to turn it into his own dream of the canyon. It just stopped.

But he remembered his dream, and realized that his dream and hers were alike. She had somebody beside her in her dream, and Mack had somebody beside him in his. Somebody you could never quite look at.

Each of us is in the other one's dream.

She needs me to kill that dragonslug. And I need her to . . . or do I? She's the one driving, if she's the person in my dream. She's the one who drives me into danger.

But in *her* dream she needs me. In her dream I'm the hero who slays the . . .

No. I'm the idiot who *tries*. Nothing to say that I succeed.

If it's me. If I'm the one who attacks that flying slug.

If I'm part of her wish, and her wish comes true, then it'll come true some ugly way, and do I want to be a part of that?

So he decided not to go up the street to her house today. Instead, though it was so early in the morning that it was still full dark, he got up and jogged down the street to Skinny House. If he woke Puck that was too damn bad. Puck was immortal—waking up early one morning wouldn't kill him.

He should have known Puck would be awake, racking up a game of pool on a table that nearly filled the living room. The other furniture was stacked up along one wall, and there was more of it than could have fit in the living room even without the pool table.

"Going into the moving and storage business?" Mack asked him.

"Quiet. This is a tricky shot."

"It's the *break*," said Mack.

Puck looked up at him, put a finger to his lips, then let fly with a sharp stroke of the cue.

The white ball struck at only the slightest angle from dead center on the front ball. All of them took off, four of them going directly into four different pockets. And after only another rebound or two, all the others but the eight ball and the cue ball were in the pockets. And the eight ball teetered on the edge.

"You distracted me," said Puck. "Ruined my shot."

Mack snorted. "Like a three-year-old. 'Look what you made me do.'"

"I don't use magic on shots like that," said Puck.

"Bullshit," said Mack.

"Not to an exorbitant degree, anyway," said Puck. "I've had a lot of practice."

"She's in my dream and it's not like the others," said Mack. "It's not her wish."

"You mind telling me who 'she' is?"

"Yolanda White. Yo Yo. Girl on a motorcycle, lives just below the drainage basin. She gave me a ride to school a couple of weeks ago."

"Stay away from women on motorcycles," said Puck. "They're usually bad for you."

"Why do I get her dream when it's not a wish?"

"Maybe she doesn't want anything."

"Doesn't explain why I dreamed her dream."

"Backup," said Puck.

At first Mack thought he was giving him a command, and he took a step back.

Puck rolled his eyes. "Come on, Mack, you're not stupid. I mean you're like a backup device for a computer. She's storing copies of her most important dreams in your head."

"I don't mean to repeat myself, but bullshit."

"You asked me a question, I did my best to answer."

"That wasn't your best," said Mack. "You know what happens with those cold dreams is magic, and magic is something you know about."

"I don't always know what *he's* doing."

"Tell me what she's doing in my dreams."

"Maybe *she's* not doing anything," said Puck. "Maybe she doesn't even know you're having her dreams."

Something occurred to Mack. "What do *you* have to do with my dreams?"

"Think of me as being an appreciative audience. Front-row seat."

"You see my dreams?"

"I see you dreaming," said Puck.

"You have anything to do with the way they sometimes come true?"

"I don't have the power to make wishes come true."

"That wasn't what I asked."

Puck sent the cue ball into the eight ball with such force that it struck the back of a corner pocket and flew straight back out, zipped across the table, and dropped into the opposite corner pocket.

"That is such *crap*," said Mack. "Why is that even fun, when you can make it go wherever you want?"

"I'm trying to entertain you," said Puck. He snapped his fingers, and the balls all flew up as if the pockets were spitting them out. They hit the table and rolled back into a triangle at the opposite end from where they had been before the break.

"Distract me, you mean," said Mack.

"Is it working?" Puck broke again. The balls flew around the table and, when they finally came to rest, they were back in their original order, except that the cue ball was where the eight ball had been, in the midst of the triangle, and the eight ball was now in the cue ball's position on the opposite dot.

"How long were you doing this before I got here?" asked Mack.

"None of this stuff was here until you slid into the yard a few minutes ago," said Puck. "When you're not around, I just hang on a hook in the closet like your pants."

"You're the one who makes them come true," said Mack. "The dreams, I mean."

"Am not," said Puck. "*He* is."

"But you . . . you *bend* them."

Puck shrugged. "Believe what you want."

"What does her dream mean? And mine?"

"Can't tell you less I know what the dreams are."

"You know all my dreams."

"I know the dreams that come from other people's wishes," said Puck. "But I don't see *her* dreams, nor yours either. Weren't wishes anyway, right?"

Mack knew that if he told Puck the dreams, there was a danger he'd meddle with them or make something out of them. At the same time, Mack had to know what that business was with the flying slug, and who it was sitting beside him in his own plunge through the flash flood in the canyon. He finally decided to tell him Yo Yo's dream, but not his own. It made him feel disloyal and hypocritical.

Puck listened with interest and, Mack suspected, amusement. He was silent for a good long while after Mack finished telling the dream. "What a dangerous girl she is," he finally said.

"Dangerous to who?" said Mack.

"She can't do anything without you," said Puck.

"That's what the dream means?"

Puck smiled. "It's the truth, whether the dream means anything or not."

"She's the one gave *me* a ride."

"Tell you what," said Puck. "I'll tell you the absolute truth. If you stay with her and help her, you'll have a thrilling time, but you'll end up dead."

"How?" demanded Mack. "A bike accident? Or something else?"

"Of course, you'll end up dead anyway," said Puck. "Being mortal and therefore built to break."

"*You* got broke up pretty bad a few years ago, as I remember."

"Never let yourself get pecked and picked up and dropped by birds when you're about an inch and a half high."

"If it comes up, I'll keep that in mind."

"Did I ever thank you for finding me?" asked Puck.

"No," said Mack. "But I never expected you to."

"Good thing, cause I'm not going to. You did me no favor."

"You called out to me, man. That's the only way I found you."

"Did not," said Puck. "That would be pathetic."

"You called my name and I heard your voice come from the bushes and that's how I found you."

A smile crossed his face. "Well, isn't that sweet."

"What's sweet?"

The smile left his face. "It wasn't me who called you."

"Who, then?"

"Must have been the Queen."

"The one in that floating mason jar?"

"She's the *only* Queen," said Puck. "All others are sloppy imitations, not worthy of the name."

"Titania. Mab."

"Only fools and mortals would try to contain her in a name," said Puck. "She is my lady."

"Not according to Shakespeare," said Mack. "You were Oberon's buddy and you put that potion in her eyes so she fell in love with the ass-faced guy."

"Ass-faced." Puck got a real kick out of that. In the midst of a great heaving laugh, he broke again. This time the balls bounced all over and every single one of them came to rest flush against one of the sides, so the middle of the table was completely clear.

"That's more like how *I* break," said Mack.

Puck proceeded to hit the balls in numerical order, putting each one into a pocket without touching any of the other balls.

"Wasn't Shakespeare right?" asked Mack.

"Shakespeare knew about me and making mortals fall in love," said Puck. "Had nothing to do with a potion, but he never forgave me for getting him married to Anne Hathaway. She was seven years older than him and her eyes were cocked. And for three years I had him so silly with love for her that he thought she was the most beautiful girl in the world. She was pregnant when he married her, but what nobody knows is that he had to beg her to marry him."

"She didn't want him?"

"She thought he was making fun of her."

"So what happened when the potion wore off in three years?" asked Mack.

"It wasn't a potion, I told you. And it didn't wear off. I got tired of it. It wasn't amusing anymore. So I set him free."

"He woke up one morning and—"

"It wasn't morning. He had just come home from a day's work at his father's glove shop and she was putting the twins to bed and he swept her up in a fond embrace and kissed her all over her face, and right in the middle of that I gave him back to himself." Puck sighed. "He didn't get the joke. I don't like assholes who got no sense of humor."

"You're such a bastard," said Mack.

"You'd know."

"I'm an *abandoned* child," said Mack. "But I didn't mean that kind of bastard anyway."

Puck smiled maliciously. "I amuse myself by watching a perpetual TV series called 'Messing with the Mortals.' I'm the host."

"What did he do?"

"To me? What *could* he do? And as for Anne Hathaway, Will was such a *nice* boy. He couldn't stand to be with her—she repulsed him physically, and he was filled with loathing for how he had been used. Very resentful. But there was no getting out of the marriage—in those days you just had to hope for a dose of smallpox or a bad childbirth to get you out of an unpleasant coupling—and besides, he knew it wasn't *her* fault, so why should he punish her for loving the only man who had ever wooed her?"

"You so understanding."

"Years of study. I know what makes these mortals tick. A hundred different hungers, but most especially the hunger to make babies, the longing to belong, the dread of death."

"Freud and Jung and you, masters of the mind."

"So Will Shakestaffe got himself taken on as a substitute in a traveling company that had a lead actor die suddenly, so they had to reshuffle all the roles. He showed them some of the sonnets he had written for his beloved wife and they mocked him for being such a bad writer—and it's true, nobody does their best poems when the love is artificial. The only one he ever allowed to be published was the one that punned on Anne's last name—'hate away' for 'Hathaway.' So he had to show them he was a good writer by rewriting some speeches and adding lines to his own bit parts. It really pissed off the big boys in the company, because he was getting laughs and tears for tiny parts, but the audience loved his rewrites and the partners weren't stupid. They had him rewrite the leading actors' speeches, too, until they had some plays that were more Shakespeare than the original writers' work. And they nicknamed him Shake-scene."

"So they accepted him."

"He hated the nickname," said Puck. "And they wouldn't even look at his first complete script. That was why he quit and joined a company that would treat him with respect and put on his plays. So you see, I did him a favor. I started him on his great career by making him fall in love with an unlovable woman."

"And broke her heart when he left her," said Mack.

"She had three good years of a husband who was completely devoted to her," said Puck. "That's two years and fifty weeks more than most wives get."

"He wouldn't have been an actor without your little prank?"

"Oh, he would have been," said Puck. "He was part-timing with a company when he met Anne."

He really couldn't see that he had caused any harm. "So you postponed his career."

"I postponed his *acting* career," said Puck. "It was loving Anne Hathaway that made a bad poet of him. And the ridicule he got for those poems that made him a great playwright."

And now Mack understood something. "You're the one who twists the dreams."

"Twists? What are you talking about?"

"Tamika dreams of swimming and you put her inside a waterbed."

"I *woke* her father up, didn't I? Not my fault if he took so long figuring out where she was and getting her out."

"And what about Deacon Landry and Juanettia Post? It was *his* wish, not hers, and why did you have to make them get found on the floor right in the middle of the sanctuary?"

"It was the deacon's wish to be irresistible to her. *She* was the one acting under compulsion, *he* could have stopped whenever he wanted. All I did was pick the place where they saw each other next. And you have to admit it was funny."

"They both had to move away, and it broke up his marriage."

"I didn't make up the wish."

"You made them get caught."

"Man has no business wishing for a woman ain't his wife," said Puck.

"Oh, now you're Mr. Morality."

"He was a deacon," said Puck. "He judged other people. I thought it was fair."

"But in the real world, without this magic, he wouldn't have done anything about it."

"So I showed who he really was."

"Having a wish in your heart, a man can't help that," said Mack. "He's only a bad man if he acts on it."

"Well, there you are. This beautiful woman suddenly offered him what he had no right to have. Nobody made him take it."

"So it was all his fault."

"I set them up. They knock themselves down."

"So you're the judge."

"They judge themselves."

"You make me sick."

"You're so sanctimonious," said Puck. "Come on, admit it, you think it's funny, too. You're only making yourself angry cause you think you ought to."

"These people are my friends," said Mack.

"You were a little boy then, Mack," said Puck.

"I mean the people in this place. My neighborhood. All of them."

"You think so?" said Puck. "There *are* no friends. There *is* no love. Just hunger and illusion. You hunger till you get the illusion of being fed, but you feel empty again in a moment and then all your love and desire go somewhere else, to someone else. You don't love these people, you just need to belong and these are the people who happened to be close by."

"You don't understand anything."

"You told me to tell you the truth," said Puck.

"You love things to be ugly."

"I like things to be entertaining," said Puck. "You have no idea how boring it gets, living forever."

"So if this furniture and this pool table didn't appear until I showed up, how were you entertaining yourself before I got here?"

"I was planning my shots," said Puck.

"You never tell the truth about anything."

"I never lie," said Puck.

"*That* was a lie," said Mack.

"Believe what you want," said Puck. "Mortals always do."

"What are you doing here?" demanded Mack. "Why are you hanging around in my neighborhood? Why don't you go and have your fun at somebody else's expense?"

Puck shook his head. "You think I picked this place?"

"Who did, then?"

"*He* did," said Puck.

"Doesn't mean *you* have to stay."

Puck stood upright and threw the pool cue at Mack. It hovered in the air, the tip right against Mack's chest, as if it were a spear aimed at his heart. "I'm his slave, you fool, not his buddy. And now not even that. Not even his slave. His *prisoner.*"

"This is a jail?"

Puck shook his head. "Go away. I'm tired of pool, anyway. Like you said, it's no challenge."

"No wonder Professor Williams wanted to kill you."

"Oh, do you want to, too? Get in line," said Puck. "You got to give Will Shakespeare credit for this: He didn't hate me. He understood."

"Yeah, right, you got no choice."

"Oh, I got choices. But you're so stupid, it don't occur to you that the other choices might be worse." Puck glared at Mack and then he reached down and started stuffing pool balls into his mouth and swallowing them. They went down his throat like a rats down a python, bulging as they passed. He was taking the balls in numerical order and after each one he gave a little belch.

It was clear the conversation was over. Mack left.

15

YO YO

Ceese Tucker heard about it from his mother, who got it from Ura Lee Smitcher, who was about out of her mind she was so angry and worried about that motorcycle mama giving rides to her boy Mack. "Corrupting a minor is still a crime in this state," said Ceese's mama as he ate his supper. "That's what I told Ura Lee and that's what I'm telling you. Now you go arrest that woman."

"Mama," said Ceese, "I'm eating."

"Oh, so you intend to be one of those *fat* cops with your belly hanging down over your belt. One of those cops that watches criminals do whatever they want but he too fat and lazy to *do* anything."

"Mama, giving a ride to a seventeen-year-old boy who's late for school is not going to get that woman convicted of anything in any court, and if I arrested her it would make me look like an idiot and I'm still on probation, so all that would happen is I might get dropped from the LAPD and your motorcycle mama would still be at large."

"Ain't that just like the law. Never does a thing to help black people."

"Just think about it for a minute, Mama."

"You saying I don't think less you tell me to?"

"Mama, if a *white* cop came and arrested a black woman for giving a ride to a high school boy, you'd be first in line to call that racial profiling or harassment or some such thing."

"You ain't a white cop," said Mama.

"The law's the law," said Ceese. "And my job is one I want to keep."

"I remember my daddy telling me," said Mama, "that back in the South, somebody got out of line, he come home and find his house on fire or burned right down to the ground. That generally worked to give him the idea his neighbors wanted him to move out."

"Now that *is* a crime, Mama, and a serious one. Burning somebody's house down. I hope I never hear you or anybody else in this neighborhood talking like that. Because now if something *did* happen to her house, I'd be obstructing justice not to tell them what you said."

"They turned you completely white, didn't they. Put a badge on you, and you a white man, just like that, turn in your own mama."

"It didn't turn me white, it turned me into a cop. I'm a *good* cop, Mama, and that means I don't just go arresting somebody because their neighbors don't like her. And it also means that when a real crime *is* committed, I will see to it that the perpetrators are arrested and tried."

"So having you here makes that hoochie mama safe to prey on the young boys of our neighborhood and makes it *un*safe for us to do a single thing about it."

"That's right, Mama. Now you got somebody to blame—me. Feel better?"

"I'm just sorry I fixed you supper. Breakfast tomorrow I ought to make you eat cold cornflakes. Ought to make you sit on the back porch to eat them."

"Mama, I love you, but you worry me sometimes."

Ceese was worried about more than Mama threatening not to fix him a good breakfast. No shortage of fast-food places with good egg-and-biscuit breakfasts before he had to eat cornflakes. And come to think of it, cornflakes weren't bad, either.

What worried him was a woman on a motorcycle taking special note of Mack Street. The memories came flooding back, of that woman in black leather and a motorcycle helmet who stood there on the landing of the stairs in the hospital and urged him—no, made him *want*—to throw baby Mack down and end his life on the concrete at the bottom.

She wanted him dead, and now she's giving him rides on a very dangerous machine. Without a helmet.

If it's the same woman.

How could it be? That was seventeen years ago. Nobody would call her a young woman *now*, the way they were all talking about Yolanda White.

Lots of people ride motorcycles. Lots of women, for that matter.

That other woman, though, she knew Mr. Christmas or Bag Man or Puck or whatever his name is. Which means she's probably just like him. A fairy. An immortal. In which case she could look as young as ever, even after seventeen years. Could be the same woman. Might not be, but *could* be.

Which is why Ceese got up from the supper table, rinsed his dishes, put them in the dishwasher, added the soap, started it up, then strapped on his gun and headed out the door to walk up the street.

It occurred to him that this might be more convincing if he arrived in a patrol car.

Then it occurred to him that if this was an ordinary woman who just moved into a neighborhood that didn't appreciate her, there really wasn't much point to the visit. And if this Yolanda was actually a fairy like Puck, he was in serious danger of getting turned upside down or inside out or something without her lifting a finger.

But if it *was* the woman from his childhood, the one who wanted Mack dead, she hadn't forced anything then. She made him *want* to kill baby Mack, but she didn't make him *do* it. And she didn't use any magic power to kill the baby herself, either.

Maybe she wasn't as powerful as he feared.

Still, he couldn't help but wish that this confrontation was happening in Fairyland, where he was very, very large, and fairies were very, very little.

Ceese walked up the hill, remembering seventeen years before when he walked up this same street with Raymo, carrying a skateboard under his arm and fake weed in his pocket. He had seen enough weed since then to know that they'd been scammed. Finding the baby probably saved him from smoking something poisonous or at least sickening. And it occurred to him right then: Did Raymo know it was fake? Was he setting Ceese up to be humiliated? Look what I got Ceese to smoke!

Well, it didn't work. Ceese was a cop now. And Raymo was . . . somewhere. Doing something. His family moved out before he got out of high school. Moved north somewhere. Central Valley. Raymo was probably the biggest hood in a small town. Well, that was all right. In LA, Raymo would have had plenty of really evil guys to imitate; in a more innocent town, he'd be limited by the evil he was able to think up for himself.

Trouble was, Raymo was kind of a creative guy.

And what if he didn't stay in Fresno or Milpitas or wherever the hell he was? After high school, why would he stay? What if he came back to LA and found himself a spot in South Central or Compton? Would there come a day when Ceese came face to face with Raymo again, only this time he's a cop with a gun and the law on his side, and Raymo is . . .

Not the same dumb malicious kid he was, that's for sure. Something more. Something worse.

If my life was touched by whatever power brought Mack and these fairies into our life, why wasn't Raymo touched? Or was he?

Ceese was standing in front of the Phelps house. Where Yolanda White lived. There were some lights on, but what did that mean? Garage door was closed so he couldn't tell if the bike was there or not.

Why was he afraid? He was a cop, but he was also a neighbor. He wished he hadn't strapped on his gun.

He passed through the low gate and walked to the front door and rang the doorbell. Still had the chimes that Mrs. Phelps liked so much. Longest door chiming in Baldwin Hills. And she'd never answer the door till they finished chiming.

Yolanda White apparently had no such qualms. The door was open less than halfway through the complicated melody. "Oh, good heavens," she said—not exactly the expletive he expected her to use. "A policeman at my door. What is it, the noise of the motorcycle or a charge that I was speeding? Or are you just here on a neighborly visit?"

Ceese was taken aback, but he let himself smile. "All of the above, Miz Yolanda."

"Miz Yolanda? Am I that old and still single?" She held the door wider so he could come in.

"Miz White, then," he said as he entered.

She asked him to sit, and when he did, on a big white furry polar bear of a couch, she sat down across from him on an ebony cube. "So," she said. "Let me guess. My bike is noisy, I drive too fast, I dress too sexy, and the Welcome Wagon wears a gun."

"Just got off work," said Ceese. "Cecil Tucker's my name. Everybody calls me Ceese."

"As in 'cease and desist'? You should have grown up to be a

lawyer, not a cop. You got a brother named Nolo Contendere? What about Sic Transit Gloria Mundi?"

"I don't speak Spanish," said Ceese. "And I don't know any Gloria."

"So you're the one they chose to come tell me what they been hinting about since I got here."

"No, ma'am," said Ceese. "I suppose I chose myself."

"So what are you? Neighborhood watch? LAPD? Or you wanting to take me dancing?"

"I wanted to meet you is all. No dancing."

"Got something against dancing?"

"I don't dance."

"Two left feet? Got no rhythm? Or just never found anybody who'd dance with you?"

"I see I'm out of my league here," said Ceese. "I just can't think as fast as you talk."

"My problem, Officer Cease and Desist, is that I never once found a man who could."

"You're a fast talker."

"There *was* one, a long time ago. With him, when we were together I didn't want him thinking and he didn't want me talking."

"I'm glad to know you have happy erotic memories," said Ceese.

"Wo, now, that was a fine speech. They teach you that in cop school?"

"The word 'erotic' comes up now and then."

"I meant irony. When you say what you don't mean. Cause you ain't happy I got erotic memories. You don't care about me at all. In fact, you look to me like you halfway afraid of me, and whoever heard of a cop scared of a motorcycle mama?"

The challenge in her voice, her words, her posture, woke a memory in him. Was that how the woman in the black helmet and black leather had stood, looking up at him from the landing on the hospital stairs? Was that how she stood when she was talking to Bag Man on the street?

At that moment the doorbell rang, startling Ceese and making Yolanda laugh. "Now *here's* the guest I was looking for."

She strode to the door, flung it open, and there stood Mack Street.

Mack looked from Yolanda to Ceese and back to Yolanda.

"Why, it's that nice boy I gave a ride to school," said Yolanda.

Mack grinned. "I didn't know you knew each other."

"Step away from the door," said Ceese.

He was pointing his gun at her.

"Is that loaded?" she said.

"Mack, go home. Now. Get out of here."

"Are you crazy?" asked Mack. "She wasn't doing anything."

"I wasn't doing anything," said Yolanda.

"You called him here," said Ceese. "You made him come."

"She did not," said Mack.

"I'm just an unforgettable woman, Mr. Cop," said Yolanda.

"I came to tell her about how they planning to sue her," said Mack. "I think that's wrong."

"Get the hell out of here, Mack," said Ceese intensely. "She's got you under her control."

But Mack was rooted to the spot. "Ceese, you lost your mind?"

"I guess he's the jealous type," said Yolanda. "And we haven't even dated yet."

"I know you," Ceese said to her.

"That line might work in bars, but not in my living room."

"We met. A long time ago."

"Well, what can I say? I'm kind of memorable, and you just ain't." Yolanda grinned. "What I do that makes you want to shoot me?"

"I was twelve. I was holding a baby."

"No sir, doesn't stir a memory," said Yolanda. "Besides which, if you was twelve then, I must have been about nine."

"You were exactly the age you are now," said Ceese.

"Then it wasn't me."

"You couldn't make me do it then," said Ceese. "So you come back to do it yourself?"

"Do what?" asked Mack.

"Kill you," said Ceese.

Yolanda laughed.

"She can't kill me," said Mack.

"Why not?" asked Ceese.

"I'm her hero."

Mack said the words with such simplicity and truth that it made Ceese lower his weapon a little.

"You are?" asked Yolanda. "I always wanted one."

"Your dream," said Mack. "When the flying slug—the dragon, whatever it is—when it comes to kill you, I'm the one who fights it."

"Well, I'll be damned," she said. "And here I thought it was just my dog."

Mack looked disappointed. "You have a dog?"

She shook her head. "Always meant to get one though."

"What are you talking about?" asked Ceese.

"Ceese, you know I see dreams," said Mack. "But I was *in* her dream."

"Mack, she tried to make me kill you. When you were a baby. The day I found you. She stood there and looked at me and all I wanted to do was kill you."

"Why?"

"I don't know why," said Ceese. "I just know that it took all the strength I had to keep from doing it. And I'm not going to let her kill you now."

Yolanda laughed. "You poor stupid sumbitch, don't you get it yet?"

And with those words, Ceese felt an overwhelming need to turn and point the gun at Mack.

"God help me," whispered Ceese. But he knew with all his heart that he was going to kill Mack. The person he loved best in all the world. There was his finger on the trigger. The gun pointed straight at Mack's heart.

"God doesn't sweat the small stuff," said Yolanda. "He ain't going to interfere."

"Like you'd know," said Ceese. He was sweating from the effort of not pulling the trigger.

"Ceese, please put down that gun," said Mack.

"Just get out of here," Ceese said between clenched teeth.

"Yolanda," said Mack. "Let go of him. Please."

"*He* the one with the gun," said Yolanda.

"Titania," said Mack, in a louder voice. "Let him go."

She laughed. "You silly boy, do you think I ever told Will Shakespeare my real name?"

"Mab," said Mack. "Don't do this to him."

"Those things are dangerous. You never know where they'll be pointing when they go off."

"He couldn't have hurt *you*," said Mack. "Your soul is in a glass jar in a clearing with a panther watching over it."

When the compulsion left Ceese it felt like somebody removed a wall he'd been leaning against. He stumbled and fell to one knee.

"Bend yo' knee, bow yo' head," said Yolanda. "Tote that barge until yo' dead."

"Mack," whispered Ceese. "I'm sorry."

"Why don't you boys just both sit down on the couch and tell me why you come to see me, 'stead of messing around with guns and shit."

Ceese wanted to plunge out that front door and run home. Or farther. As far as he could go to get the sense of helplessness off him. It clung to him like the stink of skunk.

But he couldn't go and leave Mack here alone.

So he found himself sitting on the shaggy white couch, Mack beside him, his gun still lying on the floor where he'd dropped it.

"I came to warn you," said Mack. "About the neighbors. They plan to use the law on you. Cause your house's deed got a clause in it—"

"Sandy Claus?" asked Yolanda brightly.

"Anyway, that's cause I didn't know who you were. Till you made him point the gun at me. Then I knew."

"You knew less than you think," said Yolanda. She turned to Ceese. "And *you,* did you come to kill me?"

"I had to know if it was you. The same one."

"You're very strong," said Yolanda. "Twice now, you told me no. Nobody tells me no."

"You can't kill Mack Street," said Ceese.

"Oh, you silly boy," she said. "That was then, this is now. I don't want him dead *now.* Back then he was still new, just a little wad of evil that my husband squirted out into the world. I was cleaning up. Only you wouldn't do it, Cecil Tucker. And now Mack's grown up into something else. Not just a changeling anymore."

"What's going on?" asked Mack. "Why did I suddenly dream your dream?"

"Because I came into your neighborhood," said Yolanda. "Because I needed a hero. Because nobody around here can wish for anything without it showing up in your dreams."

"Why?"

"Because you the Keeper of Dreams," said Yolanda. "You the Guardian of Wishes. Deep desire, it flows to you. From the moment you popped out of that chimney up there, all the desires around you, they got channeled. They flowed. Right to you, into you, all the power of all the wishing of your whole neighborhood."

"Why?" demanded Mack again.

"So he can worm his way back into the world."

"Who?" asked Ceese.

"My husband," said Yolanda. "The one Will Shakespeare knew as Oberon. Or as he likes to think of himself, the Master of the Universe." She laughed bitterly. "He was cruel, my husband. Not like Puck—not just playful. He was tired of flirting with the human race, he said. He was going to make an end of you and start over with some other kind of creature. One that wouldn't keep fighting him. And I didn't want to. I *like* humans. And Puck, he doesn't so much like you as like playing with you, but I was able to persuade him to help me."

"Help you what?" asked Ceese.

"Bind the old devil deep inside the earth," said Yolanda. "It took the two of us and a great circle of fairies. We danced on Stonehenge and I called out his name. Because he *told* me his name, you see."

"What is it?" Mack quickly asked.

"Don't even ask that," said Yolanda. "That's his desire, talking through you. If you say his true name, then he can come out. You're his key, don't you see? All the power of these hundreds of humans is stored up in you, except whatever got bled off to grant their foolish wishes. You've been strong for him, I can see it. You've been keeping it in, not letting any of it out for a long time. But now he wants it out, and he'll have it. If he could get you to say his name, then it would be easier. He could rise up out of the earth himself and no one could stop him then. He'd be like in the ancient days when our kind first came to earth and we all had the shape he's never given up. The first thing he'd do, Mack Street, is swallow you whole, so all that stored-up power was inside him."

"And you're here to stop him?" asked Ceese.

"I'm not here," she said. "That's what Mack understands and you don't. I'm trapped in a jar in a clearing, guarded by a panther, and so is Puck. When we bound Oberon, when he was writhing on the ground in the middle of the henge, when he was sinking down into the earth and it was swallowing him up to hold him captive so he couldn't destroy the human race, he still had his power over Puck. Once a slave to the king of the fairies, then you're never really free. He can't be trusted, poor Puck, because he's bound by my husband's will. So at the last moment, the old worm tore the light out of us and put it in two jars and hung them like lanterns in a faraway place where he thought we'd never find it."

She sighed. "It took us all these years. Nearly four hundred years. And yet we couldn't get to where he held us captive. Because we could only control bodies in *this* world. Until you were born, Mack, if you want to call it that, all we could do was petty magicks. Bending humans to our will. Puck didn't mind—it amused him—but I was tired of using castoff bodies and it didn't amuse me to torment the others who still had a firm grip on theirs. We hung around here, but we went our separate ways. Until we felt it. The surge of power. The darkness like a sudden blast of licorice. Of anise. We knew he had found a passageway that let him push something of himself out into the world. Puck found the way to you first—of course he would, he's still bound to Oberon and such binding works both ways, Oberon can't stir without Puck feeling it. I'm bound, too, but only as a wife. So you were already born when I arrived. Born and put in that shopping bag and taken back to the spout through which the old worm reaches into this world."

"There's no way that Mack is something evil," said Ceese, finally making some sense of what she was saying.

"Is a hammer a good carpenter or a bad one?" asked Yolanda. "The answer is, it's no carpenter at all, and the good or bad of the hammer depends on how the carpenter uses it."

"He's not a tool, either."

"He's a tool when Oberon says he is. He'll have the use of him when he wants."

"He's the worm in your dream," Mack said. "The slug with wings. The one I fight."

"I don't know how twisted up that dream gets, but Mack, when you go to the worm, it's not to fight him. It's to be swallowed. It's to bring the power of these people into him. Nourish him. Make him mighty again."

"No way," said Mack. "I won't do it."

"You're not like Ceese here. I think maybe Ceese *could* tell him no. But you could no more deny him than your finger could refuse to pick your nose. May not like the work, but it can't say no."

"You saying Mack's not really human?" Ceese asked.

"Mack is what he is. Once you turn magic loose in the world, it becomes what it becomes. I don't know how reliable a tool he'll be. And you can count on this—Oberon hasn't been waiting all this time just to have everything depend on a changeling who's been under the daily influence of a human as strong as you, Cecil Tucker."

"So what does that mean?" asked Mack. "What am I supposed to do?"

"You're not supposed to do anything," said Ceese. "Do you think you can *trust* this woman? She's out for herself."

"Well, of course I am," said Yolanda. "But it so happens that what I want—to keep Oberon penned up in hell, or whatever you want to call it—will make life a lot better for you mortals. Especially the ones in this neighborhood, who have already been collected."

"Collected?" asked Ceese.

"Mack here has been collecting them all for years," said Yolanda.

Mack looked stunned. "I have?"

"Every dream you saw that came from someone else, you've got their will tied up in yours. What do you think Oberon will be eating, when he swallows you? You're nothing—you're just a piece of him. It's what you collected for him that counts. He's been working through you ever since you were born."

Mack leapt to his feet. "I haven't been. I've been cutting out of those dreams. After what it did to Deacon Landry and Tamika Brown and . . . I been getting out of those dreams."

"You've been stopping up those dreams," said Yolanda cheerfully. "Like putting a cork in them. Penning them in. Putting the genie into the bottle. All those deep and powerful desires, all the wishes of their heart, locked up inside you, ready for Oberon to start using all that magic."

"What about *your* magic? Where does that come from?" demanded Mack.

"It's all locked up in a jar in the woods," said Yolanda.

"And Puck's in the other lantern. How come *he* can do things?"

"All we have is enough power to influence the desires of mortals. Puck's using *your* power, not his own. And only because *he* wants him to." She laughed, but it was a sad laugh. "If I could ever get free of that jar, you'd see what power is. After all, I beat him once. My servants and I."

"So where are they now?"

"Weak," she said. "Lost. Alone. And mostly still in England. They have to hide. I draw power from them, they draw power from me. Be glad, though—his servants are also weakened. Like Puck."

"So Puck *is* an enemy," said Mack.

"Puck is . . . Puck. He loves me. I thought you knew that much. He loves me, but he's Oberon's slave. So he can only help me obliquely. Sideways. He can't actually disobey anything Oberon thought to command him to do. That's why he couldn't tell you flat out who I am, or even who he is."

"I thought he was just a lying snake."

"Well, he *is*. But he's a lying snake who loves me, and a lying snake who would rather have his power trapped in a jar in a clearing in the woods of Fairyland than have Oberon raging through the world, sending him on cruel errands—especially errands to torment *me*."

"And I'm Oberon's slave, too," said Mack.

"Well, no," said Yolanda. "You're *part* of him. More like Oberon's goiter. But a cute one."

Ceese could see how this devastated Mack—especially the way Yolanda seemed not even to notice how hurtful her words were. Or maybe she just didn't care about humans' feelings. "Mack, you don't have to believe this."

"But it's true," said Mack. "It's what I felt all along. That I never belonged to myself. I thought I belonged—to you, to Miz Smitcher, to the neighborhood. But now I know what I been searching for all these years, all my life—it was him. It was the rest of me. He's the one driving. He's the one carrying me along into the flood."

"What are you talking about?" asked Ceese.

"Oh, he'll get used to it," said Yolanda.

"Used to it? Finding out he isn't even real?"

"Oh, he's *real*," said Yolanda. "Real as real can be. Which is why I tried to get you to kill Mack when he was a baby. Only thing I wasn't sure about was—when you didn't kill him, when you resisted me, was it because of your own strength? Or because of Oberon's power stopping you? If it was that worm doing it, then it meant he was watching closer than I thought he could. But now, I'm pretty sure it's just you. I'm pretty sure he's still blind up here. He can sense the power. He can taste the dreams. He can find dark and power-craving hearts that are looking for him. But he can't really see. It's like searching for clothes in the back of the closet."

"So what?" asked Ceese. "What can we do about it?"

"That's what I'm here to figure out," said Yolanda.

"Great," said Mack. "But what am *I* here for?"

"For Oberon to use you," she said.

"So everything would be better if I was dead."

"That's the thing," said Yolanda. "You're *part* of him. So you're immortal. Can't kill you. We stuck with you here, Mack Street." She grinned. "But you can call me Yo Yo if you want."

Mack looked downright grateful. But only for a moment. Then his eyes rolled back in his head and he slumped to the ground.

Ceese was kneeling by him in a moment, supporting his head. "What did you do to him?" he demanded of Yolanda.

"Haven't you heard a thing I said?" she answered. "All that power stored up inside him—Oberon's using it. The boy'll wake up when it's done."

16

PREACHER MAN

It was Word's first day preaching at City Haven, the storefront ministry where Reverend Theodore Lee had taken him on as an assistant pastor. "It's an act of faith, young man," said Rev Theo, as everyone called him. "Not in you, but in God's ability to transform you."

From what to what? Word wondered. But he smiled and said nothing. He had his college degree, but after trying two divinity schools he was done with education.

The first one tried to make him an expert in theology while discouraging Word from having any belief in the supernatural. Word could only shake his head at their oh-so-sophisticated religion, because he knew from experience that supernatural things could happen in LA. So why shouldn't he believe they could happen in Palestine two thousand years ago?

The second one, though, was just as annoyingly off the mark. Full of all kinds of ideology on current political issues, the professors had no idea how good and evil actually worked in the world, and no plan for how to stop evil—not when evil was capable of working dark miracles like the birth of Mack Street from Word's mother's body.

There is no one who can teach me except God, Word decided. And the only way God will teach me is if I'm hard at work trying to serve him.

That's why Word chose City Haven, which sat between two boarded-up storefronts in a failed shopping center in a neighborhood that even the Koreans wouldn't buy up and renovate. The parishioners were mostly women, and mostly elderly women at that. Children were dragged along to church meetings, but few over the age when the gangs started reaching for them. The mothers were worried sick about their children—the fathers who weren't dead, in jail, or unidentified were usually part of the bad influence.

And yet these were the hopeful women, the Christians who still had faith that God would reach out to them and save their children if they just prayed hard enough for a miracle. Behind them, out there in the deceptively sunny streets of the city, were thousands of women who had no hope, who saw their children headed down dark roads and knew they could not stop them.

Word felt them out there, the hopeless ones, and thought: I know that there are miracles. Dark ones that I've seen, and bright ones that I hope for. I will find you, I will touch your hearts, I will bring you together in faith to *demand* that God do something about this mess. And I'll do it because nobody is angrier at evil than I am. Most of the world doesn't really believe it exists. When they say "evil" they mean "sick" or "nasty." When I say "evil," I mean power that makes use of human bodies like they were puppets. Evil is the spirits that inhabited the woman who spoke filth to Jesus, and whom Jesus cast out of her and into the bodies of the Gadarene swine. That's the power we need in this world, right now, to cast out the filth-speaking devils and free the children of God to hear his sweet word and redeem their souls from despair.

I won't let them be like my mother, forgetting everything, or my father, denying everything. I will wake them up.

The trouble with all this grim determination was that Word

wasn't much of a speaker. He knew it, too. Growing up in Baldwin Hills as the son of a fine-spoken English professor and poet, Word spoke English too fluently and clearly to be credible on the street. He sounded like a foreigner here—but not foreign enough for anyone to take him for Jamaican or a highly educated British black. As one little boy said it when Word asked him where the unlocked entrance to City Haven might be, "You sound like a white man." To which Word could only smile and say, "You've never met a white man who talks this well."

He had tried for a while, back in grad school. He rented movies that were full of street slang, but the more he listened, the more it dawned on him that most of these scripts were written by white guys faking it. Spike Lee he could trust, but when he tried to talk like characters from Spike's movies, it sounded so phony that even Word himself was disgusted. It was too late for him to pick up any of the street-black dialects in America. The most he could do was lapse back into the phony Baldwin Hills version, and he knew that talking *that* way would open no doors for him in the gang neighborhoods.

And yet there were his dreams. He could see himself standing in a huge arena, with tens of thousands of people, black *and* white, screaming and chanting "Give us Word, give us Word!"

He could hear an announcer speak over the sound system, the words rebounding raggedly from every corner of the vast space: "In the beginning was the Word! And the Word was with God! And the Word *was* God." Huge cheers. Vast roaring cheers that swept wave on wave across the stage. "And here today in the name of the Word, is Word himself, Reverend Word Williams!"

In the dream, Word walked out onto the stage and saw all the faces, and in his dream he was able to see each individual of them, all at once, to understand what they wanted, to feel their need and he knew that he could grant their wishes, feed their hunger, shelter them from all that they feared. If they truly believed in him, then anything was possible, because with their faith joined together with his own, God himself could not say no to them.

He opened his mouth to speak . . .

And every time, the dream stopped there. Just a sudden flash of being in a car riding along a road between canyon walls, and then he'd either wake up or go off into some random silly dream that he couldn't even remember in the morning.

But the dream of that arena, of that audience, Word remembered every bit of it. He knew it was real. He hungered for it.

So he set out to become Reverend Word Williams, and when he gave up on divinity school, the only route left to him was apprenticeship.

He knew right away that Rev Theo was the right choice. His preaching wasn't empty—he felt the fire. More important, he really loved the people and they knew it. He cared what they were going through. He tried to help them with their children. Even their money problems. Sometimes he'd turn down their contributions—small as they were. "You can't afford that, Sister Rebecca."

"Oh, but I want to, Rev Theo."

"It's the widow's mite, Sister Rebecca, and the Lord knows you gave it. Now I give it back to you as Jesus' own blessing on your family."

But then sometimes he'd keep the contribution—and from someone in worse shape than Sister Rebecca. When Word asked him about it, he said, "It's important for her to feel like she's part of the church. Sister Rebecca contributes often and gets the blessings that come from her sacrifice. But Sister Willa Mae, this is her first time, and to refuse her gift would be to deny her a place in the Kingdom of Jesus Christ."

The man was wise, Word decided. Wise and good, and I should be like him.

Only when it came to the sermons, Word was terrified, because he knew he'd fail. Rev Theo's sermons were musical, rhythmic, passionate. Above all, though, they were personal. He knew these people, named names from the pulpit. "Don't you be afraid like Sister Ollie is afraid! You know she hears a noise in the night and she thinks it's a burglar come to steal from her! Oh, Sister Areena, you laughing, but that's cause any noise *you* hear, you hoping it's one of your men coming back to you to make another baby! You know we love you, Sister Areena, but you got to let Jesus teach you how to say no when a man wants what he got no right to have. You know that. And at least you got hope! Any kind of hope better than living all the time in fear. You can go to sleep on a dream of hope, but fear will steal the sleep right out of your bed.

"Back to Sister Ollie. I tell you, I tell you all, if you afraid of burglars, then take everything worth stealing from your house and lay it down outside your front door. Do you hear me? If you value your possessions so much that you afraid somebody steal them, you give them to God and let him lead the right person to your door! Sister Ollie got nothing to fear, nothing! When she hear that noise in the night, don't she know that it's the Lord? It's the Lord Jesus coming to her! It's the comfort of the Lord Jesus coming into her heart! But he can't get in because she so afraid, and the Lord can't get in past that triple padlock, that deadbolt, that bank vault door of fear!"

And Sister Ollie was sitting there weeping because he knew her heart, and Sister Areena, too, and now the whole congregation knew them and loved them anyway. Sister Ollie called out to Rev Theo, "I won't be afraid no more, Rev Theo! I let Jesus into my heart!" And Sister Areena cried, "I ain't lost hope yet!" And everybody clapped and cheered and laughed and wept and . . .

And how the hell was Word going to touch their hearts the way Rev Theo did? Lucky if he didn't put them straight to sleep.

So Word helped Rev Theo in his ministry, visiting people, taking notes at meetings, going with him to ask for money from ministers of richer churches or from black businessmen. Word went here and there in Baldwin Hills, asking people he knew had money if they could help sustain a little storefront church in South Central. He smiled and nodded when they patronizingly said, "I didn't know you were with the Lord now, Word. I'm glad to see you found Jesus."

I didn't, thought Word. Not yet. But I sure found the devil, and I'm hoping Jesus won't be far behind.

He was energetic. He was dedicated. Rev Theo counted on him for more and more. And one on one, Word liked talking to the members of the church. They liked him—though of course they all told him to learn from Rev Theo, because he was a real man of God. "That's what I'm here for," said Word, "but the Lord doesn't work through me the way he works through Rev Theo."

"The Lord works through everyone," said Rev Theo. "They just don't always know it."

But what Word had most hoped to learn never happened. Despite his love and faith, Rev Theo didn't have the power. People who were ailing would ask him to lay on hands and he did, but they didn't get better except in the ordinary way. "That's how healing works," Rev Theo explained to Word. "All in the Lord's own time." But Word had seen another kind of healing, where a gravely injured old man gripped the hand of a magical boy and rose up from his bed and his cast fell away from his broken leg and he walked on it, and his clothing was restored to him—filthy as it was, but when the devil worked miracles, what could you expect but filthiness?

Now it was time to preach. To stand before the congregation. It was the nighttime meeting, for the people who worked during the day, so it was a smaller group. And it included a couple of men, neither one of them married, trying to come back from drug dealing and even darker sins. At first they scared Word a little, and they knew that he was scared, and that amused them but both of them at different times had said to him, Don't be afraid of me, the only person I harm these days is me. But what could Word say to them? He'd been raised in privilege, surrounded by literature and love and the comforts of life.

But not by faith. Despite all that he had, Word had never known that magic was possible in the world. But *these* men knew. They were counting on it.

Rev Theo introduced him—including a reminder that it was his first sermon and they should be as kind to Word as Rev Theo's first congregation had been to him. Word appreciated what he said, but also resented it a little because he had hoped that Rev Theo might believe that he'd do a good job. Why should he, though? Why should anybody believe in him?

Word gripped the two sides of the pulpit and locked his knees and looked out at people he knew well and loved and cared about and he was terrified all the same. "Why am I talking to you?" he said. "What do I have to say to you? You know everything about pain and suffering. I don't know anything. You know about sacrifice. I don't know anything." He had begun this as candor. But now he was picking up the cadence of a preacher and feeling the music of it and he had a fleeting thought: Is this all? Is it this easy?

And in that moment it all dried up.

"Brothers and sisters, I don't even know humility. Just that moment I was thinking, This is easier than I thought. But it isn't easy. It's only easy if Jesus is in your heart, and I don't know if he has ever been in my heart. I know I've seen the Lord in Rev Theo's heart! I know I've seen the Lord in your heart, Brother Eddie. I've seen Jesus in your face, Sister Antoinette! So I ask you who know the Lord so well to pray for me. Let Jesus into my heart, so I can know what you know about the Lord."

Word fell silent. He had a prepared sermon but he didn't know how to get to it from where he was. Why had he started out this way? Why was he off on this tangent?

Sister Antoinette spoke up from the congregation. "Lord Jesus hear the prayer of your servant Brother Word and let him know that you already in his heart."

"Amen," said Brother Eddie loudly. "Amen to that prayer, Lord Jesus!"

And then, as a murmur of amens spread through the congregation, Word felt something astonishing. It was like somebody had reached a hand into his body, right through the back of his head and down his spine and into his heart. He was filled with fire. His heartbeat became a jackhammer.

"O Lord!" he cried. "Give me the words they need to hear!"

And the words came.

It was as if Word heard someone else speaking through his mouth. Only instead of advice and counsel from the Bible, he heard himself making specific promises. "Sister 'Cookie' Simonds, the Lord heals you of your female trouble. Go to the doctor and he'll tell you that it's not cancer. But I tell you that it *was* cancer and the Lord has taken it away. Brother Eddie, call your son again. Tonight, no matter how late, you telephone him again and I promise you that this time the Lord will soften his heart and he will listen to you, every word you say, and he will forgive you and let you be the father that you should have been all along. And Sister Missy, go home to your baby Shanice right now, get out of your chair, because she is about to choke and your daughter's watching television and won't hear her. Get home and put your finger down your baby's throat and save her life!"

Missy Dole was out of her chair like a shot and out the door, and everyone looked around with wonder, but Word was not through. The hand still had hold of his heart, the ideas and images kept flowing into his brain. He ignored Rev Theo's hand on his elbow and kept promising and prophesying until he had named every person in the congregation that night and a couple who weren't even there but usually were, and just as he was about to wind down, just as he thought, Surely there's nothing more to say, in rushed Missy Dole with her baby Shanice in her arms. Weeping, she ran to the front and laid the baby down before the pulpit and cried out, "This baby belongs to Jesus! She was choking and turning blue when I got there, and I put my finger down her throat like you said and my fingernail broke open a grape, it was a whole grape in her throat choking off the air, and I broke it and pulled it out with my fingernail and my baby took a breath! I would have come home from church and found my baby dead!"

Word knew there was nothing to say after that. So he opened his mouth and sang. A common ordinary hymn, but he put new words to it, words about baby Shanice and Sister Missy and the healing power of God. The words fit the music perfectly and Word vaguely noticed that as he sang these new words, so did the congregation. They were standing up and singing with him, rocking back and forth, many of them with their hands upraised, and they were singing along with him the very same new words, without hesitation, as if the power of God was putting those new words in everyone's mouth all at once.

And then the song was over. The room was filled with weeping and laughing and murmurs of amen, hallelujah, praise God.

Now Word felt Rev Theo's hand on his elbow and he backed away from the pulpit and sat down and numbly watched as Rev Theo said a short prayer and sent them home. "Remember the miracles you've seen tonight," he said. "The Lord has answered many prayers in this holy house."

It took an hour for everyone to leave. Word felt like his arm was about to be pumped right off his shoulder, they shook his hand so much, congratulating him on a fine sermon, thanking him for his promises. Some of them looked at him with perfect faith. Others had some doubt. But they all had an air of wonder about them. They knew that they had seen something spectacular and that it had come from God by way of Word Williams.

When they all were gone, and Rev Theo was locking the door,

he began talking softly to Word. "Don't count on it being like that every time," he said.

"Rev Theo, I can't believe it happened *this* time."

"I am a wicked man," said Rev Theo. "I doubted the power of God. He granted the very prayer I asked of him, but I doubted. I touched your arm to try to get you to sit down. I was going to tell you, Word, boy, you can't promise them things like this. It'll just break their hearts when they don't come true. But then Missy Dole came back and . . . Swear to me in Jesus' holy name that this comes from God."

"Rev Theo, I don't know, but if it saved Shanice's life, who else could it come from but God? The world is full of evil, but I've been given the power to fight it. Just a little, but power all the same. Power for good. To combat the power of evil."

"But it might just be the once. As a special blessing tonight. Do you understand me? Don't lose faith if it doesn't happen again."

Word only shook his head and smiled. "Rev Theo, don't you understand? I could open my mouth right now and it would happen again." He reached out his hand and took Rev Theo by the shoulder and said, "I promise you right now, the Lord has heard your prayer and he will take away the wickedness in your heart and turn your desire back to your wife, and your wife's desire back to you."

He let his hand fall away.

Rev Theo's eyes were wide and full of tears.

"I didn't know you were married," said Word.

"She left me ten years ago," Rev Theo whispered. "A year after I left my fine church and came to this place. She couldn't take the poverty. I couldn't take her materialism. She took my children away from me. I vowed that I could forgive every sinner but I could not forgive her."

"But you do forgive her," said Word.

"As God has forgiven me the pride of my righteousness."

Rev Theo threw his arms around him and wept onto Word's shoulder and Word embraced him as his body heaved with his sobs of relief and gratitude.

"Thank you, O King of Kings," murmured Word. The power to defeat the devil was back in the world again, and it was in his hands.

17

WISH FULFILMENT

Mack woke up lying on the white couch with Yolanda staring into his eyes. "He's awake," she said.

Ceese was apparently kneeling beside the couch near Mack's head. "I can see that."

"You really ought to speak to me with more respect," said Yolanda. "Or I'll make you fall in love with me."

"I'm already in love with you," Mack said. He hadn't realized it until he said it.

"Of course you are," said Yolanda. "Because Oberon is."

"He locked you up in a glass jar and he *loves* you?" asked Ceese.

"He locked me up in a glass jar because I was imprisoning him under the earth."

Mack closed his eyes.

"He's gone again," said Ceese.

"No, he's just got his feelings hurt," said Yolanda. "It's something Will Shakespeare taught me to recognize. Mortals get sad when their love doesn't love them in return."

"I had a terrible dream," said Mack. "A cold dream."

"Which would explain the shivering," said Ceese.

"I have these dreams," said Mack.

"I know," said Ceese. "You explained it before."

"I started having this one . . . a couple of years ago. But it's different from the others. I don't know who it is. And up to now I never let it finish. This time I couldn't stop it."

"What does *that* mean? That the wish came true?" asked Ceese.

"I don't know. Yes, maybe it does. It always did before."

Yo Yo stroked his face. "Come on, little changeling, tell me what you saw."

"He's not that little," murmured Ceese.

"Hush yo' mouth, child," Yo Yo murmured back.

"I was going on stage. In a huge arena. The first time I thought maybe I was like a gladiator because it felt like some kind of contest and I was very nervous. I was afraid I might lose. But then I realized that I was alone, going out there alone in front of the crowd, and they were chanting but I couldn't hear anything. It's like I'm deaf in the dream."

"Any of your other dreams like that? Deaf I mean?" asked Ceese.

"Don't be such a cop and ask a lot of stupid questions," Yo Yo suggested.

"Don't be a fairy queen and boss people around," said Ceese.

"I can always hear in my dreams, and in this one I could hear too, just not the crowd. What I heard was the beating of wings."

"A bird?" asked Ceese.

"No," said Mack. "Up to now I didn't know what it was. Not even that it was wings. I usually know things like that. But this dream is halfway hidden from me. And I don't like it. It feels ugly. Like the wish itself is ugly, not just the trick that it might get turned into. Tamika, her wish was beautiful. Even Deacon Landry, his dream was full of love and desire and . . . admiration. But this wish, it's dark. It's *hungry*."

"What's the wish?"

"I told you. It's hungry. I go out there and I'm so hungry and I see all these people shouting and chanting and waving only they don't make a sound and I can barely taste them, so they just make me hungrier. I hated this dream. I got out of it as fast as I could. Only this time when I tried, all I did was carry the dream with me. So it combined with my escape dream. It became the same dream. And when I looked out the window of the car in *my* dream, I saw the crowd from the other dream. So I hadn't gotten away like I usually can. And then I felt something slap the car away, just whooosh and it's gone, and there I am alone on the stage of that arena, and suddenly there's something under me. Something like a motorcycle seat. Or a horse. It moved me forward and suddenly we were right out over the audience, swooping around them, their faces looking up and filled with love and madness and it was frightening, the way we flew. I could feel the wings beating now, and hear them of course—and that's when I first realized the sound was wings. I was riding something but I couldn't see what it was."

"It was a dragon," said Yo Yo quietly.

"I guess it was," said Mack, and the realization made him sad, because he knew he should be fighting the dragon, not riding on it.

"Go on," said Ceese.

"That's it," said Mack. "That was the dream. After that it just stopped making sense."

"Tell me anyway," said Yo Yo.

"Okay, but it don't mean a thing," said Mack. "I was soaring over the crowd and I looked down and I could feel their love. Their need. Like this woman with a baby. She looked at me and stuck her finger down her baby's throat and pulled out a grape. Then she held it up to me like an offering, like it was a jewel. And a man was reaching up to us and with one beat of a wing the . . . dragon, the thing I was riding, it *blew* him clear across the arena and landed him right on top of a woman who hugged him like he was her long-lost lover. Weird stuff. Not like cold dreams. So I thought the cold dream was over."

"It wasn't over," said Yo Yo. "Oberon came into your dream and took control. He's started using the power he put in you, Mack. The power you've gathered from all those dreams. He isn't letting you plug up the stream anymore. He wants the wishes to come true now. He's letting out the flood."

"I know," said Mack, and he started to cry as he remembered. "I tried to stop it. But dream after dream. I'd hear the beating of the wings but I was into an old dream, one I've known for years. Sabrina Chum, that girl with the really big nose, in her dream she's always an elephant and comes up to a rhinoceros and it saws off her trunk. I hate that dream, the sawing-off part, and I always end the dream before we get there, but this time I saw her drunk lying on the ground. And then the beating of the wings and I was in Ophelia McCallister's dream, where she walks out onto the lawn of her house and there's her husband and he holds out his hand and hugs her and kisses her." Mack shuddered.

"What's wrong with that?" asked Yo Yo.

"Old man McCallister died a long time ago," said Ceese.

"I just know how these dreams come true," said Mack. "I can think of a lot of ways she could have her husband in her arms again but none of them is very nice."

"Any other dreams?"

"Sherita Banks," said Mack. "She just wants boys to think she's cute. She isn't. She's got a really big butt like her mother. Beyond what most guys would find attractive. Family curse, kind of. But she doesn't dream that the butt gets small, she dreams that boys come up and put their hands on her butt and tell her she's beautiful."

"Sounds kind of sweet," said Yo Yo.

"No," said Mack. "That dream could come true, all right, but it wouldn't be sweet. It could be a gang getting up a train on her."

Ceese nodded. "Anybody else?"

"I was just starting Professor Williams's dream. Not the one where he kills Bag Man. The one where he's listening while people recite his poems. Only this time of course I didn't hear the poems, I just heard the wings beating only that's when they stopped. That's when I woke up."

"So you think those wishes came true?" asked Ceese.

"They didn't always come true back when I didn't know how to stop them," said Mack. "But this time, when I didn't have any control, when I was flying on the back of that thing from dream to dream—I thought, They're coming true. I knew it. Like Yo Yo said. He wants the wishes to come true. He was going from dream to dream."

"And then he stopped when he got to Professor Williams."

Mack nodded. "Yes, but I don't care where he *stopped,* I care what he *did.* We got to get on the phone. We got to call people. Like when Tamika was inside the waterbed. If I'd known what was happening, I could have called Mr. Brown and woke him up and told him to look for Yolanda in the water."

"Right," said Ceese, "but then he might have run outside and headed for a pool and he would never have found her at all. I mean, what do we warn people *of?*"

"We got to try," said Mack. "We got to phone people. We got to go places and try to stop things."

"You got a phone here that works?" Ceese asked Yo Yo.

"Yeah. You got everybody's phone numbers memorized?"

"No," said Ceese. "But my mom does. Look, I'll go home and we'll start calling. Find out about Sherita. Where she is. I can get a patrol car to go there and stop it if it's really happening like you think. A gang rape."

"What about Sabrina and her nose?" asked Mack.

"I'll call her family. Maybe she's cut herself. Maybe they can still get her to a hospital—reattach it."

"Then why you sitting here, boy?" asked Yo Yo.

"Mrs. McCallister won't answer the phone," said Mack. "She turns it off at night."

"Then you two go there while I go home. We had . . . who was it? . . . Sabrina, Mrs. McCallister, Sherita Banks, Professor Williams, and then you woke up. I'm calling everybody and you're going over to McCallisters' house."

By the time Mack got up from the couch and outside the house, he could see Ceese already going around the bend in the road on his way down the hill to home.

Then Yo Yo brought the motorcycle out of the garage and revved it up while Mack got on behind her.

Across the street, the back of the Joneses' house looked out over the street at the bottom of the hairpin—and Yo Yo's house. Now Moses Jones was out on the back deck stark naked yelling down at them. Mack couldn't hear what he was saying because the motorcycle was so loud. But he could see how he nearly had a fit, jumping up and down and screaming after Yo Yo raised one finger. It wasn't even the bad finger. But maybe in the dark old Moses Jones couldn't tell. He was still jumping up and down when they roared on up the hill to McCallisters'.

Ophelia McCallister lived in the house she had shared with her husband before he died. It was right at the top of Cloverdale, just a couple of houses from where the road dead-ended at the always-locked and often-climbed gateway leading into Hahn Park. Mack got off the bike before it even stopped, pushing himself up like in a game of leapfrog and hopping up so the bike kept going underneath him. But of course he still had a lot of momentum, so he staggered forward and since Yo Yo had just brought the bike to a stop, he crashed into her.

She switched the motor off.

Across the street two neighbors had come to their windows to look at the motorcycle and they didn't seem too happy. Though at least they weren't naked and jumping up and down like Moses Jones had been.

They got to the door and Mack rang the bell and then he knocked loud and started shouting, "Mrs. McCallister!"

Now the neighbors were out of their houses. "What are you doing?" demanded Harrison Grand, the next-door neighbor on the park side. "Do you know what time it is?"

"Something's wrong with Mrs. McCallister," said Mack. "We got to get in. She got a spare key?"

"I don't know," said Mr. Grand. And then he looked at Yo Yo and suddenly his face brightened. "She keeps a spare key."

"Where?" asked Mack.

Harrison Grand immediately jogged to the juniper next to the front door and lifted up a rock that turned out to be a fake. He took out a key and within a few moments he and Mack and Yo Yo were searching the house.

"She isn't here," said Grand.

"I thought she would be," said Mack.

"Well she was," said Yo Yo. "Her bed's been slept in. But she's not in it now."

"Why would she leave?" asked Grand.

"Mr. Grand," said Mack, "you know where Mr. McCallister's buried?"

"Well you can bet it ain't Forest Lawn," he said.

Again he glanced at Yo Yo, and again he was suddenly enlightened. "I remember she has a cab come and drive her there every week but I took her once a few years ago and it's . . . it's . . ."

He walked to the calendar on the wall over the phone. He pointed to the name and address of the cemetery that had given it out to their customers, including Mrs. McCallister. "But you don't think she's gone to visit her husband's grave in the middle of the night."

Mack knew what would probably happen but he tried to explain anyway. "I know this sound crazy but I think she's with her husband now."

"Dead?"

"No, alive. But with him. You know where his plot is?"

"I don't think so."

Yo Yo touched his shoulder. "Yes you do."

"Yes," he said. "I do."

"Can you take me there?" asked Mack.

"Right now?" he asked.

"Before she runs out of air," said Mack.

"You saying she's down inside the—"

He fell silent for a moment, Yo Yo's hand on his shoulder. Then he got an urgent look about him and took off running for the garage of his own house. "Come on, Mack! You come along and help me dig that coffin up!"

"Better get a crowbar to open the lid!" cried Mack as he followed him over to his yard, his driveway. Before they got a pick and shovel and crowbar into the back of his SUV, they could hear Yo Yo's motorcycle taking off at top volume.

RALPH CHUM WAS WORKING late on a client's quarterlies when the phone rang. He picked it up. "Barbara?" he said.

"Mr. Chum?" asked a male voice.

"Who is this?"

"This is Cecil Tucker, sir. I apologize for calling this late, but it might be an emergency." Ralph vaguely knew that Ceese Tucker was a policeman. Sabrina had mentioned it—she once had a thing for him, though of course it came to nothing.

A policeman calls at this time of night.

"*Might* be? Is something wrong with Barbara? Was there an accident?"

"Nothing like that," said Ceese. "Sir, is your daughter Sabrina at home?"

"She's asleep, Ceese." Was he actually asking her out, this long after her high school crush on him?

"I know she is, sir. I just wanted to make sure she was home. Sir, would you be willing to go and check on her?"

"Check on her? What are you talking about?"

"Sir, this is going to sound insane. Or like a cruel joke. But I assure you it is not a joke, and I am not insane. Please go into her room and look at her face."

"Look at her—"

"Make sure that nothing has happened to her face."

"What could happen to her face!"

"I told you it would sound crazy. All I can tell you is, think of how much Curtis Brown wishes he had checked on his daughter Tamika a little bit earlier."

"What does this have to do with—Curtis is in jail!"

"Please check your daughter, sir."

Ralph knew that this was insane, but Ceese sounded so grave, and the thought of this somehow being linked to what happened to poor Tamika Brown . . . "All right," he said, but he still let annoyance come out in his voice.

"With the light on, sir," said Ceese.

"Yes, with the light on!"

Angrily, Ralph Chum got up from his desk, left his office, and padded through the house on slippered feet until he got to Sabrina's room. From the door he could see that she was fine. There was no need to turn the light on. This was some stupid prank, and now that Ceese was a cop, Ralph could complain about him to somebody with more influence on him than his parents.

He turned away but now the fear came to the surface. Was it possible that Curtis Brown was telling the truth? That something strange and terrible had happened to Tamika and, as he said when he wept on the stand, he might have saved her in time if only he had believed that such things were even possible.

What was it Ceese wanted him to check for? Poor Sabrina, with her nose that seemed to spread halfway across her face. Should he wake her up by turning on the light, and then tell her that Ceese Tucker wanted him to look at her face to see if anything was wrong with it? He knew what Sabrina would say: Of course something's wrong with it. Even plastic surgeons refuse to work on it because narrowing my nostrils enough to make a difference would leave scars and make me look like a monster instead of just a freak. And then she'd cry. And when Barbara got home from her office retreat she'd be furious at him and . . .

And he had to look.

He turned on the light. Sabrina stirred a little but did not wake. Ralph walked into the room and looked at her. She was lying on her side, facing the wall. Ralph couldn't really see. When he leaned over her, his own shadow obscured her features.

So he sighed, reached out, and pulled at her shoulder.

She rolled over and opened her eyes.

There was a growth the size and texture of a walnut on the right side of her nose, the side that had been on the pillow.

"What is that," murmured Ralph.

"What?" said Sabrina.

"There's something growing there. Near your . . . eye."

Sabrina crossed her eyes as she tried to focus on the growth. She reached up and touched it. "Ow," she said.

Where she had touched it, a little blood came to the surface.

"What is it, Daddy? It hurts. Oh, it *hurts*."

"Get up and get dressed," he said. "We're taking you to the emergency room."

"What is it!"

"Something growing there," said Ralph. "And we're getting you to a doctor right now. I'll wake your sister. We can't leave her here alone."

Before he got to Keisha's room, though, he remembered Ceese Tucker and went back to his office and picked up the receiver.

"How did you know?" he asked.

"Is she all right?"

"Don't you already know she isn't?"

"I hoped I was wrong. What is it?"

"She's got a growth on her nose. It bleeds when she touches it."

"Get her to a hospital right now," said Ceese.

"That's what I'm doing. I'm hanging up now. But we're going to talk, you and I."

"Yes sir. God be with your daughter, sir."

Ralph hung up and went back to wake Keisha so they could take Sabrina to the hospital.

WHEN MIKE HERALD PULLED his patrol car up in front of the house it was obvious there was some kind of party going on inside—the bass from the music was throbbing so loud that he could feel it even before he turned off the engine. But nobody had called to complain. This was a gang neighborhood, and they all knew better than to call in the cops.

But apparently Ceese Tucker didn't know any better. A rape in progress? How would he know that? Who would have called? These gangbangers raped girls all the time. It was like an initiation for the girl. A party favor for the boys. Nobody ever reported it. And it would be worth his life to walk up to that door alone.

Backup was coming. Maybe two minutes away.

But Ceese had been so urgent about it. "I promise you, this girl does *not* want what's happening to her. If she's at that house. Mrs. Banks said she's been hanging around with a girl who lives there. Her brother's a Paladin. A young one, wants to impress the older guys."

There were a couple of kids already out on the street, and of course they noticed the LAPD vehicle. One of them was starting to sidle toward the house. To give warning.

Mike got out of the car, drew his weapon, and pointed at the boy with his other hand. Not aiming the gun at him, just pointing. The boy froze.

Mike looked around quickly. No weapons being pointed at

him. Nobody was on alert—this wasn't a drug deal or anything they planned. Just a party. Didn't expect cops to show up.

Another LAPD vehicle turned the corner, moving fast. His backup was here. He should still wait till they were out of the car, till they could cover the back door and go in in force. But the girl was in there, and maybe there was a chance to stop this thing before it got too bad for her.

So he jogged to the door. It was a piece of crap like all the materials used in these houses. He stepped back and stomped his foot hard against the door just beside the knob. The frame broke and let the door swing free. The music was so loud nobody heard it. He also couldn't hear if the other cops were running toward him or not. Couldn't hear anything except the music.

He moved into the house. Nobody in the living room, where the stereo made the cheap furniture tremble like an earthquake.

In the kitchen was a girl making a sandwich. Probably the girlfriend. Her brother was raping her friend in the back room and she was making a sandwich. She had her back to the kitchen door and didn't hear him. He knew he should neutralize her first—get her down on the floor, out of harm's way—but he let her be and moved on toward the bedrooms.

Now the music wasn't quite so loud and he could hear a girl's voice. "Please, God, no." Or was she saying, "Please, Rod, no"? Wasn't the boy's name Rod?

The door was slightly ajar. Six boys, none of them older than fourteen, were gathered around a bed, laughing and leaning in, and some of them were holding the arms and legs of a girl who had been stripped from the waist down. She was crying, and one of the youngest boys was poised over her.

"Come on, Sherita, I *want* you so bad."

It was as if the words had plunged a dagger into her heart, the way she sobbed. But she also held still. Surrendering now.

Mike shoved the boy nearest to him, sending him sprawling

across Sherita's body, knocking Rod aside. The other boys whirled around to find Mike training his gun on each of them in turn. "All of you little bastards get down on the floor with your hands on your heads. Right now!"

No chance for them to put on their brave gang faces. No chance to go for whatever weapons they might have had.

"She wanted it!" Rod was screaming. "She just showed up here, she just showed up and she wasn't wearing pants!"

Mike pushed the barrel of the pistol into his face and Rod dropped to the floor.

Mike looked at the youngest of the boys. "You. Get up and put something over her privates. Right now!"

He did.

The stereo went silent in the living room.

Another officer stood beside him, gun drawn. "You crazy, coming in here without backup?"

"Stopped them before they got into her," said Mike.

"Well, then, it's only attempted, isn't it, you moron," said the other cop.

"Let's ask her if she wished I waited," said Mike.

Sherita rolled onto her side and curled into a ball, weeping. The young boy untucked a corner of the sheet and brought it up over her rear end. Her butt was so big that it wouldn't stay, it slipped off.

"That's all right," said Mike, holstering his weapon and putting a hand on her shoulder. He helped her off the bed, then pulled the whole sheet off and helped her wrap it around herself. Then he kicked a couple of the boys to get them out of the way so they could walk out.

The girl from the kitchen was standing in the hallway, holding her sandwich with two bites out of it. She looked genuinely horrified. "Sherita," she said, "when you get here? What's going on?"

"Your friend was about to be raped by Rod," said Mike savagely. "And don't pretend you didn't know about it. Don't pretend you didn't help him set it up."

"Swear to God!" she said. "That little shit was going to rape her?"

Mike brushed her aside, bouncing her off the wall just a little as he continued to convey Sherita Banks down the hall and into the living room where the other cop, the one who had turned off the stereo, was watching.

"I'm taking her home," said Mike. "I'll get her statement."

CEESE FINISHED HIS CALLS with his mother frantically demanding that he tell her what was going on.

"You wouldn't believe me if I told you," he said.

"Try me!" she demanded.

"Mack had a bunch of dreams. People's wishes coming true in really ugly ways."

"You're waking people up from a sound sleep because Mack had a nightmare?"

"Same kind of nightmare he had the night Tamika Brown got herself inside her parents' waterbed," said Ceese. "Same kind of dream as when Mr. Tyler got hit on the head by an I-beam cause his daughter Romaine wished he could be home with her all the time."

"What are you saying? That somebody's murdering people?"

"I'm saying somebody's making wishes come true in a sick, twisted, evil way, and it's happening tonight."

"Wishes?" she said. "Like in fairy tales?"

"No," said Ceese. "Wishes like in hell, where the devil tortures sinners by making their wishes come true."

"But Tamika Brown wasn't a sinner!"

He couldn't believe she was arguing religion with him. "Who says the devil plays fair?" said Ceese. "Now I got to go."

"Where, at this time of night?"

Ceese had his keys in his hand and was at the front door. "Professor Williams didn't answer the phone."

"All this comes from Mack Street's dreams?"

"There's more to the boy than most folks thought."

"He's got the evil eye, that's what."

Ceese whirled on her. "Don't say that," he said. "It's a lie."

She flashed with anger. "You calling your mama a liar?"

"Don't you ever speak against Mack Street," he said. "It's Mack saving all these people's lives. If we get there in time to save them."

GRAND HARRISON HAD the flashlight because he knew the way, more or less. Mack and Yo Yo followed close behind. Mack had been in cemeteries before but never at night with shadows looming and something ugly waiting for them when they got to Ophelia McCallister's husband's grave. He did have the queen of the fairies with him, but apparently she didn't have all her powers, since her soul was locked up in a glass jar hanging in midair in a clearing in Fairyland.

Not that he had anything to fear. He had just found out he was immortal. So all that worry about not falling in the river and getting drowned was a complete waste.

Then again, maybe she was lying. Puck always did, and he was the only other fairy Mack knew personally, so maybe lying was just something fairies did. He didn't intend to get himself killed just to prove she was wrong.

"Here it is," said Grand. "But look, the ground is completely undisturbed. Nobody's done anything here."

"Dig," said Yo Yo.

"No! That's just—"

Yo Yo put a hand on his cheek. "For me."

Mack was amazed. The man's whole face and posture and

everything changed. He was in love with her, right on the spot. Completely out of his mind crazy for her. Like a puppy dog.

"You want me to dig?" he said. "How deep?"

"Let's find Mr. McCallister's coffin," said Yo Yo.

And so they dug. That is, Mack and Grand dug, Grand wielding the pick to loosen things up, and Mack shoveling and then Grand joining in with the other shovel, working fast—Mack because he knew there wouldn't be much air in that coffin, and Grand because he was showing off for his new lady love.

"Yo Yo," said Mack, "you going to kill this man if he don't slow down."

"Grand," she said lazily, "take it a little slower. Don't want you getting a heart attack on me."

Grand Harrison grinned like a jack-o'-lantern and slowed down just a little.

And after a while they hit wood. They couldn't lift the lid until they cleared away the dirt the whole length and breadth of the coffin, and even when they'd done that, it took serious work with the crowbar to get the thing open. It wasn't a cheap coffin.

Yo Yo stood over the hole, looking down. "Open it," she said.

Mack lifted up and sure enough, inside the box was the rotted, desiccated corpse of Mr. McCallister, its raggedy-sleeved arms wrapped around a wide-eyed Ophelia.

She looked dead.

"We too late," said Grand.

"No," said Yo Yo. "She's just terrified. Help her out. Lift her out. Get her breathing."

A few minutes later Ophelia McCallister lay weeping in the grass beside the pile of dirt from her husband's grave.

"Carry her to the SUV," said Yo Yo. "I can only keep the security guy away from here for so long before I wear out."

"Shouldn't we fill in the hole?" asked Mack.

"All that matters," said Yo Yo, "is that when they look into the coffin, they don't find an extra body."

Mack carried Ophelia McCallister to the SUV. She was light as a pillow. He didn't know old people were so . . . empty. She clung to his neck and wept into his chest, but her sobs felt like the trembling of a tiny bird's wings and her arms around his neck were like a baby's hands, her grip was so weak.

"I couldn't breathe," she whispered between sobs. "I couldn't breathe. Thank you. Thank God."

Saved one, thought Mack. I actually saved one. So maybe I was shown those dreams for a reason. Maybe I'm not just Oberon's tool in this world.

NADINE WILLIAMS OPENED THE DOOR. A police officer was standing there. She knew immediately that something terrible had happened to Word. She had warned him about becoming a minister in such a godforsaken part of the city. They'll kill you. They have no respect for religion. And God won't protect you, you can count on that! When you trust in God, you're on your own.

And now a policeman was here to tell them that Word was dead.

She sucked in her breath and refused to cry. "Can I help you, Officer?"

"Mrs. Williams," said the policeman. "I'm Ceese Tucker. Is your husband here?"

"My husband? He's asleep. Or he was, till you rang the doorbell."

"I need to see him," said Ceese.

"You can tell me," said Nadine.

"Tell you what?" He looked genuinely puzzled.

"I thought . . . aren't you here about Word?"

"What about Word?" asked Ceese.

"He was preaching his first sermon tonight in that little church in that awful neighborhood and I thought . . . he's all right?"

"I don't know anything about Word tonight, ma'am," said Ceese. "I need to see your husband."

Nadine would have continued arguing, but she felt Byron's hand on her shoulder.

"What is it, Ceese?" asked Byron.

"Professor Williams," said Ceese. "You remember Bag Man?"

"I want nothing further to do with him."

"I know that, sir," said Ceese. "I'm just telling you that the kind of thing that happens around that man, it's happening tonight to a lot of folks, and we have reason to think it might have happened to you."

Nadine looked at Byron, puzzled. Did he know what this young man was talking about?

"Nothing like that," said Byron.

"Did you have a dream tonight, sir?" asked Ceese.

"A dream?" said Nadine. "Are you the dream police?"

But Byron answered him. "I did."

"A powerful dream. About your poetry, sir."

Nadine peered at her husband's face and could see that yes, he had dreamed such a dream. "But Byron, I didn't know you wrote poetry."

"Sir," said Ceese, "I think there's reason to be afraid that your dream has come true. In an unpleasant way."

"I've dreamed it before and it never . . ."

"Tonight is different," said Ceese. "For several other people that we know of."

Ceese's cellphone rang. "Excuse me for a moment, sir," said Ceese.

Byron stood there for a moment in the doorway, watching Ceese as he started talking on the phone. Nadine looked back and forth between them.

"So you got there in time," said Ceese into the phone. "She's okay?" He looked relieved.

Byron suddenly swung away from the door and trotted toward the "office"—the spare bedroom where the computer was always on.

When Ceese put away his cellphone he stepped into the house. "Do you know where your husband went?"

"I assume to the computer."

Ceese didn't ask if he could go back there, he just went, and Nadine didn't even protest. This was a very strange evening, and what she'd heard of the cellphone conversation led her to think that something very bad had almost happened to a girl named Sherita, and that would probably be Sherita Banks, that girl who had inherited her mother's hippopotamus thighs and buttocks at a tragically young age. Her parents had tried and tried to have a baby before they finally got Sherita. It just showed you that even the blessings in your life come with their own burdens. Like Word, with his sudden conversion to Christianity three years ago, and two failed attempts at divinity school, and now this dangerous, foolish attempt to become a preacher at a storefront church in a hellish neighborhood. All the hopes and dreams they both had for that beautiful boy, and this is what he was doing with his life.

But at least he hadn't become a policeman, like Ceese Tucker. How did *his* mother ever sleep nights? No matter how bad things were, somebody always had it worse.

Byron was sitting at the computer, his face buried in his hands.

Ceese walked around behind him and looked at the screen. Nadine followed him.

Byron had googled "Byron Williams poems" and the screen was showing the first seven of more than three thousand entries.

How could there be three thousand entries about Byron's poetry on the web, and she had never even known he wrote any?

Ceese leaned over and used the mouse to click on the first entry. A moment later, a website came up.

It was a review. "Now that the poems of Pepperdine Professor Byron Williams have been spread through the web like a virus, can anyone tell us whether this was the ultimate in vanity publication, or a cruel joke? Either way, we can all agree that Professor Williams deserves our deepest sympathy. Because it's doubtful any of his students can ever take him seriously again after reading these things."

"Oh my Lord," said Nadine. "Did you really write poetry and publish it on the web?"

"I didn't publish anything," whispered Byron Williams. "It was some hacker."

"No," said Ceese, and his voice was full of pity. "It was the deepest wish of your heart."

18

WITCH

They gathered in Ophelia's house, where Mack and Grand helped her calm down.

"There's nobody to call about this, Miz McCallister," Mack said.

"Somebody kidnapped me and put me down there." She shivered and sipped a little more tea.

"No," said Mack. "They didn't. It was your wish. To be with your husband."

"What you're talking about is magic. You should be old enough to know better."

"Mrs. McCallister," said Grand, "I don't know how, but you got down in there without the ground being disturbed. Nobody dug to put you down there. We only dug to get you out."

"Why would I wish to be with my husband's dead body?"

"You dreamed," said Mack, "of dancing with him when he was a soldier in that fine uniform. He was heading out for Germany, stationed there, same time as Elvis. You called him 'my own Elvis' and you kept saying, I want to be with you forever and he said, You can always be with me, Feely."

Ophelia McCallister leaned across the table and tried to slap him, but Mack backed away in time. "That's private!" she said. The teacup trembled in her hand so that Grand took it away from her before it tipped and spilled or broke.

"Ma'am," said Mack, "I saw your dreams. I know how these dreams come true. In an ugly way. A way you'll hate. A way that makes you wish you had never wished. Like—"

"Like Tamika Brown," Ophelia said impatiently. "But what her father did to her is nothing like—"

"Her father pulled her out of that waterbed and saved her life, just like Mr. Harrison and me saved your life tonight. We didn't put you in there, and Mr. Brown didn't put Tamika in there either. You want to believe there's no such thing as magic, fine. But I know there is, and it nearly killed you tonight."

Ophelia tried for one more long moment to hold on to a rational world. Then she gave up and burst into tears. "I want to lie down."

"We tried to get you to lie down before," said Grand.

"Nothing makes sense!"

"You love your husband," said Mack. "That was the center of your world, missing him. But there's an evil force loose in the world, making wishes come true."

"It's that witch!" cried Ophelia.

"What witch?" asked Mack.

"That motorcycle-riding witch! She did it!"

Grand helped her sit down on the sofa in her living room. "Mrs. McCallister, Yolanda White was helping us. She held the flashlight while we dug. She kept the security guard from coming over and finding out what we was doing."

"Just because she's helping now doesn't mean she didn't cause it!"

Mack and Grand looked at each other. Why would she believe such a ridiculous thing? Where did the idea come from?

"She hates me," said Ophelia, lying down on the sofa. Mr. Harrison pulled off her shoes. "Get rid of that witch . . . ," mumbled the woman. She was nearly asleep, even if she wasn't quite there yet.

"I've got to go," said Mack. "I'm worried about Yolanda. If people start thinking she's a witch . . ."

"Nobody's going to believe that."

"Ophelia McCallister does," said Mack.

"Well," said Grand, "I guess you got to believe something, strange things like this going on."

"Mr. Harrison, I—"

"After what we just did, Mack Street, I think we definitely on a first-name basis."

"Sir," said Mack, who couldn't call a man older than Miz Smitcher by his first name no matter what he said, "what's going on here is magic, and Yolanda White is a magical person, but she did not cause these things tonight. It was her worst enemy caused it, and she's trying to fight him, and if she gets blamed for it, well it's just what that enemy wants."

"I'll stay with her," said Grand Harrison. "I won't let her go calling Yolanda White a witch." He thought for a moment. "I'll call my wife to come over with me."

Mack thanked him and headed out the door.

He jogged down the steep hill and as he rounded the hairpin turn he saw two things.

First, the standpipe was glowing. No longer the color of rust, it was a deep red, and it glowed as if it were being heated by lava under the earth.

And second, there was a crowd outside Yolanda's house, shouting, and some of them were beating on the door with their fists.

Was Yolanda even in there? When she left them at Ophelia's house, she said she was going to find Ceese.

But even if she wasn't in there, she could arrive at any time, and in the mood they were in, even she might not be able to keep them from dragging her off her bike. Could she change them *all* so they loved her? Maybe there was a reason witches in the past were mobbed—if they were really malevolent fairies, it would take a mob to overwhelm them.

Was it all true? Fairies that might be tiny or regular size. Giants. Possession by devils. Witches that flew and cursed people. All distorted memories of real encounters with beings like Puck and Yo Yo, or real trips into Fairyland.

And they really were dangerous. Most of those witchhunts in the past, they were probably just what his high school teachers had taught him, a stupid excuse for a lynching, a way for people to settle old scores or try to shut out their fears, by killing somebody and feeling they were on God's errand when they did it.

But the reason people believed in witches in the first place— they didn't just make them up. Maybe they met Yolanda. Or Puck. Or Oberon. Saw their power. Felt their own helplessness. Hated them, feared them. And remembered.

Did that mean there were werewolves and vampires, too? What about Superman and Spider-Man and why not Underdog, too?

It couldn't all be true. But some of it was. There was real power in the world, and it was dark and cruel, and Mack didn't know if he was right to trust Yo Yo; he knew he was right not to trust Puck.

Maybe the human race had reason to fear little creatures lurking in the woods, or people who walked the earth in human form but were really controlled by cruel entities who could make you love them, or beings of light that could be captured in bottles or jars, and if you turned them loose they'd grant your wishes and then laugh at the agony your own wishes brought to you.

Maybe the mob outside Yolanda White's house had the right response. Maybe powers like this needed to be destroyed whenever they surfaced.

Then again, he *liked* Yo Yo.

But how could he trust that feeling, when he knew she could make him like her, make *anybody* like her?

The people gathered outside her house, pounding on her doors and getting ready to break her windows, they were his neighbors. *She* was the stranger.

Hadn't Ceese said she tried to kill Mack himself when he was a baby? He owed her nothing.

But when he tried to imagine himself joining his neighbors in attacking Yolanda, he knew he couldn't do it. She wasn't the one who put Tamika Brown in a wheelchair. There was evil in this world, but right now, at this moment, it wasn't her.

It was the hatred he saw in the faces of his neighbors. It was the wolflike howling of their voices.

So he kept jogging down the hill until he was among them, pushing his way through them. Then he stood on the porch, shoving aside the men who were kicking at the door.

"Where's your burning cross!" he shouted. "You can't have a lynching without a burning cross! Where are your white hoods? Come on, do this right! You gonna kill somebody without a trial, just because you're scared, then get the gear, wear the outfit, follow the recipe!"

By the time he was through with his little speech, they were mostly silent, watching him.

"Why are you doing this?"

"She's a witch!" shouted a man. The others murmured their assent.

"So when LAPD shows up and wonders why there's a riot in *Baldwin Hills* and maybe even a lynching, you'll all explain that you had to burn a witch, is that your plan? That's what we'll see when they show your pictures on the evening news. Niggahs riot again but this time it's cause they all 'fraid of *witches.*" He poured all the scorn he could muster into his words.

"Mack," said Ebby DeVries, "I'm scared."

"Of course you're scared," said Mack. "Ugly things happened here tonight. And it doesn't make sense, because what happened, it was magic. Evil. Just like you think. Just like poor old Curtis Brown tried to tell us all those years ago. He woke up and Tamika was swimming around inside his waterbed and he only just saved her life. Impossible! Couldn't happen! Like Deacon Landry. He *never* did nothing to Juanettia Post. He wished for it! That's all he did! Any of you men ever wish for a woman wasn't your wife? That was all it was, *wishing*. Then all of a sudden, just like Tamika in the waterbed, he's in the middle of church naked with Juanettia Post right when people start arriving for church."

"Choir practice," somebody corrected him.

"Tonight Grand Harrison and me, we dug up old Mr. McCallister's grave and opened his coffin and saved the life of Ophelia McCallister because she *wished* she could be with him and that same evil magic *granted her damn wish*."

There was a murmur through the crowd.

"And what about you? Why were you suddenly so sure you had to come attack Yolanda White? Who told you she was a witch?"

"Nobody had to tell us," said Lamar Weeks.

"That's right," said Mack. "You just *knew*. You woke up and you *knew* she was a witch and you had to go . . . do what? What were you going to *do*?"

"Get her," somebody said.

"Get her and do *what*?" demanded Mack.

They had no answer.

"Burn her alive? Was that the plan? Like they used to do when they lynched uppity niggahs in the South? String her up and light a fire under her? Don't you see? That same evil magic got into *you* and made you act like the most evil people you ever knew of. And you didn't even *try* to stop yourselves." He looked at Ebby. "Ebony DeVries, what you doing here?"

"Watching you save your loverbaby's life," she said bitterly.

"But there it is again!" said Mack. "If there's anybody in the world I got a crush on, it's you, Ebby. Not her! And I think you got a crush on me, too. But that evil magic got into you and said, Yo Yo White is stealing away your man. Isn't that right? But it's not *true*. That evil is her *enemy* and it wants you to do its dirty work."

"How do *you* know so much, Mack Street!" called out Ebony's father.

"Because that evil magic been doing ugly things to *me* my whole life. I been seeing your dreams—the deep dreams, the wishes of your heart. This whole neighborhood, I been seeing your darkest secrets in my dreams *my whole life.*"

"And you telling us there's no such thing as witches?" said Lamar.

"I'm telling you that there *is* such a thing as evil, and tonight you are his slaves! Unless you stand up and say *no* to the devil."

"*You* say no to the devil!" shouted Lamar. "Get away from the door and let us through."

"Start by killing *me*, Lamar," said Mack. "Not the whole mob here, just you. Come up here and kill me. Do murder with your own hands. Show everybody how you're the *enemy* of evil. Kill a kid."

"Nobody going to kill you, Mack," said a woman.

"I been fighting off these dreams of yours for years, ever since I figured out how it worked. If I let the dream finish, then it might come true. So I'd make myself get out of those dreams of yours. I wouldn't let them finish. But tonight, our enemy started making his move. He forced the dreams through to the end. Ophelia McCallister wishing for her husband to be in her arms again. Sabrina Chum wishing she didn't have such a big nose all over her face. Sherita Banks wishing that boys would find her desirable. Professor Williams wishing people would read his poems. The wishes of their heart. Tonight they finished those dreams. I told Ceese and Yo Yo, and they been working all night trying to stop bad things from happening to these decent people. No more like Tamika! We didn't want any more like Deacon Landry! Maybe Ceese got to the others in time. I know that with Grand Harrison's help, me and Yo Yo saved Ophelia McCallister. And now you want to do the devil's work by *killing* a woman who helped me save Ophelia McCallister from her own terrible wish!"

"He making this shit up," said Lamar.

"Find out if I am. Call the Chums. Call Sherita's house. You check with Grand Harrison."

He didn't tell them to talk to Ophelia McCallister. Not if she was going to still be babbling about Yo Yo being a witch.

Of course, they might all be infected with the same delusion. In which case, what could he do? He wasn't strong enough to fight them off.

And he couldn't explain to them about the king of the fairies. Not if he wanted anybody to believe anything he said.

He pointed at Lamar Weeks. "You, Lamar. I know about that dream of yours. Money, Lamar. It's all you want, enough money that people have to treat you with respect, you can have everything you want. Only for you it's all wrapped up in that car. That fine Lexus. Everybody see you in that car, right? Isn't that the dream?"

Lamar took a step back. "You stay out of my dreams."

"How many times have I got you out of that dream? Taken you into *my* dream, riding along in a clunky car through a canyon and water comes down . . ."

"Stop it!" shouted Lamar.

"I been keeping you all safe from your own dreams. From the wishes that come up out of that pipe in the ground!" He pointed toward where it was. It was just behind the lip of the hill—they couldn't see it from there. "Go look at it!" Mack said. "Go see the place. It flows up out of there, poisoning the street, poisoning the neighborhood. A river of power, a river of magic, taking your dreams, and *I have been protecting you.*"

They began moving away from Yolanda's house. Out of her yard. Toward the edge of the little valley where rainwater collected to flow down the drain.

Mack didn't know what they'd see. Maybe only the drainpipe just like always. Or maybe the red glow he had seen.

Ebby came up to him. "You really have a crush on me?"

"Of course I do," said Mack. "But I didn't expect to tell you standing on a porch yelling at a mob."

"I don't know what got into me," said Ebby. "I just *knew* she was evil and stealing you away, only it doesn't make sense, and now I can see that she . . . that you . . ."

"It's cool," said Mack. "It's all cool now. Nobody going to kill nobody."

"But I was so sure. Like it was the most important thing in the world. To stop her."

"Come on," said Mack. He held out his hand. She took it. They walked up the hill behind the others.

They lined up along the edge of the valley, looking down. It still glowed red, but not as strong. Could anybody see that except Mack?

If they *couldn't* see it, why were they still looking at it?

"Anybody else see what I see?" said Lamar. "That thing look hot enough to melt."

The others murmured their assent. "Red," somebody said. "Red hot."

"Red as the devil in hell," somebody else said.

"Ain't the devil," said Mack.

They were silent. Listening to him respectfully, now that he had woken them from the trance of blood lust.

"I tell you what it is," said Mack. "It's the one who made me. The king of . . . it's going to sound stupid, but it's not. The king of the fairies. The elves. The leprechauns. He's been shut up under the earth. Imprisoned for a long time. He's mad as hell and he's getting ready to make a break for it. He's been sending his power out into the world through that pipe."

Through me, Mack thought but didn't say.

"I feel it more than anybody," said Mack. "Being found by that pipe the way I was. It's inside me. That's why I see your wish dreams. But I got no power of my own. I'm nothing compared to him. We got to stop him, and I don't know how. Yolanda, she's not a witch. She's *good*. But she's got a little bit of power. That's all. She used to have more. She used to have so much, she was the one who imprisoned him. Get it? She's his most terrible enemy, so that's why he sent out his power and tried to get you to kill her tonight."

"Through that pipe," said a man.

"He going to give me that Lexus?" asked Lamar, half mocking.

"How about this," said Mack. "How about if you suddenly wake up in that Lexus, going seventy miles an hour and heading right through a guardrail and over the cliff above the Santa Monica pier?"

"Yeah, right," said Lamar.

"Or you wake up in that Lexus and the whole LAPD on your ass going down the freeway like O. J. and you all covered with blood only you don't know whose blood it is. Maybe the owner of that Lexus. Maybe that's how your wish gets fulfilled. Everybody see you in that Lexus, man! On TV! Only there's a dead Lexus owner back in his garage and your prints all over the golf club that beat his brains in. How about that for getting your wish?"

"Never happen," said Lamar.

"Ophelia McCallister woke up tonight inside her dead husband's coffin," said Mack. "That couldn't happen either."

"I think we ought to talk to these people," said Osie Fleming. "Find out what's true before we believe this bullshit."

They heard the sound of a motorcycle.

They turned and saw a single headlight coming up the hill.

Two people on the bike. Had to be Yolanda in front. And behind her, when she got close enough, when she turned into the driveway of her house, was Sherita Banks. Couldn't be anybody else, those hips.

Sherita looked up at all these people watching her from fifty yards away and buried her face in Yo Yo's back. Yo Yo turned and saw them, too. They watched her put down the kickstand and worm her way off the bike without Sherita getting off first. And when she helped Sherita off, they could see that the girl was wearing a blanket wrapped around her like a skirt.

They came down the hill. Mack let go of Ebby's hand and ran down ahead of them.

"What's happening, Mack." Yo Yo called out to him.

Mack didn't answer. He got ahead of the pack and turned and faced them. "Not one step closer," he said. Over his shoulder, he called out to Yo Yo. "Some of these folks got to thinking you a witch tonight. Came to pay a visit. Maybe have them a lynching."

"Nobody going to lynch nobody," said Lamar.

"Me? A witch?" said Yo Yo. And she laughed.

It was a glorious laugh, warm and resonant. It seemed to reverberate from the hills on either side. It seemed to make the stars twinkle clearer overhead.

More people were walking up the hill and down the hill to converge at her house.

"Sherita!" called out Ebby. "What happened?"

Sherita burst into tears and hid behind Yo Yo.

"She nearly got raped, that's what," said Yo Yo. "She was asleep in her own bed having this *dream,* and she woke up at a friend's house and there was her gangbanger brother getting all set to start a train on her. Yeah, that's what! And you know why it didn't happen? Cause Mack saw her dream and told Ceese and he called his buddies on the force and they got there in time. Isn't that right, Sherita?"

They could see that Sherita was nodding.

"What you people want here?" demanded Yo Yo. "Leave this girl alone. I just brought her here to clean up and borrow some clothes before she went home. She didn't want her daddy and mama to see her with nothing on."

Lamar turned to Mack. "All that proves is the two of you got your stories together."

"Give it a rest, Lamar," said Osie Fleming. "The girl isn't denying it. And Mack's right. It's crazy to be going after a witch like this. What were we thinking?"

"*He* believes in magic, dammit," said Lamar. "It's not like he's saying there's no such thing as a witch!"

"And I'm saying we're crazy to treat this like an emergency," said Osie. "What were we thinking? Plenty of time to talk about this tomorrow. Find out how much of what Mack Street here told us is the truth. We can talk to Ceese. We can talk to the Chums. We can talk to Byron. Let's go home and go to bed. Witch hunt in the middle of the night. We must be crazy."

That was it. The end of it. People started heading back up and down the street.

Yo Yo called out from the driveway. "Any of you need a ride up the hill, I'll be back outside in a minute!"

Shut up, Yo Yo, Mack thought but did not say. You're not making any friends teasing them like that.

"I heard that, Mack Street," she said to him as he approached.

"You did not."

"Did so."

"What did I say?"

"You said, 'I'm your hero now, Miz Yolanda, cause I kept them from breaking up your house.' "

"I didn't know you wasn't inside," said Mack.

"So you were saving my life."

"Take that girl inside, Yo Yo."

But Sherita didn't go. She turned to face Mack. Now that the crowd was dispersed, she didn't feel so ashamed. "Officer that saved me said it was Ceese Tucker told him to come save me. And Ceese told me it was you saw what I was getting into," she said.

"I know you didn't choose to do it," said Mack.

"Thank you, Mack," she said. "And for what it's worth, *I* never thought you was crazy."

Behind her, Yo Yo waggled her eyebrows. But Mack didn't laugh. "Thank you, Sherita. Now you go on inside with Yolanda."

IT WAS NEAR THREE A.M. before Yo Yo got Sherita back to her folks and extricated herself from tears and hugs and thanks. And not long after that, Mack joined her, along with Ceese and Grand Harrison down Cloverdale, between the Snipe and Chandress houses.

"What's *he* doing here?" asked Ceese. Yolanda was just as suspicious.

Mack smiled. "He was my ride?"

"You walk everywhere, Mack," said Ceese.

"He helped me dig out Miz Ophelia," said Mack. "He knows what he saw. He knows you got powers, but he believes you're not a witch. There's no reason to leave him out now. And we need all the friends we can get."

"So you're taking him across?" asked Yo Yo.

"If I can," said Mack. "I'll hold on to him and Ceese and get them inside."

"And what about me?" asked Yo Yo.

"You don't need my help."

"You ever seen me inside there?" she asked.

"No."

"Then how do you know I don't need your help?"

"Puck—Mr. Christmas—he gets in and out just fine."

"That's cause it suits my husband's purposes to let him. But me? I don't think so."

"If he's watching everything you do," said Ceese, "then how can you expect to fight him and win?"

"He's not watching," said Yo Yo. "He just made this place so it locks down hard if I come up."

"So what makes you think Mack can get you in?"

"Cause he's such a lucky boy," said Yo Yo.

"That's why I'm so rich," said Mack. "Come on, let's see if we can all go at once, holding on to each other. If we can't, I'll take you one at a time."

19

COUNCIL OF WAR

Puck was waiting for them inside the house. The living room was furnished exactly like Yo Yo's living room. In fact, it *was* her furniture, right down to having Sherita's blanket tossed on the couch.

"Puck," said Yo Yo, "just keep your hands off my stuff."

"I never know what's going to show up here," said Puck. "The boy comes in bringing you—so your stuff appears. Bingo! Presto! Abracadabra!"

"Bite me," said Yo Yo.

"Like you'd ever really let me," said Puck.

"You always offer, but you're all talk."

"I know what *he* does to his servants who, uh, bite you."

"We got a situation," said Ceese, "and we got to figure out what to do."

"You?" said Puck. "*You* don't have a situation, my lady and I have a situation."

"This shit tonight didn't happen to *you*, it happened to people in our neighborhood, and we're *going* to do something about it," said Ceese.

"Ceese, he knows that," said Mack.

Puck grinned cheesily.

"Asshole," muttered Ceese.

"Bad language exacerbates the situation," said Puck. "I know they taught you that in cop nursery. Always stay calm."

"What in the world is going on with you people?" said Grand Harrison. "Tonight I was just minding my own business, and then I get my tools and my SUV borrowed, I dig up a grave, open a coffin, and take my next-door neighbor out. Then I get brought down here into a house that doesn't exist and listen to a bunch of fools argue about nothing. You know what I want? I want to know how you all going to keep this stuff from happening again."

"What stuff?" asked Puck.

"Wishes," said Mack.

"Mack's dreams," said Ceese.

"He's cut loose a big one tonight, Puckling," said Yo Yo.

"That means he's got himself a pony to ride," said Puck—again talking as if Yo Yo were the only person in the room.

"Yes," said Yo Yo.

"A pony?" asked Ceese.

"Some human he can work through. Kind of like the way my lady and I using these two bodies."

Grand didn't like hearing that. "You telling me that you—that these bodies are *possessed?*"

"Leased," said Puck. "With option."

"This girl," said Yo Yo, "she on drugs, had two abortions, getting pimped out by a guy who beat her, plus she had a couple of diseases she didn't know about or care. I have her for nearly eighteen years now, and she hasn't aged a day, she's not addicted to anything, and she looking fine."

"This old coot," said Puck, "be eating out of dumpsters and licking sweet roll wrappers and walking around talking to his dead dog named God, cause he figured as long as he knew it wasn't really God, just a dog with God's name, he wasn't actually schizo."

"We don't take bodies somebody actually using," said Yo Yo. "And that's the truth, Mr. Harrison."

"What did you mean," said Mack, "when you said 'leased with option'?"

"Didn't mean a thing," said Puck.

"You always mean something. Usually about six things."

"He means," said Yo Yo, "that if something happens to these bodies while we using them, then our option's up."

"You die?" asked Mack.

"Not the part of us in those glass jugs," said Yo Yo. "Just the part of us that can move around on its own. Be like living in a wheelchair after that."

"Worse," said Puck. "Be like living as a human."

"So you're not completely immortal," said Mack. "Just partly immortal."

"And that's why Puck couldn't tell you the truth," said Yo Yo. "He's under strict orders. He can never tell a mortal the truth unless he's sure he won't be believed."

"That's not true," said Puck. He grinned.

"Shut up, Puckster," said Yo Yo.

"We got a situation," said Ceese, "and *you* got a situation. Not the same situation, but they got the same cause. Your husband, your master, the king of the fairies, whatever he is, he's got himself a pony, right? And doing that made all those wishes come true tonight. So to solve your problem, and our problem, what can we do?"

"Nothing," said Puck. "We are absolutely helpless. Go home. Cry into your pillows until your dreams come true."

"He's so funny," said Mack to Grand. "Always joking. You know how Puck is."

"Mack," said Yo Yo. "The thing is, it's a fight you can't fight. You already did all you could. For years you did it, deflecting his power so they never finished their dreams. That was good work, but now it's done. He's got his power out in the world."

"But how come?" asked Mack. "How come *his* . . . pony . . . can do stuff like making wishes come true, and you two can't do very much at all?"

"Oberon's pony isn't doing this stuff," said Yo Yo. "In your neighborhood, I mean."

"Who is, then?"

"Puck," said Yo Yo.

Puck elaborately curled himself into a fetal position as if he feared being struck by stones.

"This isn't funny, Puck," said Mack. "*You* did this?"

"It's in my nature," said Puck.

"That's true enough," said Yo Yo. "He can't help being a trickster. But also he has Oberon's direct command to find these twists. The thing is, Puck can't tell you because it would be the truth, but he's also deflecting them. He can't stop it from happening, but . . . well, for instance, Ophelia *and* her husband could have been entwined in a love embrace under the HOLLYWOOD sign. Or halfway to Catalina. And Sherita—it didn't have to be a boy her family knew about, it could have been some rich boy in Beverly Hills or Palos Verdes, and how would you have found her then?"

"So he was *helping*," said Mack skeptically.

"As best he could," said Yo Yo.

Puck ducked his head in a show of modesty.

"He does what he can," said Yo Yo. "Here's the thing. What he can do, what I can do, it isn't much. The part of us he locked up, it includes most of our powers except persuasion and . . . pony riding. And the way it works is, we can't get that part out. Because *this* part of us, the wandering part, the curious part, is walking around free. It makes it so we aren't *hungry* enough to force anything.

"But him," she went on, "we pushed *him* all the way under. Didn't divide him. So to do *anything* he has to squeeze it out of his captivity. Get some part of him to the surface of the earth. But that part is never completely separated from him. He's not *divided* like we are." She sighed. "Took him a long time, but the force of his wandering part was so great that it worked its way through a channel to the surface of the earth."

"And that's the pony you were talking about," said Mack.

"No, Mack," said Yo Yo. "That was you. Seventeen years ago. You the first thing he squeezed out. We could feel him breaking through like a mother hen watching her chicks jiggle their eggs and then peck a hole. But we couldn't stop him. Puck here couldn't even try—he's bound to Oberon by vows he can't break. All *I* could do was try to persuade Ceese here to kill you, and he was too strong for me. His love for you too strong."

"You people are a piece of work," said Grand Harrison.

"Now I just don't understand that saying," said Puck. "A piece of needlework? Or, like, when we call a woman a 'piece,' only she does it for money so she's, you know, *working* when—"

"Shut up, Puck," said Yo Yo.

"What you're saying," said Mack, "is you want me to break you out of your little glass jars."

"Eventually," said Yo Yo. "But not *you*. You couldn't do it."

"I couldn't?" asked Mack.

"Impossible," said Puck.

"He lying, right?" Mack asked Yo Yo.

"Do you believe him?"

"No," said Mack.

"Then it doesn't matter if it's true or not, does it?" asked Yo Yo. "Look, Mack, I've tried to tell you several times. You are the part of him that he squeezed out first. You *are* Oberon."

"Bull," said Mack.

"That's why you can find where this house is hidden," said Ceese. "And why you don't change sizes going into Fairyland."

"I'm me," said Mack. "I don't have any memory of being Oberon. I got no powers."

"Excuse me," said Yo Yo. "You think seeing dreams ain't a power?"

"It's not a power if I can't control it," said Mack.

"But you *did* control it," said Ceese. "For a long time."

"*You* wander freely through Fairyland and nothing hurts you," said Yo Yo. "*Puck* goes twenty feet in and birds pick him up and damn near feed him to their babies."

"Because I'm Oberon."

"You're part of him," said Yo Yo.

"So I'm his spy?"

"No," said Yo Yo. "He probably can't use you for that. Like I said, you're not his pony—he'll see through the eyes and speak through the mouth and hear through the ears of whoever he's inside. But you—he's about as conscious of you as a mortal normally is of his heartbeat."

"When I run hard enough, I hear my heartbeat without even taking my pulse," said Mack.

"That's right. Under stress, you're more aware. Same with him. Sometimes he notices you but only when you're in trouble."

"I'm in trouble right now," said Mack. "Cause the only fairies I know keep telling me I'm their enemy."

"You're not our—" Yo Yo began.

"We're *your* enemy," said Puck, "but you're not *ours*."

"You're not our enemy," Yo Yo said forcefully, shutting Puck up.

"And if he feels like it, he can make me betray you."

"Hasn't yet, though, has he?" asked Yo Yo.

"I'm not some discarded piece of the king of the fairies," said Mack heatedly. "I'm not some appendix or tonsil, I'm *me*. I was raised by Miz Smitcher and Ceese here. I was trained up on the Bible and I try to be a decent man. I work at whatever I'm supposed to work on. I even work to oppose Oberon, and he doesn't stop me. He's not me, I'm not him."

"You're not the part of him that chooses," said Yo Yo, gently touching his arm to calm him. "See, Mack, here's what happened. He needed a changeling here to store up the power of all these people's wishes. So he sent you. It doesn't matter to him whether the wishes come true or not, except that if they do, he has Puck here assigned to make sure something ugly happens for Oberon's entertainment. *That* he likes—so when Puck comes back, *if* he does, Oberon will want a full report."

"So what am I, then? His gas tank?"

"No," said Yo Yo. "No, you're his conscience. That's the part he had to get rid of. That's the part that was stopping him from doing something truly hideous to us and to all the mortals. By taking every good thing out of his own heart, all his decency and honor and hope and joy and love, and putting them in you and shoving you out into the world, he left only pure ambition and pride and vengefulness and power-lust and violence there in his own heart."

"He decided to be evil," said Mack. "And I'm supposed to be all the good he threw away?"

"He would say, all the weakness and softness."

"I'm not weak," said Mack.

"That's his mistake," said Yo Yo. "That's our secret weapon. He *thinks* you're weak because he always managed to hide his kind heart under a mask of jokery and rages and malice. But it was there, and it kept him from utterly destroying people. Once you were . . . born, Mack, then there was no restraint on his will to evil. It could grow and grow. Bit by bit. Without you in his heart, he turned himself into the devil."

"Not *the* devil," said Puck. "I wouldn't want you to get a swelled head thinking you seen *him*."

"Meaning that he *is* the real devil? Cause Puck lies?"

"He lies," said Yo Yo, "but it doesn't mean that whatever he says is the opposite of the truth, either. That would be just as sure a guide as telling you the truth in the first place."

"Yo Yo," said Mack. "The stuff you're telling me. What difference does it make? I think I'm a free man, you think I'm secretly Oberon. So what?"

"So you can do things that we need. We can use you," said Yo Yo, "to set up the old dragon and—"

"Kill him?" Mack whispered.

"No, but castration and stomach stapling seem appropriate," said Puck.

"Is he fat?" asked Ceese.

"No, I just want him to throw up every time he eats more than three little bites of a meal."

"We got to get out of the jugs," said Yo Yo. "And not just set free. *Protected* till our . . . souls are given back."

"Why should we free *his* soul?" asked Mack, thumbing at Puck.

Puck let out a long, loud fart. Fortunately odorless. In fact, knowing Puck, it probably wasn't a real fart.

"Don't, if you don't want to," said Yo Yo. "Just remember that without me, Puck would belong completely to Oberon. No more attempts to make it possible for you to avoid letting people hurt themselves."

"My head is spinning," said Grand. "I want to go home and go to bed."

"I didn't invite you," Puck said cheerfully. "Feel free to leave any time."

"What exactly is the plan?" asked Mack. "And what can we do to help?"

"Nothing," said Yo Yo. "It's too powerful for you. Thanks for all you did so far, but except for one tiny thing, we don't need you at all and don't intend to put you at risk."

"What's that one tiny thing?" asked Mack.

"Get us out of those jars."

"How?" asked Mack.

"Well," said Yo Yo, "that's the thing. In order for us to do that, we'd have to know the counterword. So we do need you to get that. You or somebody."

"Where do I learn this 'counterword'?" asked Mack.

"Oh, you already know it," said Yo Yo. "You just don't *know* that you know it. In fact, you think you don't know it. But you know it."

"So you *do* need me."

"Just a little bit. Then we're on our own."

"Okay," said Mack. "I'll help you find that password—"

"Counterword," said Puck with all the smugness of Alex Tre-
bek.

"But you got to help us, too."

"We *are* helping you," said Yo Yo. "Once we get out of those
jars and put back together properly, *then* we can go find Oberon's
pony and shut him down. Put him out of business. Stuff the genie
back into the bottle. So to speak."

"Won't he know you're out?"

"Well," said Yo Yo, "probably."

"So won't he come down on you the second you're free?"

"That's the other little thing we need."

"The counterword *and* something else."

"We need a distraction. We need—"

Grand Harrison interrupted her. "What you need is a fairy circle."

Yolanda looked at him like he was insane. "Do you know how
many fairies it takes to make a decent circle?"

"But it's what you need, isn't it?" said Grand.

"We got no fairies to work with," said Puck. "Oberon keeps a
tight rein on them. He only lets the ones he absolutely trusts to
come out to . . . um . . . play. So we can't raise a circle."

"He lying?" Mack asked Yo Yo.

"Do you believe him?" asked Yo Yo in reply.

"Yadda yadda," said Mack. "We never get a straight answer."

"Can't get a straight answer into a crooked mind," said Puck.

"What do you mean by that?" demanded Mack.

"I mean the only time you believe me is when I lie."

Grand Harrison spoke up again. "If he can suck our wishes out
of us, why can't *you* use us mortals in your fairy circle?"

"And that's really starting to bother me," said Puck, rising to his
feet. "What do *you* know about fairy circles?"

"It's how you do truly great magicks. You bring together a bunch of fairies and they form a circle and all of the power of all the fairies in the circle becomes part of the great thing you're trying to do."

"And you learned this where?" asked Yo Yo.

"The *Blue Book of Fairy Tales*," said Grand. "Or the *Red* one. Or whatever."

"Not *in* those books," said Puck.

"Stay on topic, Puckaroo," said Yo Yo.

"If I had any real power, she'd drop dead when she called me that," said Puck. Then he grinned at Yolanda. "Just kidding, darling."

"Fairy circle," said Ceese. "Grand's idea."

"It might work," said Yo Yo. "Except we don't know just how much of him he's put into his pony. If it's all there, except for the part that *is* Mack—then we could do it using a fairy circle made of mortals. But if part of him is here in this world, and part of him in Fairyland, that would be like lassoing a one-inch-thick snake with a lariat that won't get any skinnier than two inches in diameter."

"Will this be on the geometry test?" asked Mack.

"So to do a fairy circle in order to confine him long enough for us to get free, you have to find out where he is, exactly," said Ceese. "And in order to find out where he is, you need—let me guess— Mack, because he *is* Oberon. Sort of."

"That's right," said Yo Yo.

"Only Mack doesn't know it," said Ceese.

Puck suddenly had a moustache and twirled it. "Little does he know . . ." The moustache disappeared when everybody looked at him and nobody laughed.

"So how you going to get your counterword and your information out of a guy who doesn't actually know the things you think he knows?" asked Ceese.

"Sleep with him, of course," said Yo Yo.

"He's seventeen!" said Ceese.

"It's the time-honored tradition," said Grand. "Fairy queen needs to find out something from a mortal. She gets him into Fairyland, boffs his brains out, and then he just won't go away. Mortal stalks her until she takes pity on him and makes him forget."

"Blue Fairy Book or Red?" asked Mack.

"He's just making this up," said Puck.

"I'm a folklorist," said Grand. "Amateur. Started with slave narratives and slave magic beliefs. Then I branched out. I never thought it was real."

"If you think *this* is real," said Puck.

"Shut the Puck up," said Yo Yo.

"Ha ha," said Puck. "Aren't we the class clown."

"But you've got to do it all at once," said Grand, "which is impossible. Because you can't use the fairy circle to bind him unless you two fairies are in control of it, and you can't get control of it till you're reunited with your imprisoned selves. And you can't be liberated until the fairy circle has distracted him."

"Plus I ain't sleeping with you," said Mack.

Both Puck and Yo Yo looked at him like he was crazy. "Everybody wants to sleep with her," said Puck.

"Not me," said Mack.

"Yes you do," said Yo Yo. "You think I don't know?"

"Oh, I want to," said Mack. "But I don't *want* to."

"Try English this time," said Puck.

"I *want* to sleep with her but I don't *choose* to sleep with her."

Yo Yo was on her feet in an instant. "Why not? What's wrong with me? I have never had a mortal turn me down!"

"Because I'm not sleeping with a girl I'm not married to," said Mack.

"Wow," said Ceese. "You don't hear *that* very much."

"*You* doing it that way," said Mack to Ceese.

"Yeah, but I'm not sure how much of that is voluntary and how much is inadvertent."

Puck giggled and spoke to Mack. "So you want to get *married?*"

"She's already married," said Ceese.

"It doesn't matter," said Yo Yo.

"It does to me," said Mack.

"I mean, it doesn't matter that I'm married to Oberon. You *are* Oberon. So I could sleep with you right now."

"Oberon and you might be married, but I'm not Oberon," said Mack. "And *we're* not married."

Ceese tried to summarize it. "So this all comes down to, Mack gets it on with Yolanda White here, you find out what you need to know, then all the other stuff happens at once."

"That's it," said Yo Yo.

"Including a fairy circle," said Ceese.

"If the neighbors might be willing to cooperate."

"We form your fairy circle," said Grand, "will that make these horrible wishes stop?"

"It would give me and Puck the power we need, if there are enough of you."

"And we got to get all those people into this house?" asked Grand.

"No, dear no," said Yo Yo. "Mortals' wishes have no power in Fairyland. Especially not here in this passageway. No, the fairy circle has to be in the mortal world."

"But you're imprisoned in Fairyland," said Mack.

"Right," said Puck. "Why do you think we haven't already worked this out with some other neighborhood long ago?"

"You haven't worked it out with *this* neighborhood, either," said Ceese. "You got a long way to go before most of these folks willing to cross the street for Miz Yolanda."

"You haven't worked *any* of it out," said Mack. "Including the part where you sleep with me just to get information. It's like some bad World War One movie. What was that musical one with Julie Andrews and Rock Hudson?"

"Who are they?" asked Ceese.

"When people are watching a video, they let me stay and watch," said Mack. "I seen about everything. *Darling Lili,* that was the name of it. Mary Poppins did a striptease. Nobody wants to see Mary Poppins do a striptease."

"I wouldn't mind," said Puck.

"I'm not going to lie with a woman I'm not married to," said Mack.

"That one heavy Bible-reading boy there," said Puck.

"Good for you, Mack Street," said Grand.

"queen of the fairies wants to sleep with you," said Ceese, "and you saying *no?*"

"I'm saying, Marry me," said Mack.

"Whatever," said Yo Yo.

It infuriated Mack that she dismissed him so easily. "Marry me and mean it."

"I meant it the first time I married you," said Yo Yo impatiently. "Isn't that enough?"

"You never married *me,*" said Mack. He got up and walked out the front door.

"Oh good," said Ceese. "Now how are *we* going to get home?"

"You don't need his help to get *out,* you boneheaded mortal," said Puck with a cheery smile. "Only to get in."

"Why is that?" asked Grand.

"Because that's the world you come from," said Yo Yo. "The world of the street out there. It's where you belong. You can always go home."

"So does that mean *Mack* belongs in our world, too?" asked Ceese.

Yo Yo patted his hand. "You such a sweet boy, Ceese. Still looking out for your little Mack Street. That boy lives in both worlds. He lives in both worlds *all the time.*"

"You mean when he's in Fairyland, he's walking around here, too?" said Ceese. "I'm surprised he wasn't hit by a car."

"I mean he casts a shadow in both worlds. He makes a footprint."

Puck snorted. "That boy barely *is* a footprint. Doesn't even make it up to shadow."

"He's more than a shadow," said Ceese. "He's the best kid in the world."

"Cause he don't make no trouble," said Puck. "Exactly my point."

Ceese turned away from him and spoke to Yolanda. "I don't want him to marry you."

"Like I said, I don't care either way. I just got to know what's going on with my husband."

"I know a lot of people slept with a lot of other people and still don't know squat about any of them."

"Ceese," said Yolanda. "Didn't you ever wonder why the Queen of the Fairies kept wanting to sleep with wandering minstrels and farmboys? In all those fairy tales?"

"Same reason white women always want to sleep with black men," said Ceese.

"Poor boy," said Yolanda. "When mortals hook up like that, they don't even know each other's *bodies.* It ain't even *carnal* knowledge. But when I hook up with somebody, I know everything, I see everything. I even know stuff they don't know they know. It's all mine. *That's* what I love."

"Oberon do that too?"

"He thinks he does, but he got no idea what-all I get from it. Truly knowing everything about another person—*that* takes me *way* higher than all that trembly screechy moany stuff mortal women get so excited about."

"But fairy *men* don't do that."

"Maybe they could, if they bothered to look into their partner the way I look into mine."

"Just seems to me," said Ceese, "you taking a lot from Mack and giving him pretty damn little."

"I'm a queen," said Yolanda. "What planet *you* been living on?"

"So, you going to spoil him for other women? You going to make it so he can't be happy with somebody like Ebony DeVries?"

Yolanda almost answered. Then she shook her head. "I won't keep him from anything he ever had a chance of having."

"Oh, you're all heart," said Ceese. "You're Miss Congeniality times ten."

"Cecil Tucker," she said, "I will never do anything that harms Mack Street. But I also can't give him any happiness that is out of his reach by nature."

"Nothing natural about any of you fairies."

"I don't like the way you said 'fairies,' " said Puck.

"And I don't give a flying Puck what you like," said Ceese.

"That would be a 'plying' Puck, I think," said Puck.

"Hush," said Yolanda. "We need Ceese."

"What do you need *me* for?"

"Sometimes you got to have a giant."

20

WEDDING

All day people called and came by Rev Theo's church, wanting to know if the stories they were hearing were true. Rev Theo assured them that last night they were truly blessed by God, and yes, it was through the vessel of Word Williams, his associate pastor. If anyone noticed that "associate pastor" was a promotion, they didn't mention it.

Those who wanted to talk to Word, however, were disappointed. Word spent the morning and much of the afternoon in seclusion. From time to time, Rev Theo would knock on the door of his own office, but Word would answer, "Can I have just a little longer, sir?"

Rev Theo was telling everybody that Word was spending the day in prayer, and it was true that from time to time he prayed. But mostly he was reading scripture and trying to sort things out in his mind.

There was no denying that the gift he had received last night did good things for people. He was given knowledge he shouldn't have had; the words just flowed into his mind and he spoke them. And the healings, the saved life, those were real and definitely good.

But countering it all was the feeling of having something enter him. The Holy Spirit was supposed to be a feeling of joy, exaltation. Not like someone inserting a cold and creepy hand into the back of your head and down your spine. Like a worm insinuating itself in your flesh.

It felt like being possessed by a devil. Not that Word had ever had such a thing happen before. But how else could it feel? Or like having some alien creature get inside your nervous system and take over your body.

Only here he was, praying, reading the Bible, all those things that were supposed to make devils uncomfortable, and nothing was happening. At the same time, didn't he still feel it down his spine? A kind of thickness at the back of his head? An extra little hitch in his shoulders when he moved his arms? Or was that all his imagination?

Does the Spirit of God feel like a passenger? Does it ride you like a pony?

A pony. Word thought back to when he was a little kid and somebody had a pony ride at their birthday party. For some reason the pony decided Word was a pushover. Or maybe the pony was just done for the day. Whatever the reason, it took off out of the front yard and started off down Cloverdale, right at the steepest part. Went right past the Williamses' house and the pony's owner was yelling for him to stop, but Word had no idea how to control the pony. He kept kicking it and telling it to stop, but it just went faster, and it was scary because the road was so steep. Finally the horse scraped him off on a street sign, knocking him to the street.

So to Word, it wasn't the rider who was in control, it was the pony.

Or was that what his rider wanted him to think? Had that memory been inserted in his mind like those things he said yesterday?

How could he explain to people that it wasn't him, and it might not even have been God?

The New Testament had those stories about Jesus' enemies saying, "He casts out devils by the power of the prince of devils." But the whole point of the stories is that it was stupid to think that good works could come from evil sources.

But common sense said that if you were evil and wanted to insinuate yourself into a community, you'd come on as really nice and helpful. What community wouldn't welcome a healer?

He shook his head. Why am I resisting this? Isn't it what I dreamed of? There's a congregation that will look to me now to show them the will of God. To bring them his healing blessing. How can I disappoint them?

But if this is some kind of poison, some trick, then how can I continue to deceive them?

Another knock on the door.

"Please," said Word. "I'm not done."

To Word's surprise, it wasn't Rev Theo. "Word, it's me, Mack Street."

Mack Street—the one who had known about dreams. Why didn't Word think of him before? He might have the answers Word needed.

When he got up and let Mack in, though, Mack wasn't alone. He had a woman with him. And when Mack said her name, Yolanda White, Word remembered. The motorcycle-riding bimbo who was getting all the old farts in the neighborhood so upset because she didn't have the right dignity. And here she was with Mack showing her off as proudly as if he had just invented her.

He had all the earmarks of young love. Trouble was, she didn't. She just regarded him calmly and steadily as he invited them to sit down.

Mack came to the point pretty quickly. "We want to get married."

"I'm not licensed yet," said Word. "You got to talk to Rev Theo."

"That's the point," said Mack. "We don't have a lot of time. And even though I'm underage on the books, I'm not really. I've spent at least a whole year wandering in Fairyland while only a few hours passed here in this world."

"So you got an extra year tucked in there?" asked Word.

"Maybe as much as two years."

Word tried to make sense of that one. And failed. "So you're saying that somehow you're really over eighteen but not in a way you could prove to the authorities."

"And she'd have trouble coming up with a birth certificate," said Mack. "So what we want is a kind of unofficial marriage. As far as the government is concerned, no marriage at all. But in the eyes of God, a real one. That's as much as I need."

"That would be great," said Word. "I'm a minister for so short a time I only gave my first sermon last night, and already I'm being asked to break the law."

"But we're not asking for a legally binding marriage. More like those ceremonies they do for gay couples. No legal force, but all the same words as a church marriage."

"Still, this is for Rev Theo."

"No," said Mack. "It's you. Only you. Can't be anybody else."

"Why is that?"

"Because of . . . because you were with me. Three years ago. When you saw how that old man got healed."

There it was. The very miracle that had gotten Word started on his quest for religious enlightenment.

"Why would that matter, when it comes to marriage?" asked Word.

"Because I'm . . . she's . . ."

"Mack," said Yolanda White, "we don't need to do this. I can see Brother Word here doesn't want to do it."

"I want to do whatever will please God," said Word. "Tell me."

"The thing is," said Mack, "she's already married."

"That would probably stop Rev Theo from doing it," said Word. "Thing is, it would stop me, too."

"But the person she's married to is *me*."

Word wondered if he was crazy. All those years wandering around the neighborhood in a daze.

"Look, Word, here's how it is," said Mack. "She knows who I really am. I wasn't really a baby. I mean, not a *new* baby. I'm just a part of somebody very, very old. Split off and sent to earth to gather . . . well, dreams. Wishes."

The invisible hand that had been inserted down Word's spine shifted and shivered and Word wriggled in his seat.

"Got hemorrhoids?" asked Yolanda. She grinned at him.

What an appalling woman. "No," said Word.

"I was joking," said Yolanda. "Don't any of you people have a sense of humor?"

"You people?" echoed Word, incredulous at such a racist remark coming from a black woman.

"Word," said Mack, "by 'you people' she means 'mortals.' She's . . . uh . . . she's a fairy."

Word felt a trembling in his spine. "Lady, I salute thee," said Word. He had no idea why he had said it. His mouth no longer belonged to him.

She looked at him steadily. Warily. "I also wish thee good health, sir."

"So you've found somebody you love better than me?" Word said.

He covered his mouth. Why would he have said such a thing?

"Baby," said Yolanda, "I love everybody better than you."

The invisible hand let go of his spine. "I'll perform your wedding," said Word. This time the words were his own. "As long as you don't try to assert it in court."

"Well, I wouldn't dream of *asserting* my *wedding*. All right if I attend it?"

"Wouldn't have it any other way," said Word. And then more words came unbidden to his lips: "O Titania, *dosvidanya*."

"Cute," said Yolanda. "Now we're Russian?"

"What are you doing, Word?" asked Mack. "You two know each other?"

"Only as I know the soul of every wanton woman," said Word's mouth.

"*I'm* the one wantin' to get married," said Mack. "She's just . . . willing."

Word swallowed hard, trying to resist saying any words that came to him from his possessor. But his mouth belonged to him again. "I'll do it," he said. "When?"

"Right now?" asked Mack.

"Want witnesses?" asked Word.

"Yes," said Mack.

"No," said Yolanda.

"How about a compromise?" said Word. "Let's bring in Rev Theo."

"Won't he try to stop us?" asked Mack.

"Not today," said Word. "Today I have carte blanche."

"Oooh," said Yolanda. "*Another* language."

Word stepped to the door and called out to Rev Theo.

"Thanks for letting me back into my office today," said Theo with a wink. "Glad to see you being so respectful to your mother," he said to Mack.

Mack looked around. "This isn't my mother, sir. This is the woman I'm going to marry."

Rev Theo looked back and forth between them. "I think there's an age disparity, my children. Plus you look too young, son."

"That's why we want Word to marry us," said Mack. "Because he doesn't have any authority. So it's not really a marriage."

"So why bother doing it."

"Because she needs to sleep with me," said Mack.

"More than they need to know," murmured Yolanda.

Word didn't think it was funny, and yet a laugh came unbidden to his throat. A deep, hearty laugh, and it went on and on.

"There's more than one way to possess a changeling, my love," said Yolanda. This really confused Rev Theo, since she said it to Word.

"Word," said Rev Theo, "have you and this woman been carrying on?"

"Just met for the first time," said Word. "We only wanted you as a witness to this extralegal wedding. You need to be a witness that I didn't promise them it would be binding."

So the wedding proceeded, with Word twisting around the words of the standard ceremony to reflect their real situation. He specifically denied having any authority. And when he said the part about does anybody know any reason these two should not get married, he added, "I mean, besides me."

Rev Theo raised his hand. "Well, there you go," said Word. "It's a tie. Two of us think this is a stupid idea, and you two think it's worth going ahead with."

"Man and wife," said Mack. "Say 'man and wife.' "

It sounded like Mack was quoting. "Is that from something?" asked Word.

"*Princess Bride,*" said Mack. Then he felt stupid for having made a joke during his wedding. But then, they were treating the wedding as a joke. Everybody but him.

"I thought I recognized it," said Word. And, obediently, he cut to the chase, asking them whether, and they answered that they did, and then he pronounced them man and wife in the eyes of God but definitely not the eyes of the law. "Which means it's still having sex with a minor," he pointed out to Yolanda.

"Planning to tell on me?" she asked him. "Let's tell everybody."

"I'm just asking that you not do it right here in front of me."

"You have my word," she said. Then winked. A punster. How swell. "Of course, you'll have to cooperate by leaving the room."

She turned to Rev Theo, who still looked more than a little appalled at what had just happened inside his office. "Don't you two have work to do now?" she asked. Then she touched his shoulder.

"Yes—my associate pastor here, Word Williams, needs to prepare another sermon for tonight."

"So you don't mind if we stay and consummate our marriage vows here in your office?"

"What?" said Mack.

"We don't have a lot of time, and there isn't a decent motel within easy walking distance," she explained.

"Why, that's no problem," said Rev Theo. "Just don't spill anything on my couch." And with that, Rev Theo smiled, winked at Mack, and left the room.

Word couldn't understand why Rev Theo would act like that. These people had just asked him if they could have sex in his office and he didn't bat an eye. "Who *are* you?" he asked Yolanda.

She smiled at him. "The part of you that knows, doesn't need to be told, and the part of you that needs to be told, doesn't need to know."

Mack walked to the window and looked out onto the shabby street, where people were already lined up for the evening's service. "I don't think we'll need this room, so don't worry, Word."

"What do you mean?" Yolanda asked him.

Mack turned around with tears in his eyes. "This is nothing to you," he said to her. "But it's everything to me."

"It's very important to me," Yolanda insisted.

"*It* is very important, but I'm not."

"You're the only man I've ever married. Partly."

"I don't remember you ever loving me," said Mack. "And you sure as hell don't love me now."

"But I do," said Yolanda. "I love you with all my heart."

"Why don't I believe you?"

"Because you have a very limited view of things," said Yolanda. "And, at this particular moment, so do I. What I'm wondering is, are you planning to let *your* limited view make *my* limited view permanent?"

"What's going on here?" asked Word.

Yolanda turned to him and shook her head. "Word, the part of you that doesn't understand doesn't need to know, and—"

"Oh, shut up," said Word, and he left the room. Whatever they were doing in there was none of his business. If it didn't bother Rev Theo, it didn't bother him.

There was magic in this. And Yolanda seemed to know all about the change in him. Talking about a part of him this and a part of him that.

Whatever possessed him was *not* God. It was more like Bag Man. It was about babies being born after a one-hour pregnancy. It was about an old man reaching out to be healed by a fourteen-year-old boy who had no idea what he was doing. It was about his father finding all his poems spread all over the internet and getting reviewed scornfully—the old man was almost catatonic, refusing to go to the office, and Mother was staying with him all day because she was afraid he might kill himself.

It was about magic and evil and not Jesus' healing power.

Yet the people who were blessed last night were truly blessed. There was no trick in it. Not like what happened in Baldwin Hills.

The rumors were flying all over the neighborhood about Ophelia McCallister in her husband's grave and Sherita Banks being transported to a gang bang. And Sabrina Chum had a hideous fast-growing cancer removed from her nose. The doctors said that if it hadn't been discovered till morning, it would have spread so far through her nose that the whole thing would have had to be removed. And Madeline Tucker was spreading around what Ceese told her—that Mack Street saw these people's dreams and knew that something bad was happening and saved them.

Look at it one way, and it was a blessing, a miracle. Mack knew their dreams and he saved them.

Look at it another way, and something evil was in the neighborhood—a dark force that turned wishes into nightmares. And who was profiting from those nightmares? Mack Street and his friends.

So was Mack saving them? Or profiting from their terror and gratitude? Ophelia McCallister was in her living room telling every visitor how beautiful it felt to have that coffin lid open and Mack Street and Grand Harrison lift her up out of the grave. "It was a rehearsal for the judgment day. For the rapture!" she told anybody who came by.

And then Word came back down to the church and spent the day thinking and praying and reading the scriptures. All day he'd been telling himself that the stuff that happened in Baldwin Hills had nothing to do with the Christian miracles here in this church last night. But now he knew it wasn't true. Now he knew that it was all part of the same thing. Whatever had crept inside him, this woman knew what it was, or who it was. She claimed that Mack Street was somehow already her husband.

So by preaching to the people, was he advancing the cause of that vile man who took Mack Street out of his parents' bedroom in a grocery bag? Or opposing it? Whose side was he on? What was good?

Good was that baby being saved last night.

Good was the way Rev Theo greeted him with a hug when he came in this morning, and told him, "The blessing of God is on my house again, thanks to you."

"Thanks be to Jesus alone," said Word to him, and meant it. But now . . . now he just didn't know. Was it Jesus? Or was Jesus just . . . something like Mack? Or something like Word? Possessed. Or some divided-off part of his "father" who wasn't in heaven at all?

He went back to the office door and knocked on it. Hard. He

didn't care what they were doing. He needed answers more than they needed to consummate their marriage in the pastor's office.

He opened the door. Neither of them was inside. The windows were still closed. The door had been locked. Word had never been out of sight of the door.

But all their clothes were lying on the couch as if they had simply disappeared while embracing each other.

Frustrated, angry, afraid, Word went to the window and opened it and looked down at the hundreds of people gathering in the street. No way would they all fit inside the church.

How could he come down and say, What happened last night, that was evil. Because it wasn't evil. It was good. It was healing, and blessing, and it had to come from God.

If I preach to them tonight, just so they won't be disappointed, there'll be an even bigger crowd tomorrow. And bigger, and bigger, because these blessings work. Everybody can see it. Not some vague or phony miracles like a medicine show. He didn't have somebody out working the line, learning facts about these people in order to fake up a mind-reading act. Whatever possessed him was going to change their lives. Some of them, anyway.

How could he say no to that?

AS SOON AS THE DOOR closed, she took him by the hand and led him to the couch. "It's all right, baby," she said. "It's not like you think. I'm not just using you. I really do love you."

"But I don't love *you*," he said. "I don't even know you."

"Never knew a man to be bothered by that," said Yo Yo. "Men always find out they love me, as soon as I do this." She kissed him.

"I'm not a man," said Mack. "You said so yourself."

"That's right," she said. "You don't have to love me."

"I didn't know I'd feel this way. I just thought it would be . . . like the guys at school talk about. Getting laid."

"Not with me."

"I don't want it to be nothing," he said. "I want it to be real. I want it to last."

She giggled. "Well, if it just went on and on, you'd never get anything else done."

"Yo Yo," he said. "I want to love you forever."

"What do you think I want?" She pulled him down to sit by her on the couch. "Think I imprisoned you in the underworld because I hated you? No, I loved you. I loved this part of you. The Mack Street part. Sure, the other part was fun, the contest between us was . . . entertaining. But you never let this part of you out. This is the part you hid away, and now you threw it away, but you're wrong, Oberon, this Mack Street part of you is pure love and light."

"No I'm not," said Mack. "I'm not part of something else, I'm me."

"I know it, Mack," she said. "You don't know how important it is that I know you, and you know me."

"It's just *spying* to you."

"No, Mack. It's discovering. It's making something. It's the love of my life."

"I don't want you to be the love of my life," said Mack. "I want to love someone who thinks I'm complete by myself."

"Then that someone would believe in a lie. Because you aren't complete. You're the best part of someone great, marvelous, powerful, and addicted to cruelty. You don't know that side of you, but I do. What I never got to know was *this* part of you. Oh, Mack Street, don't hide yourself from me any longer."

Her hands were around him like vines around a tree. Her lips were on his. And this kiss—his first—was more than a kiss. For a moment he thought she was sucking the life out of him, but then he realized that it wasn't like that at all. She was, in fact, moving him, but not taking anything from him.

They weren't sitting on the couch anymore. They were sitting on a moss-covered stone, cool but not cold, and the sun was shining through the canopy of leaves and warming their naked skin. He did love her, just as she had told him he would. In fact, he discovered that he already knew her body in ways that he had not imagined. They were not strangers. They were husband and wife.

He wondered if he actually looked like Oberon, or if things like that didn't matter. What was she seeing when she kissed him and held him?

Not Mack Street.

But here, in her embrace, naked among the trees, he didn't care.

WORD AND REV THEO CARRIED their whole PA system out into the street. Once this had been a thoroughfare, and these storefronts had been full of business and the streets full of people and cars, but now hardly anybody drove along here, and if some cop came up he'd see it wasn't a riot or a demonstration, it was church, it was religion. Nobody would interfere.

Because the thing that possessed him wouldn't let them.

It doesn't rule me. If it tries to turn this thing to evil, I won't let it. I'm still Word, the same man I've always been. I searched for God and this thing came instead, but that doesn't mean it wasn't *also* an answer to my prayers. Couldn't God have sent this to him? Given him this power in order to fulfil a mission from the Lord?

Wasn't this what it felt like for Jesus, when the multitude came to listen to his word, and then he reached out and healed them, and gathered up their children and blessed them?

"No collection today," Word said to Rev Theo.

"You're joking, right?" said Rev Theo. "This ministry could use a shot of cash."

"You can set up baskets by the door. Let them come up if they want to contribute. But it can't look like people are paying to get healed. Afterward, if they want to contribute. But nothing gets passed around."

"That's just crazy," said Rev Theo.

"Please," said Word. "Don't ask for it. Let them give it out of their own hearts."

Rev Theo studied his face. "You think we'll get more that way, don't you?"

"I have no idea," said Word.

"You think it's better PR, and we'll make more in the long run."

"Rev Theo, I know your ministry takes money. But money didn't buy what happened last night."

"Money paid the rent on the roof under which it happened," said Rev Theo. "Money paid the light bill and paid for the benches and the doors and the locks on the doors that keep the vandals out. A lack of money tore my wife and me apart for a long time, and now that the Lord is bringing us back together, I got to pay for me and her to live decently. Don't despise money, Word."

"I'm just afraid that . . . I don't know if it will ever happen again."

"It happened last night and we had a collection, didn't we?" Rev Theo patted his shoulder. "But for you, tonight, we'll try it your way. A couple of deacons with bowls at the door, and those who want to walk up front and contribute, we won't refuse them. The others can do what they want."

"Thanks," said Word.

THEY LAY ENTANGLED on soft grass, and still the sun shone overhead as though time had not passed, though it felt to Mack like infinite time, and it also felt like no time at all. It wasn't over because he still held her, and her heart still beat between her breasts as if it were his own heart, pumping his own blood. His hand rested there, and he never wanted to move.

"Did you get what you needed?" he asked her.

"Mm-hmm," she said.

"And me," said Mack. "Did I get what I needed?"

"You got what *he* needed," she said. "You were already perfect."

More silence. More birdsong in the trees. More petals from blossoms falling, as if in this glen it happened to be spring.

"Yo Yo," he said.

"Mm?"

"Why aren't you small."

She giggled. "What?"

"When Puck came to Fairyland he turned small. Tiny. Why didn't you?"

"Because I'm holding *you*," she said. "I'm joined to you. You keep me from shrinking. As surely as if my soul were freed from that jar you put me in."

"I didn't—"

"Your evil . . . twin. Put me in."

"So if you were whole, you wouldn't be small."

"When I go wandering in the world, I go out like this. Wearing another body. Because mortals really couldn't bear to see me as I truly am. I'm very—"

"Beautiful."

"I'm too perfect to be seen by mortal eyes. It's not vanity, it's just the truth. So I go out incomplete, and while that's happening, the part that stays behind is like what you saw in the jar. Dazzling, but very small. And when the part of me that's in your world tries to come back wearing this mortal body, then that body becomes small, too. Unless I have power like the power stored in you to keep me whole."

"So you're taking power from the dreams of my neighbors."

"Their wishes. Yes."

"Then you—we—we're like parasites."

"No," said Yo Yo. "We're like artists. They don't make food, they don't make shelter. You can't wear a painting, you can't eat a poem, you can't put a song over your head to shelter you from wind and rain. But we feed them, don't we, because we love the picture and the poem and the song. Like we feed children, who also don't earn their place."

"We feed children because of what they can become."

"And mortals feed *me* on their dreams because only I, and others like me, have the power to make their dreams come true."

"Right, like Puck does."

"If I had my right power, and Puck too, I could keep him tame. His pranks would be nothing more than that. Not these monstrous things that Oberon is taking delight in."

"How do you do it? How can you collect a wish and turn it into—something in the real world?"

"Don't you understand? Wishes are the true elements underlying all the universe. Mortal scientists study the laws, the rules, the way the dominoes fall. But we can see underneath it all to the flow of wishes and desires. The tiny wishes of the smallest particles. The vast, complicated, contradictory wishes of human beings. If mortals had the power to see the flows, the streams of desire, if they could bend them the way we can, then they would constantly be at war with each other. They stay at peace only because they have no idea of what power is possible."

"And why do *you* stay at peace?" asked Mack.

"Haven't you been paying attention? We're *not* at peace. We *are* at war. Only there are no more than a few thousand of us, and only a handful of us have great power. The kind of power that would be dangerous. We have rules of our own, too. And one of the greatest is, we don't mess with your world too much. Petty things. Entertainment. Like setting down a piece of paper, letting an ant crawl on it, and then moving him a few feet away. Watch him scurry. But we don't stamp on the anthill. We don't burn it."

"And that's what Oberon is doing."

"That's what he *will* do, if he can break free."

"Creating me, that was the first step."

"And riding that poor boy Word like a pony, that was the second," said Yo Yo.

"What's the third step?" asked Mack.

"What we just did," she said.

"What? We set him *free*?"

"We broke the shell of the egg, so to speak. Not that he was really in an egg. But you and I were uniting. A part of him with a part of me. It opens the door for him."

"So when you were doing all this in front of Word—"

"I knew he wouldn't stop us because it sets him free now, instead of waiting until he can form a fairy circle out of Word's new converts. It would have taken enormous power to break the chains we put on him. But by marrying us, another way was opened up. It'll still be a day or two. We have time."

"Time for what?"

"To get ready for him. To put him back down, only this time deeper. And this time without me and Puck being locked in jars in Fairyland."

"Can't he figure out that that's your plan?"

"Oh, he expects tricks. We've been at this a long time. What he doesn't expect is . . . power. For us to have real power."

"And where are you getting *that* from?"

"You," said Yo Yo. "You and all your friends. Your whole life, you've been gathering power without even knowing it. You're going to use it now to help us put him back down into the underworld."

"But I'm part of him. You're going to ask me to imprison myself."

"Yes."

"Why should I do that? Why would he *let* me do that?"

"He can't stop you. He thinks he can, but he doesn't understand how strong the virtue he discarded really is. He doesn't realize that it's the most powerful part of himself."

"What you mean is, you hope so."

"Well, yes, if you want to be accurate."

"And you might be wrong."

"Wouldn't that be a disappointment."

"And I might end up . . ."

"Being swallowed up in him again."

"And you might end up . . ."

"Locked away forever. Not just the part of me he already has in prison. This part too. I would be sad. And so would the mortal world. Because what then would stop him? His own goodness suppressed, and me not there to balance him from the outside."

"So the whole future of the world is at stake, all because we did *this*, and you didn't even tell me what I was risking."

"Of course I didn't," she said. "You wouldn't have done it."

"Damn right."

"But it has to be done."

"We put everybody at risk of something terrible. We don't have the right."

"That's virtue talking. The virtuous part of me agrees with you. But the practical part of me says, We'll be virtuous after we beat the son of a bitch."

"And if we fail?"

"The virtuous part of me will feel really bad for a long, long time."

"Well, now I can see why *he* fell in love with you."

"What about you, Mack. Are *you* in love with me?"

He kissed her. "No," he said. "I'll never know who *I* might have loved. But *he's* in love with you."

She held him tighter. "Let's go back to reality now, Mack Street."

"I know roughly where we are. It's not that long a walk."

"No need to walk. Besides, we need to pick up our clothes."

And just like that, as she held him close, they were no longer on the grass in Fairyland, they were in Rev Theo's office in a storefront church in LA, stark naked with their clothes spread out underneath them, and they could hear Word's voice in the street outside.

21

FAIRY CIRCLE

Word began to preach, expecting to have words given to him like last night. But it didn't happen. He fumbled for a moment. Paused. Tried to remember the sermon he actually wrote for yesterday.

"I'm not good at this," he said. "And I think a lot of you came here hoping that you'd see something miraculous. But I . . . it's not something I control. I can pray for God's help for you. And I can teach you the words of the Lord. So you can live a better life. Do the things that lead to happiness. Love the Lord with all your heart, might, mind, and strength. Love your neighbor as yourself."

"Can you pray for my boy in prison?" called out a woman. "He didn't do it!"

"I can, Sister," said Word. "I will."

"Well is he going to get out?" she demanded.

"I don't know," he said. "I don't even know if letting him out would be the will of God. It's God's will we have to follow here. Maybe your son has things he needs to learn in prison."

A couple of men in the congregation laughed bitterly. "Learn lots of good things in prison," one of them said.

"How old is your son?" asked Word.

"Sixteen," she said. "But they tried him as an adult. Can't vote, but he can do time like a grownup!"

"If he be black, they *know* he do it." A Jamaican accent.

Word was at a loss. He also knew that a lot of blacks went to prison because they *did* do it, no matter what their mothers thought. But that wasn't a good thing to say to a grieving mother. Or to a crowd in the street that came for miracles and was already disappointed.

"Brothers and sisters," said Word. "I wish I were a better preacher."

He heard himself say it and knew that the use of the subjunctive made him sound like he thought he was something. He could see it in the faces of the people, too. And in the way some of them kind of stepped back. Not with him now.

What was he supposed to do, pretend that he grew up in South Central? What good would that do, to be a liar?

"How can I know what to say to you? I was blessed in my childhood. My parents were happily married. They still are. My father's a professor. My mother's an administrator. I got the finest education. I grew up surrounded by books. We never knew what it was to be hungry. What do I know about the life your son had?

"But Jesus knows about his life. Jesus grew up in a good family, too. A mother and father who worked hard and loved him and took care of him. Jesus kept the commandments and served God. And they took him out and crucified him cause they didn't like the things he said. You think Jesus doesn't know what it's like to be in jail for a crime you didn't commit? You think Mary didn't know what it's like to have them take your son away and put him on trial and all the people shouting, 'Crucify him!'?

"I'm not preaching here today because I know anything. I don't. I'm too young. My life's been too easy. I'm here today because Jesus knows. It's the good news of Jesus that I want to bring you."

For a lot of them, that was good. They moved a little closer, then nodded, they murmured their assent.

But for others, the ones coming to see something sensational, it was over. They started to walk away.

Rev Theo spoke from behind him. "You doing fine, Word."

Word turned gratefully to smile at him. That's when he saw Mack and Yolanda come out of the door of the church, between the two deacons watching over the collection bowls. He felt a stab of guilt over having performed what amounted to a sham marriage, just so they could hump like bunnies in the pastor's own office. What was he thinking? Even if Mack was somehow magically eighteen, he was still younger than *she* was. No way did he understand what he was doing, how he was being used. Magically and sexually and every other way.

Speaking of being used . . .

He felt the invisible hand reach up his spine and spread through the back of his head. It felt to him as if the hand was somehow connected to Mack. And as it touched him, Yolanda winked at him, as if she was aware of what was happening.

He turned back around to face the congregation in the street. "Sister," he said, "your son in prison—what you don't know is that he did the murder he was convicted of. And he killed two other boys that you don't know about. And he's not sorry about it. His heart is like stone. He lies to you and tells you that he didn't do it, but the tears he sheds aren't remorse, they're because inside that prison he is fighting for his life against men much tougher and more dangerous than he is. And all the time that he's bowing before their brutal will, he's remembering how powerful he felt when he killed those boys and dreaming of the day when he can kill again."

The woman looked like she'd been slapped. People around him were wide-eyed with horror at what he was saying.

"Sister, I pray for your son. I pray that the Lord will turn his heart to repent. But most of all I pray for you. You have another son at home, sister. He's a good boy, but you don't even notice him because he's not the one in trouble. All the time you worry about the son in prison, but what about the son who obeys you and works hard at school and gets teased by other kids because he's a good student and all the time his brother's gang is trying to get him to join up. Where are you for *that* son? The prodigal is not ready to come home. Why don't you love the son you have?"

"I love my boy! Don't tell me I don't love my boy!"

"You have the power of healing in your hands, sister," said Word. "Go home and lay your hand upon your good son's brow. Touch his head and say, 'Thank you Jesus for this good boy,' and you will see how the Lord pours out his blessing upon you."

"I didn't come here for you to tell me I'm a bad mother!" she shouted.

"You came here for the miracle you want, but I'm telling you how to get the miracle you need. When that murderer repents and turns to Jesus, then you'll see a miracle in his life, too. But he won't get a miracle while you don't even have faith enough to do what the Lord tells you to do for your good son."

A fiery young woman standing next to her yelled at him. "God supposed to bring comfort!"

"God brings comfort to those who repent. But those who still love their sins and won't give them up, God doesn't bring comfort to them! He brings *good news* to them. He brings them a road map showing how to get out of hell. But there aren't any get-out-of-hell-free cards in the game of life, because life isn't a game! You can't change the rules just because you don't like the outcome! There's a path you have to walk. Jesus said I am the way. And you, sister, you so angry with me, I'll tell you right now, the Lord knows the pain of your heart. He knows about the baby you aborted when you were fourteen and how you dream about that baby. And the Lord says, You are healed. The scars in your uterus are made into normal flesh and your womb will be able to bear a child. So go home to your husband and make the baby you both long for, because the Lord knows that *you* have repented and your sins are forgiven and your body is made whole."

The woman sobbed once, then turned and ran toward the edge of the crowd.

The people who had been wandering away were coming back now.

He heard urgent whispers behind him, and he turned around again. Mack was lying on the ground, with one of the deacons bending over him. Yolanda didn't even seem to notice. She was watching Word intently.

Word stepped away from the pulpit and asked Rev Theo what was happening.

"Woman says her husband just fainted," said Rev Theo. "Go on with your ministry, we'll take care of the newlywed groom."

Word turned back to the microphone and began to tell a man near the edge of the congregation that he needed to go to his mother and beg her for forgiveness and return to her the money he stole to buy drugs. The man fled, and Word went on to the skinny old woman with the twisted back. She straightened up even as he spoke.

MACK WOKE UP to the sound of a short burst from a police siren. He tried to sit up and found one of the deacons trying to hold him down. "Got to get up," he said.

"Don't worry, you not getting arrested today," the deacon said, smiling.

"Let me up," Mack insisted, and he rolled over and got up on his hands and knees, then stood. Yolanda was there, but not watching him, and Mack turned to see what she was looking at.

A police car was at the edge of the crowd, which was even larger than when Mack came out of the church onto the street.

"Move out of the road," said a voice from the loudspeaker

mounted on the roof of the car. "There is no permit for this assembly. Clear the street."

Mack watched as Word stepped out from behind the pulpit and walked to the police car and laid his hand on the hood.

The car's motor stopped.

The cop turned the key and tried to start it, but the only sound was clicking.

The two front doors opened and two black policemen stepped out of the car. "Step away from the car, Reverend," said the driver.

"Son," said Word, "Jesus knows you didn't mean to do it. I tell you right now, he forgives you, and so does that boy you killed. He is happy in the arms of his Savior, and the Lord honors you as a good man and his true servant."

The officer staggered and leaned against the car for a moment, then turned and leaned against the roof and hid his face in his hands and wept.

His partner looked back and forth between him and Word. "You know each other?"

"Jesus knows *you*," said Word. "Stay out of your neighbor's bed. You've got no right there."

The cop got back into the passenger's seat and leaned across and tugged at his partner's belt to get him back into the car. They tried to start the engine again. Again.

Then Word laid his hand on the hood of the car and it started right up. They backed out of the crowd, did a Y-turn, and headed away.

"Jesus met the woman at the well!" cried Word. "And he told her the truth about herself. She had five husbands, and the one she had right now was not her own! She knew that it was a miracle. Because somebody knew her. In this lonely world, there was a loving God who knew her sins and had the courage to name them to her face. Only when she faced her sins could she repent of them and become holy. That's the miracle! Do you really need to come to me to face your sins? Can't you see them for yourself, and admit them all to God, and let the miracle change your life?"

"Did he heal anybody?" asked Mack quietly.

Yo Yo turned to him and grinned. "Oh, he's been doing miracles. Mostly, though, he's been whupping ass and taking names. I tell you, if this was what Jesus did when he was a mortal, no wonder they crucified him."

"I had cold dreams again," said Mack.

"I figured you did," said Yo Yo. "But I also figured I'd best wait till you were done before I woke you up."

"It's bad stuff, Yo Yo," said Mack. "We got to get back to Baldwin Hills and talk to Ceese and get going on saving the ones we can."

"It's a shame you missed the show," said Yolanda. "This Word boy, he's good at it. Oberon's got him a fine pony this time."

"He's Oberon's pony?"

"I saw all his plans, remember?"

"Yo Yo, there's terrible things happening in my neighborhood. Worse than last night, some of them. We got to go."

"Good idea." She took his hand and led him quickly away from the sidewalk in front of the church.

When they were free of the crowd, they began to jog, then to run. "So what did you think about the sex?" asked Yo Yo as they ran.

Mack couldn't believe she was asking him like that, as if it had been a movie. What did you think about the movie? Like it? Plan to see it again? Plan to recommend it to your friends?

"Oh, I forgot, you're shy."

"There's people in trouble," said Mack. "And the sex wasn't all that."

"Don't lie," said Yo Yo. "You want me again right now."

"No," said Mack truthfully. "I don't."

They jogged in silence for a few moments. "That son-of-a-bitch made you a eunuch."

"Maybe I just felt what *he* feels when he's with you," said Mack. He knew it was cruel, but then so was she.

"Stop!" she shouted.

At first he thought she was shouting at him, but then a police car pulled over to the curb. Yo Yo grabbed the passenger door, pulled it open, and said, "Get in, Mack Street, this is our ride."

The two officers in front welcomed them cheerfully and the driver listened as Yolanda explained where they were going. He reached over and switched on the siren and they made their way quickly back toward Baldwin Hills.

"What's going on?" asked Mack.

"I made love to you, and that filled me up with some of the power that my dear husband stored up in you. I *could* make this car fly right now, but only for a little way, so I thought speeding along the ground would be good enough."

Mack ignored the fact that she thought of "my husband" as someone other than him. "What do you mean, Word's his pony?"

"He's preaching what Oberon wants him to preach. And the miracles he's doing, he's not turning them over to Puck to make them perverse. He's playing them straight. But that's the worst trickery of all, because it's all about building up Word into some kind of miracle-working saint. Wish you could have seen it. Word's a great one. He uses language almost as well as Shakespeare. And it isn't written down, he speaks it right out of his head. It's like poetry."

She quoted Word as if his sermon had been broken up into lines of verse:

> *Do you really need to come to me*
> *To face your sins?*
> *Can't you see them for yourself*
> *And admit them all to God*
> *And let the miracle change your life?*

"Shakespeare was better than that," said Mack.

"Not off the top of his head, he wasn't," she said. "He stammered, you know. When he didn't have written lines to say. Stammered. Not real bad. Just couldn't get words out. Made him quiet in company. Ironic."

"So Oberon doesn't give Word the words to say."

"Oberon gives him knowledge. Ideas. Then Word says what he says and Oberon makes it true. Or makes the people hearing him believe it's true. Whatever works."

"So the miracles aren't real?"

"Oh, sure they are," said Yo Yo. "Tells a woman to go home and save her baby from choking, and Oberon makes it so the baby chokes just as she gets there. That kind of thing. And some of it's probably true."

"So he doesn't really heal anybody."

"Of course he does. Don't you get it? That's the trick. He uses the power he stored in you to make wishes come true. But it'll also make Word famous. Important. A saint. And Word is a good boy. Smart. He understands people. Oberon doesn't understand anybody. So he trusts Word to show him what's good to do in order to win people over. By the time he's done, Word'll be king of the world."

"We don't have kings in America."

"You will," said Yo Yo. "Because the prophet of the beast is speaking, and can the beast be far behind?"

"I had a dog once," said the officer who wasn't driving. "He was always tagging along behind me. On my bike. Got killed trying to cross a street that I barely made it across before the light."

The officer's cheery little observation silenced them for the last couple of minutes of the drive.

Mack wondered what the policeman was thinking, underneath Yo Yo's control of him. Did he seethe with resentment? Would he, when his own will reemerged? Or was he oblivious?

For that matter, am I?

Nobody should have that kind of power, to make someone want what they didn't want, or feel what they didn't feel.

NOW THAT SO MANY PEOPLE were aware of the perverse way magic was invading their neighborhood, Mack and Yo Yo and Ceese had help.

They were too late to stop Nathaniel Brady from waking up in midair, having dreamed that he was flying. But Ceese phoned to waken his parents, who found Nathaniel lying on the driveway, suffering from a severe concussion and several broken bones. The paramedics assured them that he would not have wakened on his own and probably would have been dead by the time anybody found him in the morning. "What, did he think he was Superman?" asked a paramedic.

And when Dwight Majors found himself in the midst of making love to Kim Hiatt, Miz Smitcher was at the Hiatts' door and was able to calm everybody down and reassure them that it wasn't rape. It took more than a little tearful conversation before it emerged that it wasn't Dwight who had been wishing for Kim—Dwight was happily married. It was Kim whose wish brought her high school flame to her as he was making love to his wife. In fact, it was Michelle Majors who took the most persuading, even though she had seen her husband simply vanish.

Yo Yo rode on her motorcycle to the 7-Eleven at La Cienega and Rodeo Road to persuade the night manager not to call the police to deal with five-year-old Alonzo Graves, whose wish left him throwing up onto a pile of candy wrappers in the middle of the store.

Madeline Tucker was able to borrow a really huge brassiere from Estelle Woener so that thirteen-year-old Felicia Danes could deal with the enormous breasts she had grown during the night.

Grand Harrison and Ophelia McCallister helped soothe a hysterical Andre and Monique Simpson after they found the desiccated corpse of their six-month-dead baby between them in their bed.

"We knew about the wishes last night," said Andre, when he could talk. "We *tried* not to wish for our baby to be with us."

"I don't think you can tell yourself what to wish, deep down," said Ophelia. "Because I didn't wish to be with my husband, not consciously. I thought I was waiting to see him again in heaven."

Aaron Graves, Alonzo's little brother, was returned by the firefighters who found him in his pajamas, straddling a firehose at the top of a crane that was working on saving the top story of a four-story apartment building.

And Mack performed CPR on Denise Johnston until she revived. He wouldn't tell her who had wished her dead, or why.

It was after eleven at night before all the wishes had been dealt with, as much as possible, and about seventy adults were gathered in front of Yolanda White's house. This time they weren't a mob. They were frightened—more than ever—but Mack and Yolanda and Ceese had the only explanation that fit all the facts, and they were disposed to listen.

"It's going to go on like this," said Yolanda. "Night after night. Every time Oberon, bless his heart, uses his power in this world, your wishes are going to be set loose to break hearts and cause havoc."

"But we *don't* wish for these things," Ophelia McCallister insisted.

"Your wishes get twisted. And you can't stop them. They're already stored up."

Mack was grateful that she didn't explain exactly where they were stored.

"So we can't do anything?" demanded Myron Graves. "Both my boys tonight—we're lucky social services didn't come and take them away because we're negligent parents and don't watch them at night."

"Why is it happening now?" asked Denise Johnston. "And can

the same wish be granted again? I have a right to know who's wishing death on me."

"No, you don't," said Mack sharply. "The person who had that wish never would have acted on it. It was malice but not murder. And I don't think it'll happen again to anybody. Except maybe for the little kids, because they didn't understand their danger so they still wish for the same things."

Ceese brought them back to the subject. "Can't we just go to the person that Oberon is working through and ask him to stop?"

A lot of people wanted to know who it was, but Yolanda refused to tell. "He doesn't know that Oberon is using him as a tool. He's a good man and it would tear him apart to know what's happening. And it wouldn't change a thing because Oberon *will* get his way, as long as he's imprisoned and has to work through a pony here in your world."

"It's a *horse?*" asked Miz Smitcher.

"He rides a human being like a pony. His power is irresistible."

"So we can't stop him," said Grand.

"Not by talking to the poor tool he's using. But yes, I think we can stop him. And by 'we' I mean all of us. All of you."

They promised that they were willing.

"Oh, you're willing *now,*" said Yolanda. "We'll see what you think when I tell you how it's got to go."

"What can *we* do anyway?" said Romaine Tyler. "I'll do anything if it can undo the damage that's been done."

"It can't undo real things. Magic things, yes, they'll fade. But the injury to your father, that was caused by a real I-beam falling on him."

"Then why can't my wish be granted before you stop all the wishing?" said Romaine. "Because every moment of my life I wish I had never wished my stupid wish."

"How can we bury our baby again?" said Andre Simpson. "How can we explain even *having* his body?"

"We'll work it out," said Yolanda. "But first we got to stop any more of these damned wishes being granted. Or are any of you curious to see how tomorrow night's wishes turn out?"

Nobody was.

"I don't have the power to stop him, not by myself. I've never been as powerful as he is anyway, and I've spent the last few centuries with my soul divided from my wanderer."

"Whatever that means," murmured Miz Smitcher to Mack.

"Here's what has to happen. My soul has to be freed from its captivity and rejoined to me. When that happens, in that very moment, the way these things are intertwined, it means that Oberon will be freed from *his* captivity. But his wanderer is gone, too, and he'll be hungry to rejoin it. He'll come first to Fairyland, and then he'll seek a passage through to this world."

"So we kill him while he's making the passage?" asked Ceese.

"Kill him? What part of the word 'immortal' don't you understand?" said Yolanda. "No, my poor husband Oberon is dangerous right now, but it's because he isn't really himself. I wish you could have known him back in the day. He was glorious then, full of light. People thought of him as a god, and he deserved it. But over the centuries he got bored and started playing pranks to amuse himself, and after a while they stopped being funny and started being mean. He competed with Puck to see which one could be more vicious, and when Puck refused to go on because they were starting to hurt people, Oberon enslaved him and made him continue to play."

"Who *are* you people?" said Miz Smitcher. "What gives you the right?"

"That's how I felt," said Yolanda. "What gives us the right? Nothing! That's why I imprisoned my husband in the first place. Who else had the power to do it? But during his captivity he deliberately removed from himself every shred of goodness. Everything I ever loved about him, he cast out of himself and became a terrible thing. A monster."

"And you're going to let him loose?" asked Grand.

"He's going to get loose one way or the other," said Yolanda. "He's been storing up power, and his wanderer is controlling a young man that he's going to propel to power in our world. Right now the boy's own virtue is still shaping his actions, but as Oberon puts more and more power in him, he'll crush the goodness of that boy and the world will be ruled by a being more cruel than Hitler or Stalin or Saddam. That's what will happen if we do nothing—not to mention all the destruction in this neighborhood when all those wishes come true."

"How did he choose this neighborhood?" asked Andre. "What did we do?"

"If something bad coming, of course it happens to the niggahs," said Dwight Majors.

"You got no reason to be so bitter," said Miz Smitcher. "You wasn't even *alive* during Jim Crow."

"Just cause you had it worse don't mean I got to like what happens now," said Dwight.

"Maybe it was just the fact that he found that drainpipe," said Yolanda, "or it might be something more than that. Maybe your wishes drew him. Maybe black people in America are more passionate, have stronger wishes. And maybe he was drawn to Baldwin Hills because this is a neighborhood where black people actually believe they can make their wishes come true."

"You still haven't told us what you expect us to do," said Ophelia.

"I need you to form a fairy circle," she said.

Byron Williams laughed aloud. "We're supposed to dance in the meadow at dawn? Only one problem—we aren't fairies."

"You're forgetting who *I* am," said Yolanda. "If it's my circle, joined to me, then it's a fairy circle."

"So we all join hands and sing 'Ring Around the Rosie'?" asked Byron skeptically.

"Long as it ain't 'Eeny Meeny Minie Moe,' " said Moses Jones.

"We form the circle here, now," said Yolanda. "I touch you all, and a part of me is in you. Then, later on, you form the circle again in a different place, and even though this body won't be with you, I'll still be connected to you, and as you dance, your power will flow into me so I can capture him and imprison him again."

"Of course we'll all do it," said Grand impatiently.

"There's no of course about it," said Yolanda. "Before you decide, let's find out where the final circle is going to be. Mack . . . in Fairyland, there should be a place of standing stones. They might be fine columns, or they might look like boulders, or something in between."

Mack nodded. "I've been there."

"Do you know where it is in *this* world?"

"Oh, yeah. Ceese and me both know. Cause I wrote a message there for Puck, and it showed up in the real world."

"Both worlds are real enough," said Yolanda. "And that one's realer than this one."

"You want to know where the connection is?" asked Mack. "It's where Avenue of the Stars crosses Olympic. Right on that bridge."

"Then that's where the fairy circle needs to form up at dawn," said Yolanda. "Exactly at dawn."

"Whoa," said Ceese. "That's not going to work."

"Why not?" asked Yolanda.

"Century City's got security. You suddenly get seventy black people there, forming a circle that blocks Avenue of the Stars, with no parade permit, and they're going to call LAPD down on us so fast—"

"The circle doesn't have to be in place for very long," said Yolanda.

"How long?"

"Depends on how fast Oberon flies when he gets loose. And how fast *you* can run."

"Me?" asked Ceese.

"You ain't in that circle, I can tell you that," said Yolanda. "Nor Mack. I got other work for the two of you."

"So we supposed to go to the middle of Century City at dawn," said Miz Smitcher, "and form a circle that blocks Avenue of the Stars, and hold that circle long enough for you to capture your husband *in Fairyland* so we can't even see when you're done?"

"Oh, you'll see plenty," said Yolanda. "And you'll absolutely know when it's over. Whichever way it turns out."

"So you might not win?" asked Grand.

"If it was easy, I wouldn't need you-all's help."

"Is it dangerous?" asked Moses Jones.

"Oh, shut up, you girly-man," said Madeline Tucker.

"Yes, it's dangerous," said Yolanda.

"Could we, like, die?" asked Kim Hiatt.

"You're mortals," said Yolanda. "Hasn't it dawned on you that you're going to die someday, no matter what?"

That was such a stupid thing to say. Mack looked at Ceese for help.

Ceese stepped in front of her. "It's dangerous," he said firmly. "But not as dangerous as *not* stopping him. Yes, you're putting your lives at risk. But if you don't do it, then the wishes he releases in the months and years to come will put your families at risk. And what he does with his pony—his slave—*that* will put the whole human race at risk. So we're the army. We're the special forces. If we succeed in our mission, then the whole world is safe and they won't even know the battle was fought. And if we fail, then those of us who die are merely the first of many, many thousands. We're like the people on that airplane that crashed in Pennsylvania on 9/11 instead of blowing up the Capitol."

"They *all* dead," pointed out Grand.

"And they was trapped in a plane," said Willie Joe Danes. "They had no choice."

"They had the choice to sit there and do nothing and let even more people die," said Ceese. "We got the same choice. But that's why Yolanda White here wanted to make sure you understood just what's at stake, before you agree to be in the fairy circle. Because whoever's in it, they can't change their minds and run away. You got to see it through. And no shame if you say you can't do it! No shame in that! Just be truthful with yourself."

Fifteen minutes later, only five of the adults from Baldwin Hills had left, and a dozen more had arrived, so there were seventy-seven now who would form the circle. Some were young adults, some were quite old. Yolanda assured them that physical strength didn't matter. "It's the fire in your hearts that I need," she said. "That good old mob spirit you showed last night."

Mack and Ceese, who would not be part of the circle, watched as Yolanda led the volunteers to the open ground around the drainpipe and had them join hands in a huge circle. She stood at the drainpipe, watching them, assessing them. Then she slowly began to walk around the drainpipe, pointing at each person in turn. Without taking a step or moving in any way, each person was slid an inch or two until they were all exactly the same distance from the drainpipe and exactly the same distance from each other.

"Don't move," said Yolanda. "And keep holding hands."

She walked around the circle then, kissing each of them firmly but brusquely on the lips.

Mack watched from the brow of the hill, and as she made the circle he said to Ceese, "You see it? You see how each one she kissed, they got a little spark of light above their heads?"

"No, I don't," said Ceese.

"Well, it's there."

"What I been thinking," said Ceese, "is how to get the LAPD to back off long enough for this fairy circle to do its job."

"Think of anything?"

"It's coming to me," said Ceese.

"You as scared as I am?" asked Mack.

"If I had brains enough to get scared, would I be a cop?"

"I don't want Miz Smitcher to get hurt. Or your mom. Or any of them."

"You didn't bring danger to this neighborhood," said Ceese. "You part of the solution, man, not the cause of the problem."

"I feel them inside me," Mack said. "All their dreams. All so . . . wistful. And hungry. Or angry. And filled with love. So mixed up."

"When all this is done," said Ceese, "maybe they'll all have their own dreams back again, and you'll be free of them. Free to be just Mack Street again."

"Whoever the hell that is," said Mack.

22

BREAKING GLASS

They left Grand Harrison and Miz Smitcher in charge of the fairy circle with a plan that sounded so crazy to Ceese that it would be a miracle if anything worked.

Mack's part of the plan was for them all to assemble about half an hour before dawn, dropping off the more elderly members of the fairy circle and parking in the Ralph's parking lot just down the hill from the overpass. It would be a little bit of a hike, but there was no on-street parking in Century City and they didn't want to give Security an excuse to eject them too early.

Only a few watchers would wander onto the bridge, waiting for Mack's signal. And this was the weirdest part: They had no idea what it would be. "The one time I wrote something," said Mack, "the words came through, but about ten times as big and along the sides of the overpass. All the other stuff I left, it sort of got transformed. All I can tell you is, look for a change. It might even be a natural change. But there are seventeen pillars, so look for seventeen . . . things."

And then what?

"Then form a circle. Seventeen of you right on top of the

markers, the others arrange yourselves in between. And the rest I don't know."

Yolanda knew. "You'll feel it," she said. "You'll know when I'm in the circle."

"But you won't *be* in the circle," Ophelia objected, sensibly.

"I *will*, but on the other side. You'll see. Or . . . not *see*, but feel. And when that happens, you start moving. Counterclockwise. Which means, if you're facing into the circle, to your right."

"We all know what counterclockwise means," said Moses Jones.

"Except for those that don't and are too embarrassed to ask," said Yolanda with a toothy smile.

"But we don't know the dance," said Miz Smitcher.

"In a fairy circle," said Yolanda, "the dance dances *you*."

The other part of the plan was Ceese's own contribution. "Six dozen black people, even nicely dressed black people, if you start blocking the road, LAPD *will* be called and you *will* be dispersed. But if you're carrying signs, then you're black *activists*. Protestors. Got to treat you differently. Find out your grievances. A couple of you carry video cameras—prominently. The LAPD has great respect for video cameras."

"Signs saying what?" asked Grand Harrison.

That was farther than Ceese had planned. "Something that would make sense to demonstrate about in Century City."

" 'Down with Fox'?" somebody suggested.

"Don't forget that there's a big MGM building there now, too."

" 'Not enough black actors in movies.' "

" 'Racial stereotypes'!"

"Yeah," said Miz Smitcher dryly. "How about the stereotype of blacks with signs, having a demonstration."

"Can we sing 'We Shall Overcome'?" asked Ebby DeVries. "I always wanted to march and sing that."

"No," said Sondra Brown. "That song is sacred. You don't sing it for some . . . act."

"You sing it to change the world, sistah, and *that* what we *doing*," said Cooky Peabody, sounding as ebonic as she knew how. A dialect she pretty much learned from television.

To Ceese it didn't matter. He left it up to Grand and Miz Smitcher and—why not?—democracy to make the decision, while he would drive his patrol car down to the gateway between worlds. First, though, he watched Mack get on the motorcycle behind . . . his *wife*. Man, that stuck in Ceese's craw, even to think it. Wife. Mack marries a hoochie mama on a bike before he's eighteen and Ceese doesn't even have a steady girl at thirty.

All right, she wasn't a hoochie mama. She was queen of the fairies and Mack was supposedly some excrescence from the king of the fairies. To Ceese he was still a kid who had no business being that free and familiar with such a voluptuous body.

Ceese stood beside his patrol car watching them ride off on the bike. That's when Miz Smitcher came up to him. "Didn't so much as invite us to the wedding," she said.

"I don't think it really counts as a wedding. Near as I can tell, it was reconnaissance."

"Now *that's* a word for it I've never heard before. 'Hey, baby, how about a little reconnaissance.' "

Ceese chuckled.

She leaned close to him. "Ceese, give me your weapon," she said softly.

"Are you crazy?" he said. "A cop doesn't give his gun to anybody."

"You can't take it in there with you, right? Into Fairyland? I just got a feeling, Ceese. You know I'm not crazy. I got a feeling that gun's going to be needed somewhere other than locked in the trunk of your patrol car here in Baldwin Hills. You dig?"

"I can't believe I heard you say 'you dig.' "

"I been listening to Ray Charles," she said.

"He used to say that?"

"I don't know. I just know that back when I *started* listening to Ray, we were all saying 'you dig.' "

"Miz Smitcher, next thing you're going to tell me is you used to be young."

"I used to *look* young, anyway," she said. "Give me the gun."

"If you shoot that thing, and somebody does ballistics on the bullet, they'll know it was my gun which got fired in a place where I wasn't."

"That happens, I stole it from you."

She looked determined.

"Ceese," she said. "I trusted you with my baby. Now you trust me with your gun. I won't ruin your life or kill anybody doesn't need killing."

He had her get inside the car and then took out the weapon, showed her how to work the safety, and then gave her extra ammo.

"Won't be much good against fairies," said Ceese. "Especially if they're really tiny."

"Just have a feeling," said Miz Smitcher. She put it all in her purse.

A few minutes later, Ceese was down near the bottom of Cloverdale, parking the patrol car between Snipes' and Chandresses'. Yolanda and Mack were already waiting for him. "What kept you? Stop to take a leak?" asked Mack. "We got a whole woods back there."

"Yeah," said Ceese, "but like you said, stuff you leave there might be anything on this side. I'd hate to leave a bag of marshmallows or a baby stroller in the middle of some road, just because I had to pee."

"Am I going to have to listen to two little boys making peepee jokes the whole way?" asked Yolanda.

Mack took both their hands and led them through the gateway into the house.

Puck was waiting inside with two plastic 35mm film canisters.

"Planning on taking pictures?" Ceese asked him.

"They're empty," said Puck. "And look—air holes."

"Air holes?"

"We're going to get real small once we get into Fairyland. Being without our souls the way we are," said Puck. "And every creature Oberon can assemble is going to come and try to kill us. If you're holding us in your hands, you can't slap them away. Or else you're going to get excited and crush us. So you let us go inside these film tubes and then put us in your pockets. Your safest pockets that we can't fall out of."

"Oh, Puck, you're so sweet and thoughtful," said Yolanda. Only here, she wasn't Yolanda anymore, was she? She was Titania. Or Mab. Or Hera. Or Ishtar. Whatever name she went by right now.

"And something else," said Puck. "When we're small, we can't hear big deep sounds. Talk really high, Ceese, or we won't understand you. And every now and then, shut up so you can hear if we're yelling something at you."

"Which pocket?" asked Yolanda. "Not your butt pocket, get it?"

"Got it," said Ceese.

"Good," said Mack. Then he broke up laughing, for reasons Ceese didn't bother to inquire about.

"You got your stuff? For the pillars?" Ceese asked Mack.

Mack patted his own pockets.

"And a knife?"

Mack shook his head. "In my dream I didn't have a knife."

"In your dream you were fighting a slug with wings, too, not the king of the fairies."

"Um," said Yolanda.

"What?"

"That's the form we imprisoned him in," she said. "It's one of the shapes he can wear, and it's the only one where he doesn't have really dextrous hands."

"Didn't want him to have hands. So what does he have?"

"Talons like a steam shovel," said Yolanda. "But we weren't thinking about fighting him in the flesh, when we did that."

"And wings," said Puck. "With little tiny fingers on them, like a bat. They can rip your cheek right off your face in combat. You couldn't tie your shoelaces with them, though."

"Wish it were the other way," said Ceese. "These other animals—what are they going to do to me?"

"Nothing much, the size you turn into in there."

"What about me?" asked Mack.

"They won't touch you, Mack. Have they ever?"

"Panther growled at me once."

"Boo hoo," said Puck.

"So all that time I kept a watch out for predators and scavengers and heat-seeking reptiles in the night, I had nothing to worry about?"

"They obey Oberon, and to their tiny little minds you *are* Oberon."

"You do smell like him," Yolanda added.

"That's good news," said Mack. "So what are we waiting for?"

"Courage," said Ceese.

"A heart," said Mack.

"A brain," said Puck, pointedly looking at Ceese. And when Mack laughed, this time Ceese got the reference.

Everybody went to the bathroom who needed to, which meant Ceese and Mack. Then they were ready to go.

When they got out on the back porch, not a thing was changed—not even blown by the wind. But when they walked back onto the brick walkway, the forest was bedecked in the reds and golds of autumn.

"Toto, I think we're not in Southern California anymore," said Mack.

"Stop," said Yolanda.

Ceese looked at her. She was half the height she was before. And he was several feet taller, because he was looking down at

Mack almost like Mack was a kid again. Yet he hadn't felt himself grow.

"They can smell us already," Yolanda said. "They're gathering. Have those film cans ready? Mack, you hold mine and be ready to put me in. Please don't let any birds snatch it out of your fingers, all right? Or me, for that matter."

Mack looked up. So did Ceese. There were several birds hovering overhead. No, more than several—most of them were so high up they were hard to spot.

"This ain't going to be fun," said Puck. "In case you thought."

"Especially watch your eyes, Cecil Tucker," said Yolanda. "They like to go for the eyes. When they're fighting giants."

"I don't know the way," said Ceese. "I got to be able to see."

"Squint," said Puck.

"Easy for you to say," said Ceese. "You're immortal."

"But I've been blind."

This wasn't the time for a story. They took another step. Still way too big to fit into a baby stroller, let alone a film canister.

"Hold my hand, baby," said Yolanda. "I don't want you to lose me."

"Hold my hand, too," said Puck.

"I'll just hold *you*," said Ceese, picking him up and tucking him like a football.

Another step. Another. Another.

Birds were swooping now, flitting by, close over their heads. And all around them, squirrels and other animals were coming to the edges of the path and chattering at them.

The next step would take them off the brick. But the fairies now fit into the palms of their hands. Another couple of steps and they'd be film size.

They took the steps. Ceese's fingers were so big he could hardly get the lid off. And now the birds were snatching and pecking at him. Landing on his shoulders. They were small but their pecks were sharp and hard. They hurt like horsefly bites.

"I can't do this," said Ceese.

Mack looked up at him. He had the lid off his film canister, and Yolanda was crawling into it.

At that moment, a bird swooped and snatched the lid to Mack's film canister right off his palm.

"Shit!" shouted Mack.

Without even thinking, Ceese swatted the bird that had stolen the lid and knocked it to the forest floor.

Mack dove for it, found it, and put it on the canister. Then he put the canister inside his front jeans pocket. Then he reached for Ceese's film canister and got it open. All the while, Puck was yelling something, but his voice was so little and high that Ceese could hardly hear him. No wonder Puck had had to crawl closer to the house and get larger before Mack could hear him, that time when he got so badly injured.

Mack handed Ceese the canister and Puck leapt in. Again, Mack had to fasten the lid because Ceese's fingers were simply too big. Like an elephant trying to pick up a dime.

"I hate being this big," said Ceese.

"Yeah, well, try being my size and fighting off these damn birds."

"Then let's get under the trees."

It was such a good idea. Except for the part about Ceese being so tall that he wasn't under anything. He had to breast his way through the trees like he was trying to force his way against a river current. And he couldn't see the path at all.

Mack was yelling at him. Ceese bent over, pushing branches out of the way as he did.

"You're off the path!" Mack yelled.

"I can't see the path," said Ceese. "But I can see the sky."

"Great, I need a weather report, I'll give you a call. Look, Ceese, there's no way to do this unless you get down to my level. Stay under the trees."

"I'm supposed to crawl the whole way?"

Mack shrugged. "I can't help it."

Ceese saw that there was no choice. But it hurt his knees. The tree trunks were also close together, so that Ceese was constantly banging his shoulders. Not to mention breaking low-hanging branches with his head.

"I'm going to have such a headache," said Ceese.

He noticed that, along with the birds nipping at his ears and the back of his neck, there were squirrels and other creatures running over his hands and up his sleeves. "What do they think they are, ants?"

"Commandos," said Mack. "Think: fire ants."

"Squirrels aren't poisonous."

"They've got teeth and jaws so strong they can crack nuts."

"Aw no," said Ceese. "Please tell me that bastard won't make them go for my package."

"Must be a *huge* target," said Mack helpfully. "Easy to find."

Sure enough, just like fire ants, they went straight for his scrotum. Ceese pulled at the crotch of his pants and tried to pinch the creatures without mashing his own testicles.

"Ceese," said Mack, "if you stop every time some creature bites you, we'll never get there."

"I don't notice them biting *you*."

"They won't fit up my sleeve or into my pants," said Mack.

"*And* they think you're him."

"That, too," said Mack.

It was slow going—crawling, bumping into trees, scraping through branches, brushing away birds, plucking at squirrels. Ceese was bleeding from hundreds of pecks and bites and he was desperate to fling his clothes off and put Neosporin—or anything, rubbing alcohol—on the sores inside his clothes. "I always hated squirrels," said Ceese. "Now I know why."

"You think they like hanging around in your crotch?"

"Why not?" said Ceese. "Nobody's biting *them*."

Mack held up a hand. "Stop."

Ceese stopped. He saw Mack simply disappear.

Then he looked closer and realized that they were at the edge of a chasm. There was a fast-moving river at the bottom, and Mack had swung down a little way, clinging to a complicated root system.

Ceese saw the other side and it didn't look so far off. He extended his huge arm to reach for the opposite bank. But inexplicably he couldn't quite touch it. It was as if it kept retreating just enough to be a half-inch out of reach.

"I can't bridge it," said Ceese.

"I suppose I shouldn't be surprised," said Mack. "I think it's part of the protection of the place. You can't cross over the chasm, you have to get down to the river's edge."

Ceese crept along the edge. "All right, I'll climb down over here so I don't accidently kill you by brushing you off the wall of the canyon."

Ceese swung a leg down over the edge.

"Stop!" screamed Mack.

"Just a second," said Ceese, meaning to drop down to the bottom before he stopped.

"Stop *now!* Get your leg back up! Now!"

Ceese stopped. But he still felt an overwhelming desire to jump down.

The same kind of desire he felt that day Yolanda tried to get him to throw baby Mack over the stair rail. So maybe it was an impulse he ought to ignore.

Ceese pulled up his leg.

Mack ran over to him. "Your leg was shrinking. As soon as it went over the side, it was getting down to normal size. What if you aren't big when you go down there?"

Ceese understood. "More to the point, what if they aren't small?"

Mack pulled the film canister out of his pants pocket and held it up by his ear. "What should we do?"

Ceese didn't bother getting Puck out of his pocket. It was Yolanda in charge of this expedition.

"She says she has no idea what happens, she's never been here before. But maybe it's time to let them out."

Ceese pulled the canister out of his pocket. It was easier to get the top off without Mack's help.

Ceese saw Puck stick his head out. He was drenched with sweat, panting. "I want air-conditioning before I go back in there."

"Watch out for birds," said Ceese.

"Not so many around here," said Puck.

"Only takes one."

"At this point I don't care. It can't be any worse inside a bird's gut."

Ceese saw that Mack was perching Yolanda inside the collar of his shirt. A killer squirrel leapt for the spot. Mack dodged and the squirrel plunged over the side. Ceese had never heard a squirrel scream before. Now he knew why Wile E. Coyote never made a sound in the Road Runner cartoons. An animal screaming all the way down a cliff was a chilling sound.

"No way in hell I'm getting inside your collar!" shouted Puck.

"Where then?"

"Your jacket pocket."

"What if you get big real fast?" said Ceese. "I don't want to have to replace this jacket, it's real leather."

"Now it's mesh," said Puck.

Sure enough, the birds and squirrels and who knew what other creatures had pecked and torn holes all over the leather. Tiny ones, but holes all the same. Ceese realized his neck must look like that, too.

Mack called out. "Yo Yo says to go slow, and hold on to vines and roots the whole way. Plants don't obey Oberon the way animals do. Especially trees. Very stubborn. They won't let go of us." Then he added, "Nobody ever called a tree a pushover."

"Maybe it's turning over a new leaf," said Ceese.

"Shut up, you two," Yolanda shouted—loud enough that Ceese could hear her. Unless . . . yes, they were far enough down that Yolanda was now larger, clinging to Mack's back inside his shirt like a child getting a piggyback ride.

"That shirt's going to rip, you get any bigger," said Ceese helpfully.

Puck was out of his pocket now, holding on to his shoulders. And by the time they reached the bottom, Puck was as heavy as the slightly overweight older man that he was, while Ceese was just a normal-sized LAPD cop.

Also, Puck and Yolanda were stark naked.

"Our clothes didn't grow back to normal size," Puck explained. "Oberon's sense of humor."

"But my clothes shrank back to normal size with me," said Ceese.

"No way did Oberon make up this place in the split second when he realized we were imprisoning him," said Yolanda. "Not with all these complicated traps. He was already plotting this. I think we got him just in time."

Puck smiled wickedly. "Well, that's my beloved master. Mayhem with a dirty twist."

"I was counting on Ceese still being a giant when we got to the grove."

"Maybe he will be, when we go up the other side," said Mack.

"If there's any chance my clothes will get exploded when I get bigger, I'm taking them off down here," said Ceese.

Since nobody offered him any guarantees, he took off everything except his underwear. Then he jumped over the water, with Puck holding his hand. Mack brought Yolanda over the water, too.

By ten feet up the cliff on the other side, Ceese's underwear had burst open. He was growing again. And the two fairies were shrinking. Only there weren't any pockets this time.

"You're sweaty and you stink," said Puck.

"You want a bath," said Ceese, "we got running water down there."

"I was just saying: Wear some cologne."

"I do."

"What, eau de pig sty?"

"It just said 'toilet water.' "

Puck laughed—well, chirped, his voice being very high by now.

When they got to the top, the panther was waiting. It came and stood in front of Mack, not looking ready to spring but not looking particularly friendly, either. Ceese wondered if it was possible for a cat that size not to look dangerous.

Of course, to a naked guy—even a giant—any size cat was plenty dangerous. Those claws. Those teeth. Ceese's scrotum shriveled. "What if he goes for my dick?" asked Ceese.

"Then ten thousand women will mourn!" shouted Puck. "Let's get a move on!"

"It's not fair that Mack gets clothes and I don't," said Ceese.

"What are you, six?" asked Puck.

Ceese didn't bother answering. The birds were really going at him now, and with no leather jacket to protect him the branches were almost as bad.

They were at the edge of the clearing.

The two lanterns were still there.

"There I am!" shouted Puck.

"Wait!" cried Yolanda. "Let me at least *look* for traps."

In reply, Ceese handed Puck to Mack and crawled into the clearing.

The panther leapt.

Ceese swatted it away. It struck a tree trunk and dropped in a heap at the base.

Ceese reached out for the nearest floating lantern. It shied away from his hand. When he tried for the other one, it did the same.

"All right, Miss Fairy Queen, what do I do now? Keep playing this game till I die of old age?"

"Be patient," said Yolanda. "When I say the counterword, they'll stop evading you. But the moment I say it, you have to get them both at once. One can't be opened without the other. That's the way Oberon thinks. He'd make sure we can't figure out which soul is mine and then leave Puck imprisoned. So if I get free, Puck gets free, and then my darling husband will try to make Puck *do* something."

Puck just stood there and grinned.

Ceese asked him, "You couldn't just tell us what will happen, could you?"

"Of course he can't," said Yolanda. "He is *not* his own fairy. Don't worry. Now be ready, because as soon as I say the counterword, we have to move very quickly."

"I'm ready," said Ceese.

Yolanda opened her mouth and uttered a swooping cry that rose so high that it could not possibly come from a human throat. And then higher yet, so it could not be heard at all. Only then, as she screamed in utter silence, did her lips form words.

Then she slumped to her knees and her voice also became audible as the scream lowered in pitch and faded to a sigh.

Ceese reached out both hands at once and snatched at the lanterns. They held still. He caught them.

Kneeling in the grass, he got his thumbnails under the lantern roofs and tried to pry them off at exactly the same moment. "Somebody needs to bring pop-top technology to Fairyland," he said.

"Just break them. Crush them," whispered Yolanda, exhausted for the moment by the word she had uttered. "You can't hurt *us*. That's our most immortal part inside that glass."

"How can one part be more immortal than another?" grumbled Ceese as he pried.

'Immortale*r*," said Puck, correcting him like an English teacher. "Do what the lady said."

Still kneeling in the grass, Ceese pinched both lanterns between thumb and forefinger and crushed them.

With a sharp crack and a crunch of shards of glass rubbing together, the lanterns exploded.

Two tiny lights arose from the lanterns' wreckage between Ceese's fingers.

There must have been a thousand birds waiting in the trees. And now they all swooped out and down, darting for the lights.

Mack moved just as quickly. Holding Puck in one hand and Yolanda in the other, he thrust their tiny bodies toward the hovering lights.

As they neared each other, they became like magnets. The lights crossed each other's path and caught the bodies of the fairies in midair.

There was an explosion of light.

The birds veered and now were circling the clearing, around and around, like a whirlpool of black feathers. But as they flew, their colors changed, brightened. Suddenly there were as many red and blue and yellow birds as black and brown, and among them were fantastically colored parrots, and their calls changed from harsh caws to musical sounds.

The leaves on the trees changed, too, from the colors of autumn to a thousand different shades of green, and many of the trees burst out in blossoms.

In the middle of the clearing, Yolanda stood, normal size again, with her head bowed and her arms folded across her chest. Then, as she raised her head, moth wings unfolded from her back, thin and bright as a stained-glass window. She opened her eyes and looked at the birds. Then she opened her arms, opened her hands, and the birds rose up again into the green-covered branches and sang now in unison, like an avian Tabernacle Choir. The Fairy

Queen opened her mouth and joined in the song, her voice rising rich and beautiful like the warm sun rising on a crisp morning.

And then she turned her hands over, palm down, and the song ended. She looked at Mack and said, cheerily, "Honey, I'm home."

Mack took a step toward her. She smiled.

Then she whirled toward the strong and tall young black-winged manfairy that Puck had just become. With a quick movement of her hand and a brief "Sorry, doll," she shrank him down and her finger hooked him toward her as surely as if she had just lassoed him. As he approached, he shrank, until he was grasped in her hollow fist, the way a child holds a firefly.

"Give me a film canister," she said.

Mack had them in his pockets.

She held the open canister under the heel of her fist and then blew into the top. In a moment she had the lid on.

She blew another puff of air onto the film canister, and it became a small cage made of golden wire, beautifully woven.

Inside, Puck leaned against the wires, cursing at her.

Another puff of air and his voice went silent.

Then she turned to Ceese and offered him the golden cage that contained Puck. "Oberon is free now," she said. "And Puck is his slave. He must have known I'd have no choice but to do this."

"If Oberon is awake," said Mack, "we don't have much time."

"Take it," she said to Ceese. "Take him back to the house. Don't let him out of your sight. I don't want anybody stealing him and trying to control him like the poor fairies that gave rise to those genie-in-a-bottle stories."

Ceese took the cage, looking at the raging fairy whose wings fluttered madly as he ran around and around inside the cage, treating the walls and ceiling of the spherical cage as if they were all floor and there were no up and down.

"Be gentle with him," said Titania. "I owe him so much. And when this is over, he *will* be free. Not just from that cage, but from

Oberon as well. His own man again. A free fairy." And softly, tenderly, she leaned toward the cage. "You have my word on it, you nasty, beautiful fairy boy." She looked up into Ceese's face. "Get going. The animals should leave you alone now, but you want to be out of Fairyland before the dragon comes."

"Good idea," said Ceese.

Holding the cage in his giant hand like a pea on a pillow, Ceese stood upright. His head was above the treetops. He looked back the way he had come. He could see the route he had followed to get here by the broken branches and leaning trees, and instead of getting back down on all fours and crawling, he strode directly along. The chasm wasn't uncrossable this time—the magical defenses were done away with. He stepped right over it.

As he neared the place where the brick path began, he stopped one last time to look around over the beautiful green of springtime in Fairyland. He knew that he would probably never see this land again. Nor would he ever be so tall, or see so far.

When he looked south, toward where Cloverdale climbed the mountain in his home world, he saw a hot red shaft of light shoot upward, surrounded by smoke.

And in the shaft a huge black snaky thing began to writhe upward. Even at this distance, Ceese could see how the creature's slimy skin shone in many colors, like a slick of oil on a puddle.

Two great wings unfolded, shaped like enormous bat wings, but webbed like the wings of a dragonfly. They kept unfolding until they extended to an impossible span.

And two red eyes opened and blinked.

From the cage in Ceese's hand, a tiny high voice cried out. "Here, Master! I'm here! She went that way! She's over there! Head for the temple of Pan! Set me free to help you!"

Ceese dropped to his knees and closed his fist over the golden cage. Then he crawled onto the brick path until he was small enough to stand up and walk.

He strode across the patio and opened the back door. The

golden cage now was the size of a grapefruit in his hand. Inside the lacework of golden wires, Puck hung by his hands from the wires, his body racked with great sobs. "God help me!" he cried, again and again. "I hate him! I hate him!" And then, more softly, "Beloved master, beautiful king."

23

SLUG

As soon as Ceese left the clearing, bearing away Puck in his golden cage, Titania flung her arms around Mack and clung to him. "He's coming," she whispered. "I can feel him rising."

"We've got to go," Mack said. "It's a good long run."

"You forget that I'm in my power now." She kissed him. "I'm so afraid."

"There's a chance that we'll lose?"

"If he wins today, I'll win tomorrow. No, I'm afraid that if I win, he won't love me anymore. *You* won't love me anymore."

"Titania," said Mack. "I'm not sure I even love you now."

"But *he* does," she said. "The only reason *you* don't love me is you're upset because you think I betrayed Puck. You're so good and pure, Mack. But if you were a little more wicked and selfish like me, you'd realize that Puck was a tool that Oberon could have used against me. Now he can't."

"I understand that," said Mack.

"With your mind," said Titania. "But in here"—she touched his chest—"you would never be able to do such a thing. So loyal and true. Fly with me, Mack Street."

"I can't fly."

"But I can." In a quick, sudden movement she swung herself around behind him, gripped him across his chest and under his arms, then wrapped her legs around him. All the while, she was beating her wings, so she weighed nothing. Less than nothing: Under her wings they both rose from the ground.

In a moment they were above the clearing. She took one soaring circle. No birds came near them. Mack could see the glorious spring forest spreading in all directions. Only now did he realize that in all his wanderings, he had never seen spring. Perhaps there was no spring when Titania wasn't free in this world.

Not so far away, smoke was rising from a gap in the hills—the place where the drainpipe rose in the other world.

"He's coming up now," said Titania. "Away we go."

He was surprised at how fast she flew. Like a dragonfly, not a moth. She could hover in one place, then dart like a rocket. He could feel the muscles flexing in her chest and arms as they balanced and responded to the exertions of her wing muscles. As womanly as this fairy queen might be, she was also a magnificent creature, overwhelmingly strong.

"So the pixie dust thing is just a myth," said Mack.

She laughed. "J. M. Barrie knew boys. But he didn't know fairies. Not like Shakespeare. He glimpsed Puck once, and one of my daughters. He thought the sparks of light were fairy dust. He had no idea what was going on."

"What *was* going on?"

"Oberon's first attempt to make you," said Titania. "Using Puck as the father. And no humans at all. It didn't work."

"How many tries?"

"Four. Five counting you. The last two could have done it, but they were never able to connect with the people around them. Never able to catch the dreams. It takes a village to raise a changeling."

"How do you do it?" asked Mack. "Magic, I mean. What does it have to do with wishing? With dreams? You keep talking about it as if it could be stored up. In *me*."

"That's what humans never understand," said Titania. "They're so seduced by the material world, they think that's what's real. But all the things they touch and see and measure, they're just—wishes come true. The reality is the wishing. The desire. The only things that are real are beings who *wish*. And their wishes become the causes of things. Wishes flow like rivers; causality bubbles up from the earth like springs. We fairies drink wishes like wine, and inside us they're digested and turned to reality. Brought to life. All this life!"

"More to the right," Mack directed her. "That hill over there. You're heading for Cheviot Hills."

"I never did get the grasp of LA. Too much asphalt. Tar smeared over the face of the earth."

"On which you rode that motorcycle."

"It was the closest I could come to flying like this. Only they would never let me ride naked."

"So the dreams that I absorbed and stored—they're real."

"Dreams are the stuff that life is made of," said Titania.

"And what am I made of, then? Coming into the world after gestating only an hour?"

"You're Oberon's wish. All his wishes for beauty and truth and life. For order and system, for kindness and love. Poured out into the body of a woman and allowed to grow in the form that *she* dreamed of."

"So she really was my mother."

"The mother of your shape. But Oberon was father and mother of your soul."

"I thought I didn't have one."

Titania laughed lightly, like music in the hurtling wind.

"So," said Mack. "How are we going to fight him?"

"I don't know," said Titania.

That was not good news. "I thought you had a plan."

"I have a plan to make me as strong as possible. And him a little weaker. But once you start hurling unformed causality around, you never quite know what's going to happen. I'll do some things. He'll do some things. The things we do will change the way things work. So we'll do different things. Until I'm strong enough to bind him."

"What does it mean, to bind him?"

"Bound," she said. "To the rules. What people in your world think of as the laws of nature."

"So it's all about you and him."

"That's right. I draw power from the fairy circle. And he can't see it. He won't know they're there. At first, anyway."

Mack thought about that. "What am *I* here for? Why didn't you send me back with Ceese?"

No answer.

"Yo Yo?"

No answer.

"Titania, tell me. I should know."

"You're *his* fairy circle," she said. "The power he's been storing up for years. Storying up, so to speak."

"So I'm on *his* side?"

"In a way," she said. "But by having you near me, he can't do anything really awful to me."

Now he understood. "I'm your hostage."

"It's a similar relationship. Except that normally, hostages don't get eaten."

"You're going to *eat* me?"

"No, silly. I love you. *He* wants to eat you. Or the dreams stored in you, I mean. He'd spit the rest of you back out."

"So I'd live?"

"It won't happen, so don't worry about it."

"Why won't it happen?"

"Because he knows that while he's eating the dreams out of

you, I would reunite you with him. I'd restore the virtues he drove out of him."

"And he doesn't want that?"

"Suddenly he'd have a conscience again. He'd remember how much he loves me. It would completely ruin his side of this little war."

"What would happen to me?"

"You've gotten stronger in these years apart from him. His malice has been festering the whole time, too, but *you* have grown very wise and strong. I'm proud of you."

"What does that mean?"

"I don't know," she said. "Like I told you, baby. I don't know how this will all come out. We just play with the causalities he gives us, and throw our own realities back at him."

She settled lightly to the ground in the middle of the henge of seventeen columns. She unwrapped herself from Mack's body. "Time to do your art, baby."

Mack set to work at once with a red magic marker, drawing a small heart on each column and moving quickly on.

WORD WAS EXHAUSTED at the end of his sermon. His listeners weren't—after all, it was still daylight when he finished, and they were all hoping that his healing touch would come into *their* lives, too. But he was finished because the invisible hand down his back had finally let him go. He had nothing left.

He would have gone into Rev Theo's office to rest, but he remembered the use it had been put to so recently. He sat down in one of the folding chairs at the back of the sanctuary and closed his eyes.

Whatever possessed him had spoken again. This time Word wasn't taken by surprise, and he was fatalistic about it. Either it would come or it wouldn't. Either he'd be given words to say, or he wouldn't.

But by whom? He didn't like the sense that it was linked to Mack and Yolanda. What went on with them was not from God—he knew that much, at least. So why did the spirit only start working through him when the two of them emerged from their semi-holy tryst? Whatever spirit it was, it still worried him that it might not be the Holy Spirit of God.

If I don't serve Jesus with what I do, then whose service am I in?

All the things I said to people. Were they true? Or did they become true because I said them?

That was what Word had come to believe when he studied psychology as an undergraduate. He came to the conclusion that Freud wasn't discovering things, he was creating them. There were no Oedipus complexes until Freud started telling that story and people started interpreting their own lives through that lens. Like neuralgia or the vapors or UFOs or humors or any of the other weird theories—once the story was out there, people started believing it.

So now, am I doing the same thing? Do I say things, and then they become sort of true because I said them? Or are they already true, and this spirit that possesses me reveals that truth and heals whatever can be healed? Am I giving peace, or creating chaos?

Is any part of this from me, my own wish to make sense of things? Or some even deeper need that I didn't know about—a desire to dominate? Because that's what's happening. The way they look at me. Worshipful. Grateful. It's the look of faith. I've given them something I don't even have myself—certainty. Trust.

Someone turned around the chair in front of him and sat down. That was something Rev Theo did when he wanted to counsel with somebody. So Word didn't open his eyes.

"Some sermon tonight," said Theo.

"I don't know when it's going to happen," said Word. "For all I know, this was the last time."

"You doing fine before the spirit come into you tonight."

"You could tell when it came?"

"You turned around and looked back at the door, like you heard the Spirit of God coming up behind you, and then you turn around and tell that woman her son lying to her. I say it don't get much clearer than that."

"I didn't hear the Spirit of God. I heard Mack and Yolanda come out of the church."

"Well now," said Rev Theo. "How *did* you hear that? So much noise, and the door already open, and they didn't walk heavy."

"I don't know," said Word. "I don't even know if it's the Spirit of God that comes into me."

"It's the spirit of truth. Spirit of healing. Have some faith."

"It falls too close in line with the kind of thing I want and wish for," said Word.

"It's right in line with the ministry of His Majesty King Jesus," said Theo. "He said come follow me, and you doing it, Word. Even your name. In the beginning was the Word, and the Word was with God, and—"

"Don't finish that," said Word. "Or I'll change my name."

"I ain't saying that last part is about you. But it's a sure thing that Word is with God. Don't you doubt it."

"Rev Theo, I don't trust it."

"If it comes, it comes," said Rev Theo. "When it doesn't, you just tell them, the Holy Spirit comes when he comes, but the words of Jesus are always with us. We not in this to put on a show, Word. We in this to save souls."

"I know that," said Word. "What I don't trust is . . . I don't know whether it's good or not."

"Oh, it's good, Word."

"In the long run. They worship me, Rev Theo."

"Don't you mind that. They can see you. They can't see God. But they'll learn to look past you and see God over your shoulder."

"The thing that's inside me—I think it's their worship that it's after."

"Of course it is," said Rev Theo. "Didn't he say, Love the Lord your God with all your—"

"No, Rev Theo. What it wants is for them to worship *me*. To obey me. To elevate me. To give me power in this world. It wants me to rule over people because they think God is in me. It's lust. Ambition. Pride."

"If you got those sins, we can work on repentance—"

"I don't have those sins, Rev Theo. Or if I do, I don't have them so bad. It's not *my* feeling. It's what I get from the thing inside me. It doesn't feel good. It feels malicious."

Rev Theo didn't have a comforting word for him. Not a word at all.

Word opened his eyes. Rev Theo was leaning back, studying him. "You a complicated boy, Word."

"Not so complicated," said Word. "I just want to do good. For good reasons."

"Sometimes people do bad for good reasons, and God forgives them. And sometimes they do good for bad reasons, and God forgives them. And when they do bad for bad reasons, God will forgive them if they repent and come unto him. You got nothing to fear, Word."

Word pretended that this was the answer he needed, because he knew that wise as Rev Theo was, he didn't understand. He hadn't felt that hot hand down his back. He hadn't felt the glee that radiated from it when people wept as they called out: Word, Word, Word.

It's the beast, and I'm the prophet of the beast. I know that now. It's pretending to be the Holy Ghost, but it isn't. So I'm not serving God, even though that's what I meant. I'm serving . . . . someone else. Maybe someone like Bag Man. Except it's not the way Dad said it was for him. Bag Man made him *want* things he didn't want. This *thing* inside me doesn't change what I want. I'm still the same person I was.

Word let Rev Theo take him partway home in his rattletrap

ministry car, an ancient Volvo that looked like a cardboard box with wheels and rust spots. "Thing that makes me most proud of this car," Rev Theo liked to say, "ain't a mechanic left in LA knows how to fix it. So you *know* it runs on faith alone."

Rev Theo dropped him at the bus stop and not long after, Word got on the bus that ran down La Brea and dropped him at Coliseum. Word insisted on that—no need for Rev Theo to take him all the way in to Baldwin Hills, it was too far out of his way. Even though it did mean it was nearly midnight by the time Word wound his way into the neighborhood.

Walking up Cloverdale, Word saw Ceese Tucker's patrol car and Yolanda's motorcycle parked in front of Chandresses' house. But the house looked dark, like nobody was there, or at least nobody was up.

Word walked on up the street and passed so many people it made him wonder if there had been a block party. Or maybe a political meeting, since some of the people were carrying big sheets of tagboard, the kind you make political signs out of. But what cause could possibly unite all these different people—folks from up the hill talking with people from the flat, which wasn't all *that* common. Not on the street anyway.

A lot of them greeted him, but they didn't volunteer any information and Word didn't ask. Maybe they could see on his face how distracted and worried he was. Whatever they were doing, Word wasn't part of it.

He got home and Mother was drinking tea in the kitchen. "Your father's in his office and he doesn't want to be disturbed."

"I'm tired myself," said Word. "He still upset about those poems?"

"Actually, he got some complimentary emails today. There *are* people out there who like the kind of old-fashioned poetry your father has apparently been writing for twenty years without ever giving me or anyone else a hint."

"Well that's good," said Word.

"So his wish came true, I guess," said Mother. "I wouldn't mind a few of *my* wishes coming true."

Word sat down across the table from her. "What *is* the wish of your heart, Mom?"

"My children to be happy," she said.

"You're already Miss America to me, Mom," he said, grinning.

"Well, I *do* want that. But I guess that's not what you meant. I honestly don't know the wish of my heart. Maybe I like my life the way it is. I'm pretty content."

"That's what *happy* means in this world, Mom."

"Well, aren't you the philosopher."

"Not since I got that C in aesthetics."

He got up and kissed her cheek and left her to her tea and her contentment with life. Maybe she'd feel differently if she knew that a child of her loins had lived in the neighborhood for the past seventeen years, and just tonight slept with a woman at least ten years older than him after a sort of fake marriage. Maybe that would spoil her contentment just a little. Especially the part about not remembering giving birth to the kid.

Word got undressed and went to bed, but it didn't do any good. Well, maybe he dozed for a while now and then, but he kept opening his eyes and seeing the clock. One-thirty. Two-ten. Like that.

Finally at nearly four A.M. he got down on his knees and prayed. Asking all his questions. Begging for answers. If this is from you, Lord, let me know it. Let me trust it. But if it's not from you, then please, God, set me free of it. Don't make me part of some evil spirit that hungers to own people's souls.

And then, all of a sudden, right in the middle of a plea to God, he felt the hand down his spine start to stir.

I've woken it. I'm going to be punished for asking God to take this spirit away.

He felt it slide up and out of him. And just like that, it was gone.

"O God," he said out loud. "Was it thy spirit? Hast thou taken thyself from me because of my unbelief?"

But in the next moment, now that the presence down his back was gone, he felt a powerful lightness, as if the hand cupping his heart had been a great weight he was carrying around with him. And now he was at peace.

"I thank thee, O God most holy," he whispered. "Thou hast cast out from me the evil spirit."

He prayed a moment longer, giving his thanks. And with the thanks still in his heart and a murmuring prayer on his lips, he rose up from his knees and went to the window and turned the long handle on the blinds and looked out into the grayish light.

There was a red glow from behind the houses to the right of his window. A glow so intense that it could only be coming from a fire. But whose house? He could see all the houses on Cloverdale, and behind them there was nothing. Just the empty basin around the drainpipe.

At that moment, a column of red light shot upward and something dark rose within it. Word watched in fascination as the thing writhed a little. Like a slug.

A slug with wings. He saw them unfold. He saw the bright and terrifying eyes. He saw the wings spread out and beat against the red and smoky air and lift the great worm into the air.

Not a worm, really. Too thick and stubby for a worm. The ancient lore had it wrong. Not a worm, but a Wyrm. The great enemy of God. The one cast out of heaven by Michael the archangel.

He heard footsteps behind him. He glanced back and saw his father, his eyes red-rimmed as if he'd been up way too late. Or as if he'd been crying.

"So there it is, Father," said Word.

"Can you figure out what a chopper's doing flying over our neighborhood this time of night?" asked Father.

"Chopper?"

Word looked back out the window. And sure enough, the great dragonslug was gone. And in its place was a chopper. Not the police. It belonged to a TV station, but not one whose call letters Word knew.

"What were you looking at then?"

"No, I just . . . I'm kind of bleary-eyed. Didn't know it was a chopper."

"You can hear it," said Father. "Waking people up all over the neighborhood, I bet. Have you slept at all tonight, son?"

"If I have, I must have slept through it, cause I don't remember."

It was an old joke between them, and Father laughed and clapped him on the shoulder. "Guess they'll have to do without you at that church today."

"Maybe," said Word.

Father walked out of the room.

Word watched the chopper head out toward the northwest, right over the Williamses' house.

It *was* a slugdragon, thought Word. I knew it when I saw it— this was the beast.

And yet it was a chopper all along. Heading northwest.

A dragon in disguise?

Word had to see. He was responsible for this thing, somehow. It had been in him. Who knew what it took away? What knowledge it stole from him.

Word ran to his dad's office. "Can I take a car?"

"When will you be back?" asked Father.

"Don't know."

"You're too tired to drive."

"Won't be far, Dad." Word hoped he was telling the truth. And then hoped he wasn't—because whatever business that flying slug had, he didn't want it to be in his own neighborhood, among his friends.

"Take the Mercedes," said his father, and then Word caught the keys in midair and headed for the garage.

.   .   .

URA LEE WORE her nurse's uniform as she stood on the overpass with the earliest of the Olympic Avenue traffic passing under her. There weren't many cars out at this time of day—but the surprise was that there were any at all. Early shifts? Or just people who figured it was better to be at work two hours early and be productive than to arrive at work on time after an hour and a half on the 405 or the 10.

She wasn't sure how she felt about being one of the old people that had been dropped off while the younger ones went and parked and hiked. She could have hiked it easily enough—she spent all day on her feet, and the only thing interesting about the walk from Ralph's up to the overpass was that it was uphill and wound around a cloverleaf.

Folks from Cloverdale walking up a cloverleaf.

And before she let herself go off on a mental riff about that, she reminded herself: Sometimes coincidences aren't signs of anything.

Would she ever see Mack Street again?

My son, she thought. As much of a son as I could ever have had. And I raised him about as much as I ever could. I was never cut out to be a fulltime mother, that's for sure. Thank God for Ceese. That boy gave Mack Street a terrific childhood. Full of freedom and yet completely safe, with someone always watching over him.

Maybe I *could* have been a fulltime mother. Maybe I wouldn't have run out of patience if I hadn't already had a long shift of taking care of people made fretful by their pain. Not to mention the bossy people and the sneaky relatives and the selfish visitors who never noticed that their victim was worn out. The buzzers going off. The bureaucrats making demands. The incompetent trainees. The inept doctors that you had to keep covering for.

Maybe Ura Lee would have been a great mother.

In another life.

She was going to lose Mack this morning. That's what she felt in the pit of her stomach. And she didn't get to say goodbye. Did the boy even know she loved him? Did he love her? He said he did. He showed he did.

He was supposed to be with me when I died. That was the only wish of my life. To have someone to love me, to hold my hand as I leave this world. I thought it would be Mack. I thought God had granted my wish by putting this child in my life.

Selfish. To grieve more because he wouldn't be there to grieve for me, than for the life that he should have had, and now he wouldn't.

Don't be such a mope, Ura Lee! He's not going to die. Why do you think you're suddenly a psychic. When have you *ever* been able to tell the future?

She noticed a child's alphabet block up on the sidewalk right beside her. How in the world would something like that be abandoned here, of all places? Did some child throw it out of the car?

And look, there's another. Did they dump the whole thing?

Stupid. Those blocks weren't there ten minutes ago.

"Look!" she shouted to the other people on watch. "Alphabet blocks! Look! Stand on them! One of you on each of them! Get the signs! Don't let anybody drive over the blocks or move them!"

They started obeying her. She turned to face Ralph's and waved her arms. Then she remembered that it was still almost completely dark. She switched on her flashlight and pointed it at them and blinked it.

She got an answering blink, and saw some people start trotting up the sidewalk.

That won't last long, she thought. Not many of them were in shape to run uphill all the way to the overpass.

Apparently some of them had sense enough to know that, because a few cars started up in the Ralph's lot and swung out to turn left on Olympic.

Well, let them get here when they come. I've got a block to stand on.

The blocks were too spread out for anybody to hold hands with anybody else. And there weren't seventeen people up here, so they couldn't even cover all the blocks. Why didn't we think to make sure there were at least seventeen?

A single car came from the south. Not part of their group, just some early riser heading for some office in Century City. He blinked his lights when he saw the old black people standing out in the road.

"Let him through!" Ura Lee called out. "But stay close, so he'll drive slow."

They stepped back, leaving a gap barely wide enough for a car to pass. The guy pressed the button and his automatic window rolled down. "What the hell are you doing at this time of day? Stay out of the road!"

"We're here to commemorate the death of an asshole who yelled things at old people out of his car!" shouted Eva Sweet Fillmore.

The man probably didn't even hear her—he was already on his way, with his window going up.

The blocks hadn't been touched.

And now more people began to arrive, carrying signs. Now it would be obvious it was a demonstration. Now they could let them honk or turn around and head back the way they came. No explanation needed. The signs would say it all.

Ura Lee took the sign that Ebby DeVries handed her. SAVE THE CHRISTIANS IN SUDAN," it said. She looked at the others and smiled. It was actually a cause she cared about. After all, this might end up on TV, so they might as well demonstrate for a worthy cause.

REMEMBER AFRICA

AIDS IS MORE COMMON IN AFRICA THAN THE FLU

FREE THE SLAVES IN AFRICA

IF BLACK SKIN COULD RUN YOUR CAR WE'D LIBERATE SUDAN

WHAT DOES IT MATTER IF A MILLION BLACK PEOPLE DIE?

As far as Ura Lee knew, nobody in LA even knew this was a cause. They certainly didn't expect to have a bunch of black people stop traffic in Century City. So she had made them add a couple of signs:

THIS IS THE AFRICAN CENTURY!
WHY AREN'T ANY STARS LOOKING OUT FOR AFRICA?

That would explain, sort of, why they were in Century City, blocking the Avenue of the Stars.

"Are we up to seventy-seven?" shouted Grand Harrison.

Someone on the other side, where the cloverleafs were, called back, "No, we still got about six straggling up the hill."

"Well hurry! We got to close this circle."

Ura Lee felt a strange tingling in her feet. She turned to Ebby, who was now holding her hand on the left. "You feel that?"

"Tingling feet?" asked Ebby.

"Gotta dance," said Ura Lee. She yelled at the others. "No more time! It's started! Grab hands and let the latecomers join in as soon as they get up here!"

The circle formed, and they started moving—though five or six people forgot about counterclockwise and there was a moment of confusion. In a few moments, though, with hands joined around the handles of picket signs, the whole circle was slowly but smoothly walking rightward as they faced the center. The stragglers joined in as they could.

Only when the last one—Sondra Brown, wouldn't you know it—took her place did the tingling start to rise from Ura Lee's feet. Her feet began to get a little jiggy. Her hips began to sway a little as she walked. A little attitude. A little shine. A few people laughed with delight.

The circle moved faster and faster, but nobody was running out of breath. The tingling covered her whole body, every bit of her skin and deep inside as well.

No way was Yolanda White a hoochie mama. Cause if men could get this feeling just by paying a hundred bucks, she'd never have had *time* to ride that motorcycle.

They heard the hum, the roar, the *thud-thud-thud* of a helicopter. Ura Lee looked up. "Good Lord," she said. "How did we get a news chopper here already?"

"HE'S COMING," SAID MACK. "I can see him."

"Well, you done with your little hearts and flowers?"

"Just hearts," said Mack.

"Are you done?" she said impatiently.

"One on every pillar."

"All right. Stand here in the middle. And . . . how can I put this . . . when he gets here . . ."

"Keep myself between you and him," said Mack.

"That would be so very helpful," she said.

She went from pillar to pillar, kissing the hearts. "They ought to be feeling *that* now."

She ran back to the center of the circle.

The flying slug let out a cry of such rage that the pillars seemed to tremble.

"Get in front of me, Mack! Don't leave me out here alone!"

Mack ran to put himself between the Queen and her husband.

Is this the fulfilment of her dream?

In the dream she didn't even know I was there. But in reality, she needs me.

It made him feel good.

"Dammit, Mack, what's going on there? We're not connected yet."

"Maybe it took some of them longer to get up from Ralph's than they expected," said Mack. "It's not that long since I started drawing the hearts."

"What is this, a bad cellphone system?" said Titania. "Can you hear me now? Can you hear me effing *now*?"

"Please," said Mack. "Don't get angry."

"You're right," she said.

The slugdragon circled at a distance, reconnoitering. Mack sidled around her, as she pointed at each pillar in turn. "I'm not filling up, Mack. This is going to be a short fight if he's got you to draw on and I don't have anybody."

"Why don't *you* draw on me?"

"I can't, Mack, and you know why," she said. And then: "Oh, praise the Lord. They finished it."

Immediately Titania pointed at each pillar, but this time she sang a low note as she did it, and the pillars began to glow.

"Oh, he sees that," she murmured—on the note. "He knows now. Watch out, Mack. Stand up for me."

Mack could hardly think about the dragon, because he was watching the pillars. They were starting to move, sliding around the circle. Clockwise.

"I thought you said counterclockwise," said Mack.

"If the circle moved the same on both sides," said Titania impatiently, "there wouldn't be any friction, now, would there?"

"Silly me," murmured Mack.

"You do know that I love you, don't you, Mack?"

"What are you doing, kissing my ass goodbye?" he said.

"Here he comes, the son-of-a-bitch!"

The flying slug swooped down at them and a talon caught Mack a glancing blow. But it tore open his chest diagonally from waist to shoulder. Mack screamed with the pain and dropped to his knees.

"Stand up, Mack!" she cried. "He can't do that again, he can't afford to weaken you!"

"Once was enough," Mack whispered. "God help me!"

"I can't help you!" she said. "I've got to get this circle moving!"

Mack tore off his shirt to see the wound. It was deep in places—the skin gaped wide. But it hadn't opened his belly. His guts were still safely inside. "Just a flesh wound," he said.

"Well, ain't you brave."

"We'll see what you think when I poop my pants," said Mack. "He's coming back."

"I'm getting stronger, Mack. It's working. You'll see."

The dragon swooped down again, but this time a bright yellow Cadillac suddenly rose straight up from a point inside the circle and smacked into the slug and threw it off course. A moment later, before the Caddy could come back to earth, it blew up into smithereens.

No, not smithereens. Golf balls.

A thousand golf balls were pelting them.

"Damn," she said. "You got a lot of strength in you, baby. Those should have been ping-pong balls."

"Ain't I cool," said Mack, nursing a welt that was rising on his head where a golf ball had smacked him.

"LET ME OUT of this cage," shouted Puck. "She needs me, don't you understand? She thinks I'm his slave, but I'm not, I love her! She's the love of my life! I'd never hurt her! Let me out!"

Ceese knelt by the cage. "I don't even know how," he said.

"Tear it open. Get back in there where you're a giant and rip this sucker open with your teeth!"

"No," Ceese said.

All of a sudden the globe began to roll. It wasn't magic. Puck was moving it like a hamster, running inside the ball and making it move across the floor toward the kitchen.

"You're not getting out of here!"

"Try and stop me!"

Ceese stopped him.

Puck stared at Ceese's foot, which was holding the cage in place.

"Police brutality!" shouted Puck.

"Oh, shut up, nobody's hurting you."

"Rodney King!"

"Nobody can hear you, Puck. And even if they could, they can't even *see* this house."

"She needs me!"

"She needs you *here,* with me," said Ceese.

Puck reared back and let out such a piercing scream that one of the panes blew out of the window. It gave Ceese such a pain in his ears that he picked up the globe and ran back to the back of the house, intending to duck it in the toilet or stick it in the shower.

What he found was a bedroom with a closet full of police uniforms. All of them his.

"Damn," said Puck. "What is this, the Village People's dressing room?"

"I'm getting dressed," said Ceese. "But before I do . . ."

Ceese took one of the leather jackets—the one that was still dripping from having been ducked in water—and wrapped it completely around the globe.

From inside it, Ceese could hear Puck's muffled voice. "It's dark."

Ceese shook the wet jacket.

"It's raining," said Puck.

THE CHOPPER SWOOPED in low over the fairy circle. When it was exactly in the middle, a big dollop of red splashed down in the direct center of the circle, spattering everyone with it.

"What is it, paint?" called someone.

"Shut up and keep dancing!" cried Grand.

"It's blood," said Ebby.

"Keep dancing, sweetie," said Ura Lee.

Then, to Ura Lee's amazement, her feet were no longer touching the ground. Still dancing, she rose into the air and the circle began to move even faster.

The chopper returned, but this time as it passed, the red paint peeled off the pavement—and off everybody it had hit—and formed itself back into a ball of paint . . . or blood, or whatever it was . . . which then rose straight up and splashed right across the windshield of the chopper.

The helicopter immediately veered upward and away.

"Blinded him. Good," said Ura Lee.

"What's that chopper doing?" asked Ebby.

"That ain't no chopper, sweetie," said Ura Lee. "It's the devil. And that paint—that was Mack and Yolanda, over in Fairyland, doing something bad to him and making him go away."

"Not for long," said Ebby. "He's coming back."

"Dance faster."

"I want to fly higher!" said Ebby.

And she did.

The chopper came in close again, and seemed to be heading straight for the flying, dancing, spinning fairy circle. But at the last moment, what looked like a giant frog's tongue shot up from beyond the overpass and stuck to the chopper and flung it away.

"That was close," said Ura Lee.

"It was cool," said Ebby.

That happened a couple more times before the LAPD cruiser slowly coasted along the bridge and slid in under the fairy circle. Ura Lee looked down at the officers who got out of the car and thought it was rather charming the way they took off their caps and scratched their heads and spent a long time discussing whether they dared to report what they were seeing.

Suddenly the metal pipe that made up the guardrail on the overpass tore loose from the concrete and flew upward.

It hit Sondra Brown and knocked her out of the circle. She dropped like a rock onto the road below.

"Oh God help her!" cried Ura Lee. The prayer was echoed by many others.

Whatever God might be doing about Sondra Brown, the guardrail pipe was now standing on end in the middle of the circle, poised to strike at another of them.

And where Sondra had been, it took a moment for the two whose hands she had been holding to get together and close up the gap. During that moment, the circle slowed down noticeably, and sank a little toward the ground, and the tingling that gave them such pleasure as they danced began to fade.

The pipe struck again. This time Ura Lee thought it was aiming at her. But of course it couldn't aim at all—the circle was moving too fast. It hit Ebby DeVries and she flew out from the circle, over Olympic Avenue, and dropped down out of sight.

"Oh, God," cried Ura Lee. "Not Ebby!"

The cop car suddenly sprang into action. The lights came on, the engine gunned, and the cops began to run back toward it, trying to get the doors open.

The car rose up in the exact center of the circle and the guardrail wrapped itself around the car, coiled itself like a snake.

"THIS IS GETTING FUN," said Titania.

Mack, whose chest seemed to be on fire so he could hardly breathe, wasn't quite sure he agreed. The pillars were now up in the air and circling so fast that they formed a kind of wall; twice the dragon tried to swoop in and was struck by a pillar and knocked away.

But now Mack and Titania were in the air, too, and Mack looked out frantically to see where the dragon was flying now.

Only when a huge tree suddenly rose up into the air in the center of the circle did Mack realize that the dragonslug had stopped flying and had slipped in under the wall of flying pillars. It was now directly underneath them, holding a huge tree in its talons.

It swing it like a cudgel. Incredibly, the tree passed between two pillars, so they weren't disturbed at all.

But Titania gasped as if she had been struck, and the whole circle slowed down. They also sank closer to the ground, and when Mack looked down he could see the slug opening its huge, toothless, sluglike mouth to swallow them up.

The tree swung again, and again it passed between columns, seemingly without harm. But again the circle staggered in its movement and Titania and Mack sank closer to the dragon's mouth.

"Can't you do something?" demanded Mack.

"As soon as they get the circle back together," she said.

"They never will if he keeps breaking it," said Mack.

"Just hold on to me and you'll be fine!" she shouted.

Mack looked down and saw that the reason the mouth stayed directly under him was because it was catching the blood that dripped off his foot. There was a steady trickle of it. He was strengthening the monster. His own blood was being used against Titania.

Mack knew that his moment had come. In the dream he raced up to fight the dragon. Now, in reality, he'd be dropping down onto it. So it was different. But that didn't matter. The most important thing was that the dragon was gaining strength from him. He had to keep it from getting worse. If he was going to save Titania.

Only when he had shoved himself away from her and was dropping downward did it occur to him that maybe the impulse to let go and drop hadn't come from his own mind, but rather from Oberon's.

The treetrunk dropped to the ground and the slug leapt upward. Mack thought he'd simply be swallowed whole, but instead the beast leaned back and caught him in its talons. Then it began to rise up past Titania.

"No!" she howled. "Mack, baby, fight him! Don't let him take you!"

Fight him with what?

Titania let out a piercing cry. A single word, but in a language Mack didn't understand.

Then, suddenly, everything changed. There was no talon holding him. Instead, he was hanging from something by his hands, and the pain in his chest was unbearable as his body strained and stretched.

SUDDENLY, EVERYTHING CHANGED. The guardrail unwrapped itself and dropped to the ground; the patrol car fell after it, landing with such force that it blew out all four tires.

The chopper appeared in the middle of the air, the blades seeming to be only inches from the fairy circle as they spun. And hanging from the bottom skid of the chopper was . . . Mack Street.

His shirt was open and his chest was bleeding from a terrible wound from hip to shoulder. Ura Lee was relieved that no bowel was exposed, but he was losing blood steadily. And the chopper was trying to rise up and carry him away.

The circle spun faster and faster.

"No!" cried Ura Lee. "I have to get out! I have to help him!"

But Mack couldn't hear her. He grimaced and swung on the skid and pulled himself up so he was standing on the skid and holding on to the door of the chopper.

"Stay away from the door!" Ura Lee cried. For she knew—somehow—that if that door opened and Mack went inside, he would be lost. "Don't go in!" she shouted.

Mack seemed to hear her. He looked toward the rapidly spinning circle and hesitated.

At that moment, a Mercedes coasted along the bridge underneath the chopper. It stopped and Word Williams got out.

"Mack!" he shouted. "Jump! I'll catch you!"

That was about the stupidest thing Ura Lee ever heard. Mack was half a head taller than Word. Word wasn't catching anything tonight.

The door of the chopper swung open. Mack lost his balance, veered, and then, in catching his balance, swung back toward the open door. He was going to fall into the mouth of the beast.

Word jumped straight up into the air and caught the skid of the chopper and hung on. It was an incredible jump—it would have set the record in any Olympics—but more important to Ura Lee was the fact that he overbalanced the chopper, causing it to lurch and swing Mack back out of the door, which promptly slammed shut behind him.

The chopper tipped on its side.

And suddenly Ura Lee knew what she had to do.

"Hold my arms!" she demanded of the people on either side of her. Though it cost the circle a small lurch as they let go to find a new grip on her upper arm, the maneuver worked well enough. Even though her dancing stopped unabated, her hands were now free to reach down into her coat pocket and pull out Ceese's revolver. She took off the safety, aimed the gun at the broad windshield of the chopper, and fired.

The bullet ricocheted off.

"Open the door, Mack!" cried Ura Lee.

"Don't do it!" shouted Word.

"Mack, this is your mother! This is Mom! Open the door!"

MACK HUNG ON to the handle beside the door, completely baffled by what was happening. Where had this helicopter come from? Where were the pillars? Where was Titania?

Only gradually did he realize where he was—in the air above the bridge over Olympic. And the chopper must be . . .

The manifestation of Oberon in this world. The dragonslug might not be able to cross over between worlds, but like the debris that Mack had left in Fairyland, Oberon himself caused things to happen in this world, and there was a figure here that represented him. A news chopper.

Mack had almost crawled into Oberon's mouth of his own free will.

"Open the door!" he heard someone cry.

"Don't do it!" He knew both voices. The man was Word Williams. The same voice whose sermon he had listened to just last night. Or had he? Hadn't he fallen asleep?

"Mack, this is your mother! This is Mom! Open the door!"

It was Miz Smitcher. But she called herself his mother. And she wanted him to . . .

To open the door.

She understood. She wanted him to make the sacrifice. She knew it was what he had been born for. He was dragon food all along.

She had called herself Mom.

"I will, Mom," said Mack. He reached out and flung open the door.

Suddenly a shot rang out. Another.

The door slammed shut.

TITANIA WATCHED HELPLESSLY as Mack struggled in the dragon's talon. Only the heavy weight of the ice and snow Titania had summoned were keeping the dragon from soaring up and out of reach with Mack clutched in its claw.

Even with the ice and snow, the dragon somehow managed to stay in the air. But it was staggering, reeling.

One lurch brought the dragon's mouth close to Mack's head. It probably would have bitten down and swallowed the boy in two bites, but something made the dragon lurch yet again, and Mack was pulled back out of its mouth.

Titania looked down and saw a tyrannosaur, with its enormous jaws clamped down on the dragon's other leg. The weight was more than the dragon could bear. It was sinking toward the ground.

Yet Mack seemed oblivious. He reached up toward the dragon's mouth, caught hold of it, gripped its lip, and drew it downward toward him.

What is he doing? thought Titania. Volunteering to be eaten?

The dragon's mouth was now wide open, and on the same level as the pillars that still spun madly around Titania.

A shot rang out. And another.

A bloody eruption in the dragon's eye told Titania that her husband had been hit. But by what?

The dragon was spitting out blood.

Titania knew this was her chance. Whatever had hit the dragon, it had its mind on something other than the magic she might be able to bring to bear.

She said the words, sang the notes, did the quick little jig.

The wings of the dragon dropped off and the sluglike body plummeted.

Sprawled on the ground with both the tyrannosaur and Mack Street being crushed or smothered under it, the dragon stirred. But not quickly enough for Titania.

She waved her hand, and the slug was suddenly transformed. No longer a terrifying dragonslug, it was just a man.

Her man.

And Mack Street was gone. In his place was a single plastic grocery bag, rolling like a tumbleweed in a slight breeze coming in from off the ocean.

THE HELICOPTER WAS GOING to crash, and what would happen? An explosion, bringing death or injury to everybody in the fairy circle.

But Ura Lee did not regret shooting at the chopper. Whoever was flying it was trying to consume her son. What else could she have done?

The helicopter hit the ground and . . . disappeared.

Mack Street and Word Williams lay sprawled and somewhat entangled with each other on top of the patrol car.

And the helicopter was gone.

The fairy circle slowed down and sank so rapidly that in two revolutions they were on the ground, moving at no more than a brisk walk. The tingling stopped. So did the jigging.

Ura Lee shrugged off the arms of the two people holding on to her and ran toward the body of her son.

Word Williams stirred, slid away from Mack's body. He saw Ura Lee and said, "I'm sorry, Miz Smitcher. I tried to save him."

The others gathered around.

Not far away, a car caught in the traffic jam surrounding the fairy circle let out a blast of its horn.

One of the cops raised his nightstick and approached the offending car. "This is a demonstration!" he shouted. "It has a permit! Didn't you see the signs out on Pico?"

Ura Lee didn't care about the surrounding people. She made sure Mack's neck wasn't broken, then slid her arms under him and lifted him and held his head and shoulders against her like a child.

"Oh, Mack," she said. "Mack, it was supposed to be the other way. You were supposed to hold me while I died."

Yolanda White appeared out of nowhere, standing on the roof of the cop car.

"Say goodbye to him, Ura Lee Smitcher," she said. "He's coming with me."

"He's dead!" said Ura Lee. "Can't I bury him?"

"He's not dead. But his job is done. Say goodbye to him, Miz Smitcher. I've got to get my pathetic loser of a husband back down to hell."

"He's not a loser!" shouted Word. "He's a hero!"

"I didn't mean *Mack,*" said Yolanda. "I know we had that cere-mony, but . . . it's the king of the fairies that I'm married to. Only now he's the king of nothing, not even himself. Thanks to all these fine people, the fairy circle held, and we've got Oberon in chains. Thank you!"

Then she bent down to Ura Lee and held out her hand. "Give me the gun, Ura Lee Smitcher. You don't want to get caught with this gun."

"It's Cecil Tucker's gun," she said numbly.

"I know where he is. I'll give it back to him."

Ura Lee took the gun out of the pocket of her jacket and handed it to the fairy queen.

Titania smiled at her. "It will be all right, Miz Smitcher." Then she bent over, took Mack Street's limp hands, and pulled him up from his mother's lap.

"Come on, Mack," she said. "You're going home."

She held him close to her, and then unfolded her wings. The people gasped. They hadn't seen them, folded as they were on her back. "Better clear the road and let the traffic through," she said.

Word Williams helped a weeping Ura Lee away from the patrol car and over to the sidewalk.

The cops stepped out into the road and started directing traffic.

Ura Lee looked over the rim of the overpass and saw several people doing CPR on Ebby.

"Sweet Jesus," she said. "Let her live."

"I wish," said Word Williams beside her, "I wish I had the power to heal her."

"No wishing," said Ura Lee. "I don't want any wishing around me. Just *doing* or shutting up. Help me down there to look at that girl and see if I can do anything before the paramedics get here."

"Yes ma'am," said Word.

Then she burst into tears again. "Oh, Mack, my son, my sweet beautiful baby! Why couldn't I be the one to die!"

"You'll see him again, Miz Smitcher, I'm sure of it," said Word. "In the loving arms of his Savior. He'll be waiting for you."

"I know that," said Ura Lee. "I know it, but I can't help wishing. Wishing! Why can't we stop wishing and leave things alone!"

24

CHANGELING

Titania flew with Mack Street in her arms, soaring over the buildings and streets of Los Angeles. The Santa Monica Freeway like a river flowing with cars. Hills that in her own country were thick with forest, but here were thick with houses.

Still, the glory of Fairyland peeked through here and there. In the lush gardens tended by the hands of Mexican laborers. In the jacaranda that was just coming into fragrant bloom. In the moist wind off the Pacific, carrying cooler air inland, though not very far. Just to Baldwin Hills, where Titania landed on the sidewalk between two houses, with a cop car and a motorcycle at the curb.

She carried his light, almost empty body into the gap between the houses and, as far as any observer on the street could have seen, disappeared.

Inside the house, Ceese heard the door open and called out, "Who's there!"

"Bill Clinton, the first black President, what do you think?"

It was Yolanda. Ceese picked up the golden cage wrapped in a copy of his leather jacket and walked into the living room.

She was laying Mack Street down on the floor. His shirt was open and a terrible wound was seeping blood.

Ceese cried out, a terrible groan, and flung aside the cage. He ran to Mack's body and embraced it, covering himself with blood. "Mack," he cried.

"He's not dead," said Titania.

"Do you think I don't know death?" said Ceese. "He's cold, and he has no heartbeat."

"He's not dead," she said. "He's just empty."

"What do you mean?"

"In our battle, Oberon used him up. Emptied all the wishes out of him. So in the end, the old monster had nothing left to draw on. A couple of bullets from your gun took my dear husband right in the mouth and he had no strength to turn them into anything but what they were. Bullets."

"Oberon's dead?"

"He's bound. While he was lying there gasping with pain like he had never felt before, I bound him. I stripped him of that hideous shape. I sent him back down, and this time he didn't have the power to bind me in return." She walked over to the corner behind the front door, where the golden cage had rolled after it fell out of the jacket. Puck was glaring at her.

"It's over, Puck," she said.

"I could have helped. I could have saved the boy."

"You would have torn the boy into pieces and killed everybody in the fairy circle," said Titania. "There at the end, when the dragon had no more strength, he would have made you do his bidding, and you would have done it."

"Let me out."

"No revenge," she said. "I'll set you free—of this cage, of Oberon—but only if I have your solemn vow. No revenge on me or any of the people who helped bring Oberon down today."

"So now I'm your slave," said Puck.

"I'm offering you parole," said Titania. "As long as you don't try to hurt me or any of these mortals, you're free. So say it. Give me your oath."

After a moment's hesitation, Puck launched into a stream of some language Ceese had never heard before.

"What's he saying?"

"What I told him to. Only he's saying it in Sumerian, so you can't witness his humiliation."

"Sumerian?"

"It's where we first met. I found him in the wild and loved him until he awoke from his animal stupor and realized he was a man. It took a while longer to persuade him that he was really one of us, and immortal. Isn't that right, Enkidu?"

Puck answered with another stream of incomprehensible words. Titania chuckled. "That'll do." She passed her hand around the globe. As she did, the wires unwove themselves and skeined themselves around the third finger of her left hand. So fine were the wires that they became a simple gold band.

Released from his prison, Puck squatted down and strained like a dog trying to lay a turd in the grass. As he did, he grew larger and larger until he was his full height. But not the same man. No, not the old homeless guy. He was young and beautiful and seriously pissed off.

"You owe your freedom to me," said Titania.

"Only because you didn't let me help," said Puck.

"Help now. Help me waken the boy. Let him remember who he is."

Puck sighed. "Well, turnabout is fair play. He healed *me* once." He knelt on the other side of Mack from Ceese and laid a hand on the boy's head. Then he sighed, smiling. "Oh, Mack, it's good to know you."

Mack's eyes fluttered and opened. He took a huge breath. His heart started. Ceese's tears didn't stop, but they changed meaning.

"Don't get too happy," said Titania. "Say your goodbyes, Ceese. I'm taking him with me."

"No," said Ceese.

"I have to," she said. "I have to finish this. He's the last bit of business."

"He's not a bit of business," said Ceese.

"He's the most beautiful of souls," she said, "but he's been too long away from the rest of himself, and he needs to be made whole again."

"You're giving him back to Oberon?" asked Ceese. "To that damned dragon?"

"Dragon no more," said Titania. "I tamed him. He's just an ordinary fairy now, except that he's in chains, and can't find the best parts of himself, and has no idea of why."

Mack sat up under his own power, stood up, looked around. "Did we win?"

"We did, Mack, thanks to you. And to Ceese. And Ura Lee Smitcher, who shot the bastard in the mouth when he wasn't looking. And even Word Williams, who recognized the demon that possessed him and helped keep him from swallowing you up. And all those good people who made my fairy circle and freely gave me their good wishes." She turned to Puck. "Speaking of which, I'd be grateful, my dearest darling Puckaboo, if you'd go find the two people that Oberon smacked out of the circle. A girl named Ebony DeVries and a woman named Sondra Brown. They're the ones who paid the highest price for your freedom. Don't let them die. And no tricks. I want them restored to perfect health and strength with their minds intact. And while you're at it, let's see about undoing some of the other tricks you pulled with Mack's cold dreams. A little girl named Tamika. A man named Tyler. You know the list."

"Oberon made me."

"Well, I'm not making you undo it, so this isn't a punishment. It's a favor I'm asking you to do. For me. I'll owe you."

"*What* will you owe me?"

"A single sweet and precious kiss," she said softly.

Puck bowed, then spread his wings.

He shrank rapidly again, until he was the size of a moth, and not a large one. He took off flying, out a slightly opened window, and into the gathering light of morning.

"Time to go, baby," said Titania.

"So you're giving me back to him after all," said Mack.

"He's ready for you now. And you're ready for him. I promise."

"And I'll never see Ceese again? Or Miz Smitcher?"

"Mack, that's not in my hands."

Mack turned to Ceese, who was also standing now, and threw his arms around him. "You're in all my happiest memories, Ceese," he said.

"And you're in mine," Ceese answered him.

Mack clung to him a moment more, then parted. "You know what, Ceese? Miz Smitcher called herself my mother. She called herself 'Mom.'"

"Took her long enough," said Ceese.

"Ceese, there's something I got to tell you. When I had her cold dream, the thing she wished for—it was not to be alone. To have her son holding her hand in her bed when she dies. I can't now. But you can still fulfil her wish, can't you? For me?"

"We raised a bratty little kid together. We're practically married."

"That's what I thought." Mack kissed Ceese on one cheek and then turned to Titania. "Let's go."

"Let me go with you," said Ceese.

"You've already said goodbye," said Titania. "As Ura Lee did. Leave it at that."

MACK AND TITANIA HELD HANDS as they walked up Cloverdale. Mack was keenly aware that this was his last time walking this street, and it made him sad. It seemed to him as though he were five years old again, and ten, and fifteen, all at once, his feet knew the sidewalk so well at every age.

"I didn't see enough," said Mack. "I tried, but I didn't see anything as clearly as I should have."

"You saw it all, baby," said Titania. "Better than anybody."

Mack shook his head. "I know all these people so well, and now I'll never see them again."

"You know what we have to do, don't you, Mack?" said Titania.

"What I don't know is why."

"Ah. Back to causality. But Mack, you *do* know why. As long as you're out here, then his virtues are gone from him. All he's got is his malice and his chains. And with you out here, he has a tool to use. It'll all start over again—if not this year then ten years or twenty or thirty. You're immortal, Mack. You'll always be here for him to use for some despicable purpose."

"I guess," he said.

"Don't be childish about it, Mack. Be glad. I promise you, it's not death I'm sending you to."

"I don't see how it could be anything else. I won't be Mack anymore. I'll be Oberon. Which means I won't be anything, and he'll be everything."

Mack and Titania reached the hairpin turn, crested the ridge, and walked down into the basin surrounding the drainpipe. The grassy area around it had been blasted and burned and then even the ashes had blown away. There was nothing but grey California dirt.

Titania led him to the drainpipe and helped him climb up on top of it.

"What do I do, just fall down into it? It's got a grating in the way. Looks like crisscrossed rebar."

"Mack," said Titania, "your body isn't real. Not the way other bodies are. It has a whole different set of causes. So you have to trust me when I tell you that all I'm going to do is send you back down the pipe with this."

Mack looked at the gun in her hand. "That Ceese's gun?"

"Yes. And it's the gun that your mother used to stop Oberon in his tracks."

"And you're going to use it to kill me."

"Not kill. Disrupt the structure of your body and let your immortal parts back down the pipe."

"Oh, cool. Now it's fine."

"Mack," she said. "I have no choice, and neither do you. For the sake of all these people."

"I know that," he said. "That's why you didn't want to marry me, isn't it? Because you knew your victory wouldn't be complete until I was dead."

"Everything has a reason," said Titania. "But until you know all the reasons, you don't really understand any of them."

"Go ahead and shoot."

Titania aimed at him. "Bye, baby." She fired.

Mack felt nothing at all. "You missed."

"I didn't miss," she said. "It went right through your head."

"Didn't feel it."

"Jump down from there."

He did.

She aimed again, this time at his hand, and fired.

It hurt like crazy. Not as bad as the rip in his chest from the dragon's talon, but bad enough. "Why did you shoot me in the *hand!* Now you've got to do it again!"

"This is great," said Titania. "I can shoot you just fine down here, but it wouldn't do a damn bit of good. And when you're standing up there, it halfway dematerializes you so bullets pass right through."

"Oh," said Mack. "Standing over the drainpipe does that to me?"

"It's where you came from," she said. "You popped out of there and floated around till Puck sent you up the road to Nadine Williams's womb. It was his job. As it was his job to go fetch Byron Williams and get him home before you were born."

"What about Ceese? Puck fetch him, too?"

"No, baby," said Titania. "Your own goodness called out to him. As it called out to Ura Lee Smitcher. Love and honor and courage know their own kind. Even Word Williams. It was that connection between you that kept Puck from fully erasing his memory. And it was that connection that let Oberon find him and use him as his pony."

"It all comes back to me," said Mack.

"How's your hand?"

"Bloody and painful. How's your conscience?"

"Troubled," said Titania.

"You won't even miss me," said Mack.

"I will," she said, "but only for a little while."

Her words staggered him, but he nodded gravely and said, "Thank you for being honest with me."

"I'll never be anything else."

"As long as we both shall live," he said bitterly.

"How are we going to do this?"

"*We* aren't going to do anything. *I'm* going to do it."

"How?"

"If bullets go right through me when I'm over the drainpipe," said Mack, "then why would four sections of rebar stop me from dropping back down to hell?"

Again Titania spread her wings and lifted him up to stand on the rim of the pipe.

Then she backed away and hovered, watching.

"I'll do it," he said impatiently. "You don't have to watch."

"Yes I do," she said.

"Just have to make sure I don't cheat and run away," he said bitterly.

"Every voyager needs someone who loves him to say good-bye."

"Do you love me? Not Oberon, *me*?"

"I can't answer that," said Titania.

Mack turned away from her.

His feet balanced on the rim of the drainpipe, Mack made one slow turn, drinking in the hills that surrounded the little basin on three sides, and the view to the north, out over the city of Los Angeles.

I wish I'd known yesterday morning that I'd never see any of this again after today. I would have . . . I would have . . .

Only then did he realize that he wouldn't have done anything differently. Not yesterday. Not any other day of his life. There wasn't a single choice that he regretted.

Well, that's okay then, he decided. How many people get to leave this world without a single thing in their lives that they'd like to undo? Oh, there's people I wish I could have helped, but no harm that I did myself but what I set it right as quick as I could.

"Titania!" he called out.

She flew into view, a few yards away. Only now she was very small. About the size of a butterfly.

"Titania, I didn't get to tell Ebby goodbye. Will you tell her for me?"

"I will, after Puck fixes her up."

"I think maybe I might have fallen in love with her, if I'd had more time."

"In and out of love. That's what mortals do," said Titania. "Always in love yet never satisfied."

"You and Oberon are so much better?"

She smiled. "Touché, baby."

Mack smiled back. Then he drew his arms close to his body, jumped just a little bit upward into the air, pulled his feet together, and fell straight down the drainpipe. He didn't feel the rebar or the sides of the pipe or anything at all. He was just . . . gone.

25

ONE

Oberon stood wingless and in chains, guarded by two fairies with swords who never took their gaze from him. Over him vaulted a ceiling of solid rock, though if he had his freedom, the rock would not be solid if he didn't want it to be.

Out of the sometimes solid rock directly above his head, a small sprinkling of lights slid downward, forming a faint pillar that sank toward him.

Oberon recoiled, strained against his chains to keep himself from being touched by the descending column.

It came gently to the ground and there began to coalesce into a manshape, with a face gradually becoming clear. Mack Street. Oberon knew him well. A monster, that's what he was. All that he hated about himself, all he had purged from himself, now come back to torture him.

"Get away," he said. "I don't want you. You weaken me. You poison me."

The apparition did not answer. It wasn't solid enough to have a voice. All it did was drift toward Oberon. And reach out an ephemeral hand.

Oberon cried out as if it were torture to be so touched. But the moment the dust of light came into contact with his skin, the whole apparition brightened, thickened, until it was dazzling white light.

And Oberon thinned out, becoming a dust of ash in his own shape.

The two clouds of dust, bright light and infinite shadow, hovered beside each other until, with just the faintest tugging, they suddenly flew together into a single manshape.

The dust became a kaleidoscope of colors, until they finally took on a firm surface again. It was a man again, his skin warm and brown. He was still in chains, but not standing in pride as Oberon had done. Now his head was bowed, and he sank to his knees and wept, covering his face with his hands.

"What have I done," he groaned. Sobs racked his body.

As he knelt weeping, two patches of skin running up and down his back brightened, then broke open into two slits of pure light. Out of the slits emerged more of the kaleidoscopic dust. It formed a double sheath over his back. The folded wings of a moth at rest.

A faint chord of music rang through the great cavern. Fairies began drifting in. In various sizes, they hovered in the air, watching. Waiting.

Until at last a hush fell over the crowd of onlookers, and the music swelled fervently, and Titania, the queen of the fairies, flew in to the tumultuous shouts of the fairies who had not seen her in all the years of her captivity. "Titania!" they shouted, and "Queen!" and "Glory!"

She nodded graciously, waved, touched several fairies who came near her.

But nothing diverted her from the direction of her flight: toward the slab of rock where Oberon knelt in chains, his head bowed.

She stood before him. "Oberon, my husband," she said.

He did not raise his head. "I can't bear to remember what I did to you," he said.

"But I understand, my king. You suppressed the part of you that loved me, the part that knew how to love. Bit by bit and day by day you ejected it from yourself, isolated it, gave it no control over any of your choices. It was no longer part of the cause of anything you did. When there was nothing left but malice, envy, and ambition, how else could you do but the things you did?"

"I did them," said Oberon. "All my cruelties, they were my choices. I knew what I was doing."

"Yes," said Titania. "Even when you created a surrogate for no other purpose than to capture other people's wishes and keep them until you needed their power, you knew what you were doing. You were the one who chose to build them out of the very parts of you that you had driven into exile. Forming them into a living soul who walked the earth as you could not, seeing what you had forgotten how to see."

She reached down, put her hand under his chin, and lifted his face to see her.

The face that looked at her was not the proud face of the captive Oberon.

It was the face of Mack Street.

"Hello, baby," she said. "I told you I'd only miss you for a little while."

She ran her hand across his hair and behind his head. As she did, the chains dropped away.

He raised his hands, took her wrists in a firm grip, and looked intently into her face. "I didn't think it would be me," he said. "I thought it would be him."

"They're both you, baby," said Titania. "Driving together down that canyon, through the flood. But now you've got the right person in the driver's seat."

She leaned closer to him, kissed him.

"You loved so many people up there in that neighborhood, and so many people opened their homes and hearts to you, that you became too strong for him. It's everything I hoped for, baby. He didn't stand a chance."

They embraced, and as they did they rose into the air, turning, turning, their wings outspread, glorious stained-glass windows of color and light; and the fairies sang for joy.

They soared upward to the rocky ceiling of the cavern, and then began to whirl, growing smaller as they did. Below them, the other fairies also shrank and began to fly, swarming upward. Then they funneled through a ceiling passageway and the cavern was left empty and dark.

In Fairyland, in a clearing in the woods that covered a steep-rising hill, there was a small opening in the earth, surrounded by flowers from the first rush of spring that had begun only that morning. Out of the cleft there burst two tiny whirling fairies, followed by a thousand more that swarmed like bees escaping from a hive.

There were birds in the branches around the glen, and squirrels that skittered on trunks and over roots; they gave the bright cloud of fairies only a moment's glance before going about their business. The fairies formed themselves into a circle around their king and queen, who danced above the opening into the underworld.

In Baldwin Hills, Los Angeles, as tired neighbors were dropped off at their homes, or parked their cars and went inside, Word Williams walked down the hairpin curve of Cloverdale to join Ceese Tucker and Ura Lee Smitcher on the brow of the hill, looking down into the dead brown hollow surrounding the drainpipe.

In a perfect circle around the rusty red pipe, a thousand toadstools grew.

"It's a fairy circle," said Ura Lee. "The toadstools grow where the fairies dance."

"I hope she takes good care of him," said Ceese. "Where she took him."

Word took Ura Lee's other arm. "She took him home."

Together they walked her back down to her empty house, where tonight no dreams would be dreamed except her own.

But the hands that helped her make that walk despite the tears that filled her eyes were eloquent with promises. You will not die alone, Ura Lee Smitcher, they said to her. There will be two men beside you when that time comes. An LAPD cop and a preacher from a storefront church; they'll hold your hand to remind you that they also knew and in their own way loved the son you raised, the boy who never existed in this world, and yet who saved it.

ACKNOWLEDGMENTS

This novel began in 1999 with a letter from Roland Bernard Brown, a friend of mine who grew up in an upper-middle-class black family in Southern California. We had been talking about racial issues in America (and have continued the conversation for many years since then), but one of his biggest regrets was that black men get short shrift in literature. He wondered why I had never written a black hero in my fiction.

I reminded him of Arthur Stuart, a major character in the Alvin Maker books—but he reminded me that Arthur was a side-kick, not the hero.

The problem with my writing a black hero—using his point of view, seeing the world through his eyes—is that I'm not a black man myself and probably never will be. I didn't grow up in black culture and so I would make a thousand mistakes without even knowing it.

Whereupon Roland promised me that he would help. He would give me background. He would catch my mistakes and help me get back on track.

Then you should write the book yourself, too, I said.

Someday he would, he told me. But that didn't let me off the hook.

Because I was intrigued by the idea. Roland had told me stories from his life, growing up in a mixed middle-class neighborhood in Los Angeles—the subtle (and not so subtle) ways that he was told that his "acceptance" was less than total.

But I didn't want to write a novel about race—that is, I didn't want to write about racial conflict. So we decided together that the ideal place to set this book was in Baldwin Hills, a middle- to upper-middle-class black neighborhood in Los Angeles between La Cienega and La Brea. There, I could create a community of African-Americans who had made it—or whose parents had made it—out of the morass of poverty and oppression.

When next I was in Los Angeles, my cousin Mark and I drove to Baldwin Hills and took pictures. I was impressed by the great variety of the houses, from impressive demi-mansions on the slopes of the hills to the more modest, but still well-tended and attractive homes in the flat. It was a neighborhood with tire swings here and there, occasional yards with eccentric plantings or houses with odd paint jobs; the flat of Baldwin Hills, in fact, reminded me of the neighborhood I had grown up in farther north, in Santa Clara.

It felt like what I had imagined when reading Ray Bradbury's *Dandelion Wine.*

Above the neighborhood was the Kenneth Hahn State Recreation Area, which had a drainage system that funneled rainwater down into the steep valleys where the wealthiest houses of Baldwin Hills stood. The park had gorgeous views of Los Angeles to the north—and of old oil wells to the south.

And between the park and the neighborhood, there was a wild area that ended in a basin surrounding a drainpipe. In a torrential rain, the runoff from the wild hills would collect there and then be drained away so it wouldn't flood Baldwin Hills.

I knew then that my story would be about the leakage of magic into the world, right there where it would spill out over this particular neighborhood; and because no one would be likely to believe what the residents were going through, they would have to solve the problem themselves. I called it *Slow Leak.*

It's a long way from a situation to a story. It took me so many years to come up with a good character that sometimes I despaired.

I made two attempts at beginning the tale. One was the short story "Waterbaby,"* my first telling of the tale of Tamika Brown.

Later I came up with the character of Yolanda White—the motorcycle-riding "hoochie mama" who scandalized the neighborhood. And that finally led me to the character of my hero, Mack Street, the baby who was found by the drainpipe at the hairpin turn of Cloverdale. My first stab at writing it appeared as the short story "Keeper of Lost Dreams."**

Finally I found the character of Byron Williams and the way that Mack Street was born into the world, and finally this novel—which I now was calling by its present title—began to take shape. It was still painful going, and so many years had passed since my first expedition to Baldwin Hills with my cousin Mark that I had to go back and refresh my memory of the place. Aaron Johnston, one of my partners in my film company and a wonderful writer himself, came armed with a digital camera, and those were the pictures I consulted during the writing of the book.

I knew the physical place, but not the people. I don't know a single soul who ever lived in Baldwin Hills. So for those readers who do, I can tell you right now that nobody in this book is based on anybody who lives there. If you think you recognize a real person in this book, it only shows that guys who make stuff up for a living sometimes hit close to reality entirely by accident.

Then, with the book about half written, I went back to Baldwin Hills and was horrified to discover that in the process of construction of a new house just below the hairpin turn, someone had stripped all the grass and greenery from the basin surrounding

---

* "Waterbaby," published in *Galaxy Online,* May 2000, *Leading Edge* magazine, 2001, and *Bli-Panika* online fanzine (Israel), August 2001.

** "Keeper of Lost Dreams," published in *Flights: Visions of Extreme Fantasy,* edited by Al Sarrantonio (Roc, June 2004).

the drainpipe. Instead of looking like an idyllic meadow straight out of *Shepherd's Calendar*, it looked like Mordor.

Disaster! Even though it wouldn't matter to most of the readers of the book, I wanted people to be able to drive up Cloverdale and see the scene that I described!

But the solution was obvious: I would have an event in the book that explained why the basin looked burned over.

The final key to the novel did not come, however, until I was floundering about in mid-book, and it dawned on me who Yo Yo and Bag Man really were. I had once designed and built the set for a production of *A Midsummer Night's Dream*, and I realized that if Yo Yo were Titania and Bag Man were Puck, the story would take on a whole new layer of meaning.

I went back and revised and rewrote, and now the middle of the book came together. All that remained was the realization that Word Williams, instead of forgetting the birth of Mack Street, should remember it and be Oberon's tool in the mortal world. Finally, all the elements were in place and I could finish the book.

What Roland Bernard Brown asked me for, I finally was able to deliver—thanks to his help, before, during, and after the writing of the book. In fact, it turned out to be overkill, since the characters of Ceese and Word took on so much life for me that one could argue that *Magic Street* is a novel with three black male heroes.

It is too much to hope that my depiction of a culture that I have never belonged to will be error-free. I assure you that all the errors are mine, the inevitable result of being a stranger; but it is thanks to Roland and other African-American friends that the errors are not more numerous and more egregious.

Besides driving and hiking around Baldwin Hills and Hahn Park with me, Aaron and Mark helped in other ways. It's because of the boundless hospitality of Mark and Margaret Park that I have had the chance to know and love Los Angeles as I do; that magical place where Avenue of the Stars flies over Olympic is on my regular running path when I stay with them, sometimes for weeks on end, working on projects in the city. And significant portions of this book were written on the table in the spare room they let me inhabit.

Aaron Johnston obtained for me the official maps of Baldwin Hills that I used as a resource. And he worked like a crazy man to produce *Posing as People* (besides writing one of the one-act plays within it), so that I could direct the plays and still have time to write on *Magic Street* during those hot August days in the summer of 2004.

I was helped by my normal crew of pre-readers—Kathy H. Kidd, Erin Absher, and, as always, my wife, Kristine, who also had to suffer through every idea I came up with for the story over a period of five years. Kristine also performed financial miracles, keeping everything afloat while I was six months later than I thought I'd be in completing this novel.

My assistant, Kathleen Bellamy, and my resident webwright, Scott Allen, make things run smoothly and help me in uncountable ways, though to Scott's relief I didn't write a single page of this book in the car beside him, as I had done with the novel before. Not that there was no car-writing this time—but it was Kristine doing the driving on the way to and from a speaking gig in Fredericksburg, Virginia. As she drove I wrote two chapters . . . and the speech.

I'm grateful for the patience and the sense of urgency provided by my editor, the saintly Betsy Mitchell, and my agent, the long-suffering Barbara Bova.

And thanks to Queen Latifah for putting Yolanda White on a motorcycle.